CRÈME

DE LA

CRIME

CRÈME
DE LA
CRIME

Edited by

JANET HUTCHINGS

CARROLL & GRAF PUBLISHERS, INC.
NEW YORK

First Carroll & Graf edition 2000

Carroll & Graf Publishers, Inc.
19 West 21st Street
New York, NY 10010-6805

Library of Congress Cataloging-in-Publication Data is available.
ISBN: 0-7867-0738-0

Manufactured in the United States of America

CRÈME
DE LA
CRIME

CONTENTS

INTRODUCTION

LIKE A TYPICAL issue of *Ellery Queen's Mystery Magazine, Crème de la Crime* contains a mix of traditional whodunits, mean-street crime, private-eye capers, psychological suspense, historical mysteries, cops on the beat, detective puzzles, and humorous or clever twist-in-the-tail pieces. Some stories—those that fall roughly within the subgenre called "cozies"—are intended to allow the reader to escape from reality and enter a world in which he or she plays a sort of game with the author, trying to figure out ahead of the story's detective who is responsible for the crime. At the other end of the spectrum are hard-boiled crime stories that depict reality with much harsher accuracy and invite the reader to consider serious themes along with the mystery. The success of *Ellery Queen's Mystery Magazine* over its fifty-nine years of publication is proof that there are large areas of crossover among the readerships of the various subgenres of the mystery despite the great differences that exist among them in tone, style, and theme. This book is for readers who already enjoy a catholic taste in crime reading as well as for those who know less about the field but would like to be exposed to a varied selection of that which is most excellent in it.

Excellence in crime writing has many measures, one being the size and commitment of the readership the work commands. While there are in crime writing, as in every endeavour, people whose talents deserve much greater recognition than they enjoy, the converse is rarely true: Rarely does an author make it to the top of the genre's bestseller lists without having some special gift for storytelling or characterization or clever plotting or richness of writing. Most of the authors included in this book are popular favorites, at least one even has her own fan club; all have written novels as well as short stories, and most have books that can be found on the shelves of any good general or mystery bookstore. They are, in other words, those who have risen or are in the process of rising to the top of their profession in terms of name recognition and sales. Not coincidentally, all have also won or been nominated for major awards.

Mystery awards fall into two categories: those that are voted on by readers and fans and those that are bestowed by a committee of professional judges—often other writers. *Ellery Queen's Mystery Magazine* sponsors its own readers' award for best short story, for which the full readership of the magazine is eligible to vote; likewise, the fanzine *Mystery Readers Journal* takes nominations for its Macavity Awards from all of its subscribers. Fan gatherings are somewhat more restrictive in who they allow to contribute to the outcome of their awards. Conventions such as the annual Bouchercon World Mystery Convention, which each year presents the Anthony Awards, and the Malice Domestic Convention, which yearly presides over the Agatha Awards, both limit input to attendees of the convention, a tightly knit group of fans who decide, by ballot, which stories and books take the laurels. In contrast, the Mystery Writers of America's Edgar Allan Poe Awards, the Private Eye Writers of America's Shamus Awards, the Crime Writers of Canada's Arthur Ellis Awards, and Britain's Dagger Awards are all determined by committees of writers who assiduously read every new piece of crime fiction published within the specified calendar year and proffer their votes on what is purported to be a purely critical basis. As an aid to those who are not already familiar with all of the authors in *Crème de la Crime,* a short author introduction has been provided preceding each tale. As the award information included in these write-ups shows, nearly every author who has won or been nominated for a fan award has also won or been nominated for at least one of the critical awards, demonstrating that in this field at least, fans and professional judges tend to be of like mind, and the popular taste coincides with the critical.

A look at the author biographies of this volume's contributors also reveals an extraordinary amount of versatility in the talents of individual authors, many of whom regularly work in several different subgenres equally effectively. As different as the rules of the spy or thriller or private-eye story are from one another and from the classical detective or suspense story, there appear to be certain conventions they all share that make it possible for writers of one type of story to switch easily to another. A book of this sort is not the place to speculate on what the different types of stories have in common. There may be certain universal threads binding them all together, such as a craving for order or a wish to see justice served, or there may simply be a loose network of overlapping expectations linking the various parts that make up the field as a whole. In the following pages we've tried to do no more than paint a picture of the crime genre as it is today. It wasn't possible in the space allotted to include the work of every

author who rightly belongs with the crème de la crime, but we hope the
selections we have made will be interesting enough to readers to make them
want to make further explorations of the mystery shelves in their local
libraries and bookstores.

—Janet Hutchings

In for a Penny

Lawrence Block

We begin this volume with a selection from a true mystery writing pro. Lawrence Block published his first mystery, a short story, in the magazine Manhunt *at the age of nineteen. He quickly expanded from the short story to the paperback-book market, writing both under his own name and several pseudonyms before an entry in his Matt Scudder private-eye series in 1987 shot him to prominence in the mystery world. Although he is often classed with the genre's hard-boiled writers, there seems to be no area of the field in which he hasn't succeeded. His deftness in bringing humor to the mystery is evident in his Bernie Rhodenbarr novels about an erudite burglar turned occasional detective, while his knowledge of the mystery's more traditional forms shines through in the pseudonymously written books and stories about Leo Haig, a devotee of Rex Stout's Nero Wolf. Lawrence Block's mastery of the mystery in all its guises was celebrated by the Mystery Writers of America in 1994 when he was named one of the organization's Grandmasters. That distinction is one of many the author—a multiple winner of the Edgar Allan Poe and Shamus awards—has received in the course of a career that already spans more than four decades.*

PAUL KEPT IT very simple. That seemed to be the secret. You kept it simple, you drew firm lines and didn't cross them. You put one foot in front of the other, took it day by day, and let the days mount up.

The state didn't take an interest. They put you back on the street with a cheap suit and figured you'd be back inside before the pants got shiny. But other people cared. This one outfit, about two parts ex-cons to one part holy joes, had wised him up and helped him out. They'd found him a job and a place to live, and what more did he need?

The job wasn't much, frying eggs and flipping burgers in a diner at Twenty-third and Eighth. The room wasn't much, either, seven blocks south

4

of the diner, four flights up from the street. It was small, and all you could see from its window was the back of another building. The furnishings were minimal—an iron bed-stead, a beat-up dresser, a rickety chair—and the walls needed paint and the floor needed carpet. There was a sink in the room, a bathroom down the hall. No cooking, no pets, no overnight guests, the landlady told him. No kidding, he thought.

His shift was four to midnight, Monday through Friday. The first weekend he did nothing but go to the movies, and by Sunday night he was ready to climb the wall. Too much time to kill, too few ways to kill it that wouldn't get him in trouble. How many movies could you sit through? And a movie cost him two hours' pay, and if you spent the whole weekend dragging yourself from one movie house to another . . .

Weekends were dangerous, one of the ex-cons had told him. Weekends could put you back in the joint. There ought to be a law against weekends.

But he figured out a way around it. Walking home Tuesday night, after that first weekend of movie-going, he'd stopped at three diners on Seventh Avenue, nursing a cup of coffee and chatting with the guy behind the counter. The third time was the charm; he walked out of there with a weekend job. Saturday and Sunday, same hours, same wages, same work. And they'd pay him off the books, which made his weekend work tax-free.

Between what he was saving in taxes and what he wasn't spending on movies, he'd be a millionaire.

Well, maybe he'd never be a millionaire. Probably be dangerous to be a millionaire, a guy like him, with his ways, his habits. But he was earning an honest dollar, and he ate all he wanted on the job, seven days a week now, so it wasn't hard to put a few bucks aside. The weeks added up and so did the dollars, and the time came when he had enough cash socked away to buy himself a little television set. The cashier at his weekend job set it up and her boyfriend brought it over, so he figured it fell off a truck or walked out of somebody's apartment, but it got good reception and the price was right.

It was a lot easier to pass the time once he had the TV. He'd get up at ten or eleven in the morning, grab a shower in the bathroom down the hall, then pick up doughnuts and coffee at the corner deli. Then he'd watch a little TV until it was time to go to work.

After work he'd stop at the same deli for two bottles of cold beer and some cigarettes. He'd settle in with the TV, a beer bottle in one hand and a cigarette in the other and his eyes on the screen.

He didn't get cable, but he figured that was all to the good. He was better off staying away from some of the stuff they were allowed to show on cable TV. Just because you had cable didn't mean you had to watch it, but he knew himself, and if he had it right there in the house how could he keep himself from looking at it?

And that could get you started. Something as simple as late-night adult programming could put him on a train to the big house upstate. He'd been there. He didn't want to go back.

He would get through most of a pack of cigarettes by the time he turned off the light and went to bed. It was funny, during the day he hardly smoked at all, but back in his room at night he had a butt going just about all the time. If the smoking was heavy, well, the drinking was ultralight. He could make a bottle of Bud last an hour. More, even. The second bottle was always warm by the time he got to it, but he didn't mind, nor did he drink it any faster than he'd drunk the first one. What was the rush?

Two beers was enough. All it did was give him a little buzz, and when the second beer was gone he'd turn off the TV and sit at the window, smoking one cigarette after another, looking out at the city.

Then he'd go to bed. Then he'd get up and do it all over again.

The only problem was walking home.

And even that was no problem at first. He'd leave his rooming house around three in the afternoon. The diner was ten minutes away, and that left him time to eat before his shift started. Then he'd leave sometime between midnight and twelve-thirty—the guy who relieved him, a manic Albanian, had a habit of showing up ten to fifteen minutes late. Paul would retrace his earlier route, walking the seven blocks down Eighth Avenue to Sixteenth Street, with a stop at the deli for cigarettes and beer.

The Rose of Singapore was the problem.

The first time he walked past the place, he didn't even notice it. By day it was just another seedy bar, but at night the neon glowed and the jukebox music poured out the door, along with the smell of spilled drinks and stale beer and something more, something unnameable, something elusive.

"If you don't want to slip," they'd told him, "stay out of slippery places."

He quickened his pace and walked on by.

The next afternoon the Rose of Singapore didn't carry the same feeling of danger. Not that he'd risk crossing the threshold, not at any hour of the day or night. He wasn't stupid. But it didn't lure him and, consequently, it didn't make him uncomfortable.

Coming home was a different story.

He was thinking about it during his last hour on the job, and by the time he reached it he was walking all the way over at the edge of the sidewalk, as far from the building's entrance as he could get without stepping down into the street. He was like an acrophobe edging along a precipitous path, scared to look down, afraid of losing his balance and falling accidentally, afraid too of the impulse that might lead him to plunge purposefully into the void.

He kept walking, eyes forward, heart racing. Once he was past it he felt himself calming down, and he bought his two bottles of beer and his pack of cigarettes and went on home.

He'd get used to it, he told himself. It would get easier with time.

But, surprisingly enough, it didn't. Instead it got worse, but gradually, imperceptibly, and he learned to accommodate it. For one thing, he steered clear of the west side of Eighth Avenue, where the Rose of Singapore stood. Going to work and coming home, he kept to the opposite side of the street.

Even so, he found himself hugging the inner edge of the sidewalk, as if every inch closer to the street would put him that much closer to crossing it and being drawn mothlike into the tavern's neon flame. And, approaching the Rose of Singapore's block, he'd slow down or speed up his pace so that the traffic signal would allow him to cross the street as soon as he reached the corner. As if otherwise, stranded there, he might cross in the other direction instead, across Eighth Avenue and on into the Rose.

He knew it was ridiculous, but he couldn't change the way it felt. When it didn't get better, he found a way around it.

He took Seventh Avenue instead.

He did that on the weekends anyway because it was the shortest route. But during the week it added two long crosstown blocks to his pedestrian commute, four blocks a day, twenty blocks a week. That came to about three miles a week, maybe a hundred and fifty extra miles a year.

On good days he told himself he was lucky to be getting the exercise, that the extra blocks would help him stay in shape. On bad days he felt like an idiot, crippled by fear.

Then the Albanian got fired.

He was never clear on what happened. One waitress said the Albanian had popped off at the manager one time too many, and maybe that was what happened. All he knew was that one night his relief man was not the usual wild-eyed fellow with the droopy moustache but a stocky dude with a calculating air about him. His name was Dooley, and Paul made him at a glance as a man who'd done time. You could tell, but of course he didn't say anything, didn't drop any hints. And neither did Dooley.

But the night came when Dooley showed up, tied his apron, rolled up his sleeves, and said, "Give her my love, huh?" And, when Paul looked at him in puzzlement, he added, "Your girlfriend."

"Haven't got one," he said.

"You live on Eighth Avenue, right? That's what you told me. Eighth and Sixteenth, right? Yet every time you leave here you head over toward Seventh. Every single time."

"I like the exercise," he said.

"Exercise," Dooley said, and grinned. "Good word for it."

He let it go, but the next night Dooley made a similar comment. "I need to unwind when I come off work," Paul told him. "Sometimes I'll walk clear over to Sixth Avenue before I head downtown. Or even Fifth."

"That's nice," Dooley said. "Just do me a favor, will you? Ask her if she's got a sister."

"It's cold and it looks like rain," Paul said. "I'll be walking home on Eighth Avenue tonight, in case you're keeping track."

And when he left he did walk down Eighth Avenue—for one block. Then he cut over to Seventh and took what had become his usual route.

He began doing that all the time, and whenever he headed east on Twenty-second Street he found himself wondering why he'd let Dooley have such power over him. For that matter, how could he have let a seedy gin joint make him walk out of his way to the tune of a hundred and fifty miles a year?

He was supposed to be keeping it simple. Was this keeping it simple? Making up elaborate lies to explain the way he walked home? And walking extra blocks every night for fear that the devil would reach out and drag him into a neon-lit hell?

Then came a night when it rained, and he walked all the way home on Eighth Avenue.

It was always a problem when it rained. Going to work he could catch a bus, although it wasn't terribly convenient. But coming home he didn't have the option, because traffic was one-way the wrong way.

So he walked home on Eighth Avenue, and he didn't turn left at Twenty-second Street and didn't fall apart when he drew even with the Rose of Singapore. He breezed on by, bought his beer and cigarettes at the deli, and went home to watch television. But he turned the set off again after a few minutes and spent the hours until bedtime at the window, looking out at the rain, nursing the beers, smoking the cigarettes, and thinking long thoughts.

The next two nights were clear and mild, but he chose Eighth Avenue anyway. He wasn't uneasy, not going to work, not coming home, either. Then came the weekend, and then on Monday he took Eighth again, and this time on the way home he found himself on the west side of the street, the same side as the bar.

The door was open. Music, strident and bluesy, poured through it, along with all the sounds and smells you'd expect.

He walked right on by.

You're over it, he thought. He went home and didn't even turn on the TV, just sat and smoked and sipped his two longneck bottles of Bud.

Same story Tuesday, same story Wednesday.

Thursday night, steps from the tavern's open door, he thought, *Why drag this out?*

He walked in, found a stool at the bar. "Double scotch," he told the barmaid. "Straight up, beer chaser."

He'd tossed off the shot and was working on the beer when a woman slid onto the stool beside him. She put a cigarette between bright red lips, and he scratched a match and lit it for her.

Their eyes met, and he felt something click.

She lived over on Ninth and Seventeenth, on the third floor of a brownstone across the street from the projects. She said her name was Tiffany, and maybe it was. Her apartment was three little rooms. They sat on the couch in the front room and he kissed her a few times and got a little dizzy from it. He excused himself and went to the bathroom and looked at himself in the mirror over the sink.

You could go home now, he told the mirror image. Tell her anything, like you got a headache, you got malaria, you're really a Catholic priest or gay or both. Anything. Doesn't matter what you say or if she believes you. You could go home.

He looked into his own eyes in the mirror and knew it wasn't true.

Because he was stuck, he was committed, he was down for it. Had been from the moment he walked into the bar. No, longer than that. From the first rainy night when he walked home on Eighth Avenue. Or maybe before, maybe ever since Dooley's insinuation had led him to change his route.

And maybe it went back further than that. Maybe he was locked in from the jump, from the day they opened the gates and put him on the street. Hell, from the day he was born, even.

"Paul?"

"Just a minute," he said.

And he slipped into the kitchen. In for a penny, in for a pound, he thought, and he started opening drawers, looking for the one where she kept the knives.

TRIANGLE

Jeffery Deaver

Though the thriller clearly belongs under the umbrella of crime fiction, thrillers of novel length are usually found in the mainstream popular fiction displays at bookstores, not in the mystery section. As a result, names such as Jeffery Deaver are less known within mystery circles than they ought to be. With first-print runs on his thriller novels regularly running in to the six figures and several movies already out based on his books—including the recently released The Bone Collector, *starring Denzel Washington—the author is clearly one of the field's most successful writers. The key to his success lies in his uncanny ability to deliver multiple twist endings at the tail of stories fraught with suspense—he is able to do this so reliably in short stories as well as novels that his literary agent has aptly dubbed him the O. Henry of the mystery story. When writing mysteries as opposed to thrillers, the author often employs the pseudonym William Jefferies. The work he has produced under these two bylines, at novel and short-story length, have earned him two nominations for the Edgar Allan Poe Award from the Mystery Writers of America and two first-place finishes in the* Ellery Queen's Mystery Magazine *Readers Award competition.*

"MAYBE I'LL GO to Baltimore."

"You mean . . ." She looked at him. "To see . . ."

"Doug," he answered.

"Really?" Mo Anderson asked and looked carefully at her fingernails, which she was painting bright red. He didn't like the color but he didn't say anything about it. She wouldn't listen to him anyway.

"I think it'd be fun," he continued.

"Oh, it would be," she said quickly. "Doug's a fun guy."

"Sure is," Pete Anderson said. He sat across from Mo on the front porch of their split-level house in suburban Westchester County. The month was

10

June and the air was thick with the smell of the jasmine that Mo had planted earlier in the spring. Pete used to like that smell. Now, though, it made him sick to his stomach.

Mo inspected her nails for streaks and pretended to be sort of bored with the idea of him going to see her friend Doug. But she was a lousy actor; Pete could tell she was really excited by the idea and he knew why. But he just watched the lightning bugs and kept quiet. Unlike Mo, he *could* act.

"When would you go?" she asked.

"This weekend, I guess. Saturday."

They were silent and sipped their drinks, the ice clunking dully on the plastic glasses. It was the first day of summer and the sky wasn't completely dark yet even though it was nearly nine o'clock in the evening. There must've been a thousand lightning bugs in their front yard.

"I know I kinda said I'd help you clean up the garage," he said, wincing a little, looking guilty.

"No, I think you should go. I think it'd be a good idea," she said.

I *know* you think it'd be a good idea, Pete thought. But he didn't say this to her. Lately he'd been thinking a lot of things and not saying them.

Pete was sweating—more from excitement than from the heat—and he wiped the sweat off his face and his round buzz-cut blond hair with his napkin.

The phone rang and Mo went to answer it.

She came back and said, "It's your *father*," in that sour voice of hers that Pete hated. She sat down and didn't say anything else, just picked up her drink and examined her nails again.

Pete got up and went into the kitchen. His father lived in Wisconsin, not far from Lake Michigan. He loved the man and wished they lived closer together. Mo, though, didn't like him one bit and always raised a stink when Pete wanted to go visit. She never went with him. Pete was never exactly sure what the problem was between Mo and his dad. But it made him mad that she treated the man so badly and would never talk to Pete about it.

And he was mad, too, that Mo seemed to put Pete in the middle of things. Sometimes Pete even felt guilty he *had* a father.

He had a nice talk but hung up after only ten minutes because he felt Mo didn't want him to be on the phone.

Pete walked out onto the porch.

"Saturday," Mo said. "I think Saturday'd be fine."

Fine . . .

Then she looked at her watch and said, "It's getting late. Time for bed."

And when Mo said it was time for bed, it was definitely time for bed.

* * *

Later that night, when Mo was asleep, Pete walked downstairs into the office. He reached behind a row of books resting on the built-in bookshelves and pulled out a large, sealed envelope.

He carried it down to his workshop in the basement. He opened the envelope and took out a book. It was called *Triangle* and Pete had found it in the true-crime section of a local used-book shop after flipping through nearly twenty books about real-life murders. Pete had never ripped off anything, but that day he'd looked around the store and slipped the book inside his windbreaker, then strolled casually out the door. He'd *had* to steal it; he was afraid that—if everything went as he'd planned—the clerk might remember him buying the book and the police would use it as evidence.

Triangle was the story of a couple in Colorado Springs. The wife was married to a man named Roy. But she was also seeing another man— Hank—a local carpenter. Roy found out and waited until Hank was out hiking on a mountain path, then he snuck up beside him and pushed him over the cliff. Hank grabbed onto a tree root but he lost his grip—or Roy smashed his hands; it wasn't clear—and Hank fell a hundred feet to his death on the rocks in the valley. Roy went back home and had a drink with his wife just to watch her reaction when the call came that Hank was dead.

Pete didn't know squat about crimes. All he knew was what he'd seen on TV and in the movies. None of the criminals in those shows seemed very smart and they were always getting caught by the good guys, even though *they* didn't really seem much smarter than the bad guys. But that crime in Colorado was a smart crime. Because there were no murder weapons and very few clues. The only reason Roy got caught was that he'd forgotten to look for witnesses.

If the killer had only taken the time to look around him, he would have seen the witnesses: A couple of campers had a perfect view of Hank Gibson plummeting to his bloody death, screaming as he fell, and of Roy standing on the cliff, watching him. . . .

Triangle became Pete's bible. He read it cover to cover—to see how Roy had planned the crime and to find out how the police had investigated it.

Tonight, with Mo asleep and his electronic airline ticket to Baltimore bought and paid for, Pete read *Triangle* once again, paying particular attention to the parts he'd underlined. Then he walked back upstairs, packed the book in the bottom of his suitcase, and lay on the couch in the office, looking out the window at the hazy summer stars and thinking about his trip from every angle.

Because he wanted to make sure he got away with the crime. He didn't want to go to jail for life—like Roy.

Oh, sure there were risks. Pete knew that. But nothing was going to stop him.

Doug had to die.

Pete realized he'd been thinking about the idea, in the back of his mind, for months, not long after Mo met Doug.

She worked part-time for a drug company in Westchester—the same company Doug was a salesman for, assigned to the Baltimore office. They met when he came to the headquarters for a sales conference. Mo had told Pete that she was having dinner with "somebody" from the company, but she didn't say who. Pete didn't think anything of it until he overheard her tell one of her girlfriends on the phone about this interesting guy she'd met. But then she realized Pete was standing near enough to hear and she changed the subject.

Over the next few months, Pete realized that Mo was getting more and more distracted, paying less and less attention to him. And he heard her mention Doug more and more.

One night Pete asked her about him.

"Oh, Doug?" she said, sounding irritated. "Why, he's just a friend, that's all. Can't I have friends? Aren't I allowed?"

Pete noticed that Mo was starting to spend a lot of time on the phone and on-line. He tried to check the phone bills to see if she was calling Baltimore but she hid them or threw them out. He also tried to read her e-mails but found she'd changed her password. Pete was an expert with computers and easily broke into her account. But when he went to read her e-mails he found she'd deleted them all.

He was so furious he nearly smashed the computer.

Then, to Pete's dismay, Mo started inviting Doug to dinner at their house when he was in Westchester on company business. He was older than Mo and sort of heavy. But Pete admitted he was handsome and real slick. Those dinners were the worst. . . . They'd all three sit at the dinner table and Doug would try to charm Pete and ask him about computers and sports and the things that Mo obviously had told Doug that Pete liked. But it was real awkward and you could tell he didn't give a damn about Pete. He just wanted to be there with Mo, alone.

By then Pete was checking up on Mo all the time. Sometimes he'd pretend to go to a game with Sammy Biltmore or Tony Hale but he'd come home early and find that she was gone too. Then she'd come home at eight or nine and look all flustered, not expecting to find him, and she'd say she'd been working late, even though she was just an office manager and hardly ever worked later than five before she met Doug. Once, when she claimed she was at the office, Pete got Doug's number in Baltimore and the message said he'd be out of town for a couple of days.

Everything was changing. Mo and Pete would have dinner together but it wasn't the same. They didn't have picnics and they didn't take walks in the evenings. And they hardly ever sat together on the porch anymore and looked out at the fireflies and made plans for trips they wanted to take.

"I don't like him," Pete said. "Doug, I mean."

"Oh, quit being so jealous. He's a good friend, that's all. He likes both of us."

"No, he doesn't like me."

"Of course he does. You don't have to worry."

But Pete did worry, and he worried even more when he found a piece of paper in her purse last month. It said: *D. G.—Sunday, motel 2 P.M.*

Doug's last name was Grant.

That Sunday morning Pete tried not to react when Mo said, "I'm going out for a while, honey."

"Where you going?"

"Shopping. I'll be back by five."

He thought about asking her exactly where she was going but he didn't think that was a good idea. It might make her suspicious. So he said cheerfully, "Okay, see you later."

As soon as her car had pulled out of the driveway he'd started calling motels in the area and asking for Douglas Grant.

The clerk at the Westchester Motor Inn said, "One minute, please, I'll connect you."

Pete hung up fast.

He was at the motel in fifteen minutes and, yep, there was Mo's car parked in front of one of the doors. Pete snuck up close to the room. The shade was drawn and the lights were out, but the window was partly open. Pete could hear bits of the conversation.

"I don't like that."

"That . . . ?" she asked.

"That color. I want you to paint your nails red. It's sexy. I don't like that color you're wearing. What is it?"

"Peach."

"I like bright red," Doug said.

"Well, okay."

There was some laughing. Then a long silence. Pete tried to look inside but he couldn't see anything. Finally, Mo said, "We have to talk. About Pete."

"He knows something," Doug was saying. "I know he does."

"He's been like a damn spy lately," she said, with that edge to her voice that Pete hated. "Sometimes I'd like to strangle him."

Pete closed his eyes when he heard Mo say this. Pressed the lids closed so hard he thought he might never open them again.

He heard the sound of a beer can opening.

Doug said, "So what if he finds out?"

"So *what?* I told you what having an affair does to alimony in this state. It *eliminates* it. We have to be careful. I've got a lifestyle I'm accustomed to."

"Then what should we do?" Doug asked.

"I've been thinking about it. I think you should do something with him."

"Do something with him?" Doug had an edge to his voice too. "Get him a one-way ticket . . ."

"Come on."

"Okay, sorry. But what do you mean by 'do something'?"

"Get to know him."

"You're kidding."

"Prove to him you're just a friend."

Doug laughed and said in a soft, low voice, "Does *that* feel like a friend?"

She laughed too. "Stop it. I'm trying to have a serious talk here."

"So what? We go to a ball game together?"

"No, it's got to be more than that. Ask him to come visit you."

"Oh, that'd be fun." With that same snotty tone that Mo sometimes used.

She continued, "No, I like it. Ask him to come down. Pretend you've got a girlfriend or something."

"He won't believe that."

"Pete's only smart when it comes to computers and baseball. He's stupid about everything else."

Peter wrung his hands together. Nearly sprained a thumb—like the time he jammed his finger on the basketball court.

"That means I have to pretend I like him."

"Yeah, that's *exactly* what it means. It's not going to kill you."

"You come with him."

"No," she said. "I couldn't keep my hands off you."

A pause. Then Doug said, "Oh, hell, all right. I'll do it."

Pete, crouching on a strip of yellow grass beside three discarded soda cans, curled into a ball and shook with fury. It took all his willpower not to scream.

He hurried home, threw himself down on the couch in the office, and turned on the game.

When Mo came home—which wasn't at five at all, like she promised, but at six-thirty—he pretended he'd fallen asleep.

That night he decided what he had to do and the next day he went to the used-book store and stole the copy of *Triangle*.

On Saturday Mo drove him to the airport.

"You two gonna have fun together?" In the car she lit a cigarette. She'd never smoked before she met Doug.

"You bet," Pete said. He sounded cheerful because he was cheerful. "We're gonna have a fine time."

On the day of the murder, while his wife and her lover were sipping wine in a room at the Mountain View Lodge, Roy had lunch with a business associate. The man, who wished to remain anonymous, reported that Roy was in unusually good spirits. It seemed his depression had lifted and he was happy once more.

Fine, fine, fine . . .

At the gate Mo kissed him and then hugged him hard. He didn't kiss her but he hugged her back. But not hard. He didn't want to touch her. Didn't want to be touched by her.

"You're looking forward to going, aren't you?" she asked.

"I sure am," he answered. This was true.

"I love you," she said.

"I love you, too," he responded. This was not true. He hated her. He hoped the plane left on time. He didn't want to wait here with her any longer than he had to.

But the flight left as scheduled.

The flight attendant, a pretty blond woman, kept stopping at his seat. This wasn't unusual for Pete. Women liked him. He'd heard a million times that he was cute. Women were always leaning close and telling him that. Touching his arm, squeezing his shoulder. But today he answered her questions with a simple "yes" or "no." And kept reading *Triangle*. Reading the passages he'd underlined. Memorizing them.

Learning about fingerprints, about interviewing witnesses, about footprints and trace evidence. There was a lot he didn't understand, but he did figure out how smart the cops were and that he'd have to be very careful if he was going to kill Doug.

"We're about to land," the flight attendant said, "could you put your seat belt on, please?"

She squeezed his shoulder and smiled at him.

He put the seat belt on and went back to his book.

Hank Gibson's body had fallen one hundred and twelve feet. He'd landed on his right side and of the more than two hundred bones in the human body, he'd broken seventy-seven of them. His ribs had pierced all his major internal organs and his skull was flattened on one side.

"Welcome to Baltimore, where the local time is twelve twenty-five," the flight attendant said. "Please remain in your seat with the seat belt fastened until the plane has come to a complete stop and the pilot has turned off the Fasten Seat Belt sign. Thank you."

The medical examiner estimated that Hank was traveling eighty miles an hour when he struck the ground and that death was virtually instantaneous.

Welcome to Baltimore . . .

Doug met him at the airport. Shook his hand.

"How you doing, buddy?" Doug asked.

"Okay."

This was so weird. Spending the weekend with a man that Mo knew so well and that Pete hardly knew at all.

Going hiking with somebody he hardly knew at all.

Going to kill somebody he hardly knew at all. . . .

He walked along beside Doug.

"I need a beer and some crabs," Doug said as they got into his car. "You hungry?"

"Sure am."

They stopped at the waterfront and went into an old dive. The place stunk. It smelled like the cleanser Mo used on the floor when Randolf, their Labrador retriever puppy, made a mess on the carpet.

Doug whistled at the waitress before they'd even sat down. "Hey, honey, think you can handle two real men?" He gave her the sort of grin Pete'd seen Doug give Mo a couple of times. Pete looked away, somewhat embarrassed but plenty disgusted.

When they started to eat Doug calmed down, though that was more likely the beers. Like Mo got after her third glass of Gallo in the evenings. Doug had at least three that Pete counted and maybe a couple more after them.

Pete wasn't saying much. Doug tried to be cheerful. He talked and talked but it was just garbage. Pete didn't pay any attention.

"Maybe I'll give my girlfriend a call," Doug said suddenly. "See if she wants to join us."

"You have a girlfriend? What's her name?"

"Uhm, Cathy," he said.

The waitress's nametag said: *Hi, I'm Cathleen.*

"That'd be fun," Pete said.

"She might be going out of town this weekend." He avoided Pete's eyes. "But I'll call her later."

Pete's only smart when it comes to computers and baseball. He's stupid about everything else.

Finally Doug looked at his watch and said, "So what do you feel like doing now?"

Pete pretended to think for a minute and asked, "Anyplace we can go hiking around here?"

"Hiking?"

"Like any mountain trails?"

Doug finished his beer, shook his head. "Naw, nothing like that I know of."

Pete felt rage again—his hands were shaking, the blood roaring in his ears—but he covered it up pretty well and tried to think. Now, what was he going to do? He'd counted on Doug agreeing to whatever he wanted. He'd counted on a nice high cliff.

But then Doug continued. "But if you want to be outside, one thing we could do, maybe, is go hunting."

"Hunting?"

"Nothing good's in season now," Doug said. "But there's always rabbits and squirrels."

"Well—"

"I've got a couple of guns we can use."

Guns?

Pete said, "Okay. Let's go hunting."

"You shoot much?" Doug asked him.

"Some."

In fact, Pete was a good shot. His father had taught him how to load and clean guns and how to handle them. ("Never point it at anything unless you're prepared to shoot it.")

But Pete didn't want Doug to know he knew anything about guns so he let the man show him how to load the little .22 and how to pull the slide to cock it and where the safety was.

I'm a *much* better actor than Mo.

They were in Doug's house, which was pretty nice. It was in the woods and it was a big house, all full of stone walls and glass. The furniture wasn't like the cheap things Mo and Pete had. It was mostly antiques.

Which depressed Pete even more, made him angrier, because he knew that Mo liked money and she liked *people* who had money even if they were idiots, like Doug. When Pete looked at Doug's beautiful house he knew that if Mo ever saw it then she'd want Doug even more. Then he wondered if she *had* seen it. Pete had gone to Wisconsin a few months ago. Maybe Mo had come down here to spend the night with Doug.

"So," Doug said. "Ready?"

"Where're we going?" Pete asked.

"There's a good field about a mile from here. It's not posted. Anything we can hit we can take."

"Sounds good to me," Pete said.

They got into the car and Doug pulled onto the road.

"Better put that seat belt on," Doug warned. "I drive like a crazy man."

The field looked familiar to Pete.

As Doug laced up his boots, Pete realized why it was familiar. It was almost identical to a field in White Plains—the one across the highway from the elementary school. The only difference was that this one was completely quiet; the New York field was noisy. You heard a continual stream of traffic.

Pete was looking around.

Not a soul.

"What?" Doug asked, and Pete realized that the man was staring at him.

"Pretty quiet."

And deserted. No witnesses.

"Nobody knows about this place. I found it by my little old lonesome." Doug said this real proud, as if he'd discovered a cure for cancer. "Lessee." He lifted his rifle and squeezed off a round.

Crack . . .

He missed a can sitting about thirty feet away.

"Little rusty," he said. "But, hey, aren't we having fun?"

"Sure are," Pete answered.

Doug fired again, three times, and hit the can on the last shot. It leapt into the air. "There we go!"

Doug reloaded and they started through the tall grass and brush.

They walked for five minutes.

"There," Doug said. "Can you hit that rock over there?"

He was pointing at a white rock about twenty feet from them. Pete thought he could have hit it but he missed on purpose. He emptied the clip.

"Not bad," Doug said. "Came close the last few shots." Pete knew he was being sarcastic.

"So, what? We go to a ball game together?"

"No, it's got to be more than that. Ask him to come visit you."

"Oh, that'd be fun."

Pete reloaded and they continued through the grass.

"So," Doug said. "How's she doing?"

"Fine. She's fine."

Whenever Mo was upset and Pete'd ask her how she was she'd say, "Fine. I'm fine."

Which didn't mean fine at all. It meant, I don't feel like telling you anything. I'm keeping secrets from you.

They stepped over a few fallen logs and started down a hill.

The grass was mixed with blue flowers and daisies. Mo liked to garden and was always driving up to the nursery to buy plants. Sometimes she'd come back without any and Pete began to wonder if on those trips she was really seeing Doug instead. He got angry again. Hands sweaty, teeth grinding together.

"She get her car fixed?" Doug asked. "She was saying that there was something wrong with the transmission."

How'd he know that? The car broke down only four days ago. Had Doug been there and Pete didn't know it?

Doug glanced at Pete and repeated the question.

Pete blinked. "Oh, her car? Yeah, it's okay. She took it in and they fixed it."

But then he felt better because that meant they *hadn't* talked yesterday or she would have told him about getting the car fixed.

On the other hand, maybe Doug was lying to him now. Making it *look* as if she hadn't told him about the car when they really had talked.

Pete looked at Doug's pudgy face and couldn't decide whether to believe him or not. He looked sort of innocent but Pete had learned that people who seemed innocent were sometimes the most guilty. Roy, the husband in the *Triangle* book, had been a church choir director. From the smiling picture in the book, you'd never guess he'd kill a soul.

Thinking about the book, thinking about murder.

Pete was scanning the field. Yes, there . . . About fifty feet away. A fence. Five feet high. It would work just fine.

Fine.

As fine as Mo.

Who wanted Doug more than she wanted Pete.

"What're you looking for?" Doug asked.

"Something to shoot."

And he thought: Just witnesses. That's all I'm looking for.

"Let's go that way," Pete said and walked toward the fence.

Doug shrugged. "Sure. Why not?"

Pete studied it as they approached. Wood posts about eight feet apart, five strands of rusting wire.

Not too easy to climb over, but it wasn't barbed wire like some of the fences they'd passed. Besides, Pete didn't want it *too* easy to climb. He'd been thinking. He had a plan.

Roy had thought about the murder for weeks. It had obsessed his every waking moment. He'd drawn charts and diagrams and planned every detail down to the nth degree. In his mind, at least, it was the perfect crime.

Pete now asked, "So what's your girlfriend do?"

"Uhm, my girlfriend? She works in Baltimore."

"Oh. Doing what?"

"In an office."

"Oh."

They got closer to the fence. Pete asked, "You're divorced? Mo was saying you're divorced."

"Right. Betty and I split up two years ago."

"You still see her?"

"Who? Betty? Naw. We went our separate ways."

"You have any kids?"

"Nope."

Of course not. When you had kids you had to think about somebody else. You couldn't think about yourself all the time. Like Doug did. Like Mo. Pete was looking around again. For squirrels, for rabbits, for witnesses. Then Doug stopped and he looked around, too. Pete wondered why, but then Doug took a bottle of beer from his knapsack and drank the whole bottle down and tossed it on the ground. "You want something to drink?" Doug asked.

"No," Pete answered. It was good that Doug'd be slightly drunk when they found him. They'd check his blood. They did that. That's how they knew Hank'd been drinking when they got the body to the Colorado Springs hospital—they checked the alcohol in the blood.

The fence was only twenty feet away.

"Oh, hey," Pete said. "Over there. Look."

He pointed to the grass on the other side of the fence.

"What?" Doug asked.

"I saw a couple of rabbits."

"You did? Where?"

"I'll show you. Come on."

"Okay. Let's do it," Doug said.

They walked to the fence. Suddenly, Doug reached out and took Pete's rifle. "I'll hold it while you climb over. Safer that way."

Jesus . . . Pete froze with terror. Doug was going to do exactly what Pete had thought of. He'd been planning on holding Doug's gun for him. And then when Doug was at the top of the fence he was going to shoot him. Making it look like Doug had tried to carry his gun as he climbed the fence but he'd dropped it and it went off.

Roy bet on the old law-enforcement rule that what looks like an accident probably is an accident.

Pete didn't move. He thought he saw something funny in Doug's eyes, something mean and sarcastic. It reminded him of Mo's expression. Pete took one look at those eyes and he could see how much Doug hated him and how much he loved Mo.

"You want me to go first?" Pete asked. Not moving, wondering if he should just run.

"Sure," Doug said. "You go first. Then I'll hand the guns over to you." His eyes said: You're not afraid of climbing over the fence, are you? You're not afraid to turn your back on me, are you?

Then Doug was looking around, too.

Looking for witnesses.

"Go on," Doug encouraged.

Pete—his hands shaking from fear now, not anger—started to climb. Thinking: This is it. He's going to shoot me. I left the motel too early! Doug and Mo must have kept talking and planned out how he was going to ask me down here and pretend to be all nice and then he'd shoot me.

Remembering it was Doug who suggested hunting.

But if I run, Pete thought, he'll chase me down and shoot me. Even if he shoots me in the back he'll just claim it's an accident.

Roy's lawyer argued to the jury that, yes, the men had met on the path and struggled, but Hank had fallen accidentally. He urged the jury that, at worst, Roy was guilty of negligent homicide.

He put his foot on the first rung of wire. Started up.

Second rung of wire . . .

Pete's heart was beating a million times a minute. He had to pause to wipe his palms.

He thought he heard a whisper, as if Doug were talking to himself.

He swung his leg over the top wire.

Then he heard the sound of a gun cocking.

And Doug said in a hoarse whisper, "You're dead."

Pete gasped.

Crack!

The short, snappy sound of the .22 filled the field.

Pete choked a cry and looked around, nearly falling off the fence.

"Damn," Doug muttered. He was aiming away from the fence, nodding toward a tree line. "Squirrel. Missed him by two inches."

"Squirrel," Pete repeated manically. "And you missed him."

"Two goddamn inches."

Hands shaking, Pete continued over the fence and climbed to the ground.

"You okay?" Doug asked. "You look a little funny."

"I'm fine," he said.

Fine, fine, fine . . .

Doug handed Pete the guns and started over the fence. Pete debated. Then he put his rifle on the ground and gripped Doug's gun tight. He walked to the fence so that he was right below Doug.

"Look," Doug said as he got to the top. He was straddling it, his right leg on one side of the fence, his left on the other. "Over there." He pointed nearby.

There was a big gray lop-eared rabbit on his haunches only twenty feet away.

"There you go!" Doug whispered. "You've got a great shot."

Pete shouldered the gun. It was pointing at the ground, halfway between the rabbit and Doug.

"Go ahead. What're you waiting for?"

Roy was convicted of premeditated murder in the first degree and sentenced to life in prison. Yet he came very close to committing the perfect murder. If not for a simple twist of fate, he would have gotten away with it.

Pete looked at the rabbit, looked at Doug.

"Aren't you going to shoot?"

Uhm, okay, he thought.

Pete raised the gun and pulled the trigger once.

Doug gasped, pressed at the tiny bullet hole in his chest. "But . . . But . . . No!"

He fell backwards off the fence and lay on a patch of dried mud, completely still. The rabbit bounded through the grass, panicked by the sound of the shot, and disappeared in a tangle of bushes that Pete recognized as blackberries. Mo had planted tons of them in their backyard.

The plane descended from cruising altitude and slowly floated toward the airport.

Pete watched the billowy clouds, tried to figure out what they looked like. He was bored. He didn't have anything to read. Before he'd talked to the Maryland state troopers about Doug's death, he'd thrown the true-crime book about the Triangle murder into a trash bin.

One of the reasons the jury convicted Roy was that, upon examining his house, the police found several books about disposing of evidence. Roy had no satisfactory explanation for them.

The small plane glided out of the skies and landed at White Plains airport. Pete pulled his knapsack out from underneath the seat in front of him and climbed out of the plane. He walked down the ramp, beside the flight attendant, a tall black woman. They'd talked together for most of the flight.

Pete saw Mo at the gate. She looked numb. She wore sunglasses and Pete supposed she'd been crying. She was clutching a Kleenex in her fingers.

Her nails weren't bright red anymore, he noticed.

They weren't peach either.

They were just plain fingernail color.

The flight attendant came up to Mo. "You're Mrs. Jill Anderson?"

Mo nodded.

The woman held up a sheet of paper. "Here. Could you sign this, please?"

Numbly Mo took the pen the woman offered and signed the paper.

It was an unaccompanied-minor form, which adults had to sign to allow their children to get on planes by themselves. The parent picking up the child also had to sign it. After his parents were divorced Pete flew back and forth between Wisconsin and White Plains so often he knew all about airlines' procedures for kids who flew alone.

"I have to say," she said to Mo, smiling down at Pete, "he's the best-behaved youngster I've ever had on one of my flights. How old are you, Pete?"

"I'm ten," he answered. "But I'm going to be eleven next week."

She squeezed his shoulder, then looked at Mo. "I'm so sorry about what happened," she said in a soft voice. "The trooper who put Pete on the plane told me. Your boyfriend was killed in a hunting accident?"

"No," Mo said, struggling to say the words, "he wasn't my boyfriend."

Though Pete was thinking: Of course he was your boyfriend. Except you didn't want the court to find that out because then Dad wouldn't have to pay you alimony anymore. Which is why she and Doug had been working so hard to convince Pete that Doug was "just a friend."

Can't I have friends? Aren't I allowed?

No, you're not, Pete thought. You're not going to get away with dumping me the way you dumped Dad.

"Can we go home, Mo?" he asked, looking as sad as he could. "I feel real funny about what happened."

"Sure, honey."

"Mo?" the flight attendant asked.

Mo, staring out the window, said, "When he was five Pete tried to write 'Mother' on my birthday card. He just wrote M-O and didn't know how to spell the rest. It became my nickname."

"What a sweet story," the woman said and looked like *she* was going to cry. "Pete, you come back and fly with us real soon."

"Okay."

"Hey, what're you going to do for your birthday?"

"I don't know," he said. Then he looked up at his mother. "I was thinking about maybe going hiking. In Colorado. Just the two of us."

SPOOKED

Carolyn Hart

Oklahoma native Carolyn Hart is the epitome of a writer able to touch the chords of mystery fandom. Though she came to fiction writing after a successful first career as a journalist, and only settled down to write mysteries after penning several children's books and romantic suspense novels, her first mystery series, about mystery bookstore owner Annie Laurance and her soon-to-be-husband Max Darling, exhibited her knowledge of the genre's roots and delighted fans, who felt at home in the fictional bookstore's surroundings. Carolyn Hart's humorous touch with the traditional, fairly clued mystery has earned her a following that includes a fan club and a newsletter, The Hart Beat, *devoted exclusively to her work. The Annie Laurance series was already a hit when Carolyn Hart launched a very different, but still traditional, series featuring an older heroine, retired newspaper reporter Henrie O. The author describes the Henrie O. series as "my tribute to women who were young during WWII . . . a generation of women who blazed independent paths in a male-dominated society." Carolyn Hart has played an important part in revitalizing the traditional mystery in an American setting: she has received, for her work, multiple Anthony and Agatha awards and a Macavity Award from* Mystery Readers Journal.

THE DUST FROM the convoy rose in plumes. Gretchen stood on tiptoe, waving, waving.

A soldier leaned over the tailgate of the olive-drab troop carrier. The blazing July sun touched his crew cut with gold. He grinned as he tossed her a bubble gum. "Chew it for me, kid."

Gretchen wished she could run alongside, give him some of Grandmother Lotte's biscuits and honey. But his truck was twenty feet away and another one rumbled in front of her. She ran a few steps, called out, "Good luck. Good luck!" The knobby piece of gum was a precious lump in her hand.

She stood on the edge of the highway until the last truck passed. Grandmother said Highway 66 went all the way to California and the soldiers were on their way to big ships to sail across the ocean to fight the Japs. Gretchen wished she could do something for the war. Her brother Jimmy was a Marine, somewhere in the South Pacific. He'd survived Iwo Jima. Every month they sent him cookies, peanut butter and oatmeal raisin and spice, packed in popcorn. When they had enough precious sugar, they made Aunt Bill's candy, but Mom had to find the sugar in Tulsa. Mr. Hudson's general store here in town almost never had sacks of sugar. Every morning she and Grandmother sat in a front pew of the little frame church in the willows and prayed for Jimmy and for all the boys overseas and for Gretchen's mom working so hard at the defense plant in Tulsa. Her mom only came home about one weekend a month. Grandmother tried to save a special piece of meat when she could. Grandmother said her mom was thin as a rail and working too hard, but Gretchen knew it was important for her mom to work. They needed everybody to help, and Mom was proud that she put radio parts in the big B-24 Liberators.

Gretchen took a deep breath of the hot heavy air, still laced with dust, and walked across the street to the cafe. Ever since the war started, they'd been busy from early morning until they ran out of food, sometimes around five o'clock, never later than seven. Of course, they had special ration books for the cafe, but Grandmother said they couldn't use those points to get sugar for Jimmy. That wouldn't be right.

Gretchen shaded her eyes and looked at the plate-glass window. She still felt a kind of thrill when she saw the name painted in bright blue: Victory Cafe. A thrill, but also a tightness in her chest, the kind of feeling she once had when she climbed the big sycamore to get the calico kitten and a branch snapped beneath her feet. For an instant that seemed to last forever, she was falling. She whopped against a thick limb and held on tight. She remembered the sense of strangeness as she fell. And disbelief, the thought that this couldn't be happening to her. There was a strangeness in the cafe's new name. It had been Pfizer's Cafe for almost twenty years, but now it didn't do to be proud of being German. Now Grandmother didn't say much in the cafe because her accent was thick. She was careful not to say "ja" and she let Gretchen do most of the talking. Grandmother prayed for Jimmy and for her sister's family in Hamburg.

Gretchen tucked the bubblegum in the pocket of her pedal pushers. Grandmother wouldn't let her wear shorts even though it was so hot the cotton stuck to her legs. She glanced at the big thermometer hanging by the door. Ninety-eight degrees and just past one o'clock. They'd sure hit over a hundred today, just like every day for the past few weeks. They kept the front door propped open, hoping for a little breeze through the screen.

The cafe was almost as much her home as the boxy three-bedroom frame house a half-mile away down a dirt road. Her earliest memories were playing with paper dolls in a corner of the kitchen as her mother and grandmother worked hard and fast, fixing country breakfasts for truck drivers in a hurry to get to Tulsa and on to Oklahoma City and Amarillo with their big rigs. Every morning, grizzled old men from around the county gathered at Pfizer's for their newspapers and gossip as well as rashers of bacon, a short stack and scrambled eggs. But everything changed with the war. Camp Crowder, just over the line in Missouri, brought in thousands of soldiers. Of course, they were busy training, but there were always plenty of khaki uniforms in the Victory Cafe now even though the menu wasn't what it had been before the war. Now they had meatless Tuesdays and Grandmother fixed huge batches of macaroni and cheese. Sometimes there wasn't any bacon, but they had scrambled eggs and grits and fried potatoes. Instead of roast beef, they had hash, the potatoes and meat bubbly in a vinegary sauce. But Grandmother never fixed red cabbage or sauerkraut anymore.

It was up to Gretchen to help her grandmother when her mom moved to Tulsa. She might only be twelve, but she was wiry and strong and she promised herself she'd never complain, not once, not ever, not for the duration. That's what everybody talked about, the duration until someday the war was over. On summer evenings she was too tired to play kick the can and it seemed a long-ago memory when she used to climb up into the maple tree, carrying a stack of movie magazines, and nestle with her back to the trunk and legs dangling.

She gave a swift, professional glance around the square room. The counter with red leatherette stools was to the left. The mirror behind the counter sparkled. She'd stood on a stool to polish it after lunch. Now it reflected her: black pigtails, a skinny face with blue eyes that often looked tired and worried, and a pink Ship 'n Shore blouse and green pedal pushers. Her blouse had started the day crisp and starched, but now it was limp and spattered with bacon grease.

Four tables sat in the center. Three wooden booths ran along the back wall and two booths to the right. The jukebox was tucked between the back booths and the swinging door to the kitchen. It was almost always playing. She loved "Stardust" and "Chattanooga Choo-Choo," but the most often played song was "Praise the Lord and Pass the Ammunition." A poster on the wall beside the jukebox pictured a sinking ship and a somber Uncle Sam with a finger to his lips and the legend: LOOSE LIPS SINK SHIPS.

Grandmother told her it meant no one should talk about the troop convoys that went through on Highway 66 or where they were going, or talk about soldiers' letters that sometimes carried information that got past the censors. Grandmother said that's why they had to be so careful about the food, to make sure there was enough for Jimmy and all the other boys. And that's why they couldn't drive to Tulsa to see Mom. There wasn't enough gas. Grandmother said even a cupful of gas might make a difference one day whether some boy—like Jimmy—lived or died.

Two of the front tables needed clearing. But she made a circuit of the occupied places first.

Deputy Sheriff Carter flicked his cigar and ash dribbled onto his paunch, which started just under his chin and pouched against the edge of the table. He frowned at black and white squares on the newspaper page. He looked at Mr. Hudson across the table. "You know a word for mountain ridge? Five letters." He chewed on his pencil. "Oh, yeah," he murmured. He marked the letters, closed the paper, leaned back in the booth. "Heard they been grading a road out near the McLemore place."

Mr. Hudson clanked his spoon against the thick white coffee mug. "Got some more java, Gretchen?"

She nodded.

Mr. Hudson pursed his thin mouth. "Bud McLemore's son-in-law's a county commissioner, Euel. What do you expect?"

Gretchen hurried to the hot plates behind the counter, brought the steaming coffeepot, and refilled both men's mugs.

The deputy sheriff's face looked like an old ham, crusted and pink. "Never no flies on Bud. Maybe my youngest girl'll get herself a county commissioner. 'Course, she spends most of her time at the USO in Tulsa. But she's makin' good money at the Douglas plant. Forty dollars a week." Then he frowned. "But it's sure givin' her big ideas."

Gretchen moved on to the next booth, refilled the cups for some army officers who had a map spread out on the table.

The younger officer looked just like Alan Ladd. "I've got it marked in a grid, sir. Here's the last five places they spotted the Spooklight."

The bigger man fingered his little black moustache. "Lieutenant, I want men out in the field every night. We're damn well going to get to the bottom of this business."

Gretchen took her time moving away. The Spooklight. Everybody in town knew the army had set up a special camp about six miles out of town just to look for the Spooklight, those balls of orange or white that rose from nowhere and flowed up and down hills, hung like fiery globes in the scrawny bois d'arc trees, sometimes ran right up on porches or over barns.

Some people said the bouncing globes of light were a reflection from the headlights on Highway 66. Other folks scoffed, because the lights had been talked about for a hundred years, long before cars moved on the twisting road.

Gretchen put the coffee on the hot plate, picked up a damp cloth and a tray. She set to work on the table closest to the army officers.

". . . Sergeant Ferris swore this light was big as a locomotive and it came rolling and bouncing down the road, went right over the truck like seltzer water bouncing in a soda glass. Now, you can't tell me," the black moustache bristled, "that burning gas acts like that."

"No, sir." The lieutenant sounded just like Cornel Wilde saluting a general in that movie about the fall of Corregidor.

The kitchen door squeaked open. Her grandmother's red face, naturally ruddy skin flushed with heat from the stove, brightened and she smiled. But she didn't say a word. When Gretchen was little, she would have caroled, *"Komm her, mein Shatz."* Now she waved her floury hands.

Gretchen carried the dirty dishes into the kitchen. The last words she heard were like an Abbott and Costello radio show, a nonsensical mixture, ". . . soon as the war's over . . . set up search parties . . . I'm gonna see if I can patch those tires . . . good training for night . . ."

Four pies sat on the kitchen's center table, steam still rising from the latticed crusts. The smell of apples and cinnamon and a hint of nutmeg overlay the onions and liver and fried okra cooked for lunch.

"Oh, Grandmother." Gretchen's eyes shone. Apple pie was her favorite food in all the world. Then, without warning, she felt the hot prick of tears. Jimmy loved apple pie, too.

Grandmother's big blue eyes were suddenly soft. She was heavy and moved slowly, but her arms soon enveloped Gretchen. "No tears. Tomorrow ve send Jimmy a stollen rich with our own pecans. Now, let's take our pies to the counter. But first," she used a sharp knife, cut a generous wedge, scooped it out, and placed it on a plate, "I haf saved one piece— ein—for you."

The pie plates were still warm. Gretchen held the door for her grandmother. It was almost like a festive procession as they carried the pies to the counter.

The officers watched. Mr. Hudson's nose wrinkled in pleasure. Deputy Carter pointed at a pie plate. "Hey, Lotte, I'll sure take one of those." There was a chorus of calls.

Grandmother dished up the pieces, handing the plates to Gretchen, then stood at the end of the counter, sprigs of silver-streaked blond hair loose from her coronet braids, her blue eyes happy, her plump hands folded on her floury apron. Gretchen refilled all the coffee cups.

Grandmother was behind the cash register when Mr. Hudson paid his check. "Lotte, the deputy may have to put you in jail, you make any more pies like that."

Grandmother's face was suddenly still. She looked at him in bewilderment.

Mr. Hudson cackled. "You sure don't have enough sugar to make that many pies. You been dealing in the black market?"

Grandmother's hands shook as she held them up, as if to stop a careening horse. "Oh, nein, ne—no, no. Not black market. Never. I use honey, honey my cousin Ernst makes himself."

The officers were waiting with their checks. The younger blond man, the one who looked like Alan Ladd, smiled warmly. *"Sprechen Sie Deustch? Dies ist der beste Apfelkuchen den ich je gegessen habe."*

The deputy tossed down a quarter, a dime, and a nickel for macaroni and cheese, cole slaw, pie, and coffee. He glowered at Grandmother. "No Heinie talk needed around here. That right, Lotte?" He glared at the soldier. "How come you speak it so good?"

The blond officer was a much smaller man, but Gretchen loved the way he looked at the deputy as if he were a piece of banana peel. "Too bad you don't have a German *Großmutter* like she and I do." He nodded toward Gretchen. "We're lucky, you know," and he gave Grandmother a gentle smile. *"Danke schön."*

But Grandmother's shoulders were drawn tight. She made the change without another word, not looking at any of the men, and when they turned toward the front door, she scuttled to the kitchen.

Gretchen waited a moment, then darted after her.

Grandmother stood against the back wall, her apron to her face, her shoulders shaking.

"Don't cry, Grandmother." Now it was Gretchen who stood on tiptoe to hug the big woman.

Her grandmother wiped her face and said, her accent even more pronounced than usual, "Ve haf vork to do. Enough now."

As her grandmother stacked the dirty dishes in the sink, Gretchen took a clean recipe card. She searched through the file, then printed in large block letters:

LOTTE'S APPLE HONEY VICTORY PIE
6 tart apples
1 cup honey
2 tbs. flour
1 tsp. cinnamon
dash nutmeg
dash salt
pastry

She took the card and propped it by the cash register.

Back in the kitchen, Grandmother scrubbed the dishes in hot soapy water then hefted a teakettle to pour boiling water over them as they drained. Gretchen mopped the floor. Every so often, the bell jangled from the front and Gretchen hurried out to take an order.

The pie and all the food were gone before five. Grandmother turned the sign in the front window to CLOSED. Then she walked wearily to the counter and picked up the recipe Gretchen had scrawled.

"Let's leave it there, Grandmother." Gretchen was surprised at how stern she sounded.

Her grandmother almost put it down, then shook her head. "Ve don't vant to make the deputy mad, Gretchen."

Gretchen hated hearing the fear in Grandmother's voice. She wanted to insist that the recipe remain. She wanted to say that they hadn't done anything wrong and they shouldn't have to be afraid. But she didn't say anything else as her grandmother held the card tight to her chest and turned away.

"You go on home, Grandmother. I'll close up." Gretchen held up her hands as her grandmother started to protest. "You know I like to close up." She'd made a game of it months ago because she knew Grandmother was so tired by closing time that she almost couldn't walk the half-mile to the house, and there was still the garbage to haul down to the incinerator and the menus to stack and silverware to roll up in the clean gingham napkins and potatoes to scrub for tomorrow and the jam and jelly jars to be wiped with a hot rag.

Gretchen made three trips to the incinerator, hauling the trash in a wheelbarrow. She liked the creak of the wheel and the caw of the crows and even though it was so hot she felt like an egg on a sizzling griddle, it was fun to use a big kitchen match and set the garbage on fire. She had to stay until she could stir the ashes, be sure the fire was out. She tipped the wheelbarrow over and stood on it to reach up and catch a limb and climb the big cottonwood. She climbed high enough to look out over the town, at the cafe and at McGrory's gas station and at the flag hanging limp on the pole outside the post office.

If it hadn't been for the ugly way the deputy had acted to Grandmother, Gretchen probably would never have paid any attention to him. But he'd been mean, and she glowered at him through the shifting leaves of the cottonwood.

He didn't see her, of course. He was walking along the highway. A big truck zoomed over the hill. When the driver spotted the deputy's high-crowned black hat and khaki uniform, he abruptly slowed. But the deputy wasn't paying any attention, he was just strolling along, his hands in his pockets, almost underneath Gretchen's tree.

A hot day for a walk. Too hot a day for a walk. Gretchen wiped her sticky face against the collar of her blouse. She craned for a better look. Oh, the deputy was turning into the graveyard nestled on the side of the hill near the church. The graveyard was screened from most of the town by a stand of enormous evergreens, so only Gretchen and the crows could see past the mossy stone pillars and the metal arch.

Gretchen frowned and remembered the time when Mrs. Whittle caught Sammy Cooper out in the hall without a pass. She'd never forgotten the chagrin on Sammy's face when Mrs. Whittle said, "Samuel, the next time you plan to cut class, don't walk like you have the Hope diamond in your pocket and there's a policeman on every corner." Gretchen wasn't sure what the Hope diamond was, but every time any of the kids saw Sammy for the next year, they'd whistle and shout, "Got the Hope diamond, Sammy?"

The deputy stopped in a huge swath of shade from an evergreen. He peered around the graveyard. What did he expect to see? Nobody there could look at him.

Gretchen forgot how hot she was. She even forgot to be mad. She leaned forward and grabbed the closest limb, moved it so she could see better.

The deputy made a full circle of the graveyard, which was maybe half as big as a football field, no more than forty or fifty headstones. He passed by the stone angel at Grandpa Pfizer's grave and her dad's stone that had a weeping willow on it. That was the old part of the cemetery. A mossy stone, half fallen on one side, marked the grave of a Confederate soldier. Mrs. Peters took Gretchen's social studies class there last year and showed them how to do a rubbing of a stone even though the inscription was scarcely legible. Gretchen shivered when she saw the wobbly, indistinct gray letters: Hiram Kelly, age 19, wounded July 17, 1863 in the Battle of Honey Springs, died July 29, 1863. Beloved Son of Robert and Effie Kelly, Cherished Brother of Corinne Kelly. Some of the graves still had little

American flags, placed there for the Fourth. A half-dozen big sprays marked the most recent grave.

Back by the pillars, the deputy made one more careful study of the church and the graveyard, then he pulled a folded sheet of paper from his pocket and knelt by the west pillar. He tugged at a stone about three inches from the ground.

Gretchen couldn't believe her eyes. She leaned so far forward her branch creaked.

The kneeling man's head jerked up.

Gretchen froze quieter than a tick on a dog.

The sun glistened on his face, giving it an unhealthy, coppery glow. The eyes that skittered over the headstones and probed the lengthening shadows were dark and dangerous.

A crow cawed. A heavy truck rumbled over the hill, down Main Street. The faraway wail of Cal Burke's saxophone sounded sad and lonely.

Gradually, the tension eased out of the deputy's shoulders. He turned and jammed the paper into the small dark square and poked the stone over the opening, like capping a jar of preserves. He lunged to his feet and strode out of the cemetery, relaxing to a casual saunter once past the church.

Gretchen waited until he climbed into his old black Ford and drove down the dusty road.

She swung down from the tree, thumped onto the wheelbarrow, and jumped to the ground. The bells in the steeple rang six times. She had to hurry. Grandmother would have a light supper ready, pork and beans and a salad with her homemade Thousand Island dressing and a big slice of watermelon.

Gretchen tried not to look like she had the Hope diamond in her pocket. Instead, she whistled as though calling a dog and clapped her hands. A truck roared past on its way north to Joplin. Still whistling, she ran to the stone posts. Once hidden from the road, she worked fast. The oblong slab of stone came right off in her hand. She pulled out the sheet of paper, unfolded it.

She'd had geography last spring with Mrs. Jacobs. She'd made an A. She liked maps, liked the way you could take anything, a mountain, a road, an ocean, and make it come alive on a piece of paper.

She figured this one at a glance. The straight line—though really the road curved and climbed and fell—was Highway 66. The little squiggle slanting off to the northeast from McGrory's station was the dusty road that led to an abandoned zinc mine, the Sister Sue. The X was a little off the road, just short of the mine entrance. There was a round clock face at the top of the sheet. The hands were set at midnight.

She stuffed the folded sheet in its dark space, replaced the stone. X marks the spot. Not a treasure map. That was kid stuff in stories by Robert Louis Stevenson. But nobody hid a note in a stone post unless they were up to something bad, something they didn't want anybody to know about. Tonight. Something secret was going to happen tonight. . . .

Gretchen pulled the sheet up to her chin even though the night oozed heat like the stoves at the cafe. She was dressed, a T-shirt and shorts, and her sneakers were on the floor. She waited until eleven, watching the slow crawl of the hands on her alarm clock and listening to the summer dance of the June bugs against her window screen. She unhooked the screen, sat on the sill, and dropped to the ground. She wished she could ride her bike, but somebody might be out on the road and see her and they'd sure tell Grandmother. Instead, she figured out the shortest route, cutting across the McClelland farm, careful to avoid the pasture where Old Amos glared out at the world with reddish eyes, and slipping in the shadows down Purdy Road.

The full moon hung low in the sky, its milky radiance creating a black and cream world, making it easy to see. She stayed in the shadows. The buzz of the cicadas was so loud she kept a close eye out for headlights coming over the hill or around the curve.

Once near the abandoned mine, she moved from shadow to shadow, smelling the sharp scent of the evergreens, feeling the slippery dried needles underfoot. A tremulous, wavering, plaintive shriek hurt her ears. Slowly, it subsided into a moan. Gretchen's heart raced. A sudden flap, and an owl launched into the air.

Gretchen looked uneasily around the clearing. The boarded-over mine shaft was a dark mound straight ahead. There was a cave-in years ago, and they weren't able to get to the miners in time. In the dark, the curved mound looked like a huge gravestone.

The road, rutted and overgrown, curved past the mine entrance and ended in front of a ramshackle storage building, perhaps half as large as a barn. A huge padlock hung from a rusty chain wound around the big splintery board that barred the double doors.

Nothing moved, though the night was alive with sound, frogs croaking, cicadas rasping.

Gretchen found a big sycamore on the hillside. She climbed high enough to see over the cleared area. She sat on a fat limb, her back to the trunk, her knees to her chin.

The cicada chorus was so loud she didn't hear the car. It appeared without warning, headlights off, lurching in the deep ruts, crushing an overgrowth of weeds as it stopped off the road to one side of the storage shed.

The car door slammed. In the moonlight, the deputy's face was a pale mask. As she watched, that pale mask turned ever so slowly, all the way around the clearing.

Gretchen hunkered into a tight crouch. She felt prickles of cold, though it was so hot sweat beaded her face, slip down her arms and legs.

A cigarette lighter flared. The end of the deputy's cigar was a red spot. He leaned inside the car, dragging out something. Metal clanked as he placed the things on the front car fender. Suddenly he turned toward the rutted lane.

Gretchen heard the dull rumble, too, loud enough to drown out the cicadas.

Dust swirled in a thick cloud as the wheels of the army truck churned the soft ruts.

The sheriff was already moving. He propped a big flashlight on the car fender. By the time the driver turned and backed the truck with its rear end facing the shed, the sheriff was snipping the chain.

The driver of the truck wore a uniform. He jumped down and ran to help and the two men lifted up the big splintery board, tossed it aside. Each man grabbed a door. They grunted and strained and pulled and finally both doors were wide open. The soldier hurried to the back of the truck, let down the metal back.

Gretchen strained to catch glimpses of the soldier as he moved back and forth past the flashlight. Tall and skinny, he had a bright bald spot on the top of his head, short dark hair on the sides. His face was bony, with a beaked nose and a chin that sank into his neck. He had sergeant stripes on his sleeves. He was a lot smaller and skinnier than the deputy, but he was twice as fast. They both moved back and forth between the truck and the shed, carrying olive-green gasoline tins in each hand.

Once the sergeant barked, "Get a move on. I've got to get that truck back damn quick."

Even in the moonlight, the deputy's face looked dangerously red and he huffed for breath. He stopped occasionally to mop his face with an oversize handkerchief. The sergeant never paused, and he shot a sour look at the bigger man.

Gretchen tried to count the tins. She got confused, but was sure there were at least forty, maybe a few more.

When the last tin was inside the shed, the doors shoved shut, the chains wrapped around the board, the deputy rested against his car, his breathing as labored as a bulldogger struggling with a calf.

The sergeant planted himself square in front of the gasping deputy and held out his hand.

"Goddamn, man—" the deputy's wind whistled in his throat—"you gotta wait till I sell the stuff. I worked out a deal with a guy in Tulsa. Top price. A lot more than we could get around here. Besides, black-market gas out here might get traced right back to us."

"I want my money." The sergeant's reedy voice sounded edgy and mean.

"Look, fella." The deputy pushed away from the car, glowered down at the smaller man. "You'll get your goddamn money when I get mine."

The soldier didn't move an inch. "Okay. That's good. When do you get yours?"

The deputy didn't answer.

"When's the man coming? We'll meet him together." A hard laugh. "We can split the money right then and there."

The deputy wiped his face and neck with his handkerchief. "Sure. You can help us load. Thursday night. Same time."

"I'll be here." The sergeant moved fast to the truck, climbed into the front seat. After he revved the motor, he leaned out of the window. "I'll be here. And you damn sure better be."

Grandmother settled the big blue bowl in her lap, began to snap green beans.

Gretchen was so tired her eyes burned and her feet felt like lead. She swiped the paring knife around the potato. "Grandmother, what does it mean when people talk about selling gas on the black market?"

Grandmother's hand moved so fast, snap, snap, snap. "We don't have much of that around here. Everyone tries hard to do right. The gas has to be used by people like the farmers and Dr. Sherman so he can go to sick people, and the army. The black market is very wrong, Gretchen. Why, what if there wasn't enough gas for the Jeeps and tanks where Jimmy is?"

There wasn't much sound then but the snap of beans and the soft squish as the potato peelings fell into the sink.

Gretchen tossed the last potato into the big pan of cold water. She scooped up the potato peels. "Grandmother, who catches these people in the black market?"

Grandmother carried her bowl to the sink. "I don't know," she said uncertainly. "I guess in the cities the police. And here it would be the deputy. Or maybe the army."

Gretchen put the dirty dishes on the tray, swiped the cloth across the table.

Deputy Carter grunted, "Bring me some more coffee," but he didn't look up from his copy of the newspaper. He frowned as he printed words in the crossword puzzle.

Across the room, the officer who looked like Alan Ladd was by himself. He smiled at Gretchen. "Tell your grandmother this is the best food I've had since I was home."

Gretchen smiled shyly at him, then she blurted, "Are you still looking for the Spooklight?"

His eyebrows scooted up like snapped window shades. "How'd you know that?"

She polished the table, slid him an uncertain look. "I heard you yesterday," she said softly.

"Oh, sure. Well," he leaned forward conspiratorially, "my colonel thinks it's a great training tool to have the troops search for mystery lights. The first platoon to find them's going to get a free weekend pass."

Gretchen wasn't sure what a training tool was, or a free pass, but she focused on what mattered to her. "You mean the soldiers are still looking for the lights? They'll come where the lights are?"

"Fast as they can. Of course," he shrugged, "nobody knows when or where they're going to appear, so it's mostly a lot of hiking around in the dark and nothing happens."

Gretchen looked toward the deputy. He was frowning as he scratched out a word, wrote another one. She turned until her back was toward him. "They say that in July the lights dance around the old Sister Sue mine. That's what I heard the other day." Behind her, she heard the creak as the deputy slid out of the booth, clumped toward the cash register. "Excuse me," she said quickly and she turned away.

The sheriff paid forty-five cents total, thirty for the Meatless Tuesday vegetable plate, ten for raisin pie, a nickel for coffee.

When the front door closed behind him, Gretchen hurried to the table. As she cleared it, she carefully tucked the discarded newspaper under her arm.

"A cherry fausfade, please." She slid onto the hard metal stool. The soda fountain at Thompson's Drugs didn't offer comfortable stools like those at the Victory Cafe.

"Cherry phosphate," Millard Thompson corrected. He gave her the sweet smile that made his round face look like a cheerful pumpkin topped by tight coils of red hair. Millard was two years older than she and had lived across the road from her all her life. He played the tuba in the junior high band, had collected more tin cans than anybody in town, and knew which shrubs the butterflies liked. Once he led her on a long walk, scrambling through the rugged bois d'arc to a little valley covered with thousands of monarchs. And in the Thompson washroom, he had two shelves full of chemicals and sometimes he let her watch his experiments. He even had a Bunsen burner. And Millard's big brother Mike was in the 45th, now part of General Patton's Seventh Army. They hadn't heard from him since the landings in Sicily and there was a haunted look in Mrs. Thompson's eyes. Mr. Thompson had a big map at the back of the store and he moved red pins along the invasion route. Mike's unit was reported fighting for the Comiso airport.

Gretchen looked around the store, but it was quiet in midafternoon. Millard's mother was arranging perfumes and powders on a shelf behind the cash register. His dad was in the back of the store behind the pharmacy counter. "Millard," she kept her voice low, "do you know about the black market?"

He leaned his elbow on the counter. "See if I got enough cherry in. Yeah, sure, Gretchen. Dad says it's as bad as being a spy. He says people who sell on the black market make blood money. He says they don't deserve to have guys like Mike ready to die for them."

Gretchen loved cherry fausfades (okay, she knew it was phosphate but it had always sounded like fausfade to her) but she just held tight to the tall beaded sundae glass. "Okay, then listen, Millard . . ."

Gretchen struggled to stay awake. She waited a half-hour after Grandmother turned off her light, then slipped from her window. Millard was waiting by Big Angus's pasture.

As they hurried along Purdy Road, Millard asked, "You sure it was Deputy Carter? And he said it was for the black market?"

"Yes."

Millard didn't answer but she knew he was struggling with the truth that they couldn't go to the man who was supposed to catch bad guys. When they pulled the shed doors wide and he shone his flashlight over the dozens and dozens of five-gallon gasoline tins, he gave a low whistle. Being Millard, he picked up a tin, unscrewed the cap, smelled.

"Gas, all right." There was a definite change in Millard's voice when he spoke. He sounded more grownup and very serious. "We got to do something, Gretchen."

She knew that. That's why she'd come to him. "I know." She, too, sounded somber. "Listen, Millard, I got an idea. . . ."

He listened intently while she spoke, then he looked around the clearing, his round face intent, measuring. Then he grinned. "Sure. Sure we can. Dad's got a bunch of powdered magnesium out in the storeroom. They used to use it with the old-fashioned photography." He looked at her blank face. "For the flash, Gretchen. Here's what we'll do. . . ."

* * *

Gretchen could scarcely bear the relief that flooded through her when the young lieutenant stopped in for coffee and pie Wednesday afternoon. When she refilled his cup, she said quickly, "Will you look for the Spooklight tonight?"

The lieutenant sighed. "Every night. Don't know why the darned thing's disappeared just when we started looking for it."

"A friend of mine saw it last night. Near the Sister Sue mine." She gripped her cleaning cloth tightly. "If you'll look there tonight, I'm sure you'll find it."

It was cloudy Wednesday night. Gretchen and Millard moved quickly around the clearing, Gretchen clambering up in the trees, Millard handing her the pie tins she'd brought from the cafe. She scrambled to high branches, fastened the tins with duct tape.

She was panting by the time she finished. She tried to catch her breath as Millard unwrapped the chain to the big shed. The big chain clanked as he tossed it aside. Gretchen helped him tug the doors wide open. She stepped inside and carefully tucked the newspaper discarded by the sheriff between two tins.

Millard was a dark shadow behind her. "Do you think they'll come?"

"Yes. Oh, Millard, I believe they will. I do." There had been a sudden sharpness in the young officer's eyes. She'd had the feeling he really listened to her. Maybe she felt that way because she wanted it so badly, but there was a calmness in her heart. He would come. He would come.

Millard took his place high in the branches of an oak that grew close to the boarded-over mine shaft. Gretchen clutched the huge oversize flashlight and checked over in her mind which trees had the pie tins and how she could move in the shadows to reach them.

Suddenly Millard began to scramble down from the tree. "Gretchen, Gretchen, where are you?"

"Over here, Millard." She moved out into the clearing. "What's wrong?"

He was panting. "It's the army, but they're going down the wrong road. They're on the road to Hell Hollow. They won't come close enough to see us."

Gretchen could hear the noise now from the road on the other side of the hill.

"I'll go through the woods. I've got my stuff." And Millard disappeared in the night.

Gretchen almost followed. But if Millard decoyed them this way, she had to be ready to do her part.

Suddenly a light burst in the sky and it would be easily seen from Hell Hollow road. Nobody who knew beans would have thought it was the Spooklight but, by golly, it was an odd, unexplained flash in the night sky. Then came another flash and another.

Shouts erupted. "Look, look, there it is!"

"Quick. This way!"

"Over the hill!"

If Millard had been there, she would have hugged him. He'd taken lumps of the powdered magnesium, wrapped them in net (Gretchen found an old dress of her mom's and cut off the net petticoat), and added string wicks that he'd dipped, he told her earnestly, in a strong solution of potassium nitrate. Now he was lighting the wicks and using his slingshot to toss the soon-to-explode packets high in the air.

Gretchen heard Millard crashing back through the woods. He just had time to climb the oak when the soldiers swarmed into the clearing. Gretchen slithered from shadow to shadow, briefly shining the flash high on the tins. The reflected light quivered oddly high in the branches. She made her circuit, then slipped beneath a thick pine and lay on her stomach to watch.

Two more flares shone in the sky and then three in succession blazed right in front of the open shed doors.

The local *Gazette* used headlines as big as the Invasion of Sicily in its Friday edition:

ARMY UNIT FINDS BLACK MARKET GAS AT SISTER SUE MINE

Army authorities revealed Thursday afternoon that unexplained light flashing in the sky Wednesday night led a patrol to a cache of stolen gasoline . . .

It was the talk of the town. Five days later, when Deputy Sheriff Euel Carter was arrested, the local breakfast crowd was fascinated to hear from Mr. Hudson, who heard it from someone who heard it on the post, "You know how Euel always did them damfool crossword puzzles. Well," Mr. Hudson leaned across the table, "seems he left a newspaper right there in the storage shed and the puzzle was all filled out in his handwriting. Joe Bob Terrell from the *Gazette* recognized his handwriting, said he'd seen it a million times in arrest records. The newspaper had Euel's fingerprints all over it and they found his prints on the gas tins. They traced the tins to Camp Crowder and they checked the prints of everybody in the motor pool and found some from this sergeant, and his were on half the tins and on the boards that sealed up that shack by the Sister Sue. They got 'em dead to rights."

Gretchen poured more coffee and smiled. At lunch the nice officer—

she'd known he would come that night—had left her a big tip. He'd looked at her, almost asked a question, then shook his head. She could go to Thompson's for a cherry fausfade in a little while and tell Millard everything she'd heard. It was too bad they couldn't tell everyone how clever Millard had been with the magnesium. But that was okay. What really mattered was the gas. Now maybe there'd be enough for Jimmy and Mike.

OUT OF CONTROL

Clark Howard

Clark Howard the author wears several hats: short-story writer par excellence; Edgar-nominated true-crime writer; and novelist with a dozen well-reviewed books to his credit. The thread running through this incredible versatility and binding it together is his unmatched knack for storytelling. No one in the true-crime field does more scrupulous research than Clark Howard, who has been known to conduct months of personal interviews with his subjects even when that means attending them in prison. But what brings his nonfiction to life is the ability to mold the facts into a compelling tale, and that sense of how to unfold the story for the reader is what has made his fiction popular too. An Edgar Allan Poe Award winner for his short fiction, Clark Howard is also tied for the record for first-place finishes in Ellery Queen's Mystery Magazine's Readers Award competition, with four wins.

ON THE AIR traffic control tower of LAX—the Los Angeles International Airport—the tower clock showed 23:40, almost midnight. Light in the control room was subdued. A long line of men and women—air traffic controllers—sat at consoles, intently watching radar screens in front of them. Colored dots—or "blips"—appeared on the screens, indicating the positions of aircraft in landing and takeoff patterns on the vast airfield surrounding the tower. The blips were constantly moving, turning, flashing.

The controllers worked with a casualness that belied their intense concentration. Their voices, like the light in the room, were subdued:

"Delta eleven-nine-nine, use two-three-zero approach—"

"Air West seven-seven-seven, you are cleared for takeoff on runway four-one west—"

"PSA seven-three, hold your position, please—"

"American three-six-niner, you're looking good in the pattern—"

In the center of the tower, at a large, curved desk set back from the

43

control line, sat the man in charge of this shift in the tower. A nameplate in a fixed stand on the console read:

JED STAFFORD
CHIEF CONTROLLER

Stafford was fortyish, keen-eyed, alert, the kind of man who could juggle a number of responsibilities at once while remaining efficient. He had his own console at the curved desk, with a row of smaller master screens to give him an overview of what his controllers were doing. As he worked—checking flight schedules, signing forms, answering his telephone—his glance was never far away from the screens for too long. Stafford had been a tower man for sixteen years; he knew that whatever else went on up there in the control room, it was the activity on the screens that really mattered. The blips were everything—and Jed Stafford's attention rarely strayed far from them.

Those blips were life or death to thousands of people . . .

■ ■ ■

Stafford was asleep, hair tousled, face partly buried in a pillow. He was dreaming of a desert island where there were no blips when the alarm clock next to the bed buzzed and a bare arm reached across his face to shut it off. Millie, his wife, sat up in bed beside him, yawned, then started to get up. Jed suddenly opened his eyes and playfully pulled her back down. They wrestled a little, Jed getting a hand up under her nightgown, then Millie blew in his ear and managed to slip out of his grip.

"Later," Millie said, "when the kids are in school and you get back from bowling. We'll have a matinée."

Jed forced himself up, grumbling. "Whatever possessed me to join a morning bowling league in the first place?"

"To help keep your weight down, sweetie," Millie reminded him.

"Oh yeah," Jed said, patting his stomach. He was still in good shape, but ten pounds lighter would have been better.

Millie, in her robe, went down the hall, stopping at the bedroom doors of her children. "Ron, rise and shine. School day. Liza, honey, time to get up."

Downstairs, as Millie approached the kitchen, she saw over the café doors that the light was on. Shaking her head, she wondered which one of them got up in the middle of the night and forgot to turn the light off.

Entering the kitchen, Millie froze. Her eyes widened and her mouth dropped open, but before she could make a sound, both her wrists were grabbed by a rough-looking man in a leather jacket, and from behind a strong hand was clamped over her mouth. She was held like that, immobile, silent, as she stared at another man sitting at her kitchen table, calmly drinking coffee. He was rather bland looking, but his eyes, Millie thought in her moment of terror, were clearly dangerous.

A woman stepped from behind the door and moved directly in front of Millie. She looked a bit worn, a trifle cheap, but because she was a woman, Millie was instantly thankful for her presence. "Don't be afraid, honey," the woman said. "Nobody's going to hurt you. Just be quiet, understand?" She turned to the man at the table. "Tell 'em to let her go now, Harry. I'll take care of her."

The man sitting at the table bobbed his chin at the two men holding Millie. "Eddie, go watch the front. Vic, get the man down here."

Millie was released and the woman guided her to a chair at the table. The man in the leather jacket, Eddie Strake, went into the living room to the front windows. Of the two men who had grabbed Millie, he was the younger, not even thirty, and the expression on his face read slow mind, short fuse. The other one, Vic Lupo, who was going upstairs for Jed, was a decade older, better looking, a smooth ladies' man, but a snake at heart.

Jed was shaving, looking in the bathroom mirror, when he saw Vic behind him with a gun. Like Millie, he was too surprised to do anything. Vic did not even have to speak; he simply gestured with the gun and walked Jed down to the kitchen.

After Jed and Millie were sitting under guard at their kitchen table, the third man, Harry, calmly finished his coffee and went over to the kitchen extension phone. He dialed a local number. When the call was answered, he said simply, "We're in," and hung up.

The man who took Harry's call broke the connection, then immediately dialed an eleven-digit long distance call. It was answered by a man sitting in an office in downtown Kansas City. "Yeah, this is Max."

"I just got the call. They're in."

"Okay." Max hung up and turned to a man stretched out on a couch. Sixtyish; quietly reeking of power, wealth, influence, he was a ranking director of the national crime syndicate. His name was Sam Freelow. "They're in, Mr. Freelow," Max said.

Freelow put down the newspaper he was reading and looked at his watch. "Tell the boys," he said.

Max now made a call. This one was answered on a mobile telephone by a passenger in a parked gray sedan. "Our people in L.A. are in place," Max told him.

"Okay, we'll keep you posted," the man in the car said. He clicked off the mobile handset. "Everything's set in L.A.," he told the driver of the car.

"Who's this guy the old man's got in charge of the operation out in L.A.?" the driver asked.

"Harry Barrow." His partner grunted derisively. "Some kind of throwback to the Dillinger days, I think. He was in Joliet with the old man's nephew on a bank robbery rap. I think the old man is setting him up for this so it won't look like the outfit is involved."

"Smart," said the driver.

The two men lit cigarettes and looked across a large parking lot at a massive, walled compound. A sign over its main entrance read:

UNITED STATES PENITENTIARY
LEAVENWORTH, KANSAS

In the Stafford home, the man who had started the series of telephone calls, Harry Barrow, said, "Helen, take the woman upstairs and get the kids. Vic, go with her. And send Eddie back in here."

"Come on, honey," Helen said, gently taking Millie by the arm.

Vic Lupo went with the two women. In the living room, he nodded for Strake to return to the kitchen.

Back at the table, Jed Stafford locked eyes with Harry Barrow. "Why are you in my home? What do you want here?"

"I'll tell you that when I'm ready," Barrow replied quietly. "Until then, just stay calm, do as you're told, and nobody'll get hurt."

"I want to know what you're doing here," Jed insisted, putting both hands on the table as if to rise.

"Don't get ambitious," Barrow said evenly, reading Jed's body language. Eddie Strake came in then and leaned against a wall behind Barrow.

Upstairs, Millie got Ron, their fourteen-year-old, and Liza, age six, both still in their night clothes, and herded them down the stairs, parrying their fearful questions with reassurances. Liza was frightened; Ron wary, defensive; Lupo had to push him along a couple of times. Entering the kitchen, Ron's adolescent fear erupted and he suddenly broke away from Lupo, running toward the back door. He was quickly apprehended by Eddie Strake, who slapped him back across the kitchen. Infuriated, Jed leaped from his chair and threw an awkward punch at Strake, but the young gunman easily sidestepped him and with a grin shoved Jed over to Vic Lupo, who dug a vicious blow into Jed's stomach. Jed dropped to his knees. Millie yelled; Liza began to cry. Lupo and Strake were laughing. Then Harry Barrow's angry voice broke loudly through the commotion.

"Knock it off!" he stormed. "All of you!" In an instant the room was silent except for Liza's crying. "Get back in the living room," Barrow ordered Strake. To Millie, "Quiet your little girl down, lady." To Lupo, "Get Stafford off the floor."

Lupo helped Jed back to his chair as Eddie Strake sauntered out of the room. Barrow stepped over to Ron and raised the boy's chin to look at his face.

"You're okay, aren't you, kid?" he asked in a friendly tone. "Sure you are. You look like a pretty tough kid to me." He lowered his voice to a confidential level. "I'll bet you could whip Eddie in a fair fight. That is, if you could *get* him to fight fair." He patted Ron on the shoulder. "Go on, sit down by your folks."

Ron crossed the room to sit by his father. Barrow handed his cup to Helen for more coffee. Then he faced Jed. "I already told you I'm not here to hurt anybody, Stafford," he said evenly. "If any of your family get hurt, it'll be their own doing. It's up to you to keep 'em in line."

Jed, clutching his stomach, said tightly, "If you won't tell us what it's all about, at least tell us how long you're going to hold us."

"Not long," Barrow replied. "Pretty soon this'll all be over and you can go on with your lives."

"How long?" Jed insisted.

Barrow thought about it for a moment, then looked at his watch. "About ten more hours," he said.

Inside Leavenworth Penitentiary, a prisoner was escorted by two guards across the flats of a cell house and outside to the yard. A heavyset, fiftyish man, his name was Manny Fox. His escort took him to the warden's office, where two FBI agents were waiting for him.

"All right, Fox, you know the arrangements," the warden said. "You'll be flown to Los Angeles to testify against Sam Freelow before a federal grand jury. In exchange for that, you'll be given a government pardon releasing you from serving the rest of your life sentence. And the Justice Department will then put you into its witness protection program and relocate you with a new identity."

One of the FBI agents handed Fox a garment bag. "Go with the guards and change clothes."

After Fox exited the office, the warden asked, "How are you taking him to Los Angeles?"

"Private plane," an agent said. "We didn't want to use a Bureau plane, so we leased a Lear jet and brought in our own pilot."

"I hope you don't lose him," the warden said.

"Manny Fox is the last living witness in the RICO case against Sam Freelow," the agent replied. "He's the government's last chance to nail Freelow for good. We won't lose him."

At the Stafford home, Jed and his family were sitting together on the couch in the living room; Harry Barrow was in a chair facing them. The others were standing around the room.

"The kid here will go to school," Barrow said to Jed, bobbing his chin to Ron, "after you have a nice father-son talk with him. As for you, you'll go to your Thursday-morning bowling league, as usual. Your wife and little girl will stay here, as security."

"Security for *what?*" Jed asked.

"For you and the kid to behave yourselves and not bring the cops down on us."

Millie leaned forward anxiously. "Please, can't our little girl go to school, too? Just keep me—"

Barrow shook his head. "She's too young. She might slip and say something. The boy is older, and smarter. He'll keep his mouth shut."

"I'm not leaving my wife and daughter here without me," Jed said determinedly.

"Yes, you are," Barrow replied flatly. "You're going to do exactly what I tell you to do."

"If you want our cooperation," Jed said defiantly, "you're going to have to tell me just what in hell is going on."

Eddie Strake stepped forward, pulling a leather blackjack from his pocket. "How'd you like your teeth all over the floor, sport?"

"You shut up!" Barrow ordered, throwing Strake a withering look. "And put that thing away! You're scaring the little girl."

Strake and Lupo exchanged glances of mutual contempt for Barrow, but Barrow did not notice. He was studying Jed Stafford—very thoughtfully. Barrow had seen men like Stafford before, on both sides of the law. Hardheaded men. Men who usually meant what they said. "All right," he finally told Jed, "let's go in the other room and talk." To Helen he said, "Have the kids eat their breakfast and get dressed."

Jed and Barrow went into the family room and sat opposite each other at a game table. There was a chess set between them.

"Chess is a fine game," Barrow said. "I learned to play it in prison. Great way to pass time." He picked up the king. "Let's say this is the man I work for: a very important man that the government is out to get because of certain business practices they don't like. And let's say they've got a former employee of his who's willing to testify against him in a trial." Barrow put a pawn on the other side of the board and surrounded it with knights.

"This guy is very well protected by the government. But in order for this guy to testify, they have to get him from here," he traced a line across the board, "to here."

Jed shook his head in confusion. "What's all this have to do with me and my family?"

"They're bringing him here by private plane. It'll be landing in the cargo section of L.A. International sometime this evening. After you go on duty."

"So?" Jed shrugged.

"You're going to see that it doesn't have a safe landing."

Jed Stafford's expression became incredulous. "You want me to deliberately cause a *crash?*"

Barrow nodded.

Jed began shaking his head. "No," he said emphatically, "I won't do it. *I won't do it!*"

In the car on the Leavenworth Penitentiary parking lot, the waiting men, one of them with binoculars, saw the two FBI agents bring Manny Fox out of the prison. They were met by two other agents in an unmarked car. The five men got into the car and drove off the lot. As soon as the FBI car was on the road, the gray sedan pulled out and began following it. The passenger used a cellular telephone to contact another vehicle, a taxi waiting near an expressway on-ramp. "They're turning onto the Kansas City Expressway," he said. "Be ready to take over."

At the on-ramp, the FBI driver observed in the rearview mirror that the gray sedan kept going, but that a taxi twenty yards behind it followed the FBI car onto the expressway.

The driver of the taxi was already making speaker-phone contact with a van that was following both cars on an adjacent access road. In the rear of the van, there was a passenger with a mobile telephone.

"The cop doing the driving is watching his mirror pretty closely," said the taxi driver. "I can't stay on him long. But it looks like they're headed for the airport."

"Okay, wait another mile, then pass them and get off," the passenger in the van instructed. "We'll pick them up at the next on-ramp."

In the FBI car, one of the agents asked, "Anybody on us?"

"I'm not sure yet," the driver said. Then he watched the taxi pass and leave the expressway. "We're in the clear," he said.

Presently, the van moved into expressway traffic behind them.

"Look, what's the big deal anyway?" Harry Barrow was trying to reason with Jed Stafford. "The guy we're after is a mobster; he's a convicted drug dealer and a killer. He's scum."

"The men bringing him here aren't drug dealers and killers," Jed retorted. "They're federal agents, law officers."

Barrow shrugged. "They get paid for what they do. Nobody forced them to become federal cops. They're taking chances because it's their choice. Anyway, maybe some of them would walk away from the crash."

"Maybe your witness would too," Jed countered.

"It won't matter if he does. If he survives, he'll know that there are people out here who will go to any lengths to get him. He'll be too scared to testify after that."

"I won't do it," Jed reiterated. "Even if I agreed to, I'm not sure I could. There's not that much traffic in the cargo area on my shift. A runway collision with a parked cargo tractor or an anchored private plane might not be possible."

"Anything's possible if you set your mind to it," Barrow said. "Make it run into a security car, an empty fuel truck, anything. You can figure something."

"No. No, I won't do it," Jed said again.

Barrow shook his head in disbelief. "I don't understand you, Stafford. I don't understand a man who'd risk a nice family like you've got for some hoodlum and a few federal cops. I have never understood people like you."

"That's your problem."

"Well, what happens in this house is *your* problem, pal. If you don't come up with a way to do this, the man I work for is going to have those two hooligans with me wipe out you and your whole family. And there won't be a damn thing I can do to stop it."

Jed stared solemnly at Barrow. The fear he was feeling seemed to harden in his chest.

In the kitchen, the Stafford children finished their breakfast and were going up to their rooms to get dressed. Eddie Strake went with Ron, while Helen accompanied Liza. "Don't worry, I'll take care of her okay," Helen told an apprehensive Millie as they left. A melancholic expression settled on Helen's face. "I had a little girl of my own once," she said quietly. "Long time ago."

Millie was left in the kitchen with Vic Lupo. As she cleaned off the table, he eyed her appraisingly, his glance moving to her legs, hips, breasts. Millie became increasingly aware of his gaze. She glanced at him once, uncomfortably, then tried to ignore him; but it was obvious to her that his eyes were all over her, following every movement her body made. When Millie finally turned to him, Lupo made no effort to conceal the fact that he was staring at the contours her breasts made under the robe she wore.

"Do you have to do that?" Millie asked.

"Do what?" the slick gunman asked innocently, smiling.

"Look at me like that."

"Don't you like to be looked at?" Lupo asked.

Millie did not answer.

"I'll bet you do," said Lupo. His eyes swept over her again. "I'll bet there's a lot of things you like. I've heard about frustrated housewives who have sexual fantasies about different things."

Millie turned her back on him and started cleaning off the counter. Lupo rose from the table and crossed the kitchen. She was not aware that he was approaching her. When he stepped up beside her and put his coffee cup on the counter, it startled her; she screamed and jumped away from him.

Harry Barrow rushed in from the family room, followed by Jed, who hurried to his wife. Barrow, glaring angrily at Lupo, drew an automatic from a shoulder holster under his coat and walked slowly over to the gunman.

On the Kansas City Expressway, the FBI car carrying Manny Fox drove past the International Airport turnoff and continued toward the city. In the van following it, the man in the back at once turned on the mobile telephone and called Max at the downtown office. Max listened to what he had to report, then turned to Sam Freelow.

"They passed the airport, Mr. Freelow," he said. "They didn't turn in."

Frowning, the syndicate leader sat up on the couch. "I don't understand. My information from Washington was that they were taking him by plane."

"The van's in good position," Max said. "Maybe we can get the rat on the expressway."

"Great idea," Freelow said sarcastically. "Just what we need: a public shootout. Maybe kill a dozen innocent motorists in the process. How many times do I have to tell you: It's got to look like an accident! Tell the van to just stick with them for now and keep us posted."

"What the hell happened?" Harry Barrow demanded, the barrel of his automatic jammed in Vic Lupo's stomach.

Lupo, visibly frightened, instinctively knew that Barrow would not hesitate to pull the trigger. "She freaked out!" he pleaded desperately. "All I did was put my coffee cup on the counter and the broad screamed!" Jed was edging toward Lupo, fists clenched.

"Jed, don't!" Millie said urgently. "He's right, it was my fault!"

"Did he touch you?" Barrow asked Millie, without taking his eyes off Lupo.

"No! No, he didn't! I—I'm just so nervous—"

"All right, Stafford, back off," Barrow ordered Jed. To Lupo, he said, "Go out in the living room and watch the front of the house." As Lupo left and Barrow put the gun back in its holster, he said to Jed, "I could control things a lot better around here if I knew you were going to cooperate."

Millie frowned. "What does he mean, Jed? What does he want you to do?"

Jed wet his lips, thinking quickly. "These men are looking for a—a cargo plane that's coming in," he lied. "They—want me to spot it for some friends of theirs."

"Are they hijackers?"

"Yeah. Hijackers. Look, honey, why don't you go make sure the kids are all right. Go on."

Reluctantly, still frowning, Millie left the room. Barrow nodded approvingly at Jed. "That was smart, Stafford. She doesn't have to know. Neither do your kids. As far as they're concerned, you'll be under pressure from hijackers and you'll make a mistake in the tower. It'll be an accident, that's all. Accidents happen. Nobody will blame you. It'll be over, your family will be safe, and you'll be in the clear."

Again Jed Stafford stared solemnly at the leader of the gunmen. Slowly, he began to realize that he might have to do this terrible thing in order to save his family.

In the FBI car, the agent driving had finally spotted the van. "Base, this is Transport," he reported on his radio. "We're about a mile away, with a possible tail on us: a green Dodge van, just the driver visible inside. If it follows us in, be prepared to put the emergency plan into effect."

The FBI car continued to an off-ramp and exited at a sign reading: FAIRFAX.

Another call was made to Max from the back of the van, and he relayed the message to Sam Freelow. "They left the expressway at the Fairfax exit."

The syndicate leader smiled slightly and nodded. "Sure. The old Fairfax Airport. Tell the van to stay with them. We've got to find out what kind of plane it is, the numbers on it, and what time it takes off."

The men in the van were given their orders and the vehicle continued to follow the FBI car. Farther behind, the taxi came back into traffic from an access road.

In the FBI car, the agent driving said on the radio, "Green Dodge van is definitely a tail. I saw some movement in the back cargo area. Take it out as quickly as you can. We'll go directly to the plane and board."

The FBI car entered an open side gate to the small Fairfax Airport and drove across the landing field toward a white Lear jet parked on the tarmac. Moments later, the van followed it through the gate.

"They're heading toward that white plane," the driver of the van said. "Can you see the numbers on it?"

"Not yet," his partner in the back replied, looking over the seat, juggling a pair of binoculars. "I can't get focused while we're moving—"

The driver glanced in his outside mirror and saw the gate close behind them. "I think we're made," he said tightly. He knew for sure when four FBI cars with red lights on their dashboards pulled out of a nearby hangar. Accelerating, he sped across the field.

At the Lear jet, the FBI car screeched to a halt and Manny Fox, surrounded by the four agents, was hustled aboard the plane.

Across the airstrip, the van engaged in a desperate chase with the four other FBI cars pursuing it, moving in zigzag patterns trying to get away, while the cars drove in wide circles attempting to hem it in.

Inside the plane, an agent shouted to the pilot, "Get us in the air!"

The pilot looked at him in disbelief. "You expect me to try taking off with cars racing all over the field?"

Agents in the plane moved tensely from window to window, watching the scene outside, while Manny Fox cringed down in the aisle.

On the field, seeing no other way out of the trap, the driver yelled, "Take out a couple of those cars so we can crash that gate!"

His partner in the back unzipped a leather case and removed a shotgun. Kicking open the rear door of the van, he blasted the nearest FBI car. As that car careened away, the other three cars formed up behind the van and their occupants let loose a synchronized field of fire that blew the shooter far forward in the van. His body was thrown across the driver, who lost control of the wheel. The van swerved onto the runway and crashed solidly into the left landing gear of the Lear jet. The gear collapsed and the plane tilted sideways like a wounded bird.

Outside the airport, the driver of the taxi had been watching through the fence. As soon as he saw the FBI agents drag the two men out of the van, one of them apparently dead, he got on his car phone and called Max.

*   *   *

At the Stafford home, Jed and his son Ron were getting ready to leave. Harry Barrow went to the door with them. "Remember, a lot is riding on you two," he told them quietly. "Don't get clever, don't get cute, don't all of a sudden think you can outsmart me. If you do, I guarantee you'll regret it the rest of your lives." To Jed he said, "Give your kid a good talking-to while you're driving him to school. Make sure he understands this situation."

After the two male Staffords left, Barrow went into the family room where Millie and Liza were sitting apprehensively on the couch. Vic Lupo was guarding them. Presently, Helen came in with a coloring book and crayons. She sat down beside Liza. "Come on, sugar, let's you and me color."

Lupo grunted derisively at Helen. "Regular little mother, aren't you?"

Barrow's expression darkened and he walked over and got in the slick hoodlum's face. After staring him down for a very long moment, he nodded toward the door. "Go sit by an upstairs window," he ordered. "Watch the street."

Lupo tensed slightly at being ordered about so bluntly, but he nevertheless obeyed. Barrow went over to a recliner and sat down, visibly weak. Idly, he thumbed through a magazine. Millie stared curiously at him. Helen noticed her staring. Leaning over, Helen whispered, "Better not stare at him like that, honey. Harry don't like to be stared at."

"I'm sorry," Millie whispered back. "It's just that he seems so different from the other two."

"He is," Helen said. "Them other two, they're with the mob. Harry, he's a stickup man; he usually works strictly for himself. Why, he don't even like them other two."

"What's he doing with them then?" Millie asked, still whispering.

"Well, see, Harry and me is on the run. He broke out of the state pen in Illinois where he was doing forty years for a big payroll robbery. We been trying to get out of the country but haven't been able to. But Harry knew this kid whose uncle was a mob big shot, so he got in touch with the kid to see if he could help us buy passports. Well, the nephew knew his uncle needed somebody for a strong-arm job, so he steered Harry to him. Harry agreed to do this job for him, and the uncle's going to get us out of the country."

Barrow's voice cut through the room. "What's all the whispering about over there?"

"Nothing, honey," said Helen. "Just girl talk."

"How about some coffee?" Barrow said.

"Sure, honey. Right away." Helen hurried into the kitchen.

Before Millie could stop her, Liza got up and walked over to Barrow. "That's my daddy's chair," she said accusingly.

Barrow locked eyes with the child. They stared at each other for a long moment. Presently, Barrow got up and moved to another chair.

Jed Stafford, driving Ron to school, was tense, on edge. His son was equally apprehensive.

"You scared, Dad?" the boy asked.

Jed nodded. "Yeah."

"Do you think Mom and Liza will be all right?"

"Of course, I do, Ron!" Jed snapped. "Do you think I would have left them there if I didn't think they'd be all right?"

Ron looked away, hurt by the sudden hostility in his father's voice. Jed pulled himself together and patted the boy on the knee. "Sorry, son. I didn't mean that the way it sounded. Your mother and sister will be okay. Those men know that the only way they can get what they want out of me is to keep them safe."

"You mean spotting that cargo plane for them to hijack? Mom told me."

"Yeah. Spotting the cargo plane."

They arrived at Ron's high school.

"Now, listen, son," Jed said quietly. "Our family's safety and survival depends on us. If either of us slips and says something he shouldn't, it could be a disaster for all of us. So I'll be extra careful if you will." Jed put out his hand. "Deal?"

Ron shook his father's hand. "Deal, Dad."

Ron got out of the car. Jed watched him walk away, then leaned forward on the steering wheel and sighed heavily. Every part of his being felt laced with a dreadful realization of what he now was almost sure he was going to do.

In the small operations office of Fairfax Airport, a very nervous Manny Fox was sitting in a corner away from all the windows. The FBI agents were standing around silently: guarding the door, watching the windows, glancing anxiously at the telephone. All of the Fairfax Airport personnel had been herded into a far corner. There was heavy tension in the room.

Finally, like a bomb exploding, a telephone ring shattered the silence. The senior agent snatched up the receiver. His side of the conversation was brief: "Yes, sir—yes, sir—I understand, sir—" As he listened, he jotted down notes on a pad. When he finally hung up, he summoned the other agents around him.

"The Attorney General's office has decided not to get another private plane," he said very quietly. "They think it's too risky now that the syndicate knows our plan. Our orders are to take Fox to L.A. on a commercial flight."

The other agents stared at him incredulously. "A *commercial* flight?" one of them said in disbelief.

"That's right. Trans America Airlines, flight 228. Leaves in ninety minutes. We have authority from the FAA to bump all first-class passengers. We'll have the entire front cabin to ourselves."

Manny Fox, who was in the middle of the group of agents, said, "Wait a minute here. I thought the whole idea of a private plane was because a regular flight was too risky. What's with the turnaround?"

"They figure in Washington that what Freelow will least expect us to do right now is go commercial," the senior agent said.

"Freelow will know what you're doing before you even get me on the flight," Manny insisted.

"Maybe he will," the senior agent agreed. "But by the time he tries to figure out what to do about it, we'll be in the air." He nodded to the other agents. "Let's go!"

Jed parked in the bowling alley lot and went inside, carrying the bag containing his bowling ball and shoes. He checked a chart posted at the counter to see which lane his team was bowling on. Another member of the team was already at the lane.

"Morning, Jack."

"Hi, Jed. How's it going?"

"Okay. You?"

"Couldn't be better," said Jack. He was changing shirts, putting on his team bowling shirt, folding the shirt he had taken off and putting it into a zipper bag. He folded the shirt neatly, badge on top.

Jack was a Los Angeles policeman.

At the high school, Ron was on the track for his P.E. class, doing calisthenics with a classmate. Presently, they took a break and stepped over to the sidelines, where they had their towels and plastic bottles of Gatorade.

"Say, Wally," Ron asked, "you still have that Chinese pistol your uncle gave you as a souvenir from Vietnam?"

"Sure," said Wally.

"How about letting me borrow it? Just for this afternoon. I'll bring it back in the morning."

"What for?" Wally asked.

"I want to show it to this girl I know. Kind of to impress her."

"What girl?"

"You don't know her. A girl that's visiting a neighbor of ours."

"I better not," Wally said. "I promised my parents I'd never take it out of the house."

"Come on, Wally, be a pal." Ron lowered his voice. "Listen, I think I can really make out with this girl if I impress her enough. You know what I mean?" Ron glanced around at the track team working out. "Look, I'll tell you what. Let me borrow the gun and I'll fix it so you'll get to run the four-forty against St. Ignatius on Saturday. I'll tell the coach I twisted my ankle and he'll put you in as a sub."

Wally, a second-string runner, brightened at the prospect of running in the track meet. He thought about it for a moment longer, then agreed.

"Okay, we'll go over to my house at lunch break," he told Ron.

In Kansas City, a caravan of FBI cars was now on the expressway, cruising toward International Airport. Following at a discreet distance was the taxi.

When the FBI car turned off the expressway and into the big commercial airport, the taxi cut over and parked in a line at a nearby cab stand. The driver got out and casually strolled toward a row of newspaper vending machines in front of the Trans America Airlines terminal, where the lead FBI car now parked.

As the senior FBI agent alighted from the car, an airport security guard hurried over to him. "Your plane's at Gate Thirty-four," he said. "They're holding it for you."

The other agents hustled Manny Fox out of the car and they all walked him quickly into the terminal.

At the newspaper vending machines, having overheard the security guard, the taxi driver walked over to look up at a TAA monitor and check the departure schedule. Then he hurried back to his taxi to call Max.

In Max's office, Sam Freelow lighted a cigar and exhaled expansively. "We'll get him now," he said confidently.

Max, his hand still on the receiver after hearing the news he had just passed on, looked uncertainly at Freelow. "You think this Stafford guy will still do it? A big jet instead of a small private plane?"

"If he'll do a small plane to save his family, he'll do a big plane too."

"Do you want me to call Barrow and tell him?"

Freelow looked at his watch. "Not yet. We'll tell him just before it's time for Stafford to go to work. That way neither of them will have too much time to think about it. This guy Barrow's not one of us, you know, Max. He's a hooligan, a stickup artist. We can't rely on him like we can on Lupo and Strake."

"Why do we even have the guy in on this thing then?" Max asked.

"Because I have a use for him later," Freelow said. "That's why I sent Lupo and Strake with him. So somebody could be left behind to take the heat."

Max nodded as a sly smile of understanding spread on his face.

At Kansas City International Airport, four FBI agents and their witness were safely aboard TAA flight 228, and had exclusive occupancy of the first-class cabin. All five men, but especially Manny Fox, breathed an earnest sigh of relief when the flight took off on schedule for its nonstop trip to Los Angeles.

In his friend Wally's bedroom, Ron Stafford watched Wally take the top off a glass display case and remove a Chinese-made automatic pistol similar in appearance to an old German Luger. Wally handed it, a little reluctantly, to Ron, who immediately concealed it under his shirt.

The two boys left the house, and Wally turned in the direction back toward school. He stopped when he saw that Ron was not coming. "Where are you going?" he asked.

"Home," Ron told him. "My folks are going to be out and this girl I told you about is coming over for a while."

Wally gave his friend an adolescent grin. "I hope my gun helps you out."

"It will," Ron said confidently.

As he turned away from his friend, Ron's expression became hard and determined.

In the bowling alley, Jed stepped up to the lane and rolled his ball. He missed an easy spare. Sitting at the scorepad, Jack shook his head resignedly. "Boy, are you off your game today," he said nonjudgmentally when Jed sat down.

"Tell me about it," Jed replied.

Jack studied him for a moment. "Something troubling you, Jed?" he asked seriously.

"Just my bowling average," Jed answered, forcing a smile.

"We all have off days," Jack acknowledged, "but you really seem to be down, Jed. Anything I can do?"

Jed looked down at his friend's bag on the floor and saw the folded shirt lying in it. For a moment he stared at the silver policeman's badge, thinking how much of a relief it would be to tell Jack about his problem. But that, he knew, was just wishful thinking. This was his problem to solve, and his alone.

"It's just a little personal matter, Jack," he said. "It'll work out, I'm sure. But thanks for the concern."

"Sure," said Jack.

Jed then seemed to turn his attention back to the game. Jack, however, continued to study him thoughtfully, his policeman's mind in gear.

At the Stafford home, Millie was in the kitchen preparing vegetables for the evening meal. Barrow was at the kitchen table, drinking coffee again. Presently, Helen came in.

"She's taking a nap now," Helen said of Liza. "I read her a story and she went right to sleep." Helen went over to the counter where Millie was peeling carrots. "Here, let me help you with that. I swear, I don't see how in the world you organize the meals with your husband working such funny hours."

"It isn't too bad, really," Millie fell into the conversation. "Jed always has breakfast with the children; then he has a light supper before he goes to work; then the kids and I have a regular dinner around six-thirty; then Jed and I have another light supper sometime after midnight when he gets home. Of course, we all have regular meals together on his days off." She shrugged. "It works out."

Helen was amazed. "You have dinner with the kids *and* supper with your husband when he gets home? Lord, if I ate like that, I'd weigh a *ton!*"

"Well, I do have to exercise every day," Millie admitted.

Barrow, listening to the women talk, finally had enough of it and rose to leave. "I'll be in the other room," he said to Helen. "Keep an eye on the back door."

"Sure, honey."

When the women were alone, Millie said, "He certainly does trust you."

Helen was pleased by her observation. "He really doesn't trust anyone but me. We been together a long time, Harry and me."

"You said you once had a little girl, didn't you?"

Helen sighed wistfully. "A long time ago, I did. I was married to Harry's partner; I was just a kid, only seventeen. Had the baby the first year we was married. We was on the run a lot, never stayed nowhere long enough for her to get vaccinations and things like that. She caught the smallpox and died when she was two. Then my husband got killed in a bank robbery in Memphis. After that—well, Harry and me just sort of drifted together."

Millie reached out and took Helen's hand. "I'm sorry about your little girl, Helen."

Helen nodded, blinking back tears.

Outside, Ron Stafford approached the house from the rear, across the backyard. Helen, who was not watching the back door as she should have been, did not realize Ron was there until he walked in.

"Ron," Millie said, surprised. "What are you doing home so early, hon?"

Helen's suspicion kicked in immediately and she hurried to the inside door to summon Barrow. "The kid is home early," she said quietly as Barrow came in.

"Why didn't you call me *before* he got in?" Barrow asked pointedly. "You're supposed to be watching the back." Then to Ron: "How come you're home early, kid?"

"This is how come," Ron snapped, quickly pulling the gun on Barrow.

Everyone froze as a thick tension fell over the room.

"Don't you move," Ron warned Barrow.

"I'm not moving," Barrow assured him, hands half raised.

Ron was nervous, not too steady, but determined. "Call—call the others in here—"

"Whatever you say, kid." Barrow tilted his head toward the door. "Lupo! Strake! Come into the kitchen!"

The two hoods walked into the kitchen unprepared and Ron got the drop on them. "D-don't move," he warned them.

"They're not going to move," Barrow said, his words an order to the two henchmen. Barrow was remarkably calm; he'd had guns leveled at him before. "It's your show, kid," he said easily. "What now?"

"Where's Liza, Mom?" Ron asked.

"In her bedroom, asleep."

"Get her. And get out the front door, quick."

"Ron, I can't leave you alone with these people—"

"Mom, do as I say!" Ron told her urgently. His hands were trembling now. Lupo and Strake were visibly anxious about the wavering gun.

"Look, kid, you may be making a bad mistake," Barrow said. "Why don't you talk it over with your dad?"

"My dad's not here."

"Sure, he is. He's walking up to the back door right now."

"You think I'm stupid or something?" Ron said indignantly. "I wouldn't fall for a dumb trick like that—"

Just then, Jed opened the back door and walked in with his bowling bag in hand. Ron, startled by his entrance, looked around. Barrow stepped over and wrenched the gun from his hand. An enraged Eddie Strake dashed forward, pulling out his leather blackjack again. "You lousy little punk—!"

Jed dropped his bowling bag and quickly stepped in to protect his son, but Barrow was already there; he shoved Strake back. Strake, infuriated, came forward again, determined to get at Ron. This time Barrow backhanded him viciously across the mouth. Strake, stumbling back, froze.

"You want me to put one in you?" Barrow asked coldly, leveling the gun he had just taken away from Ron.

Strake, white with anger, rubbed his mouth where Barrow had hit him, but he did not press his attack any further.

Barrow whirled to face Jed. "I thought you were going to have a talk with this kid!" he accused angrily. He showed Jed the gun. "He pulled this on us!" Jed looked incredulously at Ron. The boy was terrified, trembling.

"I g-got it from Wally, Dad. I—I just w-wanted to get them out of here—"

Ron began to cry and Jed put an arm around him. "All right, son. It's all right."

"No, it's *not* all right!" Barrow snapped. "One shot from your dumb kid could have started a massacre in here!"

"It—it's not loaded," Ron said.

"What?" Barrow frowned. He checked the gun's magazine. Empty. He looked intently at Ron. "You've got a lot of guts, kid." Then to Jed, "Sit him in a corner in the family room. Lupo, you watch him; he's not to move unless I say so." Barrow bobbed his chin at the still white-faced Strake. "You go watch the front door. Keep away from everybody, got me?"

Lupo and Strake followed Jed and Ron out of the kitchen. Strake was still rubbing his mouth. "He shouldn't have hit me like that," he complained under his breath to Lupo.

"Don't worry," Lupo told him quietly. "He'll get his—before the day is over."

"What do you mean?"

"I mean, I've got special orders from Mr. Freelow for that punk. You just back whatever I do, understand?"

"Sure, Vic." He threw an angry glance back toward the kitchen. "Be glad to."

In a corner of the kitchen away from Millie, Barrow was privately chastising Helen. "You were supposed to be watching the back door. You should have warned me before the kid got inside."

"I'm sorry, honey," Helen said nervously, contritely.

"This is our last chance, you know. If we blow this deal, we'll probably never get out of the country. We'll have to stay on the run until they catch me again; then I'll be put away for life. Is that what you want, Helen?"

"Oh, Harry, honey, you know it's not. Don't say that." She was almost in tears now.

"If you want us to have any kind of life together, you're going to have to be more help to me. I've got to be able to count on you."

"You can, honey, honest. I'm sorry. I won't let you down again—" Helen began to cry. Barrow, uncomfortable because Millie could see them, nevertheless put his arm around Helen and comforted her.

"All right, don't cry now," he said gently. "We'll make it, baby. Just help me out and we'll make it." He handed her the Chinese pistol. "Here, stash this in your purse."

Just then, the Stafford telephone rang.

Barrow stared at the phone. After it rang three times, he motioned for Millie to answer it. "Be very careful," he warned coldly.

Millie answered, listened, then turned to Barrow with an uncertain look. "Someone asking for a Mr. Johnson—"

Barrow took the phone. "Yeah?"

The voice at the other end began talking. Barrow listened intently. As he listened; a slight frown appeared on his face. He blinked a few times. The frown deepened. His eyes widened slightly in surprise, his lips parted as if to speak, but he said nothing.

Helen and Millie were both watching Barrow. It was obvious that the caller's words were having some kind of impact on him. The two women glanced apprehensively at each other. Barrow, noticing the effect his call was having on them, turned away so they could not see his face.

"Yeah, I understand," Barrow said finally into the phone. His voice had tightened, as if suddenly becoming hoarse. "Sure. Right. I understand."

He hung up the phone, then stared at it for a long moment. Helen stepped around where she could see his face. "What is it, honey?" she asked, worried.

Barrow shook his head. "Nothing. Just a—a change in plans. But it doesn't affect you and me. Our plans stay the same." He started out of the kitchen. "Watch the back door. Do it right this time."

In the family room, Barrow motioned for Jed. "I want to talk to you, Stafford."

Jed, puzzled, followed as Barrow led him upstairs to the master bedroom.

In the air, TAA flight 228 continued its thus-far-uneventful trip. Manny Fox was in a window seat, eating his in-flight meal. An agent across the aisle from him was doing the same. Two other agents were sitting halfway back in the cabin, one glancing idly through a magazine. The fourth agent was in an aisle seat just inside the curtained doorway leading back to the coach section. He allowed no one to pass forward except the cabin attendants. The agents were no longer tense, but they were still alert.

Presently, the cockpit door opened and the captain came out to speak to the senior agent. "We're halfway there," he said. "There's some headwind holding us back a little, but we should be landing in about an hour and a half."

Manny Fox overheard what was said. Pausing in his eating, he anxiously looked back at the agent guarding the door to the coach section. Nervously, he wet his lips.

Now that Manny Fox was an informer, Sam Freelow haunted his every thought.

In the Staffords' master bedroom, Jed stared at Harry Barrow in utter disbelief. "What did you say?" he asked softly.

"I said our man is coming in on a regular flight instead of a private plane. He's on TAA flight 228. That's the one you'll have to do."

Jed's expression turned to revulsion. "You want me to crash a TAA flight? A regularly scheduled jetliner full of passengers?"

"That's right," Barrow confirmed. He shrugged self-consciously. "It wasn't supposed to be this way, Stafford, but that's how it's turned out. There's nothing we can do about it—"

"There's something *I* can do about it!" Jed snapped. "I can tell you to go to hell!"

"That wouldn't be very smart," Barrow said calmly. "Not for a man interested in saving his family." A sudden irritation surfaced in the gunman. "Look, do you think I like this? If I'd known it was going to turn out this way, Helen and me wouldn't have had anything to do with it. But we made a deal and we have to stick to it. I've got a lot riding on this too, you know. This is the last chance for Helen and me. You're not the only one who wants a future, Stafford." He looked away, slightly embarrassed by his words.

"Then, for God's sake, man, be reasonable," Jed pleaded. "I've gone along with you, I've cooperated right down the line up until now. It was one thing when you were talking about a private plane: this witness, some FBI men; but now we're talking about a major crash: a jetliner with a hundred or more people on board. You *can't* go through with the plan now—"

"I've *got* to!" Barrow said insistently. "It's the only plan I've got!"

Jed shook his head emphatically. "Then you'd better think of another one, because this one is canceled. You might as well shoot me right now, because I won't do it."

"I won't shoot you at all, Stafford," Barrow said evenly. "The worst thing that can happen to you is to let you live—after your family pays for your mistake."

Jed studied Barrow closely. "I don't believe you," he said flatly. "I don't believe you'd do it. I don't believe it's in you to murder a woman and two kids."

"It doesn't have to be in *me*," Barrow reminded him. "I'm not alone in this, remember. There's Lupo. And Strake."

Jed looked toward the closed bedroom door, uncertainty registering on his face. "You—you wouldn't let them—"

Barrow grunted softly. "I probably couldn't stop them. It's been all I could do to keep them in line up to this point. Both of them have had about all of me they're going to take."

Now Jed's expression filled with desolation. He sat down on the bed and stared into space. "But—a hundred people—maybe more—"

"Strangers," Barrow told him. "Not people, not as far as you're concerned. No faces, no voices. Just a list of names in the next day's newspapers."

Jed looked at him in revulsion again. "I was wrong about you, Barrow. You're no different from Lupo and Strake."

"Maybe it'll turn out that you're not either, Stafford. You're not going to sacrifice your family for a plane load of strangers. I know it—and you know it. You're doing the same thing we're doing. The only difference is your reason. When it gets right down to the bottom line, you're not any better than we are."

The two men locked eyes, each seeking the truth in the face of the other.

Aboard TAA 228, the captain came out of the cockpit again to speak to the senior FBI agent.

"Message just came in from LAX security. Agents from your L.A. office will be on the airfield with a car and two escort vehicles. We'll let you off through the forward cabin door, down mobile deplaning stairs. They'll bring the cars right up to the plane."

"Good. What's our estimated time of arrival?"

"Four forty-five L.A. time."

At three-fifteen, Jed was preparing to leave for work. Everyone was now in the family room. Millie and her children were again visibly nervous at the prospect of Jed leaving the house.

"It'll be all right," he assured them. "Just keep as calm as possible and don't do anything foolish. As soon as I've done what they want me to do, they're going to leave. I'll be back home as soon as I can."

Anxiously, they watched him leave the room with Barrow. As Jed opened the front door, Barrow said quietly, almost ominously, "Remember, Stafford, no slip-ups."

Jed's eyes turned cold with hatred. "There'd better not be any on your part either, Barrow. If there are, I swear to God I'll hunt you down, no matter how long it takes."

"I'll keep my end of the bargain. I want this thing to be as clean as possible. The minute I hear the bulletin about the crash on TV, we'll get out of your house and out of your life. Everything will be—"

Barrow's words suddenly stopped as he saw a police car pull up to the curb in front of the house. His face froze as he looked accusingly at Jed Stafford. Snatching his automatic from its holster, he thumbed the hammer back.

"Lupo, get out with me!" he ordered. "Strake, cover everybody in there! Helen, take a look out back!"

Jed saw that the man getting out of the police car was his bowling partner, Jack. "Wait a minute!" he said urgently to Barrow. "It's a guy I bowl with. There's no problem. I'll handle it."

Lupo had moved to the other side of the front door, gun drawn. In the family room, a nervous Strake had a gun on the other Stafford family members. Helen hurried back in from the kitchen. "It's clear out back, Harry."

Barrow, expression grim, stared flatly at Jed.

"It's just a coincidence that he's here," Jed said, half pleading now as Jack started up the walk. "You don't want to blow this thing now, Barrow. Let me handle it."

Barrow and Lupo exchanged glances. "Okay, go ahead," Barrow quickly told Jed. "Handle it. Just remember, if you don't, I will."

Jed eased out the door and closed it behind him. Walking out, he met Jack halfway to the house. Jack had one hand behind his back. "You lose anything today?" he asked Jed.

"What do you mean?"

Jack pulled his hand around from his back. "A left bowling shoe, maybe?" he said, holding it up with his thumb and one finger.

Inside the house, Barrow and Lupo watched intently. Presently they saw Jed and the policeman laugh together. The two men outside exchanged a few more words, then Jed glanced at his watch and started toward his car, carrying the bowling shoe with him. Jack went back to his patrol car and drove away. Jed then backed out of the driveway and drove off in the other direction.

Sighing quietly, Barrow put his gun away. For a moment, he pinched the top of his nose to see if he could get some relief from a brutal tension headache he'd had ever since the telephone call from Sam Freelow. *Jesus,* he kept thinking, *a whole plane full of ordinary people.* Looking up, he saw Lupo staring at him.

"Go back in the family room," he said brusquely to Lupo. "Send Strake to watch the back of the house."

Lupo's expression had just become relaxed, relieved by the cop leaving; now it tightened again at being spoken to in that manner by Barrow. He forced a hard smile.

"Yes, sir, Mr. Barrow, sir!" he said in mock subservience.

Walking away, his face became a mask of hatred.

Jed Stafford arrived at the airport and parked his car in the employee lot next to the tower. Walking toward the tower entrance, he noticed a group of men in suits standing with a number of LAX airport security guards around three civilian cars parked nearby. He stopped at the employee entrance gate and routinely showed his identification to the regular security guard posted there.

"What's going on, Pete?" he asked.

"FBI," the gate guard said as he logged in Jed's ID number. "They've got somebody high priority being brought in on a TAA from Kansas City." He bobbed his chin up toward the tower. "Couple of FBI agents upstairs waiting for you, too. They're with the airport manager."

Jed raised his eyebrows. "Oh?"

At the house, Millie and her children were in the family room. Millie was trying to sew a button on a shirt, but kept nervously sticking herself with the needle. Ron was slumped on the couch, sullen, doing nothing. Liza was on the floor with several Barbie dolls. At the sliding glass door to the patio, Helen was staring out, smoking nervously. Lupo was in a chair across the room, munching on an apple.

Barrow entered the room just as Helen lighted a fresh cigarette with the butt of the one she had just smoked. "You're smoking too much." Barrow said critically.

"I'm a little nervous, Harry, all right?" she snapped. Everyone looked over; it was the first time any of them had heard her speak curtly to him. But it did not seem to bother Barrow. He glanced at a clock over the fireplace. It was five past four. He gave Helen a brief hug around the shoulders.

"Try to relax," he said quietly. "It'll be over soon."

When Jed arrived at his master console in the tower control room, two FBI agents were introduced to him by the airport manager.

"Mr. Stafford," one of the agents said, "when TAA 228 arrives, we'd like to have it directed to the farthest apron on the TAA sector and held there long enough for five passengers in the forward cabin to deplane."

Jed looked inquiringly at the airport manager. "It's approved right up to the top, Jed," the manager confirmed.

"Okay," Jed replied. "I'll hold it on the Gate Sixty-four apron."

"We'll have several cars there," the FBI agent said. "As soon as they're clear, the pilot can advise you."

"I don't like cars on the aprons," Jed said to the airport manager.

"Neither do I, Jed. But this has been cleared with the FAA chief."

"Don't worry, Mr. Stafford, we'll be careful," one of the agents said. "There won't be any accidents."

At the house, Barrow had left the family room again; he was prowling the house like a caged cat. Helen was still chain-smoking at the patio door. Her nervous smoking and sudden withdrawal from conversation began to affect Millie, who finally gave up on her sewing and put it aside.

"How is my husband supposed to let you know about the plane you're going to hijack?" Millie finally asked, looking from Lupo to Helen and back again.

Helen turned and gazed at her with an odd expression. Across the room, Lupo frowned. "The plane we're going to *what?*" he asked.

"Hijack," Millie said. "How is he going to let you know so that you'll leave?"

"I don't think your husband has been completely honest with you, lady," Lupo said with a sneer. "This has got nothing to do with hijacking. Your old man's going to *crash* a plane for us."

Millie stared at Lupo in disbelief. Before she could say anything, Barrow's voice interrupted from the doorway.

"You stupid punk," he said coldly to Lupo.

"Is that true?" Millie asked Barrow. She rose from her chair, bottom lip trembling. "What he said—is it true?"

"Calm down now, sugar," Helen said, going over to her at once.

Lupo was on his feet, facing Barrow, angry at being called a punk by someone *he* considered a punk. Barrow, glaring icily at him, said, "Freelow must have scraped the bottom of the barrel to find you and that psycho in the kitchen. From now on, keep your mouth shut unless I ask you something, understand?"

Lupo took a step forward, very close to challenging Barrow now. Helen moved away from Millie and edged toward Barrow's side.

"Understand?" Barrow asked again, hooking one thumb on his belt close to where his shoulder holster hung.

With everyone else in the room caught up in the confrontation that was taking place, Millie, still horrified at what she had just learned, backed slowly over to an extension phone and quietly lifted the receiver behind her back. Biting her bottom lip, she pictured a dial pad and felt with her fingers until she found the right buttons. She pressed nine-one-one.

Barrow and Helen both noticed at the same time what Millie was doing. Together they bolted across the room toward her. Millie was just a shade too slow; she got the receiver to her face, but before the connection could be made, Barrow snatched it out of her hand and Helen hit the disconnect button.

"I don't believe this!" Barrow proclaimed in frustration. "What the hell else is gonna go wrong on this goddamned job?"

"Just one more thing, tough guy," Lupo said from behind him.

Barrow turned to find Lupo and Strake holding their guns on him.

In the air traffic control tower, Jed looked at the clock. It was 16:35— twenty-five minutes before five o'clock. He left his master position and walked down the line to the air traffic controller operating the console for the TAA sector of the field. "You having trouble with your screen, Phil?" he asked.

"Not that I've noticed," Phil answered. "Why?"

"I'm getting a fault light from you on the master board. Why don't you go get a cup of coffee and let me take your position for a few minutes."

"Sure, glad to," Phil said. "Call on me any time for extra coffee breaks."

Phil got up and Jed slid into his place. He began handling the incoming calls.

"Tower, this is TAA four-one-five requesting takeoff pattern—"

"TAA four-one-five, taxi to north six-one," Jed replied. "Hold and advise."

"Tower, this is TAA nine-two-one requesting takeoff pattern—"

"TAA nine-two-one, taxi to east five-three. Hold and advise."

The routine of the console continued for several minutes, then Jed received the call he was waiting for. "Tower, this is TAA two-two-eight, entering your approach pattern twelve. Over."

"Roger, TAA two-two-eight," Jed replied. "Continue in AP twelve to two thousand feet and advise."

Watching the blip on the radar screen that represented TAA 228, Jed Stafford took a handkerchief from his pocket as he began to sweat.

At the house, Barrow faced Lupo and Strake. Lupo obviously was relishing the moment. "You're through, hotshot. Washed up. Finished."

"You're the one who'll be finished when Freelow finds out about this," Barrow threatened.

"Freelow already knows, *punk*. This is Freelow's idea. You don't think he'd let a hooligan like you be in on something like this unless he had a reason, do you?"

Some of Harry Barrow's icy calm diminished as he realized that he had been used. For the first time, he seemed not quite so sure of himself.

"Let me tell you how it's going to look," Lupo said importantly. "You're an escaped con on the run. You've been trying to get out of the country but haven't had any luck. You and your girlfriend have run out of money in L.A. You've got no place to stay and you're desperate. So you pick a house—this house—and take it over. You figure to stay here for a few days; there shouldn't be any trouble as long as you always keep a member of the family with you to make sure the others stay in line. But things don't go like you planned. The kid here," he nodded his head at Ron, "tries to be a hero. He grabs for your gun; the two of you wrestle; the gun goes off, and she," he pointed to Helen, "takes the slug. When your girlfriend dies, you go postal. You kill the whole family. Then you turn the gun on yourself. All very neat."

"Except for Stafford," said Barrow. "He's not here to kill."

"He will be," Lupo shrugged. "After the crash, that airport will be in a panic. Stafford will find a way to call here and see if everything's okay. He won't get an answer, so he'll rush home to find out what's wrong. Eddie and me will be waiting for him. Like I said, neat."

While Lupo was talking, Helen sat down, nervously put another cigarette between her lips, and was fumbling with a book of matches to light it. Her purse was on the table where she reached for the matches. After she lighted the cigarette, she put the matches back and left her hand near the purse.

Inside the slightly open purse was the Chinese pistol that Barrow had taken from Ron.

At the TAA console, Jed was giving takeoff instructions to flight 921. "Hold on five-three east until advised, TAA nine-two-one."

Then, to flight 228, which was making its final approach, he said, "TAA two-two-eight, use runway five-three west."

On the screen, the blip that was flight 228 moved along a course that was directly toward the stationary blip that was the waiting flight 921.

"TAA nine-two-one, begin your taxi," Jed instructed. He was tense, sweating, his hands trembling.

TAA 921 began moving slowly down the east end of runway five-three, as TAA 228 dropped lower in the sky and approached the same runway from the opposite end.

Helen's hand moved quickly to her purse and she snatched out the Chinese automatic. "You pull that trigger on Harry and you're dead, Lupo," she warned.

Lupo and Strake tensed. Helen was slightly off to their side; they could not see her and Barrow at the same time. As they kept their guns on Barrow, their eyes flicked from one to the other.

"That's the gun the kid had," Strake said. "It ain't loaded."

"You sure it's the same gun?" Lupo asked.

A tight smile broke on Barrow's face. "He'd *better* be sure, Vic." Barrow felt himself coming back into control. "If he's wrong, you'll get it from one of us."

"Let me waste him, Vic," Strake said. "The broad can't shoot. The gun's empty, I tell you!"

"Wait a minute!" Lupo replied shakily. He wet his lips. His eyes continued to flick from Barrow to Helen and back again. He could not make up his mind, and Barrow's knowing smile was unnerving him.

"What's the matter, Vic, don't you know what to do?" Barrow laughed quietly, closely watching Lupo's shifting eyes. "Let me decide for you—"

Timing the movement of Lupo's eyes, Barrow drew his gun with incredible speed and began firing.

Millie Stafford screamed, "Ron, get down!" She threw herself onto the floor to protect Liza.

Lupo was hit by Barrow's bullets and pitched back violently. But as he went back, his arm swung to the side and he was able to fire one shot. The single slug slammed into Helen's chest.

Strake, meanwhile, leveled his own gun at Barrow, just as Barrow turned on him.

The two fired simultaneously.

Jed watched the monitor as if in a stupor. The two blips were moving ever closer to each other, flashing on and off almost ominously.

TAA 921, still on the ground, taxied slowly to the east. Because of the length of the runway, and the usual haze over the airport, the pilot could not see the opposite end. To him, it looked like a clear takeoff pattern.

"Tower, TAA nine-two-one increasing speed," he radioed.

TAA 228, landing gear down, was just approaching the far east end of runway five-three. Just before touchdown, the pilot frowned, peering ahead. "Do you see anything at the other end of five-three?" he asked his co-pilot.

"No," the co-pilot said, squinting at the distance ahead. "Do you?"

"I'm not sure. Reconfirm our landing pattern."

At the console, Jed received the reconfirmation call. "Tower, this is TAA two-two-eight. Reconfirm clear landing pattern on runway five-three west, please. Over."

Jed, lips parted slightly, stared fixedly at the screen. After several long moments of silence, the call came in again.

"Tower, TAA two-two-eight now touching down on runway five-three west. Reconfirm this pattern, please, urgent. Over."

Then another call came in: "Tower, TAA nine-two-one beginning power-up for takeoff on five-three east—"

Suddenly, Jed Stafford came to life.

"TAA nine-two-one, abort takeoff! Repeat, abort takeoff! Turn into five-four east at next crossover!"

He watched the blips. They continued to move closer together.

The pilot of TAA 921 powered down and made a right turn off runway five-three. Seconds later, TAA 228 rushed past where 921 had just been.

In the tower, Jed watched the two blips miss each other. He expelled a deep sigh. Then, when he realized what he had probably done to his family, his expression became agonized. He sprang from the console and waved the regular controller back to his place. Then he hurried from the control room.

At the house, Millie looked up from the floor. The room was filled with acrid wisps of gun smoke. Across the room, Lupo and Strake lay dead. Near the chair where she had been sitting when shot, Helen also lay motionless. Only Barrow was still on his feet. With two spreading spots of blood on his shirt, he staggered over to Helen. Lowering himself to the floor beside her, he put down his gun and gently touched the fallen woman's face. As he saw that she was dead, tears began to streak down his cheeks. Sadly, he shook his head in utter despair of it all.

"We—almost made it—baby—" he said to Helen.

Then he leaned over, closed his eyes, and died.

Millie leaped to her feet and rushed to the phone.

Jed was on his way out of the tower when a security guard shouted at him, "Stafford! Phone! Your wife—"

Jed hurried over and snatched up the phone. "Millie—?"

As Jed listened, his strained expression relaxed and his tense shoulders slumped. He began to nod gratefully as his wife's voice continued to reassure him.

Outside, all around Stafford, the huge LAX airport complex continued to function, everything again under control.

DA CAPO

Janet LaPierre

The creation of atmosphere is an important, if intangible, element of successful mystery writing. Janet LaPierre is one of the field's best practitioners when it comes to conjuring a feeling of unease out of the fixtures and conditions of natural and man-made environments. Most of her novels and stories are set on the foggy California north coast where she and her family have resided for many years, and she uses the haunting beauty of that locale to create tales in which pure suspense rather than the solution of a puzzle predominates. LaPierre's fine touch with the atmospheric suspense story has earned her nominations for the Agatha, Anthony, and Macavity awards.

———

THE NEIGHBORHOOD, A mix of two-and three-story apartment buildings from the fifties, with the occasional older cottage, looked deserted in the weak winter sunlight. At almost five P.M. workers weren't home yet and kids were probably glued to television sets.

Teri Gowan made a bet with herself as she turned her elderly Toyota into the driveway of the cottage she'd been renting for the past six months. She stopped in front of the garage door, put the transmission in park, got out—and won her bet.

"Just in time!" James D. Worth strode past her, bent, and gripped the handle of the garage door. One hearty pull and the door screeched up onto its overhead track.

"Voilà!" he announced, brushing his palms together. "That big heavy door is a job for a man, not for a pretty little girl like you."

"Pretty" was stretching it a bit, although she made an effort. But at five feet six and one hundred forty pounds, Teri didn't think of herself as little. "Thank you, Mister . . . uh, James," she said. Over the space of two months, she'd finally given in on that.

Teri got back in her car and drove into the garage, pulling close against the right wall. Now he couldn't get between her and the kitchen door. And she wouldn't be able to get out that door tomorrow morning. Shit.

She turned off the engine, grabbed shoulder bag and laptop computer, and was out of the car, out of the garage in the space of two breaths. Worth, waiting, now moved to reach up for the door but she beat him to it and jerked the thing down with more complaint from tortured metal.

"Needs oil," he advised. Tall body decked out in navy sweats with red cording, he looked ready to sprint the half-dozen blocks to his apartment for an oil can.

"I'll deal with it," she told him. "My father thought his little girl should be able to take care of herself."

"What did your father do?"

Beats me, she thought. You'd have to ask my mother. If you can find her. "He was a logger. Got killed when a tree fell on him."

"That's sad."

"Right. Excuse me," she said, and edged past him to head for the curb and her mailbox.

"It's okay, I already got it."

Teri spun on her heel to glare at him. He grinned and flourished a rubber-banded packet: a magazine folded around several envelopes.

She reached for the packet, and he held onto it a moment too long. "James, I'd prefer to pick up my own mail."

"Just trying to be helpful," he said plaintively.

"I know." Teri shoved the mail into her bag and set off for her front door.

"I'm off to Caesar's for Happy Hour." James was right on her heels. "I thought you might join me."

Up the two steps to the small porch; then she half turned and spoke over her shoulder. "James, I told you this afternoon I'd be bringing home work tonight, for Professor Magowan." Teri was a clerk in the Communications Department of California State College at Santa Luisa. "And I've asked you please not to call me at work. They don't like it."

"Don't call you at work, don't bother you at home. You make it hard for a man, Teri. Is this professor male?" His face was expressionless, the eyes ice-blue marbles.

"No," she lied. The little computer in its leather case was a weapon-weight to her hand; she resisted a strong urge to sling it at his head. Key in keyhole, door open. "Good night, James." Inside, she leaned against the door for a moment before turning the night lock and pushing off toward the kitchen, where she poured herself a glass of wine. She figured she had an hour before the first telephone call.

Friday morning Teri put her contacts in, brushed her unruly hair into submission, and considered her situation. James Worth had telephoned four times last night—to invite her out to lunch today, an offer she'd refused. To describe at length a television program he was watching and was sure she'd enjoy.

To tell her answering machine that it would be good for her to take a break. Finally, to read to her—to the machine—a short poem that ended with dead lovers, or at least that's the way it had sounded to Teri.

Wondering now whether the poem was meant as whine or threat, she smeared cream cheese on a bagel and ate that with a glass of orange juice while coffee dripped into her travel mug.

Coat. Umbrella; it was gray out there. Shoulder bag, keys, lidded coffee mug. Hand on the kitchen doorknob, Teri remembered last night's defensive parking, bit back one of those words she was trying to erase from her vocabulary, and went out the front door. She juggled the coffee mug while opening the garage door, hurried to her car with a niggling sense of something amiss, stopped short and stared before snatching the sheet of paper from under the windshield wiper.

"Dearest Teri, I want to apologize if I've made you feel I was hurrying things. Put it down to my eager and loving heart. I'll be out of town on business for several days. I trust my absence will make your heart, and all the rest of your lovely self, grow fonder. Your James."

"The son of a bitch," Teri snarled, forgetting her resolve. He'd come here, sometime in the night, and oiled her garage door, which was why it had swung up so easily and quietly just now. Then he'd sneaked inside to leave this slimy, insinuating . . . She squeezed her fist tight around the note, then thrust the crumpled result into her bag.

Midmorning, James called Teri at work to ask whether she'd received his note. With the department secretary and several other people listening, Teri didn't feel free to tell him how she felt about his invasion of her garage.

When she had hung up, Maggie Kline gave her a cold look and said, "I don't like to seem authoritarian, but you know department policy opposes receiving personal calls except those of an emergency nature."

"I'm sorry," Teri muttered. "I've told him. I'll tell him again. Believe me, I don't encourage him. He's a . . . problem."

"Not the kind who'll turn up here waving an automatic weapon, I hope!"

Head high and eyes showing a lot of white, Kline looked like a spooked horse.

"No no, I'm *sure* he won't." Teri wasn't sure at all, but she wasn't willing to jeopardize this job. "He's an educated man, with a business of his own."

"You just make sure he *minds* his own business." Kline moved away to her desk, but continued to toss the occasional suspicious glance Teri's way. Teri kept her head down and her hands busy until Carol Daley, another clerk, came by to suggest they go to lunch.

"I owe you, Teri, for the distraction. Usually it's me in the shit about telephone calls." Carol, a divorced thirty-something raising two children, leaned plump elbows on the cafe table and picked up her iced tea. "So, tell me all about this guy."

"He's a pest," said Teri flatly.

"One woman's pest is another woman's treasure, I always say. Come on, what's he look like? How old?"

"Maybe forty."

"God, Teri, talking to you is like breaking rocks. How *tall?*" At five feet ten, Carol was a big woman in every way.

"A little over six feet."

Carol's sigh mixed pleasure and exasperation. "Is he fat, medium, skinny? Does he have all his hair?"

A waitress set food before them and went on her way. Teri picked up her fork and cut into a quesadilla; Carol frowned at her salad and then at Teri.

"Okay, okay. He has plenty of hair, brown. He's fairly skinny; he runs." She took a bite of the crisp-surfaced beef-and-mushroom quesadilla, and felt better than she had in hours.

Carol ate a piece of roasted pepper. "How many ex-wives and kids?"

"None that I know of."

"Incredible."

"Carol, he's *hassling* me, even though I've never given him the least encouragement. He comes by my house every day, he calls me three or four times a night. He keeps asking me out for a drink, or lunch, or dinner, however many times I say no."

Carol's expression suggested that Teri belonged on some other planet.

"Last night he got into my garage and left this on my windshield." Teri pulled the crumpled paper from her bag and smoothed it out on the table.

" 'My eager and loving heart'!" Carol clasped both her hands over her own heart.

"Yuk."

"Look, Teri . . ." Carol reached over and cut herself a bite of Teri's quesadilla. "God, I don't see how you can eat stuff like this and stay in the
shape you're in. Speaking of which." She cocked her head and gave Teri
an assessing look. "Even if you insist on dressing like a virgin right out of
Sacred Heart High . . ."

Teri's long-sleeved white blouse, with a bit of lace in the demure vee of
the neckline, was tucked into straight-legged black wool pants. "Mrs. Kline
wants a businesslike appearance."

Carol ignored this. "But you don't talk like one, or move like one. And
you've gotta be what, twenty-seven, twenty-eight?"

"Twenty-five."

"Really? Still, in this day and age I'm surprised an independent woman
of twenty-five would be scared of guys."

"I have no trouble dealing with a pat on the butt or a straight come-on.
But a grown-up man who won't hear 'no' and just keeps hanging around
smiling—that's creepy."

"Has he tried to get physical?" asked Carol.

"Not yet," said Teri.

Carol munched a forkful of lettuce. "So why not go out with him one
time? Then if you still don't like him, you can say you gave him a chance,
and it just didn't work, and he should look elsewhere."

"That doesn't . . . feel right." Teri picked up the note and returned it to
her purse.

"Think about it, okay? And let your Auntie Carol know what happens."

Afternoon in the office was enlivened by the arrival, at hourly intervals, of
florists' bouquets. Although all were addressed to Teri, from James, with
love, she took care to spread them around, so that by the end of the day
each of the four desks bore a vaseful of color and fragrance. Teri made
sure Margaret Kline got the prize offering, an elegant arrangement of sagey-
smelling green spears and branches of spring blossoms.

Her job not at hazard for the moment, Teri drove home that evening in
some uneasiness, wondering what James's latest ploy meant. Was he giving
her up, saying a flamboyant floral goodbye?

Or was he underlining the verse he'd read her? "Lovers lying two and
two/ Ask not whom they sleep beside,/ And the bridegroom all night
through/ Never turns him to the bride." Teri had asked Professor Magowan
about the lines; he said they were by a minor English poet named Housman
who wrote catch-in-the-throat stuff about love and death.

She pulled into her driveway, stopped, and counted off a minute, and another; but James didn't appear. Really gone? Merely holding back to torment her, the way he'd held onto her mail yesterday?

Teri put the car away, checked her mailbox, and waved to the gangly orange-haired adolescent boy saluting her from the balcony of the apartment building across the street—Mike something. Inside the cottage, she did her usual check-over. She had never invited James in, and she had no evidence that he'd ever managed entry on his own; but she figured he would, one day.

Not today, so far as she could tell. She changed into old Levi's and a purple sweatshirt, took out her contacts, poured herself a glass of chardonnay, and felt her whole body relax, like a too-tight guitar string as its tuning peg was eased back. What had James said, several days? So she had the weekend at least.

Putting the wine bottle back in the refrigerator, she checked dinner options and found bread, eggs, oranges, and a brown-edged head of lettuce. Never mind, she wasn't hungry yet. With Shawn Colvin, then Nancy Griffith, and later the Indigo Girls filling the house with music, the dining-area window open slightly to let in rain-washed air, Teri sat at the table, finished her wine and switched to mineral water, and put in some overtime-pay work on Dr. Hal Magowan's class notes.

The telephone did not ring, the neighborhood was quiet. Once, thinking she sensed movement in her backyard, she got up to peer out the window; nobody, probably one of the local cats. At eight o'clock she saved her work, stood to stretch, and decided she was very hungry.

The sky was black but flecked with stars. Teri turned off the music and the computer, closed the window and made sure it and others were latched, then pulled on her anorak. She shifted wallet, lipstick, and comb from her shoulder bag to the anorak's belly pocket, collected flashlight and keys, and set off to walk to the Mexican restaurant less than a mile away.

Two blocks along, hearing footsteps behind her, she stopped and turned quickly, catching a blinking adolescent face in the beam of her light. "Mike's friend Bobby, right?"

"Unh, yeah." This one was shorter and solider than Mike, with ponytailed hair and a smear of dark fuzz on his upper lip.

"Were you looking for me?"

"No way. I was just headin' home."

"Good." Teri lowered the light and went on her brisk-paced way to the double doors of Rigoberto's Cantina.

Inside was warmth, chatter, music. Teri took a stool at the bar and ordered a margarita over, with salt.

"Hey, been awhile!" Bartender Dave Ramos brought her drink and an admiring gaze. "You are lookin' *good*. All pink-cheeked and everything," he added, brushing a finger lightly against her face. "Out for a run?"

"Thanks for that *good*. Just a walk, for the fresh air." Dave, probably mid-twenties, wore a macho-stud manner contradicted by an ain't-it-ridiculous grin. Teri liked him.

"Hey," he said softly, leaning closer to look at her. "How come I never noticed you got green eyes?"

She blinked and realized she'd come out without her contacts. "My eyes are light-sensitive, so I sometimes wear colored lenses. What's good tonight?"

"You mean besides me? Tamales, like always. Or the carnitas, if you're real hungry. You want to eat here at the bar?"

"Why not? After I finish this drink and probably one more."

Dave nodded, handed her a menu, and moved off to tend to other thirsty people. When he came back fifteen minutes later with her second drink, he leaned close again. "I'm off at ten tonight. Give you a ride home?"

"If I'm still here."

Dave drove an old Mustang, lovingly restored. He parked in Teri's driveway, saw her to the door, and didn't have much trouble promoting an invitation inside. About an hour later, two glasses of wine and some silly chatter led to a soft kiss, which led to a deeper one, which led inexorably to Dave's warm hand pushing under her clothes to find her breast.

Teri leaned into the touch for a moment, then gently pushed the hand away. "No, Davey." Aunt Lou and Uncle Matt had been loving but stern in laying down the rules for moral behavior; after nearly ten years on her own, she still envisioned the pair of them and Jesus shaking sad heads whenever she went astray. Not that she didn't short-circuit that picture fairly often. But right now her life was complicated enough.

"Really?"

"Sorry, but really."

He drew his mouth down in mock sorrow. "Too bad. But there's always another time, right?"

"Or another girl," she said, grinning to take any sting from her words. "But thanks for the ride."

Teri slept poorly and woke early. With the fridge nearly empty, she ate an orange, drank a cup of coffee, and set off for the working woman's Saturday round: supermarket, drugstore, dry cleaner's. The entire thirty-five-thousand population of Santa Luisa seemed to be on the same run this morning, most of them looking as glum as she felt.

At home, the telephone was silent, the answering machine unblinking. Teri put her purchases away, half wishing that she'd let Dave stay last night, that he was even now sprawled across her unmade bed waiting for her. She'd thought to find ease in this break, the first she'd had from James Worth's attentions since the day he'd interrupted his run to help her replace a radiator hose in her Toyota. But the tension was still there: an ache in the jaw she hadn't realized was clenched, a hitch in her breathing. It was like the waiting-around time on a Forestry Department firefighting team, just before the fire season explodes.

The rest of Saturday dragged past; she ran three miles, read two magazines. Sunday she ran four miles, went to the laundromat, cleaned her sparsely furnished house. The neighborhood was quiet, lots of adolescents, mostly boys, hanging about but nobody making any trouble.

When the telephone rang Sunday afternoon, she picked it up only when she heard an unfamiliar voice begin to leave a message. Chuck Bernstein, a computer-science instructor she'd met at work, wondered whether she'd be interested in a concert next weekend by a well-known Baroque music group.

Music was a part of her youth she missed. Deciding she could allow herself this one treat, she agreed to go. Saturday, he said. He'd get the tickets, let her know later about time.

Good heavens, a date. She settled into her most comfortable chair with a pot of tea and a paperback mystery novel, and came back to her own life only when the telephone rang again, just before five o'clock. This time she answered on the second ring.

"Teri, I just got back to town." James, not bothering with identification. "I trust you missed me."

In a way, she had. "I've been busy."

"So have I, and I'm ready for some relaxation. Won't you let me take you out for dinner? Or if you like, I'll pick up something good and bring it over."

Do it and get it over with. "Not here, my house is a mess. But I have to be home early."

"Wonderful! I'll pick you up at seven."

Teri shaved her legs, showered, gave her hair a touch-up dark rinse. At six-thirty she poured herself a glass of chardonnay and began to dress, in a flared dark skirt and a silky white blouse, with dark hose and black ballet-slipper flats. She smoothed her hair into a twist, applied lipstick, eyeliner, and shadow. Put in her contacts. Raised her glass to her image in the mirror. "The devil we know, and the ones we don't—to hell with them all."

When the doorbell rang at ten to seven, Teri stepped outside with coat on, pulling the door shut behind her. James, in gray slacks and blue blazer, cocked an amused eyebrow and took a firm grip on her elbow, to guide her to his BMW.

"We have a reservation at L'Etoile," he told her. "I think you'll like it."

L'Etoile was the most expensive and reputedly the best restaurant in Santa Luisa. While waiters and the wine man, whatever he was called, and the bread-and-ice-water boy hovered and murmured, Teri made an inward vow not to be intimidated.

James ordered for both of them and then talked of his trip to Sacramento and his work as a CPA. Teri sipped champagne, nibbled at pâté (good) and caviar (not), spooned up shellfish in broth, drank a little cabernet, and ate every bite of rare lamb medallions on creamy risotto.

When the dessert tray was presented, she shook her head, took a sip of very good coffee, and waited until James's chocolate mousse was in front of him.

"James. Thank you for a wonderful meal."

James picked up a spoon and tasted the mousse, then looked at her with a broad smile that showed lots of large white teeth. "I'm glad you enjoyed it. There'll be many more."

"No."

His spoon hit the dish with a *ching* that brought glances from the next table.

She took a deep breath. "I'm sorry you feel a—romantic interest in me, because I can't return it. I haven't been able to make that clear in other ways, so I'm telling you straight out."

Face an ugly red, James lifted his napkin to his lips with a hand that shook. He took two deep breaths of his own, put the napkin down, and signaled for the check. As Teri pushed her chair back, he snapped, "Stay where you are. I will take you home."

It really wasn't a good place for a scene; and she did need a ride home. The check was paid, her coat was presented. The valet brought the car. Teri let herself be handed in, wishing she'd stopped in that fancy restaurant to pee. Without a word James pulled smoothly away from the curb, headed toward her neighborhood.

And stopped, not on a dark street as she'd feared, but in front of Rigoberto's.

"What . . . ?"

"This is a favorite place of yours, I believe? I think we should end the evening with a drink."

The Cantina looked familiar and friendly. Teri got out of the car on her own and led the way inside to the bar. "Two margaritas, over," James said to the bartender. "That's right, isn't it?" he asked Teri.

"Fine." The bartender mixing the drinks was an older man, Miguel. When he set the glasses on napkins before them, Teri said, "Where's Dave? He usually works Sunday."

"Oh, you didn't hear? Dave, he got the shit—Excuse me, Miss Teri. Dave got beat up last night by this bunch of gringo punks, kids. He's gonna be okay," he added quickly, as he saw her reaction. "Got his nose broke and some teeth knocked loose, the rest is just bruises. What hurt him most, they smashed his car with baseball bats."

He reached across the bar and patted her hand. "I'll tell him you asked after him." Someone at the other end of the bar called, and he moved away.

Teri turned just her head to look at James. His narrowed eyes gleamed, and his tight smile hid all those teeth.

"You? What is *wrong* with you?"

"I feel sure you didn't willingly let him into your house Friday night; you've never even let *me* in. I know you had sex with him, but I believe he forced you. You need someone to take care of you."

"You're crazy! Davey is a nice, good-looking guy who wouldn't force himself on anybody; he can get all the girls he wants!"

He took hold of her left forearm and squeezed so hard she thought she felt the bones grind together. "Not mine."

Reaching out blindly with her right hand, Teri swept up her full glass and flung it at him. "Get away! *Get away!*"

The bartender vaulted over the bar, a surprising act for a man not young; he wrapped an arm around Teri while several waiters converged on James, who was palming liquid and ice from his face and hair.

"He's crazy! Get him away from me!"

Hands high, James backed to the doors, bumped one open, and disappeared.

"Miss?" Miguel squeezed her shoulder. "You all right?"

Not very. "I'm sorry for the fuss." She stepped free of him, and realized she needed to get to the bathroom fast. "Would you please call me a cab?"

Teri had the cabbie drop her off on the street behind her own, and was slipping silently between buildings toward her cottage when she saw a figure ahead, beside her back fence. Tall enough to be James.

A shaft of light from a window glanced off orange hair. Suddenly remembering the hovering teenagers of the weekend, she hurried after this one in her soft slippers and reached him just as he sensed something and began to turn.

"Wha . . . ? Ow! Shit, you're breaking my arm!"

"Down," she said through her teeth, and gave the armlock a twist as she hooked a foot around his ankle. "Or the elbow goes."

He fell to his knees and then forward, Teri moving with him and planting a knee on his back. "What are you—Ow!—some kind of nut?"

"The kind of nut you don't want to screw around with." A reminder with the elbow brought a moan from Mike. "You and your buddies stay away from me and my windows, hear?"

"We didn't do nothin'. Hey, it's a free world."

Teri slapped the back of his head, hard. "When I tell all the guys at Rigoberto's who it was beat up Davey Ramos and his car, you'll find out how free the world is."

Mike groaned and Teri felt his long body abandon resistance. "And the man who paid you won't be any help at all." She released him and sprang to her feet, stepping well clear. "Believe it."

He stayed where he was; she moved past him and hurried to her own empty porch and locked front door.

". . . you'll have to change your mind, because I love you so much."

Teri's jolt of fear faded as she realized James's voice was coming from the answering machine. She closed and locked the door, hung up her coat, went into the bedroom to strip off muddy slippers, dirt-streaked skirt, ruined pantyhose. Her blouse was damp; some of the margarita must have splashed her.

". . . public humiliation, but I forgive you because I know God meant us for each other . . ."

In flannel nightgown, quilted robe, and slippers with woolly linings, Teri scrubbed her face and brushed her teeth. When she turned off the water, James's voice was still there; she looked in the bathroom mirror and saw not her own reflection but Davey Ramos's straight nose and beautiful teeth.

James was still ranting as she unplugged the phone from the wall. No more, not tonight.

Monday morning James sent an enormous box of candy to the office, for "Teri and all her friends." Later in the day came a bouquet of balloons that nearly filled the office. When one of them popped, Maggie Kline screamed.

At home, Teri found a valentine in her mailbox: a fat heart made of padded red felt, with a tiny knife plunged deep into the felt and strands of red yarn streaming bloodlike from the cut. In the house, she set the monstrosity on the telephone table and plugged the telephone in, and James was with her via the answering machine within half an hour. He loved her to death. She was pushing him to the brink of insanity, would have to hold herself responsible for any acts he committed.

Tuesday was blessedly quiet at the office until the early afternoon delivery of a large cake, colorful frosting-drawn figures dancing on its flat white surface. As Carol approached with hungry eyes and a knife, Teri realized that the figures were not exactly dancing.

Carol looked, too, and dropped the knife. "My God! Porno cake!"

That evening, Teri huddled in her armchair sipping sour-tasting wine while a sometimes-sobbing James told her he loved her and described in detail the things he planned to do to her and with her. The phrases quickly assumed a surreal ordinariness, something like "slide tab A into slot B."

After a pause—for God knew what purpose and Teri didn't want to— he said very clearly, "Understand me. If anyone else tries to have you, he'll be sorry."

Teri broke the phone connection, left the receiver off, rewound the message tape, and then turned off the answering machine. Receiver back in place, the phone began to ring at once. In a moment of respite after more than twenty rings, she made a quick call to nice Chuck Bernstein, to tell him she'd be unable to attend the concert Saturday. Then she unplugged the phone.

"Don't bother taking your coat off!" snapped Maggie Kline.

More than an hour late to work after a sleepless night, Teri peered around the office, saw a shiny cardboard box on each desk, hunched her shoulders. "What?"

Edith, the oldest of the clerks, looked as if she might cry. With a rustle of tissue paper, Carol flourished a pair of filmy red panties in one hand, a matching bra in the other. "Nipple cut-outs, open crotch," she remarked cheerfully. "Unfortunately, too small for me."

"I'm sorry," Teri said. "I swear I've done nothing to encourage this man."

"You're on unpaid leave until you get your life straightened out. Assuming you can do that," Maggie Kline added.

At the police department a blond and buffed young cop took her complaint: personal details about her and, so far as she knew them, her alleged harasser; specific incidents of harassment; her responses to these incidents. When she produced her message tape, he put it on a machine and listened.

And then sighed. "Sounds like one sick puppy. Thing is, our justice system really isn't set up to deal with this kind of problem."

"I beg your pardon?"

"Ms. Gowan, we—you—basically have two options. We can talk to the guy, point out he's heading for trouble. Since he apparently leads an otherwise stable life, he may decide to knock it off."

"*May?*"

"If he keeps it up, we go to court for a restraining order; he violates that, maybe he gets some jail time, more likely probation. Some people think this is the right approach. Others, and this is my view, think it just makes the guy mad and doesn't change his behavior except maybe for the worse."

"So if he doesn't rape or kill me, there's nothing I can do except something that might push him into raping or killing me."

Officer Burdett looked offended. "The other option I was about to mention, probably your best bet, honestly, would be to move away. Especially since you don't have family or long-term connections here."

"That's it?" Teri's sleep-deprived eyes filled with tears.

"Ms. Gowan, we can go for a restraining order. It's your call."

"Thanks a lot," said Teri as she got to her feet.

Burdett got up as well, to see her to the door. "I'm sorry. I'll talk to the guy, okay? Then you can decide where you want to take it."

An older uniformed man sitting at a desk across the room called out, "Hey, ma'am? I'd get a gun."

"We don't recommend that," said Burdett quickly. "A dog, maybe."

"Woof woof," said Teri.

Lunchtime, but she wasn't hungry; she went back to the campus and spent the afternoon in the library, working quietly on her laptop. By the time it began to get dark she was ready for food and drove downtown to a Thai place she liked.

Well fed but still edgy, she headed not for home but for a nearby multiplex movie theater, where she bought one ticket and managed to see two movies. It was close to one A.M. when she put her car away in the garage at the cottage.

She unlocked the kitchen door, closed it behind her, dropped bag and coat on a chair, and hurried to the bathroom. Even as she reached for the light switch she knew someone had been there.

The lid of the toilet seat, which she always left down, was up, the bowl full of brown water, the tile floor sticky under her shoes. Holding her breath, she pulled a strip of toilet paper from the roller and used it to shield her fingers as she pushed the flush lever.

Cabinet doors and drawers were ajar, water trickling from the sink faucet. On the edge of the sink a red toothbrush lay wetly in a puddle of toothpaste. He'd used her toothbrush! She picked it up with thumb and finger and dropped it in the wastebasket.

Teri washed her hands with soap, then wet the hand towel and scrubbed it over the soles of her shoes before moving out of the bathroom to stand in the hall and listen. She heard no human sound, had no sense of any presence.

In her bedroom, her lingerie drawer stood open, its contents spilling out. Several things—a couple of pretty nightgowns, a lacy black half-slip and matching chemise, three or four pairs of panties—were wadded up in the middle of her bed, which looked as if it, and the lingerie, had been rolled on.

The small second bedroom looked undisturbed. Teri knelt beside the daybed, thrust a hand under the mattress, and sighed with relief. She pulled out the small red-leather book just to be sure, then replaced it and smoothed the bed cover.

A chair stood askew at her dining table, before a scatter of crumbs and a crumpled paper napkin. In the living room her favorite chair and ottoman had been moved across the room; there were flecks of mud on the ottoman and the carpet. Everything in the room—books in the bookcase, magazines, pictures on the wall—looked somehow *off.*

In the kitchen, she saw nothing amiss until she opened the refrigerator to find a bottle of champagne—the same French champagne they'd drunk Sunday night.

Teri eyed the silent telephone and decided that tomorrow would be soon enough to talk to the police. She put on rubber gloves and scrubbed the bathroom; then she took a quilt into the second bedroom and curled up on the daybed and slept.

Next morning, Teri scrubbed the bathroom again before showering. The telephone began to ring as soon as she plugged it in; she unplugged it, had a quick cup of coffee, and drove to the police station.

Burdett got quickly to his feet as she approached his desk. "Ms. Gowan, we've been trying to call you. Our records show that—"

"About a year ago—before Officer Burdett's time—another young woman from your neighborhood came in with a complaint against James Worth." The speaker was a bulky, graying man whose nametag identified him as Sergeant Dennis Malloy. "She looked quite a bit like you, smaller maybe."

"What did he do to her?"

"She said he pursued her constantly, drove away her music students, and cost her her job playing cello with our regional symphony orchestra."

"Did she get a restraining order?"

"She chose to move away," said Burdett.

"She was a quiet little thing, and real spooked," Malloy added.

Teri gave her attention to the older man. "Did he ever hurt her physically?"

Burdett said, "The department can't comment on . . ."

"Not long after she talked to us," said Malloy, "we got a call from a neighbor, what sounded like trouble at the victim's house. Patrol got there and found her alone, bruised and bleeding, clothes torn. She just kept crying and saying she didn't know what had happened. Refused to be taken to the hospital. Next day she was gone."

Teri sat down in the nearest chair, clutching her shoulder bag in front of her like a shield. " 'Spooked' is about right. James Worth got into my house last night."

Half an hour later the two policemen prowled the cottage. The only fingerprints on doorknobs, window latches, and refrigerator door were Teri's, mostly smeared. None at all on the champagne bottle. In the bedroom, the three of them viewed the disordered bed.

"Probably masturbated, wearing a condom," said Malloy. "And tossed it in the toilet," he added glumly.

Teri had already defended her cleaning of the bathroom.

"And you're sure you locked up?" asked Burdett.

"I *told* you. He must have gotten keys somewhere." Teri's voice wobbled, and her eyes filled with tears.

"So we'll check the key shops," said Malloy. "What we need is a big fat piece of evidence proving the intruder was Worth."

"Yesterday," said Burdett, "Mr. Worth told me you and he were lovers who'd had a little misunderstanding."

"What he said last time," growled Malloy. "I'll see him today, Miss Gowan. And I strongly suggest you make application for a restraining order."

"I'll—think about it." Teri found a tissue in a pocket and wiped her eyes. "Yes, I'll do it. But not today."

Malloy sighed. "Right. Well, it'd be a good idea to get your locks changed."

*   *   *

"Teri, I know your touch-me-not behavior is just your own kind of foreplay. Like my anger at the lies you're telling. I love imagining the things you'll do to appease me, soon."

As if he might detect her presence, Teri stood motionless. When she heard the hang-up click, she continued her survey of the cottage. All windows latched, curtains drawn, lights off except for the twenty-five-watt bulb in the garage. In the long mirror on the closet door she was more shadow than reflection: black pants and sweater and shoes, froth of hair tucked under a dark stocking cap. She pulled on a navy wool jacket and went out the kitchen door to the garage. Moments later she drove off into the gathering dusk, leaving the garage door up.

At two-ten A.M. by the luminous numerals on the microwave oven, sounds of movement came from the garage. A key rattled faintly in the lock, the kitchen door opened, and a tall figure with a misshapen head was silhouetted there. The door closed; feet squeaked on the floor; the green numerals disappeared and reappeared.

When light burst into the room like a silent explosion, the figure spun around and froze, arms wide. "Aaugh!" With a yellow plastic shower cap hiding his hair, Worth's big face looked doughy. "Where's your car?"

"A mile away with a flat tire. *Sit down!* On the floor against the fridge." Astride a reversed straight chair in the doorway between kitchen and dining area, Teri rested her forearms on the chair's back, her right hand holding a short-barreled dark revolver.

Eyes on the gun, Worth sat, slowly. "I mean no harm, Teri. While I'm waiting for you to come to the end of your game-playing, I need to be where you've been, touch your things, smell your smell."

"Leave souvenirs?"

"Live with you. Where did a nice girl like you get a gun?"

"I'm the kind of girl that knows how to get guns." He drew his legs closer, as if to rise, and she shifted her grip to brace her right wrist with her left hand. "Jenny Lamb was the *nice* girl."

He held his face very still. "Jenny Lamb?"

"Jenny's mother is my mother's half-sister," said Teri, her voice low in her throat. "She took me in after my mom hit the road when I was eight and Jenny was ten. Jenny shared everything with me. I watched out for her and didn't ever let anybody mess with her until she went away to college and I—hit the road."

"I don't see what this has to do with me." He shifted position, and she snapped, "Stay still!

"Last summer," she continued, "it looked like I was really getting my life together, so for the first time in years I called Aunt Lou, to ask for Jenny's address. She told me Jenny had just been shipped home to Chicago in a coffin."

"That must have been sad for you."

"Sad for you, too, you slimy son-of-a-bitch. Aunt Lou asked me to go to Denver and pack up Jenny's apartment, and I found her diary, she always kept a diary. So Jenny herself told me all about James D. Worth of Santa Luisa, California." Her gaze steady on him, she thumbed back the revolver's hammer.

"For Christ's sake, be careful!"

"After you'd ruined her—Isn't that funny? From a different angle, that dumb old word still means pretty much the same thing—after that, she'd started to make a new life in Denver. Then one day she answered her door and there you were. The next day she drove her car off a mountain into a ravine."

"She belonged to me. She shouldn't have run away, either time."

Teri sat a little straighter, feet flat on the floor. "And what about me?"

"You?"

"You've been harassing me. People at work have seen that, and the police know how frightened I am. They told me you stalked Jenny. Raped her."

"She never accused me of rape!"

"Then you turn up in my kitchen in the middle of the night, in latex gloves and a plastic shower cap, with a set of keys to this place in your pocket."

Face reddening, he snatched off the cap he'd apparently forgotten. "You dressed like Jenny, acted like her. You moved to my neighborhood and dangled yourself around me. That's entrapment."

He pulled his feet close again and when she didn't object, he stood up slowly. "Entrapment," he repeated with relish. "When the police find out who you are, they'll arrest *you*. Now give me that gun."

"Who's going to tell them?"

A step closer to her, hand out, he stopped. "What?"

Teri squeezed the trigger.

THE SERPENT'S BACK

Ian Rankin

Like the classic novels of Simenon, Ian Rankin's books generally deal with the policing of a particular region—in the case of his best-known series, the Rebus novels, that region is Edinburgh. In the Rebus books, Rebus's personal life is often of as much interest to the reader as the cases he tries to solve. The BBC is currently making a television series based on the character, capitalizing, perhaps, on the character's huge popularity in Scotland and the rest of the United Kingdom: At last count, Rankin's novels occupied seven of the top ten spots on Scotland's bestsellers' list. Not that Rankin writes only of Rebus; he is the author of several large-scale thrillers, and he is a favorite of the critics with a Gold Dagger Award for Best Novel, multiple short-story Dagger Awards, and Edgar and Anthony Award nominations to his credit.

THIS WAS, MIND you, back in 1793 or '94. Edinburgh was a better place then. Nothing ever happens here now, but back then . . . back then *everything* was happening.

Back then a caddie was indispensible if you happened to be visiting the town. If you wanted someone found, if a message needed delivering, if you wanted a bed for the night, fresh oysters, a shirt-maker, or the local hoor, you came to a caddie. And if the claret got the better of you, a caddie would see you safely home.

See, the town wasn't safe, Lord no. The streets were mean. The hifalutin' were leaving the old town and crossing the Nor' Loch to the New. They lived in Princes Street and George Street, or did until they could no longer stand the stench. The old loch was an open sewer by that time, and the old town not much better.

I was called Cullender, Cully to my friends. No one knew my first name. They need only say "Cullender" and they'd be pointed in my direction.

That's how it was with young Master Gisborne. He had newly arrived by coach from London, and feared he'd never sit down again. . . .

"Are you Cullender? My good friend Mr. Wilks told me to ask for you."
"Wilks?"
"He was here for some weeks. A medical student."
I nodded. "I recall the young gentleman particularly," I lied.
"I shall require a clean room, nothing too fancy. My pockets aren't bottomless."
"How long will you be staying, Master?"
He looked around. "I'm not sure. I'm considering a career in medicine. If I like the faculty, I may enroll."
And he fingered the edges of his coat. It was a pale blue coat with bright silver buttons. Like Master Gisborne, it was overdone and didn't quite fit together. His face was fat like a whelp's, but his physique was lean and his eyes shone. His skin had suffered neither disease nor malnourishment. He was, I suppose, a fine enough specimen, but I'd seen fine specimens before. Many of them stayed, seduced by Edinburgh. I saw them daily in the pungent howffs, or slouching through the narrow closes, heads bowed. None of them looked so fresh these days. Had they been eels, the fishwives would have tossed them in a bucket and sold them to only the most gullible.
The most gullible, of course, being those newly arrived in the city.
Master Gisborne would need looking after. He was haughty on the surface, cocksure, but I knew he was troubled, wondering how long he could sustain the act of worldliness. He had money but not in limitless supply. His parents would be professional folk, not gentry. Some denizens would gull him before supper. Me? I was undecided.
I picked up his trunk. "Shall I call a chair?" He frowned. "The streets here are too narrow and steep for coaches. Haven't you noticed? Know why they're narrow?" I sidled up to him. "There's a serpent buried beneath." He looked ill at ease so I laughed. "Just a story, Master. We use chairmen instead of horses. Good strong Highland stock."
I knew he had already walked a good way in search of me, hauling his trunk with him. He was tired, but counting his money too.
"Let's walk," he decided, "and you can acquaint me with the town."
"The town, Master," I said, "will acquaint you with itself."

We got him settled in at Lucky Seaton's. Lucky had been a hoor herself at one time, then had been turned to the Moderate movement and now ran a Christian rooming house.
"We know all about medical students, don't we, Cully?" she said, while

Gisborne took the measure of his room. "The worst sinners in Christendom."

She patted Master Gisborne on his plump cheek, and I led him back down the treacherous stairwell.

"What did she mean?" he asked me.

"Visit a few howffs and you'll find out," I told him. "The medical students are the most notorious group of topers in the city, if you discount the lawyers, judges, poets, boatmen, and Lords this-and-that."

"What's a howff?"

I led him directly into one.

There was a general fug in what passed for the air. Pipes were being smoked furiously, and there were no windows to open, so the stale fumes lay heavy at eye level. I could hear laughter and swearing and the shrieks of women, but it was like peering through a haar. I saw one-legged Jack, balancing a wench on his good knee. Two lawyers sat at the next table along, heads close together. A poet of minor repute scribbled away as he sat slumped on the floor. And all around there was wine, wine in jugs and bumpers and bottles, its sour smell vying with that of tobacco.

But the most noise came from a big round table in the furthest corner, where beneath flickering lamplight a meeting of the Monthly Club was underway. I led Gisborne to the table, having promised him that Edinburgh would acquaint itself with him. Five gentlemen sat round the table. One recognised me immediately.

"Dear old Cully! What news from the world above?"

"No news, sir."

"None better than that!"

"What's the meeting this month, sirs?"

"The Hot Air Club, Cully." The speaker made a toast of the words. "We are celebrating the tenth anniversary of Mr. Tytler's flight by montgolfier over this very city."

This had to be toasted again, while I explained to Master Gisborne that the Monthly Club changed its name regularly in order to have something to celebrate.

"I see you've brought fresh blood, Cully."

"Mr. Gisborne," I said, "is newly arrived from London and hopes to study medicine."

"I hope he will, too, if he intends to practise."

There was laughter and replenishing of glasses.

"This gentleman," I informed my master, "is Mr. Walter Scott. Mr. Scott is an advocate."

"Not today," said another of the group. "Today he's Colonel Grogg!"

More laughter. Gisborne was asked what he would drink.

"A glass of port," my hapless charge replied.

The table went quiet. Scott was smiling with half his mouth only.

"Port is not much drunk in these parts. It reminds some people of the Union. Some people would rather drink *whisky* and toast their Jacobite 'King O'er the Water.' " Someone at the table actually did this, not heeding the tone of Scott's voice. "But we're one nation now," Scott continued. That man did like to make a speech. "And if you'll drink some claret with us, we may yet be reconciled."

The drinker toasted Bonnie Prince Charlie; another lawyer, whose name was Urquhart, now turned to Gisborne with his usual complaint to Englishmen. " 'Rule Britannia,' " he said, "was written by a Scot. John Bull was *invented* by a Scot!"

He slumped back, having to his mind made his point. Master Gisborne looked like he had tumbled into Bedlam.

"Now, now," Scott calmed. "We're here to celebrate mont-golfiers." He handed Gisborne a stemless glass filled to the brim. "And new arrivals. But you've come to a dangerous place, sir."

"How so?" my master enquired.

"Sedition is rife." Scott paused. "As is murder. How many is it now, Cully?"

"Three this past fortnight." I recited the names. "Dr. Benson, MacStay the coffin maker, and a wretch called Howison."

"All stabbed," Scott informed Gisborne. "Imagine, murdering a coffin maker! It's like trying to murder Death himself."

As was wont to happen, the Monthly Club shifted to another howff to partake of a *prix fixe* dinner, and thence to another, where Scott would drink champagne and lead a discussion of "the chest."

The chest in question had been found when the Castle's crown room was opened during a search for some documents. The crown room had been opened, according to the advocate, by special warrant under the royal sign manual. No one had authority to break open the chest. The crown room was locked again, and the chest still inside. At the time of the union with England, the royal regalia of Scotland had disappeared. It was Scott's contention that this regalia—crown, sceptre, and sword—lay in the chest.

Gisborne listened in fascination. Somewhere along the route he had misplaced his sense of economy. He would pay for the champagne. He would pay for dinner. A brothel was being discussed as the next destination. . . . Luckily, Scott was taking an interest in him, so that Gisborne's pockets were still fairly full, though his wits be empty.

I sat apart, conversing with the exiled Comte d'Artois, who had fled France at the outset of revolution. He retained the habit of stroking his neck for luck, his good fortune being that it still connected his head to his trunk. He had reason to feel nervous. Prompted by events in France, sedition was in the air. There had been riots, and now the ringleaders were being tried.

We were discussing Deacon Brodie, hanged six years before for a series of housebreakings. Brodie, a cabinetmaker and locksmith, had robbed the very premises to which he'd fitted locks. Respectable by day, he'd been nefarious by night. To the Comte (who knew about such matters), this was merely "the human condition."

I noticed suddenly that I was seated in shadow. A man stood over me. He had full thick lips, a meaty stew of a nose, and eyebrows which met at the central divide the way warring forces sometimes will.

"Cullender?"

I shook my head and turned away.

"You're Cullender," he said. "This is for you." He slapped his paw onto the table, then turned and pushed back through the throng. A piece of paper, neatly folded, sat on the wood where his hand had been. I unfolded it and read:

"Outside the Tolbooth, quarter before midnight."

The note was unsigned. I handed it to the Comte.

"You will go?"

It was already past eleven. "I'll let one more drink decide."

The Tolbooth was the city jail where Brodie himself had spent his final days, singing airs from *The Beggar's Opera*. The night was like pitch, nobody having bothered to light their lamps, and a haar rolled through from the direction of Leith.

In the darkness, I had trodden in something I did not care to study and was scraping my shoe clean on the Tolbooth's cornerstone when I heard a voice close by.

"Cullender?"

A woman's voice. Even held to a whisper, I knew it for that. The lady herself was dressed top to toe in black, her face deep inside the hood of a cloak.

"I'm Cullender."

"I'm told you perform services."

"I'm no minister, lady."

Maybe she smiled. A small bag appeared and I took it, weighing the coins inside.

"There's a book circulating in the town," said my new mistress. "I am keen to obtain it."

"We have several fine booksellers in the Luckenbooths. . . ."

"You are glib, sir."

"And you are mysterious."

"Then I'll be plain. I know of only one copy of this book, a private printing. It is called *Ranger's Second Impartial List . . .*"

"*. . . of the Ladies of Pleasure in Edinburgh.*"

"You know it. Have you seen it?"

"It's not meant for the likes of me."

"I would like to see this book."

"You want me to find it?"

"It's said you know everyone in the city."

"Everyone that matters."

"Then you can locate it."

"It's possible." I examined my shoes. "But first I'd need to know a little more. . . ."

When I looked up again, she was gone.

At The Cross, the caddies were speaking quietly with the chairmen. We caddies had organised ourselves into a company, boasting written standards and a Magistrate of Caddies in charge of all. We regarded ourselves superior to the chairmen, mere brawny Highland migrants.

But my best friend and most trusted ally, Mr. Mack, was a chairman. He was not, however, at The Cross. Work was nearly over for the night. The last taverns were throwing out the last soused customers. Only the brothels and cockpits were still active. Not able to locate Mr. Mack, I turned instead to a fellow caddie, an old hand called Dryden.

"Mr. Dryden?" I said, all businesslike, "I require your services, the fee to be agreed between us."

Dryden, as ever, was willing. I knew he would work through the night. He was known to the various brothelkeepers and could ask his questions discreetly, as I might have done myself had the lady's fee not been sufficient to turn me employer.

Me, I headed home, climbing the lonely stairs to my attic quarters and a cold mattress. I found sleep the way a pickpocket finds his gull.

Which is to say easily.

Next morning, Dryden was dead.

A young caddie called Colin came to tell me. We repaired to the Nor'

Loch, where the body still lay, facedown in the slime. The Town Guard—
"Town Rats" behind their backs—fingered their Lochaber axes, straightened their tall cocked hats, and tried to look important. One of their number,
a red-faced individual named Fairlie, asked if we knew the victim.

"Dryden," I said. "He was a caddie."

"He's been run through with a dagger," Fairlie delighted in telling me.
"Just like those other three."

But I wasn't so sure about that. . . .

I went to a quiet howff, a drink steadying my humour. Dryden, I surmised, had been killed in such a way as to make him appear another victim
of the city's stabber. I knew, though, that in all likelihood he had been
killed because of the questions he'd been asking . . . questions I'd sent him
to ask. Was I safe myself? Had Dryden revealed anything to his killer?
And what was it about my mistress's mission that made it so deadly dangerous?

As I was thus musing, young Gisborne entered the bar on fragile legs.

"Did I have anything to drink last evening?" he asked, holding his head.

"Master, you drank as if it were our last day alive."

Our hostess was already replenishing my wine jug. "Kill or cure," I said,
pouring two glasses.

Gisborne could see I was worried and asked the nature of the problem.
I was grateful to tell him. Any listener would have sufficed. Mind, I held
back some. This knowledge was proving dangerous, so I made no mention
of the lady and her book. I jumped from the messenger to my words with
Dryden.

"The thing to do, then," my young master said, "is to track backwards.
Locate the messenger."

I thought back to the previous evening. About the time the messenger
had been arriving, the lawyer Urquhart had been taking his leave of the
Monthly Club.

"We'll talk to Urquhart," I said. "At this hour he'll be in his chambers.
Follow me."

Gisborne followed me out of the howff and across the street directly into
another. There, in a booth, papers before him and a bottle of wine beside
them, sat Urquhart.

"I'm pleased to see you," the lawyer announced. His eyes were bloodshot, his nose like a stoned cherry. His breath I avoided altogether. Aged
somewhere in his thirties, Urquhart was a seasoned dissolute. He would
have us take a bumper with him.

"Sir," I began, "do you recall leaving the company last night?"

"Of course. I'm only sorry I'd to leave so early. An assignation, you understand." We shared a smile at this. "Tell me, Gisborne, to which house of ill fame did the gang repair?"

"I don't recollect," Gisborne admitted.

Urquhart enjoyed this. "Then tell me, did you awake in a bed or the gutter?"

"In neither, Mr. Urquhart. I awoke on the kitchen floor of a house I did not know."

While Urquhart relished this, I asked if he'd taken a chair from the tavern last night.

"Of course. A friend of yours was front-runner."

"Mr. Mack?" Urquhart nodded. "You didn't happen to see a grotesque, sir?" I described the messenger to him. Urquhart shook his head.

"I hear a caddie was murdered last night," Urquhart said. "We all know the Town Rats can't be expected to bring anyone to justice." He leaned toward me confidentially. "Are you looking for justice, Cully?"

"I don't know what I'm looking for, sir."

Which was a lie. For now, I was looking for Mr. Mack.

I left Gisborne with Urquhart, and found Mack at The Cross.

"Yes," he said, "I saw that fellow going in. A big fat-lipped sort with eyebrows that met in the middle."

"Had you seen him before?"

Mack nodded. "But not here, over the loch."

"The new town." Mack nodded. "Then show me where."

Mack and his fellow chairman carried me down the steep slope towards the building site. Yes, building site. For though Princes Street and George Street were finished, yet more streets were being artfully constructed. Just now, the builders were busy on what would be called Charlotte Square. We took the simpler route, down past Trinity Hospital and the College Kirk, then along Princes Street itself. There were plans to turn the Nor' Loch into either a canal or formal gardens, but for the moment it was a dumping ground. I avoided looking at it and tried not to think of poor Dryden. Joining the loch to the old town sat The Mound, an apt name for a treacherous heap of new-town rubble.

"All change, eh, Cully?" Mr. Mack called to me. "Soon there'll be no business in the old town for the likes of you and me."

He had a point. The nobility had already deserted the old town. Their grand lands now housed wheelwrights and hosiers and schoolmasters. They all lived in the new town now, at a general distance from the milling rabble. So here the foundations were being laid not for the new town alone but for the death of the old.

We passed into George Street and the sedan chair was brought to rest. "It was here I saw him," Mr. Mack said. "He was marching up the street like he owned the place."

I got out of the chair and rubbed my bruised posterior. Mr. Mack's companion had already spotted another likely fare. I waved them off. I must needs talk to my mistress, and that meant finding her servant. So I sat on a step and watched the work carts grinding past overloaded with rocks and rubble. The day passed pleasantly enough.

Perhaps two hours had passed when I saw him. I couldn't be sure which house he emerged from; he was some way along the street. I tucked myself behind some railings and watched him head down towards Princes Street. I followed at a canny distance.

He was clumsy, his gait gangling, and I followed him with ease. He climbed back up to the old town and made for the Luckenbooths. Here he entered a bookshop, causing me to pause.

The shop belonged to a Mr. Whitewood, who fancied himself not only bookseller but poet and author also. I entered the premises quietly and could hear Whitewood's raised voice. He was towards the back of his shop, reciting to a fawning audience of other *soidisant* writers and people to whom books were mere fashion.

The servant was pushing his way to the front of the small gathering. Whitewood stood on a low unsteady podium, and read with a white handkerchief in one hand, which he waved for dramatic effect. He needed all the help he could get. I dealt daily with the "improvers," the self-termed "literati." I'll tell you now what an improver is, he's an imp who roves. I'd seen them dragging their carcasses through the gutter and waylaying hoors and scrapping with the tourists.

The servant had reached the podium, and the bookseller had seen him. Without pausing mid-stanza, Whitewood passed the wretch a note. It was done in an instant and the servant headed back towards the door. I slipped outside and hid myself, watching the servant head as if towards the courts.

I followed him into the courthouse. I followed him into one particular court . . . and there was brought up short.

Lord Braxfield, the Hanging Judge, was deciding a case. He sat in his wig at his muckle bench and dipped oatcakes into his claret, sucking loudly on the biscuits as he glared at the accused. There were three of them, and I knew they were charged with sedition, being leaders of a popular convention for parliamentary reform. At this time, only thirty or so people in Edinburgh had the right to vote for the member of parliament. These three sad creatures had wanted to change that, and a lot more besides.

I glanced at the jury—doubtless hand picked by Braxfield himself. The accused would be whipped and sent to Botany Bay. The public gallery was restless. There were guards between the populace and the bench. The servant was nodded through by one of the guards and handed Whitewood's note to Braxfield. Then he turned quickly and left by another door. I was set to follow when the Hanging Judge noticed me.

"Cullender, approach the bench!"

I bit my lip, but knew better than to defy Braxfield, even if it meant losing my quarry. The guards let me through. I forbore to look at the accused as I passed them.

"Yes, my Lord?"

Braxfield nibbled another of his infernal biscuits. He looked like he'd drunk well, too. "Cullender," he said, "you're one of the least honest and civil men in this town, am I correct?"

"I have competitors, my Lord."

He guffawed, spitting crumbs from his wet lips. "But tell me this, would you have a man live who committed treason?"

I swallowed, aware of three pairs of eyes behind me. "I might ask myself about his motives, my Lord."

Braxfield leaned over the bench. He was unquestionably ugly, eyes black as night. In his seventies, he grew increasingly eccentric. He was what passed for the law in this city. "Then it's as well *I'm* wearing this wig and not you!" he screeched. He wagged a finger, the nail of which was sore in need of a trim. "You'll see Australia one day, my friend, if you're not careful. Now be gone, I've some justice to dispense."

It had been a long time since Braxfield and "justice" had been even loosely acquainted.

Outside, the servant was long gone. Cursing my luck and the law courts both, I headed down to the Canongate.

I engaged Mr. Mack's services regarding my lady's book, warning him to be extra vigilant and telling him of Dryden's demise. He suggested going to the authorities, then realised what he was saying. The law was as effectual as a scented handkerchief against the pox, and we both knew it.

I sat in a howff and ate a dish of oysters. Having been to look at the university, Master Gisborne joined me.

"It'll be fine when it's finished," was his opinion.

I supped the last of the juice and put down the platter. "Remember I told you about the serpent, Master?"

His eyes were red-rimmed, face puffy with excess. He nodded.

"Well," I continued thoughtfully, "perhaps it's not so far beneath the surface as I thought. You need only scratch and you'll see it. Remember that, even in your cups."

He looked puzzled, but nodded again. Then he seemed to remember something, and reached into his leather bag. He handed me a wrapped parcel.

"Cully, can you keep this somewhere safe?"

"What is it?"

"Just hold it for me for a day or so. Will you do that?"

I nodded and placed the parcel at my feet. Gisborne looked mightily relieved. Then the howff door swung inwards and Urquhart and others appeared, taking Gisborne off with them. I finished my wine and made my way back to my room.

Halfway there, I met the tailor whose family lived two floors below me.

"Cully," he said, "men are looking for you."

"What sort of men?"

"The sort you wouldn't have find you. They're standing guard on the stairwell and won't shift."

"Thanks for the warning."

He held my arm. "Cully, business is slow. If you could persuade some of your clients of the quality of my cloth . . . ?"

"Depend on it." I went back up the brae to The Cross and found Mr. Mack.

"Here," I said, handing him the parcel. "Keep this for me."

"What's wrong?"

"I'm not sure. I think I may have stepped in something even less savoury than I thought. Any news of the *List?*"

Mack shook his head. He looked worried when I left him; not for himself, but for me.

I kept heading uphill, towards the Castle itself. Beneath Castle Hill lay the catacombs where the town's denizens used to hide when the place was being sacked. And here the lowest of Edinburgh's wretches still dwelt. I would be safe there, so I made my way into the tunnels and out of the light, averting my face where possible from each interested, unfriendly gaze.

The man I sought sat slouched against one of the curving walls, hands on his knees. He could sit like that for hours, brooding. He was a giant, and there were stories to equal his size. It was said he'd been a seditionary, a rabble-rouser, both pirate and smuggler. He had most certainly killed men, but these days he lay low. His name was Ormond.

He watched me sit opposite him, his gaze unblinking.

"You're in trouble," he said at last.

"Would I be here otherwise? I need somewhere to sleep for tonight."

He nodded slowly. "That's all any of us needs. You'll be safe here, Cullender."

And I was.

But next morning I was roused early by Ormond shaking me.

"Men outside," he hissed. "Looking for you."

I rubbed my eyes. "Is there another exit?"

Ormond shook his head. "If you went any deeper into this maze, you could lose yourself forever. These burrows run as far as the Canongate."

"How many men?" I was standing up now, fully awake.

"Four."

I held out my hand. "Give me a dagger; I'll deal with them." I meant it too. I was aching and irritable and tired of running. But Ormond shook his head.

"I've a better plan," he said.

He led me back through the tunnel towards its entrance. The tunnel grew more populous as we neared the outside world. I could hear my pursuers ahead, examining faces, snarling as each one proved false. Then Ormond filled his lungs.

"The price of corn's to be raised!" he bellowed. "New taxes! New laws! Everyone to The Cross!"

Voices were raised in anger, and people clambered to their feet. Ormond was raising a mob. The Edinburgh mob was a wondrous thing. It could run riot through the streets and then melt back into the shadows. There'd been the Porteous riots, anti-Catholic riots, price-rise riots, and pro-revolution riots. Each time, the vast majority escaped arrest. A mob could be raised in a minute and could disperse in another. Even Braxfield feared the mob.

Ormond was bellowing in front of me. As for me, I was merely another of the wretches. I passed the men who'd been seeking me. They stood dumbfounded in the midst of the spectacle. As soon as the crowd reached the Lawnmarket, I peeled off with a wave of thanks to Ormond, slipped into an alley, and was alone again.

But not for long. Down past the Luckenbooths I saw the servant again, and this time he would not evade me. Down towards Princes Street he went, down Geordie Boyd's footpath, a footpath that would soon be wide enough for carriages. He crossed Princes Street and headed up to George Street. There at last I saw him descend some steps and enter a house by its servants' door. I stopped a sedan chair. Both chairmen knew me through Mr. Mack.

"That house there?" one of them said in answer to my question. "It used to belong to Lord Thorpe before he left for London. A bookseller bought it from him."

"A Mr. Whitewood?" I asked blithely. The chairmen nodded. "I admit I don't know that gentleman well. Is he married?"

"Married, aye, but you wouldn't know it. She's seldom seen, is she, Donald?"

"Rarely, very rarely," the second chairman agreed.

"Why's that? Has she the pox or something?"

They laughed at the imputation. "How would we know a thing like that?"

I laughed too, and bid them thanks and farewell. Then I approached the front door of the house and knocked a good solid knock.

The servant, when he opened the door, was liveried. He looked at me in astonishment.

"Tell your mistress I wish to speak with her," I said sharply.

He appeared in two minds at least, but I sidestepped him and found myself in a fine entrance hall.

"Wait in here," the servant growled, closing the front door and opening another. "I'll ask my Lady if she'll deign to see you."

I toured the drawing room. It was like walking around an exhibition, though in truth the only exhibition I'd ever toured was of Bedlam on a Sunday afternoon, and then only to look for a friend of mine.

The door opened and the Lady of the house swept in. She had powdered her cheeks heavily to disguise the redness there—either embarrassment or anger. Her eyes avoided mine, which gave me opportunity to study her. She was in her mid twenties, not short, and with a pleasing figure. Her lips were full and red, her eyes hard but to my mind seductive. She was a catch. But when she spoke her voice was rough-hewn, and I wondered at her history.

"What do you want?"

"What do you think I want?"

She picked up a pretty statuette. "Are we acquainted?"

"I believe so. We met outside the Tolbooth."

She attempted a disbelieving laugh. "Indeed? It's a place I've never been."

"You would not care to see its innards, Lady, yet you may if you continue in this manner."

No amount of powder could have hidden her colouring. "How dare you come here!"

"My life is in danger, Lady."

This quieted her. "Why? What have you done?"

"Nothing save what you asked of me."

"Have you found the book?"

"Not yet, and I've a mind to hand you back your money."

She saw what I was getting at, and looked aghast. "But if you're in danger . . . I swear it cannot be to do with me!"

"No? A man has died already."

"Mr. Cullender, it's only a book! It's nothing anyone would kill for."

I almost believed her. "Why do you want it?"

She turned away. "That is not your concern."

"My chief concern is my neck, Lady. I'll save it at any cost."

"I repeat, you are in no danger from seeking that book. If you think your life in peril, there must needs be some other cause." She stared at me as she spoke, and the damnation of it was that I believed her. I believed that Dryden's death, Braxfield's threat, the men chasing me, that none of it had anything to do with her. She saw the change in me and smiled a radiant smile, a smile that took me with it.

"Now get out," she said. And with that she left the room and began to climb the stairs. Her servant was waiting for me by the front door, holding it open in readiness.

My head was full of puzzles. All I knew with certainty was that I was sick of hiding. I headed back to the old town with a plan in my mind as half-baked as the scrapings the baker tossed out to the homeless.

I toured the town gossips, starting with the fishwives. Then I headed to The Cross and whispered in the ears of selected caddies and chairmen. Then it was into the howffs and dining establishments, and I was glad to wash my hard work down with a glass or two of wine.

My story broadcast, I repaired to my lodgings and lay on the straw mattress. There were no men waiting for me on the stairwell. I believe I even slept a little. It was dark when I next looked out of the skylight. The story I'd spread was that I knew who'd killed Dryden and was merely biding my time before alerting the Town Rats. Would anyone fall for the ploy? I wasn't sure. I fell to a doze again but opened my eyes on hearing noises on the stair.

The steps to my attic were rotten and had to be managed adroitly. My visitor—a lone man, I surmised—was doing his best. I sat up on the mattress and watched the door begin to open. In deep shadow, a figure entered my room, closing the door after it with some finality.

"Good evening, Cully."

I swallowed drily. "So the stories were true then, Deacon Brodie?"

"True enough," he said, coming closer. His face was almost unrecognisable, much older, more careworn, and he wore no wig, no marks of a gentleman. He carried a slender dagger in his right hand.

"I cheated the gibbet, Cully," he said with his old pride.

"But I was there, I saw you drop."

"And you saw my men cut me down and haul me away." He grinned with what teeth were left in his head. "A wooden collar saved my throat, Cully. I devised it myself."

I recalled the red silk he'd worn ostentatiously around his throat. A scarf from a female admirer, the story went. It would have hidden just such a device.

"You've been in hiding a long time," I said. The dagger was inches from me.

"I fled Edinburgh, Cully. I've been away these past five and a half years."

"What brought you back?" I couldn't take my eyes off the dagger.

"Aye," Brodie said, seeing what was in my mind. "The doctor who pronounced me dead and the coffin maker who was supposed to have buried me. I couldn't have witnesses alive . . . not now."

"And the others, Dryden and the wretch Howison?"

"Both recognised me, curse them. Then *you* started to snoop around and couldn't be found."

"But why? Why are you back?"

The dagger was touching my throat now. I'd backed myself into a corner of the bed. There was nowhere to go. "I was *tempted* back, Cully. A temptation I could not resist. The crown jewels."

"What?"

His voice was a feverish whisper. "The chest in the crown room. I will have its contents, my last and greatest theft."

"Alone? Impossible."

"But I'm not alone. I have powerful allies." He smiled. "Braxfield, for one. He believes the theft of the jewels will spark a Scots revolution. But you know this already, Cully. You were seen watching Braxfield. You were seen in Whitewood's shop."

"Whitewood's part of it, too?"

"You know he is, romantic fool that he is." The point of the dagger broke my skin. I could feel blood trickle down my throat. If I spoke again, they would be my last words. I felt like laughing. Brodie was so wrong in his surmisings. Everything was wrong. A sudden noise on the stair turned Brodie's head. My own dagger was hidden beneath my thigh. I grabbed it with one hand, my other hand wrestling with Brodie's blade.

When Gisborne opened the door, what he saw sobered him immediately.

Brodie freed himself and turned to confront the young Englishman, dagger ready, but not ready enough. Gisborne had no hesitation in running him through. Brodie stood there frozen, then keeled over, his head hitting the boards with a dull dead sound.

Gisborne was the statue now. He stared at the spreading blood.

I got to my feet quickly. "Where did you get the blade?" I asked, amazed.

Gisborne swallowed. "I bought it new today, heeding your advice."

"You saved my life, young Master." I stared down at Brodie's corpse. "But why are you here?"

Gisborne came to his senses. "I heard you were looking for a book."

"I was. What of it?" We were both staring at Brodie.

"Only to tell you that I am in possession of it. Or I was. The lawyer Urquhart gave it to me. He said I would doubtless find it useful. . . . Who was this man?"

I ignored the question and glared at him. "*You* have the book?"

He shook his head. "I daren't keep it in my room for fear my landlady might find it."

I blinked. "That parcel?" Gisborne nodded. I felt a fool, a dumb fool. But there was Brodie's corpse to dispose of. I could see little advantage in reporting this, his second demise, to the authorities. Questions would be asked of Master Gisborne, and a young Englishman might not always receive a fair hearing, especially with Braxfield at the bench. God no, the body must be disposed of quietly.

And I knew just the spot.

Mr. Mack helped us lug the guts down to the new town, propping Brodie in the sedan chair. The slumped corpse resembled nothing so much as a sleeping drunk.

In Charlotte Square we found some fresh foundations and buried the remains of Deacon Brodie within. We were all three in a sweat by the time we'd finished. I sat myself down on a large stone and wiped my brow.

"Well, friends," I said, "it is only right and proper."

"What is?" Gisborne asked, breathing heavily.

"The old town has its serpent, and now the new town does too." I watched Gisborne put his jacket back on. It was the blue coat with silver buttons. There was blood on it, and dirt besides.

"I know a tailor," I began, "might make something fresh for an excellent price. . . ."

Next morning, washed and crisply dressed, I returned to my Lady's house. I waved the parcel under the servant's nose and he hurried upstairs.

My Lady was down promptly, but gave me no heed. She had eyes only for the book. Book? It was little more than a ragged pamphlet; its pages were thumbed, scribbled marginalia commenting on this or that entry or adding a fresh one. I handed her the tome.

"The entry you seek is towards the back," I told her. She looked startled. "You are, I suppose, the Masked Lady referred to therein? A lady for daylight assignations only, and always masked, speaking in a whisper?"

Her cheeks were crimson as she tore at the book, scattering its shreddings.

"Better have the floor swept," I told her. "You wouldn't want Mr. Whitewood to find any trace. That was your reason all along, was it not? He is a known philanderer. It was only a matter of time before he got to read of the Masked Lady and became intrigued to meet her."

Her head was held high, as if she were examining the room's cornices.

"I'm not ashamed," she said.

"Nor should you be."

She saw I was not mocking her. "I am a prisoner here, with no more life than a doll."

"So you take revenge in your own particular manner? I understand, Lady, but you must understand this. Two men died because of you. Not directly, but that matters not to them. Only one deserved to die. For the other . . ." I jangled the bag of money she'd given me that first night. "These coins will buy him a burial."

Then I bid her good day and left the whole shining new town behind me, with its noises of construction and busyness. Let them build all the mighty edifices they would; they could not erase the stain. They could not erase the real town, the old town, the town I knew so intimately. I returned to the howff where Gisborne and Mack awaited me.

"I've decided," the young master said, "to study law rather than medicine, Cully." He poured me a drink. "Edinburgh needs another lawyer, don't you think?"

The image of Braxfield came unmasked into my mind. "Like it needs another plague, Master."

But I raised my glass to him anyway.

SAINT BOBBY

Doug Allyn

A rock musician by night, Doug Allyn rises at dawn to pursue his second career as a mystery writer. His seemingly boundless energy has enabled him to launch three successful mystery series with entries at both novel and short-story length, while also finding time for the occasional non-series book or short story. With a spontaneousness and innovativeness that sometimes results in his making sudden changes of key—like when he decided to transform his first series hero, Mitch Mitchell, who'd been a man in the first tales, into a woman for the ensuing adventures—Doug Allyn has worked his way into the hearts of hundreds of thousands of readers. He has claimed the Ellery Queen's Mystery Magazine *Readers Award four times and is behind only the great Stanley Ellin in the number of Edgar Allan Poe Award nominations his short stories have earned from the Mystery Writers of America (MWA). In 1994, he won the prestigious MWA Edgar. Whether he is writing about private eye Ax Axton, veterinarian sleuth Dr. David Westbrook, or the aforementioned Mitch Mitchell, the author delivers appealing characters that readers look forward to seeing again.*

SHE'D WISHED HIM dead and now he was. For a disjointed moment Colleen McKenzie thought she was dreaming, that the tall, well-dressed police detective standing in front of her desk was a figment. . . . He was eyeing her oddly. She swallowed, hard.

"I'm sorry, Sergeant. I've forgotten your name."

"Dylan, ma'am. John Dylan. Are you all right, Dr. McKenzie? Can I get you a glass of water or something?"

"No, I'm . . . a bit shaken, that's all. How did it happen?"

"Traffic accident. It appears he was sideswiped on Balfour Road a few miles from your home. There's a steep embankment there and your husband's Porsche went over. It apparently happened sometime last night. He was pronounced dead at the scene. I'm sorry."

Her mouth narrowed as she visibly tried to control her emotions. She looked vaguely Irish, rangy, with auburn hair, fair skin, and a spray of freckles on her throat. A cool professional, though, polished as a porcelain doll. Dylan waited, watching her, wondering if her composure would crack. He hoped not. Tears were tough to handle. None came, though. After a moment, she gathered herself, straightened her white lab coat, and took a deep breath.

"I don't understand," she said. "This happened last night?"

"Yes, ma'am, but the wreck wasn't discovered until this morning. Do you know where your husband was going last night?"

"No idea. Ian and I separated last year. Our divorce will be final in six weeks."

"Or would have been."

"Or—yes, I suppose so, I . . ." She hesitated, sensing something in his tone. "What was that supposed to mean? Is there something you haven't told me?"

Dylan considered the question a moment, then shrugged. "It appears the collision was intentional, Dr. McKenzie. From the skid marks it looks like the vehicle that rammed your husband's Porsche veered into it sharply, forced it over the embankment, then drove on without offering assistance. We're treating it as a possible homicide, ma'am. Do you feel up to answering a few questions?"

"What kind of questions?"

"At this point we're just trying to gather as much information as possible."

"Don't patronize me, Detective. Most of my clients here at the Institute have been ordered into treatment by the courts. As a clinical therapist, I work with cops and parole officers every day. I'm reasonably familiar with the criminal justice system. So, one professional to another, did someone ram Ian's car deliberately or not?"

"Let's just say we haven't ruled anything out yet, ma'am. May I sit?" He eased down on the metal chair facing her without waiting for an answer and they eyed each other a moment across the desk. Her eyes were an odd shade of green, ice cold at the moment.

"Would you like to have an attorney present, ma'am?"

"Don't be ridiculous. Ian and I have been on lousy terms lately but I certainly didn't wish him harm. I don't need a lawyer."

"Maybe not, but if you're familiar with the system, Dr. McKenzie, you know that in a homicide a spouse in the middle of a divorce automatically lands on top of my list."

"Fair enough. Then let's get me off your list so we can both get back to work. What do you want to know?"

"Your whereabouts last night?"

"I was at home all evening. Alone."

"Did anyone see you? Did you talk to a neighbor, anything like that?"

"I'm afraid not. Sorry, I didn't know I was going to need an alibi or I'd have made a better job of it."

"You said your divorce was nearly final? How would you characterize your recent relationship with your husband?"

"Divorces aren't usually friendly, Sergeant. Ours definitely wasn't. It was businesslike, though. My husband is an attorney, a good one. I didn't consider our settlement equitable but fighting it would have delayed things, so I took it and ran."

"What was the reason for the divorce?"

"Infidelity. His. And . . . a car key," she added.

"Car key?"

"I was waiting for Ian in the parking lot of his club when I saw him gouge the paint of a new Pontiac. It belonged to a guy who'd just beaten him at squash. It was such a . . . damned petty thing to do that I realized our problems weren't ever going to work out. Perhaps I didn't want them to. As simple as that, and as complicated. Does that sound too cerebral, Sergeant?"

"It's not how most people would describe a divorce, but then you're a psychologist. So, the divorce may not have been friendly but it wasn't hostile either. Is that a fair statement?"

"Close enough."

"Do you stand to gain financially because of what happened?"

"I—suppose so, I haven't really thought that far ahead. Do you have a description of the car involved?"

"Not at this time, no."

"Well, I drive a secondhand blue Volvo. It's parked in my slot in the lot. You're welcome to check it over."

"Thank you, ma'am. Do you own or have access to any other vehicles? Family or friends? Anything like that?"

"My God, you're serious, aren't you?"

"We take homicide pretty seriously, yes, ma'am. And if you don't mind my saying, you're taking this quite calmly."

"It's not the first time I've heard bad news, Sergeant. I deal with grief every day."

"And it gets easier with practice?"

"Not easier, but when you've been through a tunnel a few times you know there's daylight on the other side. I've got a therapy session in five minutes. Is there anything else?"

"Just a few quick questions. Do you know of anyone who might wish your husband harm?"

"Ian handled a lot of divorce cases. In the three years we were married he got a few phone threats and his car was vandalized once, but I'm not aware of any current problems. His office staff would know more than I do."

"Are you seeing anyone now?"

"I occasionally have dinner with friends who aren't female. I'm not in a romantic relationship, if that's what you mean."

"What about these wackos you treat, are any of them violent?"

"Wackos?"

"Well, they're seeing a shrink, so by definition they're running a quart low, right?"

A rosy glow crept above the collar of her lab coat, suffusing the freckles on her throat. But when she spoke, her voice was calm. "That was pretty good," she said evenly. "I almost bit. Actually, my clients are mostly ordinary people who are trying to improve some aspect of their lives. We can all use a little help sometimes, Sergeant. I'd guess your Rottweiler interview style has landed you in trouble more than once. Does that make you a wacko?"

"It might if I were compulsive about it, ma'am, but I'm not. You're an educated woman and you play mind games for a living. If I tried fencing with you, I'd probably lose. Sometimes crude works better than finesse."

"Or maybe you're just a jerk."

"My ex-wife would agree with you a hundred percent. But she's still breathing. Your ex isn't. So if you don't mind, Dr. McKenzie, do any of your clients have a history of violence?"

"Client medical records are protected by doctor/patient privilege, as I'm sure you're aware, Detective. But just to ease your mind, this is a publicly funded clinic. We deal in court and social services referrals. The work we do here is considered mental health lite: depression, grief counseling, substance abuse, and domestic-assault counseling. We mostly meet in therapy groups because that's all the HMOs pay for. Violent patients aren't candidates for group therapy and none of my clients know anything of my personal life. They'd have no reason to act out against my husband. Are we done?"

"Yes, ma'am," he said, rising. "I really am very sorry for your loss, and

if my questions seemed a little rough I apologize. No offense intended."
He handed her his card. "If you think of anything that might help, please
call me, day or night."

"Yeah," Colleen said, leaning back in her chair, massaging her eyes.
"Right."

For a moment her professional facade slipped and she was only a woman
who'd just received some very bad news. Dylan hesitated in the doorway,
watching her. She glanced up.

"Was there something else?"

"No, ma'am," he said. "Sorry."

Rob Bergstrom already had the therapy session underway when Colleen
walked in, thank God. Groups at the Institute were led by male/female co-
therapists to offer patients a semblance of a nuclear family. Thirtyish, with
thinning blond hair and a wardrobe of corduroy sport coats and faded jeans,
Rob seemed a tad young for a father figure. He was a good listener, though,
and offered perceptive advice, which made him a first-rate partner for Colleen. For therapy sessions, at least.

Colleen took the chair beside Rob in the circle, nodding an apology to
the seven members of the group. Three were middle-aged women coping
with grief: a murdered child, an incompetent invalid mother, and a husband
who'd taken off with a waitress.

The fourth woman, Sherry Stringer, was working through an ugly divorce. Her ex had been stalking her, slashing her tires, spraying her rented
home with graffiti. Unfortunately, he was a small-town cop who knew precisely how to avoid being caught.

Sherry'd been an emotional shambles for months, held together by a few
threads of hope and the support of the group. She looked a bit more cheerful
today, though.

The oldest men in the group were in their early sixties, but they were
diametric opposites. Frank Thomas was a retired college prof who'd lost
his wife to cancer. Dapper, gracious, and shell-shocked, he seemed to drift
through the sessions like a silver-maned, courteous cloud, so insubstantial
that Colleen sometimes wondered if she could pass her hand through him.

Jesse Ortiz was Frank's opposite, squat, grizzled, and grumpy as a caged
bear. He'd lost his family farm paying for his wife's medical treatment.
After her death he'd gone on a six-week bender, got busted in Dearborn,
drunk and disorderly, and was ordered into treatment as a condition of
probation. Grimly sober now, Jesse was impatient with the sessions. He
needed a job, but for a manual laborer whose only work experience was
farming, Detroit was a lousy place to be unemployed.

The third man, Gary Noreski, was a balloon, six-three and crowding four hundred pounds, suffering through a work-required weight-loss program. He'd been withdrawn the past few sessions. Was it his medication or more trouble with his promiscuous shrew of a wife? Colleen meant to probe that area in today's meeting.

Not likely. She tried to focus on Mrs. Metcalfe's complaints about her aging mother's irrational demands, but Colleen's memory kept flashing back to fragments of Ian. In the dawn light, unshaven and surly. But beautiful. Ian's compact frame was as firm as coiled hemp, corded by years of devoted weight training. Unfortunately, his heart was similarly steeled. . . . They were all looking at her.

"I'm sorry," she said. "I lost concentration for a moment."

"Mrs. Metcalfe asked if you thought it was more a woman's place to care for a parent," Rob said smoothly. "Her brothers haven't responded to her requests for help."

"A woman bears no more responsibility than a man in such instances, of course," Colleen said, taking Rob's cue. "But with your brothers so far away, the weight may fall more heavily on you. Is that fair? Nope, but there it is. How do the rest of you feel about it? Comments?"

She shot a glance of thanks at Rob as several members offered opinions. The consensus was that Mrs. Metcalfe might have to cope on her own but she was up to it, especially with the encouragement of the group.

Colleen stumbled through the hour like a sleepwalker, half hearing her clients' problems, distracted by flickers of memory. Just as the session was closing, Sherry Stringer, the battered wife, raised her hand to speak.

"I don't know what to make of this, but apparently someone had a . . . serious talk with my husband last week. For the first time since our breakup he's acting halfway human about things. I want to thank the group for helping me through all this. But"—she looked hopefully at each of the men in the circle—"I especially want to thank my guardian angel."

"Praise be," Mrs. Metcalfe said.

"I wasn't talking about a heavenly angel," Sherry continued. "I think mine is a little closer to home."

"How do you mean that?" Gary Noreski asked.

"Somebody broke Tod's arm in three places," Sherry said, trying not to sound smug and failing. "And I hope you all won't think I'm a bad person, but it's the best damned thing that's happened to me in a year."

"*Broke* it?" Noreski pressed. "You mean in a fight?"

"Tod wouldn't say how it happened. He never was much on explanations. But he's definitely had an attitude adjustment. Maybe it'll last as long as the cast stays on."

"But you have no idea who did it?" Colleen pressed.

"Not a clue," Sherry said, glancing around the group. "But I'm grateful to whoever it was, and to the group, of course. Thank you all."

"We're here for you," Rob nodded, "and for each other. Okay, let's sum up what we've covered today to see what we've gained."

Rob deftly carried the ball for the final ten minutes, making each client feel special, offering positive reinforcement to help them through the week; he then dismissed the session. He saw the group out, shaking hands at the door like a country parson. Colleen was still in her seat, staring into space.

"Earth to Colleen, what's up? Are you all right?"

"Actually I'm not. I'm sorry about bailing on you."

"Don't be a twerp, McKenzie, the session went fine. Back in L.A. I worked with a psych who not only nodded off in sessions, she even snored sometimes. On the worst day of your professional life you're the best therapist I know, so what's wrong?"

"My . . . my ex-husband was killed this morning. Auto accident."

"Jeez, Colleen, that's awful. I'm so sorry. What happened?"

"A hit-and-run, apparently. Somebody ran him off the road a few miles from our . . . from his house."

"Awful," Rob repeated, shaking his head. "For crying out loud, why didn't you just bag the session? I would have coped."

"You *did* cope," she corrected. "I was absent without leave the whole session. The only thing that registered was Stringer's guardian angel. What was that about?"

"I don't know. Her husband's a cop who likes to muscle people, maybe somebody muscled him back. I'm more concerned about you. Why don't you skip the substance-abuse session this afternoon. I'll be happy to fill in for you."

"You're sure you don't mind subbing?"

"Not at all, but you'd better clear it with the boss. I'm still the new kid on the block."

"She'll be okay with it, especially when I mention the way you carried the weight this morning."

"All praise gratefully accepted. Look, I've got to get home to make lunch for my dad. He hassles the caregiver about meals and I can't afford to have another one quit. Tell Mrs. Dellums I may be a few minutes late but I'll definitely take the session. And you take care of yourself, okay? What do you say we do dinner later in the week, blow off a little steam? My treat."

"I'd like that. Thanks, Rob, for everything."

"You bet." He trotted off, lanky and collegiate in his rumpled jacket, looking more like a grad student than a therapist.

Colleen rapped once on the director's office door and went in. Mavis Dellums was knitting, as usual, one of the countless colorful scarves she gave away to friends and family. She was a matronly African-American grandmother who rarely raised her voice yet ran a multi-million-dollar public mental health clinic with Prussian efficiency.

"Hi," Mavis said. "I heard about your ex. Are you okay?"

"No. I want the afternoon off. Rob Bergstrom offered to take the substance-abuse session."

"Is he up to it?"

"Absolutely. He's a keeper, Mavis, bright, empathetic, good with patients. I'm jealous."

"Glad to hear it. How's he to work with personally?"

"A solid pro, perceptive, quick on the uptake. I think he'll work out fine."

"Good. He had great references, and a guy who quits a good job to come home and care for his dear old dad can't be all bad no matter what they say."

"No matter what who says?"

"I heard a few rumors from L.A. that he tended to be overly attentive to female clients and had some weird New Age therapy ideas. Any sign of trouble along those lines?"

"You mean does he hit on female clients? Not at all. If anything he's more attentive to the men in the group. As for New Age ideas, he's offered a few suggestions but we're not chanting mantras yet."

"And off the job? Anything there?"

"How do you mean?"

"I thought you two were dating?"

"You're a nosy old woman and no, there's nothing going on. Rob and I had dinner a few times, probably will again, but strictly as friends."

"Good. I hate it when therapists get involved. They always analyze their relationship to death and I end up juggling everybody's schedules to keep the peace. I don't mind juggling yours, though, considering what's happened. Take as much time as you need. How long will that be, do you think?"

"A few days should do it."

"That's not long."

"Ian and I were finished a lifetime ago, Mavis. I've only seen him twice this past year, both times in lawyers' offices. Still, I thought I was in love with him once and . . . frankly, I'm not sure how I feel about it now."

"Divorces are messy even when they're the right thing to do. And yours was. The police were here, by the way. A tall hunk of a detective named Dylan asked me some questions about you."

"You're kidding."

"When you grow up where I grew up, honey, you learn not to joke about cops. He seemed straight enough, might even be a nice guy. But then I'm not the one he had in his sights."

"Neither am I."

"I certainly hope not, hon," Mavis said, returning to her knitting. "We'd sure miss you around here."

Paranoia about Mavis's last crack or raw nerves from the day? Crossing the Institute parking lot, Colleen had an uneasy sense of being watched. She quickly unlocked her car, then scanned the lot. And spotted him hurrying after her with his rolling farmer's gait, a man used to walking with a foot in each furrow.

"Doc, can I talk to you? It's important."

"Mr. Ortiz, you know the rules about seeing me after hours. Anything important should be discussed within the group."

"Yeah, well I ain't sure all this talk is helpin' me much anyway. I'd rather be doin'. My only real trouble was losin' Vera and fallin' into a bottle. I'm past that now and I got a chance—"

"Mr. Ortiz," Colleen said, cutting him off, "I don't mean to be rude, but I have to go. If you have problems you don't feel comfortable discussing in the group, please phone the Institute for a private appointment."

"You ain't listenin'! I ain't worked a real job since I brought my wife up here to the hospital and I can't land nothin' steady if I'm stuck in some meeting."

"Mr. Ortiz—" Colleen fought to control her irritation—"you aren't in group therapy voluntarily, it's a condition of your probation. Any changes have to be okayed by the court. If you make an appointment with either Mr. Bergstrom or myself we'll try to work something out for you. I know you've had a tough time—"

"Lady, you wouldn't know a tough time if one kicked you in the ass. All you people know is talk!"

"Mr. Ortiz, I'm sorry, but I can't do this now. Please make an appointment—"

"—and we can gab some more. Thanks, Doc, you been a big help." He wheeled and stalked off, a gnarled stump of a man as out of place in Detroit as a farm wagon on a freeway.

Damn. Colleen had troubles of her own and seeing clients outside a clinical setting is almost always a mistake. Their needs can overwhelm you, leaving no resources for yourself or anyone else. Colleen knew that, yet the old farmer seemed so . . . lost, that she almost called out for him to come back.

Almost.

Instead she watched him clamber into a battered blue pickup truck and roar angrily off in a cloud of gray exhaust.

It was the last time she saw him alive.

The next few days weren't the breather Colleen needed. Ian's death was not only an emotional minefield, it was news.

She turned a half-dozen reporters from her door with no comment and began screening her calls. Her unlisted number was no help. Newspeople scored it with ease. So much for privacy.

Another development: Ian's death knocked their divorce agreement into a cocked hat. Terms she and her attorney had grimly fought out with Ian's firm were suddenly void. Instead of being stuck with the short end of a settlement, she was suddenly the sole titleholder of their home, a boat, and two cars. Even Ian's pension fund and life insurance were hers. Like a roofer whose house leaks like a springtime in Seattle, Ian the meticulous attorney hadn't gotten around to rewriting his will.

The windfall made her feel guilty, but she was too busy settling Ian's affairs to worry about her own emotions. His elderly mother was in the early stages of Alzheimer's and could barely comprehend what had happened. She'd completely forgotten that Colleen and Ian were divorcing, so their conversations were doubly difficult.

The detective, Dylan, left a message on her answering machine one afternoon. No progress to report. Had she thought of anything helpful?

Not a blessed thing. But she almost called him anyway. There was something about him, his spare smile, the intelligence in his eyes, something. They'd met under the lousiest circumstances imaginable. Hell, she was probably still a suspect. What would she say to him? That she was shaken by Ian's death? And felt lousy about profiting from it? Right.

He'd probably lock her up on general principles.

All in all, it was a crummy, nerve-grinding week. And then it crashed.

Late Thursday night Colleen was sipping a glass of white wine, reading while the TV flickered with the sound off, when the phone rang.

"Colleen, it's Rob Bergstrom. God, look, I'm sorry to bother you but . . . it's awful—Colleen, my dad's dead. Shot. Mr. Ortiz shot him."

"What? Rob, slow down, you're not making sense."

"I'm sorry, I—Mr. Ortiz, from our Tuesday therapy group? Jesse Ortiz?"

"Right, the farmer. What about him?"

"He killed my father, Colleen. And himself. Could you come to my house, please? I called nine-one-one. I don't know what else to do, who else to call. Please come."

"Try to stay calm, Rob. Don't touch anything. Go outside and wait for the police. I'll be there as quickly as I can."

Rob's home, his father's actually, was a massive two-story Beaux-Arts brownstone in a cul-de-sac full of them near Douglass High on the east side. The massive old monstrosities had been the rage among Detroit's new rich at the turn of the century, pretentiously styled with tall windows and mansard roofs, but built on lots so small the driveways dividing them could only pass one carriage at a time.

A prowl car and an EMT van were already jammed beside the house, flashers flickering eerily off the rain-slick bricks. Colleen parked at the curb behind an unmarked police car, Dylan's, as it happened. He met her halfway up the front walk.

"Dr. McKenzie? What are you doing here?"

"Rob called me. He said his father had been killed."

"Yeah, I'm afraid so. Why did he call you specifically? Why not a clergyman or a lawyer? Why you?"

"Because I'm a friend. Why all the questions?"

"We've got a multiple homicide, ma'am, so bear with me, please. Do you know a Jesse Ortiz?"

"He's one of our clients, yes."

"Client? You mean he's a mental patient?"

"No, I mean client, Detective. He was ordered into therapy as part of a plea-bargain agreement and assigned to one of our groups by the Institute."

"What was his plea agreement about?"

"Drunk and disorderly. His wife died a few months ago. He went on a bender, got into a scuffle in a bar, got arrested, and the judge sent him to us."

"Then he was violent, right? Dangerous?"

Colleen hesitated. "Technically, his treatment is shielded by doctor/patient confidentiality—"

"Technically is the operative word, Doc. You just said he wasn't mental and he's dead anyway so let's not waltz around the rule book, okay? You said he was arrested after a fight. Didn't you and Dr. Bergstrom consider him dangerous?"

"No. He was drunk when he was arrested, nearly toxic in fact, but he had no history of alcohol abuse or violence, no police record at all. The incident was anomalous, triggered by the death of his wife. He got drunk and got into a jam, end of story. He was doing well in therapy. We would have discharged him with a recommendation of unsupervised probation."

"Even so, a guy who gets loaded and beats people up doesn't sound like somebody I'd hire to babysit my dad. Why did Bergstrom do it?"

"Is that what happened?"

"I'm asking you, Doc."

"All I can tell you is that Mr. Ortiz needed work and neither of us considered him a threat. He was a nice old guy who caught a few bad breaks, that's all. Rob's dad is incompetent and I know Rob's had trouble keeping caregivers, so if he hired Mr. Ortiz to babysit, as you put it, I'd have no problem with it. I told Jesse to use me as a reference if he needed one. Now please, what happened here?"

"Well, offhand it looks like your nice old guy killed Dr. Bergstrom's father and then himself, with a handgun. Murder-suicide. He also left a note in which he admitted killing your husband."

"What?" Colleen stared at him, as stunned as if he'd struck her. "What are you saying? Ian? Mr. Ortiz killed Ian?"

"That's what the note said, he—Hey, are you all right?"

She wasn't. The world had suddenly gone dark and started wobbling. Dylan seized her shoulders, holding her upright. "Take a deep breath, Doc, that's it. Now, I'm going to ease you down to—"

"It's all right," Colleen said, swallowing hard, gathering herself. "I'm okay."

"You don't look okay."

"Well, I am, dammit! Let me go."

"Okay, okay, ease up. You looked a little shaky, that's all. You still do."

"I'll be all right. Now what the hell do you mean, he killed my husband?"

"He admitted doing it in his note, Doc, plus, a paint scrape on his pickup looks like a dead-bang match for your husband's red Porsche. I think he did it all right."

"My God. I—don't understand."

"Yeah, well, for what it's worth, Dr. McKenzie, some homicides don't even make sense to the guy who does 'em. This one has a certain logic to it, though. It looks like Mr. Ortiz decided to check out and wanted to tie up a few loose ends before he went. Do you know a Dearborn cop named Tod Stringer?"

"I—know of him. He's the ex-husband of a patient of mine."

"A domestic-violence case?"

Colleen nodded. "What about him?"

"In the note Ortiz admitted he roughed up Stringer last week. Broke his arm. I just got off the phone with Stringer and he described Ortiz right down to the dirt under his fingernails. If you don't mind my asking, are you and Dr. Bergstrom involved? Romantically, I mean?"

"Romantically? No. Why?"

"No offense, just being thorough. Dr. Bergstrom did call you."

"As a friend and colleague, which I am. We are not now nor have we ever been romantically involved. Is that specific enough for you, Detective?"

"Absolutely. Last question. You and Dr. Bergstrom are both psychologists, right? Would it be possible for a therapist like yourself to influence a patient to commit a crime?"

She stared at him as though he'd grown a second head. He expected her to blow up. She took a deep breath instead.

"Theoretically, Sergeant Dylan, a dysfunctional, tractable patient prone to violent behavior could probably be influenced to commit a violent act by anyone he perceived as an authority figure. A psychologist, say, maybe even a *cop*. But Mr. Ortiz was neither violent nor particularly receptive to treatment. In fact, he—" She paused, frowning. "I think he wanted to quit."

"Quit what?"

"The therapy group. He stopped me in the parking lot a few days ago. To be honest, I . . . don't know what he wanted. I was upset, I'd just finished talking to you. And so I just . . . brushed him off." She swallowed. "My God, he may have been trying to talk to me about Ian then."

"Whoa, Doc, take it from a pro, killers are a mixed bag. Some are brainfried street thugs and some are poor bastards like Ortiz whose lives crash and burn. They're not predictable, so don't beat yourself up; you're a shrink, not a psychic. Besides, if you couldn't make him commit this crime, why would you think you could prevent it?"

Their eyes held for a moment, then Colleen nodded. "I know what you're saying, Detective, but it's not much comfort. He came to the Institute for counseling and . . . here we are. I should have realized he was dysfunctional. It's my job to know. Are we done?"

"Yeah. Look, I'm really sorry about this, not just the questions, but . . . all of it. But I meant what I said about not blaming yourself, Doc. It's a dead-end street. Don't go there. This wasn't your fault."

"Maybe not," Colleen said, "but it sure feels like it. Can I see Rob?"

"Yes, ma'am. I'll take you to him."

They found Bergstrom in the kitchen, making coffee. Rumpled and red-eyed, he looked even younger than usual. He embraced Colleen long and hard. "Thanks for being here for me."

Dylan cleared his throat. "Do you mind if I have some coffee?"

"Let me get it," Rob said, separating from Colleen and hurrying to the coffee maker. "I thought we could all use some. Do you have any more questions for me?" The remark was offhand but there was an edge in his tone.

"Not just now. Everything seems to be in order, Dr. Bergstrom, if that's possible in a shambles like this."

"Sorry if I seemed touchy earlier, Detective. I'm a bit dazed."

"Perfectly understandable. Let me know when you're ready to go, Dr. McKenzie, and I'll have a patrolman see you home." He glanced at them over his coffee cup, then wandered out.

"How are you holding up?" Colleen said, turning to Rob.

"I'll live. I know it was selfish of me to call you but I'm glad you came. I was . . . pretty confused at the time. I saw that detective talking to you in front. What did he want?"

"Nothing, really, just background information on Jesse."

"What information?" he asked sharply. "What did you tell him?"

"The truth. That Jesse had an anomalous incident with alcohol and neither of us considered him at all dangerous."

"Good, that's fine. You're right, of course, but it's one of those situations a nonprofessional might not understand. Maybe we'd better get our stories straight for the boss."

"Our stories?"

"About my hiring Ortiz. I was just trying to give him a break, but with all that's happened it might look better if you said you okayed it."

"I would have, if you'd asked."

"Still, it could help if—"

"Rob, you're overreacting. No one will blame you for what happened, least of all Mavis. I told Mr. Ortiz he could use me as a job reference and—"

"But I'm the new kid, remember," Rob snapped. "It'd just look better if you said you okayed it. Is that asking too much?"

"If you're asking me to lie, then yes, it is too much! Look, I didn't consider Ortiz dangerous either. I'll back you a hundred percent and make sure everyone understands the situation. You won't have any trouble at work, I promise. Okay?"

"Yeah, okay. Sorry if I bit your head off, I'm halfway up the wall. Thanks for coming out, Colleen. And for standing up for me."

"No charge. Take care, Rob, we'll get through this." She bussed him lightly on the cheek and left him in the kitchen.

Two EMTs were bringing a stretcher down the stairs and she hurried past to avoid seeing it. Her memories of Ortiz were troubling enough already.

Dylan was on the porch, staring out into the rainy darkness.

"How's Dr. Bergstrom doing?"

"He's shaken up, wouldn't you be? No, maybe *you* wouldn't."

"A brilliant psychologist once told me that when you've been through a tunnel a few times you know there's light on the other side," Dylan said drily. "Some people go into a funk around violent death, some get wired on adrenaline like your friend in there. I'll have a patrolman drop you off."

"I'm all right now."

"Humor me, okay? The body count in this case is too high already. I'd drive you myself but I'll be stuck here most of the night. I'll call you tomorrow."

"Why?"

He hesitated. "Actually, I'm not sure why I said that. Reflex, I guess. What do you suppose Freud would make of it?"

"He'd probably say you're getting overly analytical from hanging out with too many therapists."

"He'd be wrong," Dylan said. "Anyway, would you mind if I called you? Just to be sure you're okay?"

Colleen glanced up at him, surprised. His face was a professional mask that hid his thoughts well. But it wasn't a bad face.

"No," she said. "I wouldn't mind."

The viewing room in the funeral home had deep green carpeting that contrasted beautifully with the oaken furnishings and the burled walnut casket on the dais. Colleen recognized a few coworkers from the Institute but most of the mourners were a generation older, contemporaries of the deceased. Generic organ music droned softly below the muted hum of conversation.

Scanning the room for Rob, Colleen nearly missed him. He was standing near the casket talking with a heavyset woman in a flowered dress and a bearded clergyman. Rob looked strikingly different. Wearing a dark suit, with his hair neatly trimmed, he could have passed for his own older brother. Even his mannerisms seemed weightier, as though he'd aged overnight.

The casket lid was open, so Colleen decided to wait for a better moment to offer condolences. She'd never met Rob's dad in life. It seemed a bit late now.

She found a bench in a corner of the room and glanced around. The room had no obvious connection with faith or mortality. Canned music, plastic plants, as impersonal as a Formica burger joint. McBurials or Kentucky Fried Funerals . . .

"Excuse me, you're Dr. McKenzie, aren't you?" The woman was willowy, with loose, sandy hair, a narrow mouth, and foxy eyes, cover-girl pretty. "I'm Lily Bergstrom, Rob's sister. He's spoken of you so often, I feel like we've already met." She slid smoothly onto the seat beside Colleen.

"I wish we could have met at a better time," Colleen said. "I'm sorry for your loss."

"No great loss," Lily said bluntly. "I haven't seen my dad in years. I wouldn't have come today except that Bobby insisted I should show up. I hardly recognized the old man. The stroke sucked all the anger out of his face. The way they've got him made up, he looks more like a Cabbage Patch Kid than the pig he was."

Colleen stared.

"Sorry," Lily said. "I assumed Rob told you about our dear old dad."

"No, he didn't, actually. I knew he was ill, but—"

"Not ill, sick. He was one sick bastard," she said acidly. "A drunken, abusive bastard. My mom ran off when I was five to get away from him. I took off when I was fourteen. Hated to leave Rob behind alone but I had to get out or die trying. The old man took up with Rob where he left off with me, groping him, taking pictures for his sick friends. The kid was tougher than I was, though. He didn't run. Saint Bobby."

"Saint Bobby?"

"That's the way he struck me, next time I saw him. He'd turned into the perfect kid, trying to keep Pop out of his bedroom. Top grades, active in church, star ballplayer, a regular saint. When he finally left, he didn't have to run away. Full scholarship to UCLA. Got a good job after graduation. But when the old man had his stroke, Rob bagged it all to come home and take care of him. Saint Bobby."

She was smiling, but there was a vicious edge to her tone and she was taut as a pole vaulter on takeoff. "It must have been quite a sacrifice," Colleen said cautiously.

"Personally, I thought he was nuts. Caring for Pop in the same house where he abused us? It may be a classy place, but the memories . . . I don't know how he did it. Or why. You're a shrink, does it make any sense to you?"

"I . . . I really couldn't say."

"No? From what Bobby said, I thought you two were pretty tight."

"We're friends, but we haven't known each other very long."

"Friends? I thought—well, never mind. Sometimes Saint Bobby has trouble talking to us earthly types, especially me. Him and the old man both. I'm sorry, but I've enjoyed about as much of this as I can stand. I've gotta get out of here."

She rose and hurried out of the room, dabbing at her eyes. She was a handsome woman, expensively dressed, and men's heads turned as she passed. But Colleen wouldn't have traded places with her for all the tea in Tijuana.

Rob eased down beside her a moment later. "I saw you talking to Lily. I hope she didn't upset you."

"Not at all, she was . . . interesting. You've never mentioned her."

"We're not close. She ran away when I was a kid and still blames my dad for the problems in her life."

"What kind of problems?"

"Bad marriages, bulimia, drugs, and those are just the troubles I know of. Doubtless there are deeper dysfunctions. Maybe she'll open up a bit more now."

"With your father gone, you mean?"

"Partly that, but I expect I'll have more time for her, too."

"Caring for your dad must have been quite a burden."

"Not really, he was so . . . childlike near the end that it was like we'd traded roles. He could be difficult, but how can you be angry at someone who doesn't know who he is, much less who you are?"

"I can see why Lily calls you Saint Bobby."

"That's her idea of a joke. I've never liked it."

"Sorry. There is something I need to ask you, though, about what happened."

"The gory details have been covered pretty well in the press."

"Not all of them. There's still something I don't understand. Dylan said Mr. Ortiz was trying to . . . tie up the loose ends of our lives before taking his own. He considered your dad a burden and wanted to free you. But how could he know about my problems with Ian? I certainly never told him."

"Perhaps you did, indirectly. Patients are always curious about our private lives. A word here, a slip there, a rumor somewhere else. He probably knew more than you think."

"But he was from out of town and he resented the group. I doubt he gossiped with anyone after hours. And I *never* discuss my personal affairs around the Institute."

"But I knew about it? Is that where you're going with this? All right, maybe it was my fault. I hired Jesse to sit with my dad a few days a week so I could have *some* kind of a life. A few times after I came home he stayed on and we'd have a beer and talk. Your name may have come up."

"*May have?*" she echoed in disbelief. "Are you saying you told a patient about my private life?"

"I said *maybe*. It was late, I don't recall all we talked about, and it's a moot point anyway. Let's just put it behind us and move on. And I'd better get back to glad-handing my guests. Thanks for coming by."

He bussed her coolly on the cheek, rose, and sauntered back toward a group near the casket. As he approached them his face assumed a somber cast of melancholy, utterly sincere.

Colleen sat a few minutes, watching him thoughtfully. Then, just before the services began, she rose and slipped out.

She was wandering down the corridor, lost in thought, when a wall placard beside another viewing room caught her eye. Ortiz. Damn. She was strongly tempted to move on. Instead, she squared her shoulders, took a deep breath, and opened the door.

The chapel was a smaller version of the one she'd just left, but with no minister, no mourners. A stocky young girl, visibly pregnant, sat alone in the front row near the closed casket. She was wearing a faded denim shift and her dark hair hung to her waist in a thick braid.

The girl glanced up as Colleen approached. She seemed dazed, numb.

"Hello," Colleen said. "Are you Jennifer Ortiz?"

The girl nodded. "Did you know my dad?"

"He was my client. I'm Dr. McKenzie."

"McKenzie?" She blinked, then her face flushed with rising anger. "Sweet Jesus, you've got a lotta sand, lady. The judge sends him to your clinic for gettin' drunk and now the cops say he killed people he didn't even know? And then himself? What the hell did you people do to him?"

"Jennifer, believe me, I'm as much at a loss—"

"Believe you, my ass. All I know is he went to you for help and he's dead. The rest don't matter anymore. Leave us alone."

"I'm sorry," Colleen said. "I truly am. I know you're angry with me and you probably have a right to be, but if I can help in any way . . . call me, please."

"I think you've helped enough already. If I was you I'd get goin' while you still can." But as Colleen turned away, Jennifer grabbed her arm.

"Hey! Just tell me one thing, Doc. Was this—was it my fault? Bein' pregnant with no husband? Is that why he did it?"

"No, it wasn't that. He was angry at first, but the last few sessions he said he was looking forward to the baby. To having new life in the family."

"But if it wasn't me, why did he do this? You're the big head doctor. Why did my dad crack up?"

"I don't know. I'm very sorry, I—" But Jennifer turned abruptly away, burying her face in her hands. And Colleen had no answers for her anyway.

Colleen climbed into her Volvo and automatically checked her cell phone for messages. The screen showed two calls while she'd been inside. Her mother and a number she didn't recognize. She tapped it in.

"Salvati Lawn Care, Geno speaking."

"Hello, this is Dr. McKenzie returning your call?"

"Oh yeah, thanks for callin' back. Hey, I hired a guy last week, older guy named Ortiz? He listed you as a reference."

Colleen's heart sank. "Yes?"

"So he worked a few days, did a helluva job, then he never came back. No answer at the number he gave me. What's up with him? Didn't seem like the kind to just take off. Besides, I still owe him three days' wages."

Colleen started to explain, then hesitated. "You said he worked three days?"

"Yeah, he was a godsend. Knew the mowin' machinery backwards and forwards; he liked bein' outside and he could outwork any three of the young punks I usually hire. I bumped him up two bucks over minimum wage the second day and said if he stuck with me a couple weeks I had a foreman's slot opening up."

"A foreman's slot?"

"You know, runnin' his own crew? It's still outside work, but it pays twenty-two bucks an hour."

"Twenty-two . . . and he knew about this?"

"Sure. Seemed real keen on the idea. Said he'd have to get his schedule squared away, so when he missed a couple days I figured he was gettin' things straight. Does he work for you?"

"No, he doesn't. Mr. Salvati, there's no easy way to say this. Mr. Ortiz passed away a few days ago."

"You're kiddin'."

"No, sir, I'm not."

"But—Jesus, he seemed strong as a horse. What happened?"

"I honestly don't know," Colleen said. She gave him the name of the funeral home and suggested he contact Ortiz's daughter about his unpaid wages. Then she sat in the parking lot for what seemed like a very long time. A rumble of thunder snapped her back to reality. It was starting to rain, a chill autumn drizzle coming on with the dusk. She fished through her purse, found a business card, and made a call.

It was a handsome older home in a solid working-class neighborhood, a large porch with a swing, lilacs in the yard.

Colleen couldn't see any lights but hurried to the porch through the rain and rang the buzzer. Dylan answered the door in a dark shirt with a tie and dress slacks.

"Hi," Colleen said, "I'm sorry to bother you at home."

"No problem, I just finished dinner. Come on in."

An old-fashioned living room, hardwood floors, comfortable leather furniture, a small fire smoldering in the grate. In the adjoining dining room the table was formally set with white linen and silver candlesticks, the candles burned a quarter of the way down.

"I'm sorry, am I interrupting something?"

"Not exactly. *Hoy de mi alma.* Soul day. My ex-wife's idea. She said I was spending so much time with street thugs that I was turning into one. So, once a week I try to have a real meal and behave like a human being. One day for my soul. The rest of the week . . ." He shrugged. "I can turn up the lights if you like."

"No, this is fine. It suits my mood."

"That bad, huh? Sit down, please. I was going to have some wine, a zinfandel, would you care for some? No? Then I'll wait too. This isn't social, is it?"

"I'm not sure where to start," Colleen said, taking a seat mid-way down the table. "Look, I know we can't be totally off the record, so I won't ask for that, but I really need some straight answers from you. Okay?"

"If I can, sure."

"Okay. Question one: Do you have any . . . misgivings about this Ortiz business?"

"Should I have?"

"Tell you what, Detective, if you'd rather not discuss this, I understand. But if you're just going to answer my questions with more questions, I'm outa here. Okay?"

"Okay." He smiled. A good smile. "That's another reason I hate shrinks. You're hard to snow. Okay, straight up, yes, I have some reservations about the Ortiz case. But homicide's a messy business. Most cases have loose ends, contradictory evidence, witness statements, whatever. Misgivings are normal. Why are you asking?"

She took a deep breath. "A few things have come up, nothing concrete, you understand, just . . . things that make me wonder about what happened."

"What things?"

"Jesse Ortiz was in therapy as a condition of a plea bargain for a drunk and disorderly bust, but his real problem was depression. His wife had died, her illness cost him a farm he'd owned for thirty years, and he couldn't find work."

"Sounds like he had reason to be depressed."

"You bet he did. Behavioral problems are often rooted in reality. But today I learned that Jesse found a job last week, a good job doing the kind of work he liked."

"So you're saying he wouldn't have committed suicide?"

"It's not that simple. Sometimes a positive development can intensify depression. A good thing happens but you're still drowning in darkness. Life seems even more hopeless than before. It sounds backwards, but a positive development can actually push a depressive over the line into violence or suicide."

"Okay, I follow that. Is that what happened with Ortiz?"

"In my professional opinion, Jesse Ortiz wasn't that sort of patient. His depression was conditional and an improvement of his situation—a new job—should have helped him. But another therapist could look at the same circumstances and draw the opposite conclusion."

"But they'd be looking at his record. You knew him."

"And maybe that's my problem. His suicide means I did a lousy job of diagnosis and I'm partly responsible for his death."

"You're being kind of rough on yourself, aren't you?"

"Just being . . . what did you call it? Straight up."

"Fair enough. But for the record, Doc, this is a closed case. We have a gun, a note, the guy had a history of violence. The pieces all fit."

"You had all of those pieces at the scene, but you still asked me if Ortiz could have been brainwashed into doing what he did. So you had some doubts too, right? Why?"

"There were a couple of small things," Dylan admitted. "Dr. Bergstrom had an alibi. He'd been to a movie and they remembered him there, joking with the ticket taker. Afterward, he had a bite at Denny's and a waitress remembered him kidding around, a real charmer."

"Let me get this straight. It bothered you *because* he had an alibi?"

"A little," he said, smiling. "Most people don't have alibis. You didn't, remember? They're asleep or watching TV alone, assuming they can even remember where they were. But Bergstrom? He could account for his movements to the minute and knew he could prove it. And I got the feeling he enjoyed telling me about it, like he'd aced an exam or something. His attitude didn't match up with the situation."

"Maybe that's because the situation wasn't quite what you thought it was. I thought Rob was caring for his father out of the goodness of his heart, but his sister tells me the father was an abusive drunk that they both despised. Apparently Rob had no reason to mourn his father's death."

"And most kids hate their fathers at some point, then change their minds later. Bergstrom's a trained therapist. He probably reacts to things differently than Joe Six-pack might."

"The fact that he's a trained therapist is the second part of my problem," Colleen sighed. "Mr. Ortiz confessed to killing Ian. But he had no reason to."

"We assumed he did it for the same reason he took out Bergstrom's father, as a kind of going-away present for you."

"But I don't believe he knew about my problems with Ian. Therapists never discuss their private lives with patients. I certainly didn't with Ortiz. But Rob implied that I may have, then admitted he told Ortiz about Ian. And he's far too good a therapist to make a mistake like that."

"Even so, talking to Ortiz about you is no crime."

"All I'm saying is that it doesn't fit. I've got this awful feeling that something's wrong about this. I'm just not bright enough or experienced enough to know what it is."

"And you think I am?"

"I don't know. If my car was running rough, I'd see a mechanic. Well, this case is running rough for me. I guess what I'm asking you for is a professional opinion."

"Okay, professionally speaking, Doc, you've got zip. I got a hinky feeling about the way Bergstrom answered questions and you have doubts about Ortiz's mental state, but those aren't facts. Here's the hard evidence: Ortiz was dead at the scene and had a history of violence. Paint found on the bumper of his pickup truck matched your husband's Porsche, and Tod Stringer, that wife-beater Ortiz roughed up, positively identified him. Ortiz left a suicide note and the handwriting's definitely his. Any more questions?"

"Just one. The suicide note? Did it say something like, I feel bad about my wife and Mrs. McKenzie's husband and Rob's dad and Tod Stringer—"

"Not Stringer. He mentioned him, but said he wasn't sorry he knocked him around. But the rest, yeah, that's roughly what it said."

"And was it crumpled?"

Dylan eyed her a moment. "Yes, it was. Like it had been wadded up then smoothed out. Why?"

"There's a technique some New Age therapists use. You list the things that are contributing to your feelings of depression then put them behind you by wadding up the list and throwing it away."

"Doesn't sound very scientific."

"It's not meant to be a cure, it's just part of a process and not one I use myself."

"Did Bergstrom?"

"He mentioned using it once in L.A. We never tried it in our therapy group, but he and Jesse were together in the evenings. It's possible he did it then."

Dylan shook his head slowly, a faint smile playing about his mouth. "Now *that's* interesting. Not evidence, exactly, but interesting. Because if you take away the note—No, wait a minute—Stringer identified Ortiz."

"That part fits. Jesse was impatient with therapy. Mrs. Stringer's husband was giving her a tough time so Jesse did something about it."

"Yeah, he broke Stringer's arm in three places."

"Trust me, it couldn't have happened to a nicer guy."

"Even so, it indicates Ortiz was violent."

"It also shows that he dealt with problems head-on. Most suicides can't cope with their problems, so they bail out. Jesse worked at a new job three days and the boss wanted to make him a foreman. He was a problem solver, not a quitter, and things were looking up for him."

"I see." He bridged his fingers and eyed her across them. "Have you considered where this is going? I mean, *really* considered it? Because if Ortiz wasn't suicidal, that only leaves two alternatives. One: that he was conned into committing murder with some mind game, which you say is impossible, or two: He didn't do it at all. Which leaves me with only one viable candidate. You."

"*Me?*"

"Sure. Bergstrom's got an alibi, you haven't. You were angry with your husband, you profited by his death, plus you play mind games for a living. Maybe you conned Ortiz into killing your husband then did Bergstrom senior and Ortiz to cover your tracks."

"For pete's sake, Dylan, I came to you! I'm . . . you're jerking my chain, aren't you?"

"Yeah, just a little. Payback for having my nice neat murder case kicked slightly in the head. The thing is, Doc, if everything you told me is true, pulling off a multiple homicide as cold as this one would take one very special cat. So what's your best guess? Is Bergstrom capable of something like this?"

"No. I mean, I don't . . ." She shook her head. "I don't know. I don't think so. His sister calls him Saint Bobby. Maybe she's right. Maybe I'm misreading the whole thing."

"Is that what you think?"

"No. I hate what I'm thinking. I can hardly believe it. But I can't ignore it either. What are we going to do?"

"What *you* do is pretend we never had this conversation and get on with your life. I'm going to do what the city pays me for and look into things. Meantime, maybe we should have that glass of wine now."

"No, thank you, I'd better go. I'm sorry if I messed up your special day."

"You didn't. In fact, while we're being straight up with each other, I'll tell you one last thing. I wanted to meet you outside of business hours that first day. I thought you were bright and interesting and . . . well, anyway, you didn't mess anything up by coming here."

"Except your neatly closed murder case."

"Yeah. You may have done a number on that. Too early to say. Thanks for coming by anyway."

She turned to go, then hesitated. "Dylan? What you said about wanting to meet off duty? Your timing is terrible."

"You're right. Sorry."

"Oh, I didn't say it was a bad idea," she said with a wan smile, "just bad timing. You'll call me if anything turns up?"

"Yes, ma'am. Count on it."

The Tuesday session was quiet as a tomb when Colleen walked in, no conversational buzz, none of the usual pre-meeting banter. Gary Noreski, the obese schoolteacher, was absent. Couldn't blame him. The press had a field day with the story. "Deranged Mental Patient Kills Therapists' Kin." Mavis had barred reporters from the building but they were still staked out across the street filming clients and trying to interview them as they entered or left the parking lot.

Bergstrom hadn't shown up either, no surprise considering all that had happened. Colleen waited a few minutes past the hour to give any latecomers time to arrive, but as she was closing the door it was suddenly blocked from the other side. Rob met her eyes from inches away.

"Starting without me?" he asked, breezing past her. "Hi, everybody, sorry I'm late. I had to crawl on my belly like a reptile to sneak past the reporters." He flopped his briefcase on the desk, then took a moment to scan the faces in the room, as if memorizing them.

"I can't tell you how much it means to me that you all came today. As you know, Colleen and I have both suffered a loss, but so have you. A member of our extended family is gone. But make no mistake, despite what the press says, Jesse Ortiz didn't throw his life away." Colleen slipped into her usual seat. No one noticed; Rob had their total focus.

"After such a terrible incident, it's a time for truth," he continued, pacing like a tiger in the ring of chairs, "a time for learning. And this is the lesson I've taken from Jesse's death: Jesse was willing to give everything for us. Not just for Dr. McKenzie and myself, but for all of us here. Our family. Because he understood that we truly are a family. That's why he sacrificed himself.

"We aren't a 'birth' family, accidentally tied by DNA or marriage vows. Jesse's truth is that we have more in common with the people in this room than we ever did with our blood relatives. We've all shared things with each other that we never told our parents. Isn't that so?"

Nods and murmurs of assent rippled around the ring. They were rapt as rabbits dazzled by headlights. When Rob asked for their personal thoughts about Jesse's death and his own and Colleen's situation, the group offered an outpouring of support and empathy that would have warmed a Tartar's heart.

But it chilled Colleen. The change in Bergstrom's personality was so profound she scarcely recognized him. His boyishness had burned away, leaving a reptilian charm glossed with a warm sheen of confidence.

The group sensed the transformation too, and were drawn to him like travelers warming themselves at a fire. They'd been walking wounded, hoping therapy would heal their pain, but Rob was offering a stronger solution, something larger and better than themselves, a New Age family bonded by a blood sacrifice. Headed by their own personal saint.

Colleen tried to redirect the group to a standard therapy session but it was like wrestling a sponge. They politely absorbed her efforts then veered back to the exciting idea of the group as a supportive New Age clan. When she walked out near the session's end, no one noticed.

Afterward, Colleen was in the closet bathroom in her office, splashing cold water on her face, when her office door opened.

"Are you all right?" Rob called.

"I'm fine." She stepped out, drying her face with a towel.

"You left early," he said, casually parking a hip on her desk. "Still upset?"

"I'm more upset by what you were doing in there. That wasn't group therapy. It was more like a revival meeting in a cargo cult."

"That's a little heavy, isn't it?"

"No, I don't think so. You know damned well that involving clients in one another's lives isn't proper therapy, and what's all this talk about the group as an extended family? What the hell methodology is that?"

"We gave Jesse Ortiz traditional, by-the-book counseling and look what it got him. And us. I'm just trying to expand the envelope a little. I used some of these techniques in L.A. and they were quite effective. And if I go a little overboard, you're there to haul me back, right?"

"I'm there to help our clients, not keep you on track. You're over the line and you know it!"

"Hey, hey, chill out, Colleen. After what we've been through it's no wonder we're barking at each other. Tell you what, let's take off next weekend. Catch a little sun, relax. Cozumel, maybe. Ever been there?"

She stared at him as though he'd suddenly started speaking Cantonese. "You mean . . . Mexico?"

"That's where it was the last time I looked. The Mayan ruins are wonderful and I'll grab the tab. I'm a man of means now. What do you say?"

"I—don't know what to say—" The phone on her desk gurgled. Rob picked it up and handed it to her.

"Hi," Dylan said. "Is my timing any better?"

"Hi, Mom," she answered. "Not really. I'm kind of busy now."

"Is Bergstrom with you?"

"Sure, that'll be fine. Why don't I meet you and Aunt Gertrude for lunch? The Capri, one o'clock? Good. Love ya. Bye.—My mother," she said, replacing the handset.

"I gathered. Lunch date? I was hoping we could go someplace, maybe talk through a few things. Heck, let's do it anyway. I'd love to meet your family. I'll even buy."

"No, today wouldn't be a good time. My mom thought the sun rose and set on Ian. This business has her pretty upset. I'd better go alone. We can do something later in the week, okay?"

"And Mexico?"

"Let's talk about it then. To be honest, I don't think I'm quite as . . . resilient as you are. Right now I'm just getting through the day an hour at a time."

"I understand," Rob said, bussing her on the temple. "I really do. Enjoy your lunch. We'll talk later."

Villa Capri was as Italian as its name: dark wood, small booths, fragrant ferns, and a staff that actually enjoyed their work. Dylan was waiting at a corner booth away from the windows. He rose as she approached.

"Hi, I hope you don't mind munching in the shadows. I doubt I could pass for your mom."

"You think he'd follow me?"

"To be honest, I think I've underrated this guy from the git. And you look as worried as I feel. What's up?"

"Saint Bobby is. He's like a new man." She slid into the booth across from him. "He was more like an evangelist than a psychologist today. As though he buried his boyhood with his father. He not only tossed out the rule book, he didn't even pretend to care. Then he invited me for a weekend in Cozumel."

"Well, he can probably afford it. His father's estate is substantial and he padded dear old Dad's insurance policy to boot, added a term life policy that pays double in case of accidental death. And surprise, according to the policy, murder qualifies as an accident."

"But doesn't that prove he was planning something?"

"Nope. It looks suspicious, all right, but buying insurance isn't illegal, I've done it myself. There's more. His alibi isn't as tight as I thought. The movie he went to was at a multiplex. He could have left anytime, walked home, and made it back in time to join the post-movie crowd at Denny's. I can't prove he did, of course, but it's possible."

"Terrific."

"Don't give up, I've saved the best for last. The paraffin test on Ortiz was positive—he definitely fired a weapon—but an area on the back of his hand showed very little gunpowder residue, which strongly indicates someone held his hand when Ortiz fired the gun. It's the first solid bit of evidence we've turned up."

"I'm not sure I understand."

"It means the killer understood the paraffin test. There were three shots fired. He popped Ortiz, then the old man, then put the gun in Ortiz's hand and fired again to be sure he'd test positive."

"And that's why there was no residue where he held his hand . . ." Her voice trailed off.

"What is it?"

"I guess I hadn't thought through the . . . mechanics of it, how cold-blooded and brutal it must have been. To plan and carry it out . . . my God. But that's how it happened, isn't it? The paraffin test proves it."

"It's a strong indication, but it's not enough. Any competent attorney could blow it off as a faulty test. My best shot would be to question Bergstrom about it, try to break him down."

"I don't think so," Colleen said thoughtfully. "Rob's a trained psychotherapist. He's conducted thousands of interviews, alert to every word, every shift in body language. He wouldn't break. It'd put him on his guard and we'd lose our only edge."

"What edge? Near as I can see, the guy's batting a thousand."

"And that's our edge. His confidence. Right now he's skying, on top of the world. He destroyed the monster who abused him, he's going to be rich and free as the air. He's smashed the ultimate taboo. He thinks he's gotten away with murder."

"Yeah, well, maybe he has."

"But it won't be enough," Colleen mused. "You said when he told you about his alibi, he almost gloated, remember? That's the key to him. He was abused as a child, abandoned by his mother and then his sister. So he became this charming overachiever his sister calls Saint Bobby. We all want to be admired, but he *needs* it, just to feel whole. It must be terribly frustrating for him. He's pulled off this amazing feat but no one knows it."

"But that's the point, isn't it?"

"But it's also our edge. Because deep down, he really wants people to know how clever he is. And how powerful."

"I don't think I like where you're going with this."

"Neither do I, but I think under the right circumstances he might tell me about it."

"Why you?"

"Because he likes me. A feeling that's reinforced because we serve as a family unit in the group. But most of all, because—" she took a deep breath—"because I think he killed my husband for me."

"*For* you? You want to run that by me in English?"

"The way I see it, he came back for revenge. Abused children who run away often continue to see the adult abuser as powerful, even after they're adults themselves."

"So when Bergstrom's father had a stroke . . . ?"

"Exactly. He knew he'd be helpless and wanted to get even. He was probably already planning the killing when Ortiz told him about roughing up Tod Stringer and Rob realized he had a perfect fall guy. But if he framed Ortiz for killing his father, there might be questions."

"So you think he used Ortiz's truck to kill your husband to make it look like a serial crime? And also set you free?"

"Something like that." She nodded.

"It's possible," Dylan conceded. "It's also possible he was setting you up to take the fall. Think about it. The evidence could easily apply to you: motive, opportunity, the works. So maybe he wasn't helping you out; maybe he was just covering his tracks and doesn't give a damn about you.

And if you casually ask him about it, how long do you think you'll keep breathing?"

"Then what should I do? Admit he's outsmarted us and pop off for a wild weekend in Cozumel?"

"Dammit, Doc, this is no joke! If this guy's guilty, it means he screwed that pistol into Ortiz's ear, scattered his brains all over the wall, shot his father, then waltzed into Denny's a few minutes later and yukked it up with a waitress!"

"Lower your voice, people are staring! I know there are risks but I'm not an amateur and I have some insight into the way he thinks. But we can't wait. He's a danger to my patients, and if I try to have him removed his guard will go up. We have to try while he's still cocky and hope he'll make a mistake. Bottom line: I don't see any other way. Do you?"

Dylan hesitated, then slowly shook his head. "No, dammit, I don't."

"All right then, how do we go about it? You're the expert."

"No, I'm not. Most homicides I handle are gang killings or family fights. Saint Bobby's something else. So far, he's outsmarted me every step of the way. I've never tangled with anyone like him before and neither have you. He's bright, he's dangerous, and he's not gonna give it up just because you flash him a smile over lunch."

"Actually, I can only think of one place where he might feel free to talk to me. But I don't think you'll like it."

"I don't like it already. What is it?"

Colleen left the restaurant first, blinking as she stepped into the autumn afternoon. Deep in her own thoughts, she didn't notice a hunter-green Bravada with blacked-out windows parked up the street.

Sitting behind its wheel, Rob stiffened when Colleen emerged. He reached for the ignition, hesitated, then he settled back to wait. When Dylan came out of the restaurant ten minutes later, Rob nodded to himself, fired up the Bravada, and eased slowly into traffic.

"It looks a lot different from the other night," Colleen said, glancing around Rob's living room. "Did the police make much of a mess?"

"Nothing the maid service couldn't handle. I cleaned up my father's room myself, of course, I couldn't ask them to do that."

"Did it bother you? Cleaning up, I mean?"

"A little, but it's my home now and it had to be done. I picked up some Hunan Chinese for dinner, is that all right?"

"Perfect."

"Here, let me take your coat," he said, helping her slip off her windbreaker. She was wearing a two-piece Armani business suit, ecru. "You look lovely. I'll admit I was a little surprised when you suggested a quiet dinner here."

"You invite me for a wild weekend in Cozumel and you're surprised I'd rather spend time with you first? What kind of girl do you think I am?"

"I'm looking forward to finding out," he said blandly, hanging her coat in the closet. "How was lunch with your mother yesterday?"

He was facing away from her, but she caught the faintest hint of an edge in his tone. "I . . . didn't have lunch with my mom, actually. I wound up seeing that cop, Dylan, instead."

"No kidding? How did that happen?"

"He called and asked me to lunch so I canceled Mom. I thought talking to him might be more helpful."

"Helpful how?"

"I wanted to know where the investigation was and what he thinks."

"And what *does* the good detective think?"

"Not much. He's like a puppy who smells smoke on the wind. He has a vague sense that something's wrong but no idea what. So eventually he'll lose interest and go back to chasing his tail."

"Very poetic. But if he's chasing his tail, why did he ask you to lunch?"

"Don't be dense. He's got a thing for me. Is that so hard to believe?"

"Not at all. And do you have a *thing* for him?"

"For Dylan? Hardly. He's a drone, an ordinary little man. I suppose he's attractive in a way, but not very bright. Let's eat, supper's getting cold."

On the rooftop of the building next door, Sergeant Linell Tatum winced as he tugged his headphones off, then rolled his bulky frame over to face Dylan, who was watching the house across the narrow alley with binoculars.

"She's right about one thing, Dylan, you're not very bright. And now he's turned on the freakin' stereo. Damn it, we're too high up here, too much wind. With all the background noise I'm only getting every other line. This shotgun mike's too touchy at this distance."

"She'll get him upstairs," Dylan said. "In the room right across from us. We'll get better reception there."

"Assumin' the freakin' wind ain't blown us both offa here by then."

"It's only a two-story drop, Linell. You're so big you'll probably just bounce anyway."

"No way. I'll make a dent so deep they'll just fill in the hole and drop a stone on top. Here lies Linell Tatum, frozen to death in the line of stupidity." Still grumbling, he turned back to refocus the shotgun mike on the window below.

*   *   *

They had white wine with dinner, but only one glass each, both wary. "I have a confession to make," Colleen said abruptly. "I had an ulterior motive for inviting myself over tonight."

"Really? Will I like it?"

"I don't know. Can I see the room where it happened?"

"That's a bit morbid, isn't it?"

"I'll admit I'm curious. Wouldn't you be?"

"Yes, I suppose so. All right, if you're sure it's what you want, it's this way." He led her up the broad staircase to the second floor. "In there."

She glanced around the immaculate bedroom, her lips pursed. The drapes were open and the tall casement window offered a clear view of the building next door. Colleen moved past it and sat on the edge of the bed. Rob stayed in the doorway, watching her.

"Well? What do you think?"

"I think it wasn't your father's room originally," she said, quietly. "It was your room, wasn't it? When you were a kid?"

"A lucky guess?"

"No, your roles were reversed. He was the child and you were the man. It's natural that you'd put him here. A kind of poetic justice."

"I'm not sure I follow you."

"I think you do. I know you're bright, Rob, everyone does. But I also think there's more than self-interest in some of the things you do."

"You're talking in circles, Colleen. You're usually pretty direct."

"Sorry, I'm a little nervous about this. If I'm wrong, you'll think I'm a fool and I'd hate that. But you're right, between us, direct is better. So: I told you that Ian and I separated because he cheated on me. Classic midlife crisis, the shiny new sports car, a younger woman. It was pathetic, but it still hurt, especially when he threatened to stall our divorce indefinitely unless I settled. So I did."

"That doesn't sound like you."

"It wasn't the brave choice, but it was the smart one. A court battle would have wiped me out financially. Still, you can't imagine how much I hated him. And that damned adolescent car of his. Or can you?"

"I suppose I can empathize, sure."

"I'm not talking about empathy, Rob, I'm talking about action. I'll spell it out. I know you had your own reasons for . . . doing what you did. But I'd like to know one small thing: Did you consider, even for a moment, the poetry in killing Ian in that car? Or was it just convenient?"

He eyed her in silence a moment. "What on earth are you talking about?"

"I'm sorry," she said, rising abruptly from the bed. "I've apparently misread things completely. I'd better go."

"Wait a minute," he said, waving her back. "One day you're having lunch with a cop, the next you're asking me about murder. What am I supposed to think?"

"Nothing. It was my mistake. I thought . . . it doesn't matter what I thought now. Let's call it a night."

He seized her arm as she moved past him. "It was both," he whispered. "It was convenient *and* it was poetic."

Only inches apart, their eyes held for what seemed like a lifetime to Colleen. His gaze was so intense she fought to remind herself that evil or not, psychotic or not, he was only human. He couldn't read her thoughts. Could he?

"I . . . knew it," she breathed. "I knew you were special the first time Mavis introduced us. I want to know about it. It must have been difficult, Ian was an excellent driver."

"Ninety-one percent of American males think they're excellent drivers. Some of us actually are, but Ortiz's pickup was no match for a Porsche on the open road so I scouted out a side road that offered the right angle for the collision."

"But how did you get Ortiz's truck?"

"He let me borrow it when he sat with my dad. I said my car was on the blink and he never questioned it. After the crash I said someone clipped his bumper in a parking lot and gave him a few hundred bucks to repair it. I knew he'd keep the money and skip the repairs. One more dent hardly mattered."

"I knew you were bright," she breathed, "but even so, I think I underestimated you."

"People often do," he said, running his hands down her body. "In more ways than you can imagine."

"Stop that!" she said sharply.

On the roof across the alley, Dylan bolted to his feet. Stunned, Rob stared at him, wide-eyed, then whirled on Colleen.

"You incredible bitch!" he roared, flailing wildly at her. "You set me up!"

Ducking his first blow, she swung back hard and caught him flush on the jaw, snapping his head around. But he was too strong, too enraged. Grabbing her lapels, he slammed her into the wall, stunning her, then snaked his forearm around her throat and hauled her to the window in view of the roof across the alley.

"Back off!" he roared at Tatum, who'd risen and drawn his weapon. Dylan had vanished. "Back off or I'll jump and take her down with me! I swear to God, I'll—"

He never finished. Dylan suddenly sprinted past Tatum. Running full tilt to the edge of the roof, he launched himself across the gap between the buildings, pinwheeling his arms to maintain his balance.

The bedroom window exploded inward in a maelstrom of splintering wood and shattered glass as Dylan cannoned into Rob and Colleen, knocking them sprawling back into the room.

Colleen slammed into a dresser and went down, stunned, unable to think or even breathe. In the sudden silence the only sound was the tinkling of glass shards dropping from the ruined window.

Groaning, Dylan tried to raise himself, then slumped facedown beside the wall. The sound of his pain galvanized Colleen with a strength she scarcely recognized. Struggling to her hands and knees, she shook her head to clear it, then crawled to Dylan through the broken glass on the carpet.

He was unconscious, bleeding from a dozen gashes in his face. She groped for the pulse at his throat. It was racing but seemed strong. Her hand came away bloody.

"Dylan? Are you okay?" Tatum called from across the alley. "Damn it, answer me!"

His voice roused Bergstrom instead. He sat up stiffly and looked around, dazed, until his eyes came to rest on Colleen. Then awareness flooded into them, and madness, and a killing rage. Staggering to his feet, he cast about for a weapon, snatched up a brass lamp, yanked the cord out of the wall, and started for her.

Desperately she fumbled inside Dylan's coat and pulled his weapon free. Her hands were trembling so fiercely it was all she could do to point the ugly black automatic in Rob's general direction. Still, he hesitated.

"You have no idea how to fire that gun," he said, licking his lips. "I can brain you before you get off a shot."

"Maybe you're right," she admitted. "But you're a bright guy, Doctor. Do you really want to bet your life on it?"

Dylan groaned as Colleen brushed past the curtain into the cubicle in the emergency room. "Go ahead and say it," he said. "I blew it. I almost got you killed."

"By standing up when you did? Well, you certainly brought things to a head. Why did you do it, by the way?"

"I've been asking myself the same damn thing every time they tweeze another glass splinter out of me. Blind instinct is the best I've been able to come up with. When I heard you tell him to stop, I thought you were being hurt and I . . . reacted. It was a bone-head move. I'm really sorry."

"Don't be. You didn't see his eyes," she said, shivering. "I counted on his intelligence, thought I could reason with him. I was wrong. I've seen a lot of troubled people in my work, kids who've killed parents, husbands who've killed wives, but never anyone like Rob. I hope to God you got a good recording of his confession."

"A ten-by-ten perfect take. With luck, he'll draw triple life, thanks to you. And speaking of thanks, I guess I should thank you for saving my neck. Tatum said when he got there you were holding Bergstrom off with my weapon."

"A bluff. I don't know doodley about guns. I didn't know how to fire it."

"Then it was an even braver thing to do."

"You've got to be kidding. Jumping across that alley was the bravest thing I've ever seen. I'll never . . . why are you smiling?"

"To tell you the truth, I'd been watching the building through binoculars for a while and I completely misjudged the distance. I thought it was a lot closer than it was."

"So you're not really brave, only stupid? That's your story? Are you always this modest?"

"Not modest, just honest. I deal with so many lies every day, sometimes I almost lose track of what's true. I don't want that to happen with you."

"Why not?"

Their eyes met and held a moment. "You're the doctor. You can probably guess."

"You said once I was a shrink, not a psychic. You were right. So suppose we discuss this later, under more . . . comfortable circumstances. Meanwhile, would you mind if I keep on thinking you were just a little bit brave?"

"No," he said, easing back on his pillow, closing his eyes. "I can live with that."

BEST BEHAVIOUR

Simon Brett

Like his best-known character, struggling actor Charles Paris, Simon Brett has deep roots in the performing arts. A producer for BBC radio for ten years, during which time he was responsible for such phenomenally popular shows as The Hitchhiker's Guide to the Galaxy, *the author has an unfailing ear for dialogue and a keen understanding of how to incorporate humor in fiction. Though he has written non-series novels, including* A Shock to the System, *which was made into a movie starring Michael Caine in 1990, his forte is the lighthearted series mystery. For the past thirteen years, he has had two series running concurrently, the Paris books and those featuring the widowed Mrs. Pargeter, a lady who, surprisingly, has underworld connections. Brett has been honored with nominations for both the Edgar and Anthony awards.*

I KNOW HOW to behave. I do. That's one thing my papa taught me. It's really the most important thing he left me with—knowing the right way to behave.

And I never thought it was cruel. He had my best interests at heart. I know he did. If there was any cruelty involved, then he was only being cruel to be kind. He often used that expression. "Edmund," he'd say. "I'm only being cruel to be kind." And I respected that. Even though the things he did sometimes hurt, I could still respect his reasons for doing them.

It's a matter of justice, you see. Being fair to people. Not just being fair to yourself—that could so easily become selfishness—but being fair to everyone else you come into contact with. "We're social beings," Papa would say. "Humankind're social beings, and one's success as a member of humankind is demonstrated by how well one relates to other human beings. You have to behave, Edmund. Never knowingly do harm to another member of the human race."

Those were the values Papa dinned into me from a very early age and, from the time I could understand what he was talking about, I very quickly came to respect what he stood for.

He was entirely consistent, you see. His rules were clear. He never punished me for something that I didn't know at the time—or at least understood pretty soon afterwards—was wrong. "Bad behaviour must never go unpunished," Papa used to say. "Otherwise it's bound to lead to worse behaviour."

He didn't have any truck with the view that, equally, good behaviour should be rewarded. "Good behaviour should be instinctive. Good behaviour brings its own reward. Though, in fact, for you, Edmund, good behaviour is not good enough. Any son of mine must always be on his *best* behaviour."

So that's what I always aspired to. And, most of the time, achieved. When I fell short of Papa's high standards—no, of *my* high standards ("It's within *you*, Edmund," he always used to say. "It should be instinctive within yourself.")—then I knew punishment was inevitable. But it was perfectly fair. I knew the rules. I'd broken them. I had failed as a member of humankind.

Papa himself avoided doing unwitting harm to other members of the human race by not having a lot to do with them. We didn't see many other people as I was growing up. There was just Papa, Mama, and me. "We don't need other people," Papa used to say. "We're self-sufficient. We are fortunate—unlike a lot of the poor bastards out there—to be a secure, loving family unit."

And he was right—we were fortunate. Money was never a problem— we always had enough to eat, we lived in a nice house, I was sent to a private school. It was all very nice.

And I'm proud to say, Mama and Papa never had any of the problems with me that you read about other families having with growing children. They were never going to see my name in the papers . . . well, that is, until this current business. And now they're both dead, so it's not as if any amount of cruel lies in the tabloids can cause them any anxiety. Not now. Not anymore.

My father's teaching stood me in good stead, though, you know. I didn't backslide after he died. No, the training Papa had given me was so good that Mama never had to raise her voice to me. I was permanently on my best behaviour.

But I don't want to sound like I'm a goody-goody, not to give that impression, no. I do have my . . . I was about to say "vices," but I think vice is probably too strong a word. Vice means doing things to other people, body things,

things with your secret bits. And I've never felt the urge to do any of that, don't understand why people make such a fuss about it. No, for what I do, "indulgences" is the word I prefer. Yes, I do have indulgences.

There are only two, really. Two big ones. They're hot buttered toast with Golden Syrup on, and Children's BBC. And, well, actually, now I come to think of it, there is sort of a third. My parents always hated the idea of my name being shortened, but now I tell people to call me not "Edmund" but "Eddie."

All right, you could say I'm reacting, greedily taking the things I wasn't allowed when I was a child, but I don't think mine're too bad, as indulgences go. Other people do a lot worse things.

And by Papa's rules—you know, about not doing harm to another member of humankind—well, I can't honestly think that my indulgences harm anyone. No matter how much Children's BBC I watch and video, no matter how much hot buttered toast with Golden Syrup I eat, nobody else gets hurt by it.

Mind you, the Golden Syrup does make me fat. I was always big—used to get rather unkind things said about my size when I was at school—but since Mama died, I have got a lot bigger. She used to keep an eye on how much Golden Syrup I ate, used to say, "Hold back, Edmund, enough is enough, you know," but since she died . . . well, there's no one to stop me. But like I said, nobody gets hurt by it.

I'm lucky. I know I'm lucky. My parents left me enough money so that I won't ever have to work. Probably that's just as well, because the few interviews I did have for jobs didn't turn out very well. I think my size put the people off, partly, and then they did seem to ask very difficult questions. I admit there are a lot of things I don't know about, and the subjects on which I am good . . . like Children's BBC . . . well, they didn't ask about them. The experience rather put me off applying for other jobs.

But I'm lucky too, in that I have friends. Not that many, but there are some children round where I live and I get on well with them. They know about Children's BBC, you see, so we've got things to talk about. I often meet them in the park, near the children's playground. I'm too big to go on any of the swings or anything . . . I'd probably break them if I did, I'm such a big lump . . . but it's a good place to meet the children.

I get on better with them when they're on their own. I buy sweets for them. Never go out without a couple of bags of Jelly Babies in my pockets. The children like those. (So do I, actually!) But I only give them sweets when they're on their own. Their parents don't seem to like the children talking to me. Sometimes they say rather cruel things. Things that wouldn't pass muster under Papa's rules. I'm another member of humankind, and the things they say do do harm to me. What's more, I think they do it knowingly.

Still, in the park I do quite often see children on their own, so it's not all bad. I tell them to call me "Eddie." I like it when I hear their little voices call me Eddie. Of course, the children get bigger and seem to lose interest in talking about Children's BBC with me. But there's always another lot of little ones growing up.

I've got so many children's programmes videoed that I sometimes think I should ask some of the children to come back home with me to have a good watch and lashings of hot buttered toast with Golden Syrup. But I haven't done that yet. I don't know why, but something told me it was a bad idea.

And now, after some of the questions I've been asked in the last few months, I know my instinct was right. It would have been a very bad idea.

My problems . . . yes, I suppose I have to call them problems . . . began in relation to a little girl called Bethany Jones. I didn't know her second name when I met her. She just told me she was called "Bethany." But recently her name's been so much over the newspapers and the television that everyone in the country knows she's called Bethany Jones.

I met her in the park, like the other children. She was six—just been six, just had her sixth birthday party, she was very proud of that. She lived quite near the park, over the other side from my house. Her parents didn't like her going to the children's playground on her own, but she was so close she used to sneak out when they weren't looking.

That's when I'd meet her. And we'd talk about Children's BBC. She didn't call me Eddie. She used to call me "Fat Boy," which I suppose could have been cruel, but I didn't mind it from Bethany. She didn't mean any harm. That's what they said in the papers. Her mother said, "Bethany never did any harm to anyone."

I didn't know what had happened to Bethany before the police arrived. I don't have a paper or watch the news—well, except for *Newsround* on Children's BBC. And that's on at five, and she wasn't found till four-thirty, so they'd have been hard put to get it on that day's programme. Anyway, *Newsround* wouldn't have covered a story like Bethany Jones. It was too unpleasant for a children's audience.

The police arrived very quickly. Children's BBC had just ended, at five thirty-five, as usual, and *Neighbours* had just started. Sometimes I watch *Neighbours* and sometimes I don't. It's not proper Children's BBC, though I know a lot of children watch it. For me, I'll watch it if I like the story. If there's too much kissing and that sort of thing, I'll switch it off. I don't like stories with kissing in them. I never saw Papa and Mama kiss, and the thought of people doing it sort of like in public, on the television . . . well, I don't think it's very nice.

The day the police arrived, there wasn't a kissing story in *Neighbours* and I was watching it. And videoing it, obviously. I video everything I watch. I had to switch off the television when the police came in. But I left the video running.

The first thing the police asked me was if I knew Bethany and I said, yes, of course I did. And they said they'd been talking to some of the other children and was I the "Eddie" who used to give them Jelly Babies, and I said, yes, I was.

There was one of them, the policemen, who seemed to be in charge. He was not wearing a uniform and he was very forceful. Detective Inspector Bracken, he was called. Not the sort of person you'd argue with. He reminded me of Papa, and in the same way that I'd never have contradicted Papa, I found it difficult to stand up to this man and say he was wrong, even when the suggestions he was making were absolutely untrue. It seemed rather rude for me to disagree with him.

"And did you ever give Jelly Babies to Bethany?" Detective Inspector Bracken demanded.

"Yes," I said. "Of course I did. I like Bethany. She's one of my friends."

"So she was one of your friends, was she?"

"*Is* one of my friends," I said. "*Is* one of my friends."

Detective Inspector Bracken looked at me thoughtfully. But his expression wasn't just thoughtful. There was something else in it too, something that almost looked like distaste. He kept on looking at me.

I suddenly remembered that the police were guests in my house and I hadn't even offered them anything. ("Black mark, Edmund," Papa would have said. "Black mark on the hospitality front.") "Could I get you some tea or something?" I asked. "Something to eat, perhaps? I often have buttered toast with Golden Syrup round this time. Maybe you'd like—?"

"No, thank you," said Detective Inspector Bracken. And he kept on looking straight at me. I found it embarrassing. I tried not to look him in the face.

"So . . ." he said, after what seemed a long silence, ". . . have you always had this urge to hang round little girls?"

He was getting the wrong end of the stick. I had to explain it to him. "It's not just little girls," I said. "It's little boys, too."

"Is it?" he said. "Really?" And somehow he didn't say it in a kind way. Then he went on, "Can you tell us what's happened to Bethany Jones?"

"Happened to her? Why should I be able to tell you?"

"I just thought you might be able to." Detective Inspector Bracken was looking at me in the way Papa used to look when I'd done something wrong and he was just waiting for me to own up to it. I always did own up; Papa knew he only had to wait. But with Detective Inspector Bracken it was different. There was nothing for me to own up to.

"Save us the trouble of doing it," he went on after a silence. "Save us the trouble of telling you what's happened to Bethany Jones."

And then he did tell me what had happened to her. It was horrid. I don't like things like that. It's like kissing, and people's secret bits . . . I don't like it.

Apparently she'd been attacked in the park by someone. She'd been dragged off into the bushes by the children's playground. Then she'd been "sexually assaulted." And then she'd been beaten on the head with a stone until she was dead.

"Bethany—dead?" I said in disbelief. "But I was talking to her only yesterday."

"Yesterday," Detective Inspector Bracken repeated. "Were you? And what about today?"

"No, I didn't see her today."

"Where were you, Mr. Bowman," asked Detective Inspector Bracken, "between three-thirty and four-thirty this afternoon?"

I smiled at the question. Anyone who knew me at all—and granted there weren't that many people who did know me—but anyone who knew anything about me would know the answer to that. I was where I am every weekday afternoon at that time.

"I was here," I replied. "Here watching Children's BBC. I always am. Go on, I can prove it. You ask me any questions you like about this afternoon's Children's BBC. I bet I can give you the right answers."

Detective Inspector Bracken smiled wryly and looked across at my video recorder. "Yes, I'm sure you can, Mr. Bowman. Pretty unusual habit for a grown man, I'd have thought, videoing children's television programmes. . . ."

"Oh, but I like to have a full record," I told him. "I feel awful if I think I've missed a single minute of Children's BBC."

"I see," he said. But he didn't look at me as if he did see. Soon after that, he said he wanted me to accompany him and the others to the police station. ". . . if I didn't mind . . ." No, I said, I didn't mind. I knew it didn't do to be difficult with forceful people like Detective Inspector Bracken. Best behaviour, Edmund, best behaviour.

They kept explaining things to me. They kept stopping and checking that I understood what was going on. Then, after I was charged, they got a lawyer for me, and she kept explaining things too. And yes, I did understand. I understood the words and I understood what they meant. What I didn't understand was how they could manage to get it all so wrong.

I think a lot of the trouble was Detective Inspector Bracken. His manner, the way he put things, was so like Papa's that . . . well, I still found it very difficult to argue with him. He'd say something which was complete nonsense and I'd . . . well, I'd try to point out, sort of, why what he was saying wasn't true, but somehow my words didn't come out right.

I felt very trapped. I wanted to get back to my house, put on a video of some old *Tom and Jerry* or something like that, and let it wash all the horrid thoughts and images out of my mind. But they wouldn't let me do that.

I felt very lonely, too. Although there were always people around— indeed, they wouldn't leave me on my own for a second—none of them were friendly. They all looked at me as if I was carrying some awful infectious disease. I wanted someone there who'd just talk to me in a relaxed, simple way. I'd've loved to have one of the children from the park there to talk to. At one moment, when I was particularly stressed, I said that to Detective Inspector Bracken. He gave me a very strange look.

The lawyer they got me—there was no way I could have got one for myself, I've never had any cause to need a lawyer—was, I'm sure, fine, but she didn't seem very interested in my case. Maybe it was just a job of work for her. She didn't seem concerned about putting my side of things. But maybe that wasn't what she was there for. Certainly she didn't stand up to Detective Inspector Bracken much. He was so strong, so dominant, so like Papa.

It was the same at the trial. There was this woman barrister who defended me. I've nothing against women. I like women. But I don't think of them as strong. Probably that comes from having grown up with my parents. It was always Papa who was in charge. Mama was a kind of shadowy figure in the background. So I never really expected the judge and the jury to take much notice of my barrister.

Also I don't think she took the right approach for my defence. She kept saying it wasn't just Bethany Jones who was a victim. I was a victim too. Then she said things that were a bit hurtful. She said just because I was odd, it didn't automatically make me a criminal. She said, yes, I was a sad, rather pathetic figure, somebody who didn't fit society's norms. But that didn't make me a murderer.

I'm not sure that was the right way to go about it. Calling me "odd" and "sad" and "pathetic" made me seem as if I was all those things. I thought she was playing into the hands of the other barrister. He was a man, much more forceful in his manner. He was like Papa, or Detective Inspector Bracken. He spoke in a way that didn't brook argument. I'm not surprised that the jury believed what he said rather than the arguments my barrister put forward. If I'd known nothing about the case and I'd been sitting in that jury box, I'd have done the same.

But of course I did know something about the case. I knew I'd never touched Bethany Jones, never touched any of the children. At the time those dreadful things happened to her, I was in my house watching Children's BBC.

There was another thing I knew too. I knew my secret bits didn't work like men's are supposed to. I knew my body wasn't capable of doing the things that had been done to her body. But I didn't like to mention that. It was a bit embarrassing. Maybe, if I'd had a male barrister . . . But to talk to a woman—any woman—about that kind of thing . . . well, I couldn't ever have done that.

It wasn't nice before the trial, or while the trial was going on. I was kept in this prison. "On remand," they called it. They didn't have any Golden Syrup in the prison. I asked for it, but you couldn't get it. And you weren't allowed to watch Children's BBC.

Also, the other prisoners were horrid to me. They all seemed to take it for granted that I'd done all those things to Bethany Jones. There was more than one occasion when only the intervention of the prison officers stopped something rather unpleasant happening.

After the trial was over, though, and that horrid wrong verdict had been given, the prison officers' attitude seemed to have changed. I was taken back to prison—the remand prison, that is; I was going to another one to serve my sentence—in a van with barred windows. Inside the prison, the guards were leading me back to my cell, I still had handcuffs on, and we were going through one of the corridors, when suddenly this man stood in front of us, blocking our progress.

I'd seen him round the prison before. He wasn't a nice man, very rough. He didn't speak nicely, didn't have good vowels. He was the kind of man Papa would have told me not to mix with. "They're not our sort of people," he'd have said. "You steer clear of them, Edmund."

And it was good advice. If I could have steered clear of him, I would have done. But there was nowhere to go. It was a narrow corridor. The prison officers who were leading me along just drew back as the man launched himself at me. He hit me in the stomach first. "Take that, you filthy fat pervert!" he said.

And when I fell down and tried to scramble away from him along the wall, he started kicking me. All over. My stomach, my arms, my legs, even my secret bits. With the handcuffs on, I couldn't protect myself. He kicked my face as well. Two of my teeth were broken. I could taste the blood and feel their jagged edges.

Then he stopped and laughed. "That's just a taster," he said. "A taster for what they'll do to you when you get in the real nick. They don't like nonces in the real nick."

After he'd finished kicking me, the prison officers came and moved him away. But they'd been there all the time, watching. They could have come to my rescue more quickly, I'm sure they could. I hope the prison officers in "the real nick" are a bit more efficient.

They took me to "the real nick" in another van with barred windows. When I was leaving the remand prison, they asked if I wanted a blanket over my head. Why would I want a blanket over my head? I'd had few enough chances to see the outside world in the last few months. I wanted to see everything I could out of the van's windows.

The trouble is, what I did see, when the van emerged from the gates, was a crowd of people. There were photographers, and a lot of women were there too, women probably about the same age as Bethany Jones's mother. But they weren't like women should be. They weren't quiet and well behaved like Mama always was. No, they were shouting and scream-ing. As the van went slowly through the crowd, they started banging on the sides. Some of them threw things and spat. I saw one face quite close to mine through the window. It was contorted with hatred. It wasn't nice.

The drumming sound they made against the walls of the van stayed with me. It kind of reverberated in my head. And now I've arrived at the new prison, I can hear it again. I've met the governor, I've been through all the en-try procedures, and now I'm being led to my cell. The drumming sound comes from all the other prisoners, banging things against the doors of their cells.

I can hear things shouted too. Not nice things. I can hear that word "nonce" that the man in the remand prison used. I wonder what it means.

Still, I'm sure it'll be all right. They may find the person who really did those horrid things to Bethany Jones, and set me free. Or they may reduce the length of my sentence. I've heard they do that for some prisoners. They reduce the sentence "for good behaviour." And I'm going to continue to do what Papa told me. All the time I'm here, I'm going to be on my absolute best behaviour.

I wonder what it'll be like here. I know there are only certain times when you're allowed to watch television in prison. Maybe here Children's BBC is one of those times.

I hope they have Golden Syrup in this prison.

HOOPS

S. J. Rozan

S. J. Rozan is breaking new ground in the mystery field. She is one of only two women recipients of the Shamus Award for best novel. She reached this milestone with a most unusual series in which a female Chinese private eye, Lydia Chin, and her sometime partner Bill Smith, alternate, on a book-by-book basis, the first-person narration of their cases. Whatever book you pick up, whoever's telling the story, the New York atmosphere is evoked through telling details about the city's neighborhoods. But then, author Rozan should know her New York. She had a first career as an architect, and has worked on many of the city's notable buildings. In addition to her Shamus Award win, the author has claimed an Anthony Award for best novel and an Edgar Allan Poe Award nomination for best short story.

A COLD WIND was pulling sharp waves from the Hudson as I drove north, out of town. The waves would strain for height, pushing forward, reaching; but then they'd fall back with small, violent crashes, never high enough, never breaking free.

I was heading to Yonkers, a tired, shabby city caught between New York and the real suburbs. I'd been there over the years as cases had taken me, but I'd never had a client from there before. I'd never had a client who was just eighteen, either. But it was a week since I'd closed my last case. Money was a little tight, I was getting antsy, and working was better than not working, always.

Even working for a relative of Curtis's. I'd been surprised when he'd called me. The ring of the telephone had burst into a practice session where a Beethoven sonata I'd thought I had in my fingers was falling apart, where rhythm, color, texture, everything was off. I usually don't like being interrupted at the piano, but this time I jumped at it.

Until I heard who it was, and what he wanted.

"A nephew of yours?" I said into the phone. "I didn't know scum like you had relatives, Curtis."

"Now, you got no call to be insulting," Curtis's smooth voice gave back. "Though it ain't surprising. I told the boy I could get him a investigator do a good job for him, but he gonna have to put up with a lot of attitude."

"What's he done?" I asked shortly.

"Ain't done nothing. A friend of his got hisself killed. Raymond think someone should be paying attention."

"When people get killed the cops usually pay attention."

"Unless you some black kid drug dealer in Yonkers, and you the suicide half of a murder-suicide."

He had a point. "Tell me about it."

He told me. An eighteen-year-old high school senior named Charles Lomax had been found in a park where the kids go at night. His pregnant girlfriend, beside him, had a bullet in her heart. Lomax had a bullet through his head and the gun in his hand.

The bodies had been discovered by the basketball coach, who said he'd gone out looking after Lomax hadn't shown up for practice. He hadn't shown up for class, either, but apparently that wasn't unusual enough for his classroom teachers to be bothered about. Lomax had been a point guard with a C average. He'd been expected to graduate, which distinguished him from about half the kids at Yonkers West. He'd been in trouble with the police all his life, which distinguished him from nobody. There was nothing else interesting about him, except that he'd been a friend of Raymond Coe, and Raymond wasn't happy with the official verdict: murder-suicide, case closed.

"What's Raymond's theory?" I asked Curtis, shouldering the phone so I could close the piano and stack my music.

"Let me put it to you this way," Curtis oozed. "I ain't suggested the boy hire hisself a honky detective because I admire the way you people dance."

I pulled slowly around the corner, coasted past the cracked asphalt playground I'd been told to find. The late-day air was mean with the wind's cold edge, but six black kids in sweats and high-tech sneakers crowded the concrete half-court. Their game was fast, loud, and physical, elbows thrown and no fouls called. One kid, tall and meaty, had a game on a level the others couldn't match: Faster and smarter both, he muscled his man when he couldn't finesse him. But it didn't stop the rest. No one hung back, no one gave in. Slam dunks and three-pointers flew through the netless rim. They didn't seem to be keeping score.

A kid fell, rolled, jumped up shaking his hand against the sting of a scrape. Without missing a beat he was back in the game. I parked across the street and watched. One of those kids was Raymond; I didn't know which. Right now I knew nothing about any of them, except for what I could see: strength, focus, a wild joy in pushing themselves. I finished a cigarette. In a minute I'd become part of their world. This moment of possibility would end. Knowledge can't be shaken off. And knowledge is always limiting.

The game faltered and then stopped as I walked to the break in the chain-link fence. They all watched me approach, silent. A chunky kid in a hooded sweatshirt shifted the ball from one hand to the other. To the one who'd fallen he said, "Yo, Ray. This your man?"

"Don't know." Raising his voice as though he suspected I spoke a different language, the kid said, "You Smith?"

I nodded. "Raymond Coe?"

"Yeah." He jerked his head at the others. "These my homeboys."

I glanced at the tight, silent group. "They in on this?"

"You got a problem with that?"

"Should I?"

"Maybe you don't like working for a bunch of niggers."

I stared into his dark eyes. It seemed to me they were softer than he might have wanted them to be. "Maybe I don't like having to pass an exam to get a case." I shrugged, turned to go.

"Yo," Raymond said, behind me.

I turned back.

"Curtis say you good."

"I don't like Curtis," I told him. "He doesn't like me. But we're useful to each other from time to time."

Surprisingly, he grinned. His face seemed, for a moment, to fit with what I'd seen in his eyes. "Curtis tell me you was gonna say that."

"What else did he tell you?"

"That you the man could find out about my man C."

"What's in it for you?"

A couple of the other kids scowled at that, and one started to speak, but Raymond silenced him with a look. "Nothing in it for me," he said.

"I cost money," I pressed. "Forty an hour, plus expenses. Two days up front. Why's it worth it to you?"

The chunky kid slammed the ball to the pavement, snatched it back. "Come on, Ray. You don't need this bull."

Raymond ignored him, looked steadily at me. "C was my main man, my homie. No way he done what they say he done. Somebody burned him. I ain't gonna let that pass."

"Why me?" I asked. "Curtis knows every piece of black slime that ever walked the earth, but he sent you a white detective. Why?"

" 'Cause the slime we looking for," Raymond said steadily, "I don't believe they black."

Raymond, his homies, and I made our way to the end of the block, to the pizza place. The day had gone and a tired gray evening was coming in, studded with yellow streetlights and blinking neon. The homies gave me their names: Ash, Caesar, Skin. Tyrell, the one who could really play. The chunky one, Halftime. None of them offered to shake my hand.

Inside, where the air swirled with garlic and oregano, we crowded around a booth, hauling chairs to the end of the table. Halftime went to order a pizza. He came back distributing Cokes and Sprites, and he brought me coffee. Across the room, from the jukebox, a rap song began, complicated rhythm under complex rhyme, music with no melody. I drank some coffee. "Well?"

Everyone glanced at everyone else, but they all came back to Raymond. Raymond looked only at me. "My man C," he started. "Someone done him, make it look like suicide."

"People kill themselves," I said.

Some heads shook; Tyrell muttered, "Damn."

"You don't know him," Raymond said. "C don't never give up on nothing. And he had no reason. He was gonna graduate, he was gonna have a kid. The season was just starting."

"The season?" I left the rest for later.

"Hoops," Raymond told me, though it was clear I was straining the patience of the others. "My man a guard. Tyrell, Ash, and me, we on the squad too." Tyrell and Ash, a round-faced quiet kid, nodded in acknowledgment. "The rest of them," Raymond's sudden, unexpected grin flashed again, "they keep us on our game."

"So you're telling me if Lomax was going to kill himself he would have waited until after the season?" I lit a cigarette, shook the match into the tin ashtray.

"Man, I am telling you no way he did that." Raymond's voice was emphatic. "C don't have no reason to want out. Plus, Ayisha. Ain't no way he gonna do her like that, the mother of his baby."

"He wanted the baby?"

Halftime grinned, poked at something on the table. Raymond said, "He already buying it things. Toys and stuff. Bought one of them fuzzy baby basketballs, you know? It was gonna be a boy."

"How was he planning to support a family?"

Raymond shrugged. "Some way. Ayisha, she bragging like he gonna get tapped to play for some big school and they gonna be rich, but she don't believe it neither."

"It wasn't true?"

"Nah." Raymond shook his head. "Only dude around here got that kind of chance be my man Tyrell. He gonna make us famous. Put us on the map."

I turned to Tyrell, who was polishing off his second Coke in the corner of the booth. "I watched you play," I told him. "You're smart and fast. You have offers?"

Tyrell stared at me for a moment before he answered. "Coach say scouts coming this season." His voice was deep, resonant, and slow. "He been talking to them."

Halftime's name rang out; he went to the counter for the pizza. I looked around at the others, at their hard faces and at their eyes. Seventeen, eighteen: They should have been on the verge of something, at the beginning. But these boys had no futures and they knew it; and I could see it, in their eyes.

I didn't ask where the money was coming from to pay me. I didn't want to know. I didn't ask what would happen to Tyrell if he didn't get a college offer, or whether the others, the ones who weren't on the squad, were still in school. So what if they were? Where would it get them?

I asked a more practical question. "Who'd want to kill Lomax?"

Raymond shrugged, looked at his homeboys. "Everybody got enemies."

"Who were his?"

"Nobody I know about," he said. "Except the cops."

"Cops?" I looked at Raymond, at the other grim faces. "That's what this is about? You think this was a cop job?"

Halftime came back, with a pizza and a pile of paper plates. Everyone reached for a slice but me; Raymond made the offer but I shook my head.

Raymond didn't answer my question, gave Tyrell a look. Tyrell's deep voice picked it up. "C and me was in a little trouble last year. Gas-station holdup. It was bull. Charges was dropped."

"But them mothers didn't let up," Raymond said impatiently. "Tyrell, nobody care, but C been a pain in the cops' butt for years. You know, up in their face, trash-talking. I tell him, man, back off, you leave them alone and they leave you alone. But he don't never stop. C like to win. Also he like to make sure you know you lose. Cops was all over him after he get out."

"And?"

"And nothing. They couldn't get nothing else on him."

"And?" I said again, knowing what was coming.

"I figure they get tired waiting for him to make a mistake and make it for him."

I pulled on my cigarette. There was nothing left; I stubbed it out. I wanted to tell them they were wrong, they were crazy, that kind of stuff doesn't really go on. But that would be pointless. They might be wrong, in this case, but they weren't crazy and we all knew it.

"Anyone in particular?" I asked.

Raymond shook his head. "Cops around here, they run in packs," he said. "Could be anyone."

Two slices were left on the tray. Without discussion, and seemingly by general consent, Raymond and Tyrell reached for them.

"Okay," I said. "Tell me about her."

Tyrell looked away, as though other things in the room were more interesting than I was.

"Ayisha?" Raymond asked. He seemed to think about my question as he ate. "He can't get enough of her," he finally said.

"But you didn't like her?"

"Nah, she okay." He flipped a piece of crust onto the tray, sat back, and popped the top of a Sprite. "She sorta—you know. She got a smart mouth. And she been around."

A couple of the other guys snickered. I wondered whom she'd been around with.

"She have enemies?"

"I don't know. But like I say, everybody got them. Can't always tell what you done to get them, but everybody got them."

I left, trading phone numbers with Raymond. I took the homies' numbers too, though I was less than certain that getting in touch with any of them would be as easy as a phone call. But I might want to talk to some of them, separately, later. Now, I wanted to talk to a few other people.

The first, from a phone booth down the street, was Lewis Farlow, the basketball coach who'd found the bodies. I called him at the high school, to find a time he'd be available. Half an hour, he told me. He knew about me; he'd been expecting my call.

Next I called the Yonkers PD, to find the detective on the Lomax case. Might as well get the party line.

He was a high-voiced Irish sergeant named Sweeney. He wasn't impressed with my name or my mission, and he wasn't helpful.

"What's to investigate?" he wanted to know. "That case has already been investigated. By real detectives."

"My client's not sure it was suicide," I said calmly.

"Yeah? Who are you working for?"

"Friend of the family."

"Don't be cute, Smith."

"I'm just asking for the results of the official investigation, Sweeney."

The grim pleasure in Sweeney's voice was palpable. "The official results are, the kid killed the girlfriend. Blam! Then he blew his own brains out. Happy?"

Start out with an easy one. "Whose was the gun?"

"The Pope's."

"You couldn't trace it?"

"No, Smith, we couldn't trace it. Numbers were filed off, inside and out. That a new one on you?"

"Seems like a lot of trouble to go to for a suicide weapon."

"Maybe suicide wasn't on his mind when he got it."

"Why'd he do it?"

"How the hell do I know why he did it? You suppose it had anything to do with her being pregnant?"

"And what, his reputation would be ruined? Anyway, his friends say he wanted the baby."

"Yeah, sure. Da-da." Sweeney made baby noises into the phone.

"Sweeney—"

"Yeah. So maybe he did. And then maybe he finds out it isn't his. You like that for a motive? It's yours."

"You have any proof of that?"

"No. Matter of fact, I just thought it up. I'll let you in on something, Smith. I got better things to do than bust my hump to prove a kid with his brains in the dirt and the gun in his hand pulled the trigger."

"I understand you guys knew this kid."

"We know them all. Most of them have been our guests for short stays in our spacious accommodations."

"I hear you couldn't hold onto this one."

"What, for that gas-station job?" He didn't rise to the bait. "Way I look at it, it's just as well. If we could hold them all as long as they deserve, the streets would be clean and I'd be out of a job."

"Come on, Sweeney. Didn't it steam you just a little when the kid, walked? I hear it wasn't the first time."

"Matter of fact, it wasn't."

"Matter of fact, I hear there were cops who had this kid on a special list. Was he on your list, Sweeney?"

"Now just hold it, Smith. What are you getting at? I killed him because I couldn't keep his ass in jail where it belonged?"

I'd made him mad. Good; angry men make mistakes.

"Not necessarily you, Sweeney. It's just that I'll bet there weren't a lot of tears in the department when Lomax bought it."

"Oh," he said slowly, his voice dangerously soft. "I get it. You're looking for a lawsuit, right?"

"Wrong."

"Crap. The family wants to milk it. You find a hole in the police work, they sue the department. The city settles out of court; it's got no backbone with these people. You drive off in your Porsche and I get pushed out early on half my stinking pension. That's it, right?"

"No, Sweeney, that's not it. I'm interested in what really happened to this kid. That's what any good cop would be interested in, too."

"You know what, Smith? You're lucky I don't know your face. Here's some advice for free: Don't let me see it."

The phone slammed down; that was that.

Yonkers West High School filled the entire block, a sulking brick-and-concrete monster whose windows were covered with a tight wire mesh. I asked the security guard at the door the way to the gym. "I'm here to see Coach Farlow," I said.

"You a scout?" he asked after me, as I started down the hall.

"No. You have something worth scouting?"

The guard grinned. "Come back tomorrow, at practice," he said. "You'll see."

I found Lewis Farlow behind his desk in his Athletic Department office, a windowless, cramped, concrete-block space that smelled of liniment, mildew, and sweat. Dusty trophies shared the top of the filing cabinets with papers and old coffee cups. Here and there a towel huddled on the floor, as though too exhausted to make it back through the connecting door to the locker room.

I knocked, checked Farlow out while I waited for him to look up from his paperwork. He was a thin white man, smaller than his players, with deep creases in the sagging skin of his face and sparse, colorless hair that might once have been red.

"Yeah." Farlow lifted his head, glanced over me swiftly with blue eyes that were bright and sharp.

"Smith," I said.

"Oh, yeah. About Lomax, right? Sit down." He gestured to a chair.

"The guard at the door asked me if I was a scout," I said as I moved into the room, trying to avoid the boxes of ropes and balls that should have been somewhere else, if there'd been somewhere else for them to be. "He meant that big guy? Tyrell?"

Farlow nodded. "Tyrell Drum," he said. "Best thing we've had here in years. Everybody's just waiting for him to catch fire. You seen him play?" He looked at me quizzically.

"He was with Raymond Coe just now," I explained. "You have scouts coming down?"

"I already had some stringers early last season. Liked what they saw, but the big guns didn't get a chance to get here while Drum was still playing."

"He didn't play the whole season?"

"Sat it out." One corner of Farlow's mouth turned up in a smile that wasn't a smile.

"Hurt?"

"In jail."

"Oh," I said. "The gas-station job?"

"You heard about that?"

"He told me. It was him and Lomax, right?"

"They say it wasn't either of them. Charges were eventually dropped, but the season was over by then."

"Did he do it?"

"Who the hell knows? If he didn't, he will soon. Or something like it. Unless he gets an offer. Unless he gets out of here. Look, Smith about this Lomax thing."

Farlow stopped, turned a pencil over in his fingers as though looking for a way to say what he wanted. I waited.

"The guys are pretty upset," Farlow said. "Especially Coe; he and Lomax were pretty tight. Coe's got this half-assed idea that the cops killed Lomax. He's sold it to the rest of them. They told me they were going to hire a private eye to prove it."

"How come they told you?"

"I'm the coach. High school, that's like a father confessor. Wasn't it that way when you were there?"

"The high school I went to, all the kids were white."

"You surprised they talk to me? They gotta talk to someone." He shrugged. "I'm on their side and they know it. I go to bat for them when they're in trouble. I bully them into staying in school. Coe wouldn't be graduating if it weren't for me."

He threw the pencil down on the desk, slumped back in his chair. "Not that I know why I bother. They stay in school, so what? They end up fry cooks at McDonald's." Farlow paused, rubbed a hand across his square chin; I got the feeling he was only half talking to me. "Eighteen years in this hole," he went on, "watching kids go down the drain. No way out. Except every now and then, a kid like Drum comes along. Someone you could actually do something for. Someone with a chance. And the stupid sonuvabitch spends half his junior year in jail."

He looked at me. The half-grin came back. "Sorry, Smith. I get like this. The old coach, feeling sorry for himself. Let's get back to Lomax. Where the hell was I?"

"The guys came to you," I said. "They told you they wanted a P.I."

"Yeah. So I told them to go ahead. Coe's like Lomax was, a stubborn bastard. Easier to agree with than to cross. So I said go ahead, call you. He probably thinks I think he's right, that there's something fishy here. But I don't."

"What do you think?"

"I think the simple answer is the best. Sometimes it's hard, but it's the best. Lomax killed the girl and he killed himself."

"Why?"

"Some beef, I don't know. Old days, he'd have knocked her around, then gone someplace to cool off. Today, they all have guns. You get mad, someone's dead before you know it. By the time he realizes what he's done it's over. Then? She's dead, the baby's dead, what's he gonna do? He's still got the gun."

He reached for the pencil again, turned it in his hand, and watched it turn.

"A guy's best friend turns up dead," he said in a quiet voice, "he wants to do something. Hiring you makes them feel better. Okay." He looked up. "So what I'm asking you is, go through the motions. You gotta do that; they're gonna pay you for it. But try to wrap it up fast. The sooner they put this behind them the better off they'll be."

I had my own doubts about how easy it ever was to put a friend's death behind you, but that didn't make Farlow wrong.

"If there's nothing to find, I'll know that soon enough," I said.

Farlow nodded, as though we'd reached an agreement. I asked him, "You found the bodies?"

"Yeah." He threw the pencil down again.

"What did it look like?"

"Look like?"

"Tell me what you saw."

Farlow's bright eyes fixed me. He paused, but if he had a question he didn't ask it.

"She's lying on her back. Just this little spot of blood on her chest; but God, her eyes are open." He stopped, licked his dry lips. "Him, he's maybe six feet away. Side of his head blown off. Right side; gun's in his right hand. What do you need this for?"

"It's the motions," I said. "What kind of gun?"

"Automatic. Didn't the police report tell you?"

"They won't let me see it."

"Jesus, don't tell Coe that. Is that normal?"

"Actually, yes. Usually you can get someone to tell you what's in it, but I rubbed the detective on the case the wrong way."

"Jim Sweeney? Everything rubs him the wrong way."

"How about Lomax?"

"You mean, Coe's theory? There's not a cop in Yonkers who wouldn't have thrown a party if they could make something stick to Lomax. Backing off wasn't something he knew how to do. They all hated him. But I don't think Sweeney any more than anyone else."

"Tell me about Lomax. Was he good?"

"Good?" Farlow looked puzzled; then he caught on. "Basketball, you mean? He was okay. He could wear better guys out, is what he could do. He'd get up for balls he couldn't reach and shoot shots he couldn't make, even after the bell. He was everywhere, both ends of the floor. Bastard never gave up."

"Did he have a future in the game?"

"Lomax? No." There was no doubt in Farlow's voice. "Eighteen years in this place, I've only seen two or three that could. Drum is the best. An NCAA school could make something out of him. Right school could get him to the NBA. Even the wrong school would get him out of here." I thought back to the concrete playground, to the eyes of the boys around the pizza-parlor table. Here, I had to admit, was a good place to get out of. "But Lomax? No."

"About the girlfriend," I said. "Had you heard anything about trouble between them?"

"No. She had a rep, you know. But all the guys seemed to think she'd quieted down since she took up with Lomax."

"Who'd she been with before?"

"Don't know."

"Do you know anyone with a reason to kill Lomax, or the girl?"

He sighed. "Look," he said. "These kids, they talk big, they look bad, but these are the ones who're trying. Coe, Drum, even Lomax—still in school, still trying. Like something could work out for them." He spread his hands wide, showing me the shabby office, the defeated building, the dead-end lives. "But me, all my life I've been a sucker. My job, the way I figure, is to do my damndest to help, whenever it looks like something might. That's your job too, Smith. You're here because it makes Coe feel like a man, avenging his buddy. That helps. But you're not going to find anything. There's nothing to find."

"Okay." I stood. I was warm; the air felt stuffy, old. I wanted to be outside, where the air moved, even with a cold edge. I wanted to be where everything wasn't already over. "Thanks. I'll come back if I need anything else."

"Sure," he answered. "And come see Drum play Saturday."

Seeing the family is always hard. People have a thousand different ways of responding to loss, of adjusting to their grief and the sudden new pattern of their lives. A prying stranger on a questionable mission is never welcome; there's no reason he should be.

Charles Lomax's family lived in a tan concrete project about half a mile from the high school. There were no corridors. The elevators went to outdoor walkways; the apartments opened off them. The door downstairs should have been locked, but the lock was broken, so I rode up to the third floor, picked my way through kids' bikes and folding beach chairs to the apartment at the end.

The wind and the air were cold as I waited for someone to answer my ring, but the view was good, and the apartments' front doors were painted cheerful colors. Here and there beyond the doors I could hear kids' voices yelling and the thump of music.

"Yes, can I help you?" The woman who opened the door was thin, tired-looking. She wore no makeup, and her wrists and collarbone were knobby under her shapeless sweater. Her hair, pulled back into a knot, was streaked with gray. It wasn't until I heard her clear soft voice that I realized she was probably younger than I was.

Electronic sirens came from the TV in the room behind her. She turned her head, raised her voice. "Darian; you turn that down."

The noise dropped a notch. The woman's eyes came back to me.

"Mrs. Lomax?" I said. "I'm Smith. Raymond Coe said you'd be expecting me."

"Raymond." She nodded slightly. "Come in."

She closed the door behind me. Warm cooking smells replaced the cold wind as we moved into the living room, where a boy of maybe ten and a girl a few years older were flopped on the sofa in front of the TV. An open door to the left led into a darkened bedroom. On the wall I glimpsed a basketball poster, Magic Johnson calling the play.

Charles Lomax's mother led me to a paper-strewn table in one corner of the living room, offered me a chair. "Claudine," she called to the girl on the sofa, "come and get your homework. Don't you leave your things around like that." The girl pushed herself reluctantly off the pillows. She looked me over with the dispassionate curiosity of children; then, fanning herself with her papers, she flopped onto the floor in front of the TV.

Sitting, Mrs. Lomax turned to me and waited, with the tired patience of a woman who's used to waiting.

"I'm sorry to bother you," I began. "But Raymond said you might answer some questions for me."

"What kind of questions?"

I looked over at the children, trying to judge whether the TV was loud enough to keep this discussion private. "Raymond doesn't think Charles killed himself, Mrs. Lomax."

"I know," she said simply. "He told me that. I think he just don't want to think it."

"Then you don't agree with him?"

She also looked to the children before she answered. "Raymond knew my boy better than I did. If he says someone else had more reason to kill Charles than Charles had, might be he's right. But I don't know." She shook her head slowly.

"Mrs. Lomax, did Charles have a gun?"

"I never saw one. I guess that don't mean he didn't have one."

A sudden sense of being watched made me glance toward the sofa again. My eyes caught the boy's; the girl was intent on the TV. The boy turned quickly back to the set, but not before Mrs. Lomax lifted her chin, straightened her shoulders. "Darian!" The boy didn't respond. "Darian," she said again, "you come over here."

Darian sullenly slipped off the sofa, came over, eyes watching the floor. His sister remained intent on the car chase on TV.

"Darian," his mother said, "Mr. Smith asked a question. Did you hear him?"

Hands in the pockets of his oversized jeans, the boy scowled and shrugged.

"He asked did your brother have a gun."

The boy shrugged again.

"Darian, if you know something you ain't saying, you're about to be in some serious kind of trouble. Did you ever see your brother with a gun?"

Darian kicked at a stray pencil, sent it rolling across the floor. "Yeah, I seen him."

I looked at Mrs. Lomax, then back to the boy. "Darian," I said, "do you know where he kept it?"

Without looking at me, Darian shook his head.

"You sure?" said his mother sharply.

" 'Course I'm sure."

Mrs. Lomax looked closely at him. "Darian, you know anything else you ain't saying?"

"No, 'course not," Darian growled.

"If I find you do . . ." she warned. "Okay, you go back and sit down."

Darian spun around, deposited himself on the sofa, arms hugging his knees.

I turned back to Mrs. Lomax. "Can I ask you about Ayisha?"

She shrugged.

"Did you like her?"

"Started out I did. She was smart to her friends, but she was polite to me. I remember her when she was small, too. Bright little thing. . . . But after I found out what she did, no, I didn't like her no more."

"Do you mean getting pregnant?" I asked.

She frowned, as though I were speaking a foreign language she was having trouble following. "Not the baby," she said. "The baby wasn't the problem. Though she didn't have no right to go and do that, after she knew. You got to see I blame her. She killed my son."

"Mrs. Lomax, I don't understand. According to the police, your son killed *her*, and himself."

"Oh, well, he pulled the trigger. But they was both already dead. And that innocent baby, too."

"I don't get it."

"Raymond didn't tell you?" Her eyes, fixed on mine, hardened with sudden understanding, and the realization that she was going to have to tell me herself. "She gave him AIDS."

Back on the winter street, I dropped a quarter in a pay phone, watched a newspaper skid down the walk, and waited for Raymond.

"Your buddy Charles was HIV positive," I said when he came on. "Did you know that?"

A short pause, then Raymond's voice, belligerent around the edges. "Yeah, I knew it."

"And his girlfriend, too."

"Uh-huh."

"Why didn't you tell me?"

"What difference do it make?"

"Sounds like a motive to me."

"What you talking about?"

"Hopelessness," I told him. "Fear. Not wanting to wait around to die. Not wanting to watch his son die."

"Oh, man!" Raymond snorted a laugh. "C didn't care. He say he never feel better. He tell me it gonna be years before he get sick. Not even gonna stop playing or nothing, even if it do piss Coach off. Just 'cause you got the virus don't mean you sick, you know," he pointed out with a touch of contempt. "You as ignorant as some of them 'round here."

"What does that mean?"

"Some of the homies, they nervous 'round C when they find out he got the virus. Talking about he shouldn't be coming 'round. Like Ash, don't want to play if C stay on the squad. I had to talk to that brother. But C just laugh. Say, some people ignorant. Don't pay them no mind, do what you be doing. Maybe someday I get sick, he say, but by then they have a cure."

"Goddamn, Raymond," I breathed. I stuck a cigarette in my mouth, lit it to keep from saying all the angry things I was thinking, things about youth, strength, arrogance not lasting, about consequences, about decisions closing doors behind you. I took a deep drag; it cleared my head. Not your business, Smith. Stick to what Raymond hired you for. "All right: Ayisha," I said. "Who else was she with?"

"Ayisha? She been with a lot of guys." Raymond paused. "You thinking some jealous dude gonna come after C and Ayisha 'cause they together?"

"It happens."

"Oh, man! Ain't no homie done this. Black man do it, it be straight up. Coming with this suicide bull, this some crazy white man. That why you here. See," he said, unexpectedly patient, trying to explain something to me, "C and me and the crew, we tight. Like . . ." He paused, reaching for an analogy I'd understand. "Like, you on a squad, maybe you don't like a brother, but you ain't gonna trip him when he got the ball. You got something to say to him, you go up in his face. You do what you gotta do, and you take what you gotta take."

Uh-huh, I thought. If life were like that.

"Okay, Raymond. I'll call you."

"Yeah, man. Later."

I turned up the collar of my jacket; the wind was blowing harder now, off the river. You could smell the water here, the openness of it, the movement and the distance. To me there had always been an offer in that, and a promise: Elsewhere, things are different. Somewhere, not here, lives are better; and the water connects that place and this.

That offer, that promise, probably didn't mean much to Raymond and his buddies. This was what they had, and, with a clear-eyed understanding I couldn't argue with, they knew what it meant.

Except Tyrell Drum, of course. "Offer" meant something different to him, but maybe not all that different: a chance to start again, to climb out of this and be somewhere else.

I started back to my car. I was cold and hungry, and down. I'd been buying into Raymond's theory. A conspiracy, the Power bringing down a black kid because they couldn't get him legally and they knew they could get away with it. I'd bought into it because I'd wanted to. Wanted to what, Smith? Be the righteous white man, the one on their side? The part of the Power working for them? Offering them justice, this once, so the world wouldn't look so bad to them? Or so it wouldn't look so bad to you? So you could sleep at night, having done your bit for the oppressed. Terrific.

But now it was different. Lomax had a motive, and a good one, if you asked me. Teenage swagger can plunge into despair fast. One bad blood test, one scary story about how it feels to die of AIDS: Something like that could have been enough. Especially if he really loved Ayisha. Especially if he already loved his son.

Running footsteps on the pavement behind me made me spin around, ready. The electricity in my skin subsided when I saw who it was.

"Mister, wait." The voice was small and breathless. Jacket open, pink backpack heavy over her arm, Claudine Lomax stopped on the sidewalk, caught her breath. She regarded me with suspicion.

"Zip your jacket," I said. "You'll freeze."

She glanced down, then did as she was told, pulling up her hood and tucking in her braids. She narrowed her eyes at me. "Mister, you a cop?"

"No," I said. "I'm a private detective."

"Why you come around asking questions like that?"

I thought for a moment. "Raymond asked me to. There were some things about Charles he wanted to know."

She bit her lower lip. "You know Raymond?"

"I'm working for him."

"Raymond was Charles friend."

"I know."

She nodded; that seemed to decide something for her. Looking me in the eye, she said, "You was asking Mama about Charles' gun."

"That's right. I was asking where he kept it. Do you know?"

"Yeah. And so do Darian. He gonna kill me when he find out it gone. But he just a *kid*. I been crazy worried about this ever since Charles . . ." She trailed off, looking away; then she lifted her head and straightened her shoulders, her mother's gesture. Putting her backpack on the ground with exaggerated care, she pulled a paper bag from it, thrust it at me. "Here."

"What's this?" It was heavy and hard and before I looked inside I knew the answer.

"I don't want it in the house. Mama don't know nothing about it. I don't want it where Darian can get it. He think he stepping like a man, gonna take care of business. Make me laugh, but he got this. Boys like that all the time, huh?"

"Yeah," I said. "Boys are like that all the time."

"I thought Charles took it with him. Meeting some guy at night like that. But he must have—he must have had another one, huh?"

"Maybe," I said carefully. "Claudine, what do you mean, 'meeting some guy at night'?"

"Charles don't like to go do his business without his piece. But maybe it wasn't business," she said thoughtfully. " 'Cause usually he tell Ayisha stay home when he taking care of business."

I asked her, "What guy was Charles meeting? Do you know?"

"Uh-uh. He just say he gotta go meet some guy, and Ayisha say she want to come. So Charles say okay, she could keep him company. Then he tell me I better be in bed when he get back, 'cause I got a math test the next day and he gonna beat my butt if I don't pass." In a small voice she added, "I passed, too."

I opened the bag, looked without taking the gun out. It was a long-barreled .32. "Claudine, how long had Charles had this?"

"About a year."

"How did you know he had it?"

"I hear him and Tyrell hiking on each other when he got it. Tyrell say it a old-fashioned, dumb kind of piece, slow as shit. Oh." She covered her mouth with her hand. "Sorry. But that what Tyrell say."

"It's okay, Claudine. What did Charles say?"

"He laugh. He say, by the time Tyrell get his fancy piece working, he gonna find out some guy with a old-fashioned dumb piece already blowed his head off, every time."

She stared at me under the yellow streetlights, a skinny twelve-year-old kid in a jacket not warm enough for a night like this.

"Claudine," I said, "did Charles and Tyrell argue a lot?"

"I hear them trash-talking all the time," she answered. "But I don't think nothing of it. Boys do that, don't they?"

"Yeah," I said. "They do."

Tyrell, then. Claudine told me where to go; I drove over. Tyrell Drum lived with his family in a run-down wood-frame house with a view of the river in the distance and the abandoned GM plant closer in. Towels were stuffed around the places where the warped windows wouldn't shut. The peeling paint had faded to a dull gray.

My knock was answered by a young boy with hooded eyes who left me to shut the door behind myself as I followed him in. From the room to the left I heard the canned laughter of a TV game show; from upstairs, the floor-shaking boom of a stereo. "Tyrell be in the basement," the boy told me, pointing without interest to a door under the stairs.

"Who's that?" a woman's voice called from above as I opened that door, headed down.

"Man to see Tyrell," the boy answered, and the household went about its business.

The basement was a weight room. The boiler and hot-water tank had been partitioned off into dimness. On this side of the partition were bright fluorescent lights, mats, weights, jump ropes. The smell of damp concrete mixed with the smell of sweat; the hum of the water heater was punctuated by grunts. Tyrell was on the bench, working his left biceps with what looked like sixty pounds. He lifted his eyes to me when I came down, but he didn't move his head out of position, and he finished his set. He was shirtless. His muscles were mounds under his glinting skin.

When he was done, he clanked the weights to the floor, ran a towel over his face.

"Yeah?" he said. He took in air in deep, controlled breaths.

"I want to talk about Ayisha," I said. "And Lomax."

"Go ahead." He kept his eyes on me for a few moments. Then, straightening, he picked up the weights with the other hand, started pumping. "Talk."

"She was your girl once, wasn't she?"

He smiled, didn't break his rhythm. "She been everyone's girl once."

"Maybe everyone didn't care."

"Maybe not." Nineteen, twenty. He put the weights down, left the bench, moved over to a Universal machine. He loaded it to 210, positioned himself, started working the big muscles in his thighs.

"But you did."

He stopped, looked at me. He held the weights in position while he spoke. "Yeah. I cared. I was so glad get rid of her and C at the same time I coulda went to Disney World." Slowly, in total control, he released the weights. He relaxed but didn't leave the seat, getting ready for his next set.

"What does that mean, get rid of them?"

Either he really had no idea what I was getting at, or he was a terrific actor. "Didn't have no time for her." Pump, breathe. "For him neither. C always got something going, some idea." Hold. Release, relax. "Always talking at you. Get me confused. Lost my whole last season because of him."

"The gas-station job was his idea?"

He gave me a sly grin. "Charges was dropped." He strained against the weights again. "C talking about, only way to make it be stealin' and de-alin'." Pump, release, pump. "I try that, ain't no good at it. Now Coach be telling me—" pump, breathe, "—say, I got a chance, a real chance. But I ain't got all the time in the world. Got to do it now, you understand?"

He looked at me. I didn't respond.

"C, he don't never shut up. Don't give a man no chance to think." Hold, release, relax. He swung his legs off the machine, picked up the towel again, wiped his face. "C don't like to think. Don't like it quiet. Dude get nervous if horns ain't honking and sirens going by." He laughed. "Surprise me him and Ayisha end up where they do."

"Meaning?"

"C don't never go to the park. They got nothing there but trees and birds, he say. What I'm gonna do with them?"

"His sister says he was going to meet someone that night."

Tyrell shrugged. He put his legs back in position, started another set.

"And that was it?" I said. "You were through with Lomax and his ideas? You weren't helping him take care of business anymore?"

This time he ran the set straight through before he answered. When he was done, he looked at me, breathing deeply.

"Coach be talking at me, I'm seeing college, the NBA, hotels and honeys and dudes carrying my suitcase. C up in my face, I'm looking at the inside of Rikers. Now what you think I'm gonna do?"

"And that was what you thought of when Lomax took up with Ayisha?"

"Damn sure. They both out my face now, I can take care my business."

"Your business," I mused. "You have a gun, right? An automatic. Can I see it?"

"What the hell for?"

"Lomax was a revolver man, wasn't he?" I asked conversationally. "He had a .32."

Tyrell shook his head in mild disbelief. "Man, Wyatt Earp coulda carried that piece."

"Why do you carry yours, Tyrell?"

"Now why the hell you think I carry mine?" He scowled. "You some kind of detective, can't figure out why a man got to be strapped 'round here?"

"Is it like that around here?" I asked softly. "A man has to have a gun?"

"God*damn!*" Tyrell exploded. "You think I like that? Watching my back just whenever I'm walking? Can't be going here, can't be going there, you got beef or your homies got beef and someone out to get you for it, go to school, everybody packing, just in case. You think I like that?" A sharp pulse throbbed in his temples; his eyes were shining and bitter. "Man, you can forget about it! I'm gonna make it, man. I'm gonna be all that. C, he got this idea, that idea, don't never think about what come next, what gonna happen 'cause of what he do. I tell him, you got Ayisha, now get out my face, leave me be. I got things to do."

His hard eyes locked on mine. The stereo, two floors up, sent down a pounding, recurring shudder that surrounded us.

"Tyrell," I said, "I'd like to see your gun."

For a moment, no reaction. Then a slow smile. He sauntered over to a padlocked steel box on the other side of the room. He ran the combination, creaked the top open, lifted out a .357 Coonan automatic. Wordlessly he handed it to me.

"How long have you had this?" I asked.

"Maybe a year."

"You sure you didn't just get it?"

He looked at me without an answer. Then, climbing the stairs to where he could reach the door, he opened it and yelled, "Shaun!" He paused; then again, "Shaun! Haul your ragged ass down here!"

The boy with the hooded eyes appeared in the doorway. "You calling me, Tyrell?" he asked tentatively.

Tyrell moved aside, motioned him downstairs. The boy, with an unsure look at me, started down. He walked like someone trying not to take up too much room.

"Shaun, this my piece?"

The boy looked at the gun I held out. "Yeah," he said. "I guess."

"Don't be guessing," Tyrell said. "This my piece, or ain't it?"

The boy gave Tyrell a nervous look, then peered more closely at the gun, still without touching it. "Yeah," he said. "It got that thing, here."

"What thing?" I asked. I looked where the boy pointed. A wide scrape marred the shiny stock.

Tyrell said, "Shaun, where that come from?"

Shaun answered without looking at Tyrell. "I dropped it."

"When?"

"Day you got it."

"What happen?"

"You mean, what you do?"

"Yeah."

The kid swallowed. "You be cursing at me and you smack me."

"Broke your nose, didn't I?"

The kid nodded.

"So you remember that day pretty good, huh?"

"Yeah."

"When was that?"

"About last year."

"You touched it since?"

"No, Tyrell." The kid looked up quickly.

"Good. Now get the hell out of here."

Shaun scuttled up the stairs and closed the door behind him.

"See?" Tyrell, smiling, took the gun from me. "My heat. Had it a year. How about that?"

"That's great, Tyrell," I said. "It must be great to be so tough. Two more questions. Where were you the night Lomax and Ayisha died?"

"Me?" Tyrell answered, still smiling, looking at the gun in his hand. "I was here."

"Can you prove that?"

"Depends. You could see if my two cousins remember. I went to bed early. Coach say discipline make the difference. You got to be able to do what need to be done, whether you want to or not."

"Uh-huh. You're a model citizen, Tyrell. One more thing. Did you know Lomax was HIV positive?"

Tyrell shrugged, locked his gun back in the box.

"Did it bother you? Friend of yours, with a disease like that?"

"Uh-uh," he said. "Don't got no time to worry about C. He got his troubles, I got mine."

I drove south, found Broadway, stopped at a tavern near the Bronx line. It was a half-empty place, the kind where dispirited old-timers nurse watery drinks and old grudges. In a scarred booth I lit a cigarette, worked on a Bud. I thought about Raymond, about the simple desire to do something, to try to help. About wanting justice, wanting what's right.

Of course, that meant so many things. To Sweeney it could mean taking a taunting, slippery drug dealer out of the picture. To Tyrell Drum it could mean getting rid of a smooth-talking, dangerous distraction. To Lomax himself, it might have meant having the last laugh: not cheating death, but choosing it, choosing your time and your way and your pain. None of these kids had ever had a lot of choices. This was one Lomax could have given himself.

But I didn't like it.

I had a couple of reasons, but the biggest was what Raymond had instinctively felt: Lomax wasn't the type.

I hadn't known Lomax, but the picture I'd gotten of him was consistent, no matter where it came from. Suicide is for when you give up. Lomax never gave up. Taunting cops. Trying to fast-talk Tyrell into his kind of life. Going up for balls he couldn't reach and shooting shots he couldn't make. That's what the coach said.

Even after the bell.

I lit another cigarette, seeing in my mind the asphalt playground in the fading light, watching the kids charge and jump, hearing the sound of the pounding ball and of their shouts. I saw one fall—I knew now it was Raymond—roll to his feet, try to shake off the sting of the scrape on his hand. Then, immediately, he was back in the game.

Even after the bell.

Suddenly I was cold. Suddenly I knew.

Wanting justice, wanting to help.

There was something else that could mean.

The next day, late afternoon again. The same gray river, the same cold wind.

It would have been pointless to go earlier. I would have been guessing, then, where to look; at this hour, I knew.

I'd made one phone call, to Sweeney, just to check what I already was sure of. He gave me what I wanted, and then he gave me a warning.

"I'm giving you this because I know you'll get it one way or another. But listen to me, Smith: Whatever road you're heading down, it's a dead end. The first complaint I hear, you'll get a look up close and personal at the smallest cell I can find. Do I make myself clear?"

I thanked him. The rest of the day, I worked on the Beethoven. It was getting better, slowly, slowly.

Yonkers West loomed darker, bigger, more hostile than before. At the front door I greeted the guard.

"You were here yesterday." He grinned. "Go on, tell me you're not a scout."

"Practice in session?" I asked.

"Uh-huh. Go on ahead. I'm sure Coach won't mind."

I wasn't. But I went.

The gym echoed with the thump of the basketball on the maple. The whole team, starters and bench, was out on the floor, practicing a complicated high-low post play. They were rotating through it, changing roles so that each man would understand it in his gut, know how each position felt; but in play, the point would be to get the ball to the big man. To Tyrell. As many times as the play was called, that's how it would end up. Tyrell shooting, Tyrell carrying the team's chances, carrying everyone's hopes.

Coach Farlow was standing on the sideline. He watched the play as they practiced it, following everyone's moves, but especially Tyrell's. I walked the short aisle between the bleachers, came and stood next to him.

He glanced at me, then turned his eyes back to his players. "Hi," he said. "Come to watch practice?"

"No," I said. "I came to talk."

He looked over at me again, then blew the whistle hanging around his neck. "All right, you guys!" The sweating players stopped, stood wiping their faces with their shirts, catching their breath. He rattled off two lists of names. Four guys headed for the sidelines; two teams formed on the court. Raymond, on one end of the floor, caught my eye. I nodded non-committally. The others looked my way, curious, but snapped their attention back to Farlow when he shouted again.

"Okay, let's go," he called. "Hawkins, take the tip. You and Ford call it."

One of the guys who'd been on his way off the court chased down the ball. Another trotted over to take the coach's whistle. The ball was tossed up in the center of the circle; the game began.

"You let them call games often?" I asked Farlow, as he stood beside me, following their movements with his sharp blue eyes.

"It's good for them. Forces them to see what's going on. Makes them take responsibility. Most of them get pretty good at it."

I said, "I'll bet Lomax wasn't."

"Lomax? He used to tick them all off. He'd call fouls on everyone, right and left. Just to throw his weight around."

"Did you stop him?"

Farlow watched Raymond go for a lay-up and miss it. Tyrell snatched the rebound, sank it easily. Farlow said, "The point is for them to find out what they're made of. What each other's made of. Doesn't help if I stop them."

"Besides," I said, "you couldn't stop Lomax, could you?"

This time his attention turned to me, stayed there. "What do you mean?"

"No one could ever stop Lomax from doing whatever he wanted. No matter how dangerous it was, to him or anyone else. He wouldn't stop playing, would he?"

"What?"

"That was it, wasn't it? He had AIDS and he wouldn't stop playing."

A whistle blew. Silence, then the slap of sneakers on wood, the thump of the ball as the game went on. Farlow's eyes stayed on me.

"You couldn't talk him out of it," I said. "You couldn't drop him, because he was too good. You'd have had to explain why, and the law protects people from that kind of thing. He'd have been back on the court and you'd have been out of a job.

"But you couldn't let him keep playing. That could have ruined everything."

Shouts came from the far end of the court as Tyrell stole a pass, broke down the floor, and dunked it before anyone from either team got near him.

"Could have ruined what?" Farlow asked in a tight, quiet voice.

"You're going through the motions," I said. "You know I have it. But all right, if you want to do that."

I watched the game, not Farlow, as I continued. "If Lomax had stayed on the team there might have been no season. Some of his own buddies didn't want to play with him. Guys get hurt in this game. They bleed, they spit, they sweat. The other guys were afraid.

"That's what happened to Magic Johnson: He couldn't keep playing after everyone knew he had AIDS because guys on the other teams were afraid to play against him. Magic had class. He didn't force it. He retired.

"But that wasn't Lomax's way, was it? Lomax felt fine and he was going to play. And if it got out he had AIDS his own teammates might have rebelled. So would the teams you play against. The whole season would have collapsed.

"That's what you were afraid of. Losing the season. Losing Drum's last chance."

We stared together down the court, to where a kid was getting set to take a foul shot.

"Lomax killed himself," Farlow said, harshly and slowly. "He took his gun and shot his girl and shot himself."

I said, "I have his gun."

"He had more than one. He bragged about it."

"Maybe," I said. "Maybe not. But the one I have is a revolver. Guys who like revolvers—I'm one—like them because they're dependable. You can bury a revolver in the mud for a month and it'll fire when you pull it

out. Lomax was like that about this gun. There've been times when I've
had to carry an automatic, and it always makes me nervous. Even if I owned
one, it's not the gun I'd take if I were going out to shoot myself."

Farlow said nothing, watching his kids, watching the game.

"Then there are the guys who like automatics," I said. "They're fast.
They're powerful. That's what you have, isn't it?"

"Me?" Farlow tried to laugh. "You're kidding. A gun?"

"An automatic," I said. "Same make and model as the one that killed
Lomax and Ayisha. Drum got me thinking about it. He said everyone
around here was packing. I started to wonder who 'everyone' was. I
checked your permit with Sweeney. He told me about it, and said if I
harassed you he'd throw me in jail. Does he know?"

The ball was knocked out of bounds, near us. The officials and players
organized themselves, resumed the game. The ball flew out again almost
immediately. Another whistle blew, play began again.

"No," Farlow said quietly.

We watched together in silence for a while. Some of the ball handling
was sloppy, but the plays were smart, and every player played flat out,
giving the game everything he had.

"Not every coach can get this from his players," I said.

Farlow asked, "How did you know?"

"Little things. They all clicked together. The gun. The fact that Lomax
didn't like the park."

"Didn't like the park?" Farlow said. "A guy might pick a place he doesn't
like, to die in."

"Sure. But his coach wouldn't think to go looking for him there, unless
he had some reason to think he might be there."

Farlow didn't answer. He glanced at the clock on the gym wall; then he
stepped onto the court, clapped his hands, and bellowed, "All right, you
guys! Looking good. Showers! Stay and wait. I'll talk to you afterwards."

The kid with the whistle brought it back to the coach; the kid with the
ball sent it Farlow's way with a bounce pass. Raymond raised his eyebrows
as he went by on his way to the locker room. I shook my head.

Farlow watched them go. When the door swung shut behind them he
stayed unmoving, as though he were still watching, still seeing something.

"One kid," he said, not talking to me. "One chance. Year after year, you
tear your heart out for these kids and they end up in the gutter. Then you
get one kid with a way out, one chance. Drum's ready, but he's weak. Not
physically. But he can't keep his head in the game. If he loses this season
too, there'll be nothing left. He'll hold up another damn gas station, or
something. It has to be now."

"Lomax was eighteen," I said. "Ayisha was seventeen. She was pregnant."

"They were dead!" The coach's eyes flashed. "They were dead already. How many years do you think they were going to have? Baby born with AIDS, it wouldn't live through Drum's pro career."

"You did them a favor?"

He flinched. "No." His voice dropped. "That's not what I mean. But Drum—so many people are waiting for this, Smith. And they were already dead."

I needed a cigarette. I lit one up; the coach didn't try to stop me.

"You asked him to meet you at the park?"

He nodded. "In this weather, there's no one there. I knew he didn't like it there, but . . ." He didn't finish.

"But you were the coach."

"I knew Lomax. He'd never let me see he was nervous. Afraid. It never occurred to me he'd bring her along."

"For company," I told him. "That's what his little sister said."

"I almost didn't—didn't do it, when I saw she was there. I tried one more time to talk him out of it. Told him I'd get his academic grades raised so he'd be sure to graduate. Told him I'd get him a job. Told him Drum needed him to quit."

"What did he say?"

The coach looked across the gym. "He said if scouts were coming down to look at Drum, maybe they were interested in point guards, too."

He brought his eyes back to me. "It was the only way, Smith."

"No," I said.

I smoked my cigarette. Farlow looked down at his hands, tough with years of balls and blackboards.

"What are you going to do?" he asked. "Will you tell Sweeney?"

"Sweeney won't hear it. I have no hard evidence. To him this case is closed."

"Then what?" he asked. His eyes lit faintly with something like hope.

I looked toward the door the players had disappeared through. "I have a client," I said.

"You'll tell Coe?"

I crushed the cigarette against the stands, dropped the butt back in the pack. "Or you will."

We stood together, wordless. "You know what's the worst part?" he finally said.

"What?"

"Coe's twice the man the rest of them are. Drum's a bully, Lomax was a creep. Ash is a coward. But Coe, he's tough but not mean. He can tell right from wrong and he doesn't let his ego get in the way. But there's nothing I can do for him. I can't help him, Smith. But I can help Drum."

"Yesterday," I said, "you told me I was here because avenging his buddy made Raymond feel like a man. And that that helped."

He stared at me. He made a motion toward the door where the players had gone, but he stopped.

"I'll wait for Raymond to call me," I said. "I'll give him a few days. Then I'll call him."

I looked once more around the gym, then walked the short aisle between the stands, leaving the coach behind.

I was at the piano the next afternoon when Raymond called. No small talk: "Coach told me," he said.

I shut the keyboard, pulled a cigarette from my pocket. "What did you do?"

"First, I couldn't believe it. Stared at him like an idiot. Coach, man! You know?"

I did know; I said nothing.

"Then I feel like killing him."

I held my breath. "But?"

"But I hear C in my head," Raymond said. "Laughing. 'What so damn funny, homey?' I ask him. 'This the guy burned you.' C keep laughing, in my head. He say, 'For Tyrell, brother? This about the funniest thing ever.' Just laughing and laughing."

"What did you do?"

"Slammed out of there, to go and think. See, I was stuck. What you gonna do, Ray, I be asking myself. Go to the cops? Give me a break."

"If you want to do that," I said, "I'll see it through with you."

"No," he said. "Ain't my way. Another thing, I could do Coach myself; but that ain't my way neither. So what I'm gonna do, just let him walk away? He done my main man; got to pay for that. Got to pay. But in my head, C just laughing. 'For Tyrell, man?' And then I know what he mean. And I know I don't got to do nothing."

"Why not?" I asked.

" 'Cause Tyrell, he been with Ayisha before C."

It took a second, then it hit.

"Jesus," I said.

"Yeah," Raymond agreed. "What Coach done, he done to get Tyrell his shot. But Tyrell ain't gonna have no shot."

No shot. No pro career, no college years. Two murders. A lifetime of hard-won trust, everything thrown away for nothing. Tyrell might be able to avoid going public, might be able to keep his mouth shut the way Lomax hadn't; people might not know, at first. But the virus was inexorable. It would get Tyrell before Tyrell had a chance to make everyone's dreams come true.

"Raymond," I said, "I'm sorry."

"Man," he said, "so am I."

There wasn't anything more. I told Raymond to keep in touch; he laughed shortly and we both knew why. When we hung up I stood at the window for a while. After the sky turned from purple to gray, after the promise faded, I pulled on my jacket, went over to the 4th Street courts, and watched the kids play basketball under the lights.

THE CARER

Ruth Rendell

Ruth Rendell is the winner of three Edgar Allan Poe Awards, three Gold Dagger Awards, and nominations and other honors too numerous to mention. But all these distinctions pale beside the CBE (Commander of the Order of the British Empire) she was awarded in 1996. In 1997, she was made a life peer. Now entitled to sit in Britain's House of Lords, which it is said she attends on a regular basis, the author continues to write and to achieve the highest level of literary excellence. To many, Ruth Rendell is as much a mainstream novelist as a crime writer. Although her longest running series features a police chief inspector, Reg Wexford, the exploration of relationships between the characters always forms as important a part of her stories as does the mystery itself. The author's novels under the pseudonym Barbara Vine are even more explicitly a probing of relationships and psychology than the Wexford novels. There is perhaps no one else currently writing who is on a par with Rendell in the realm of psychological suspense. Amazingly, she appears to be able to engage readers in the inner lives of her characters as easily in the few pages that comprise a short story as in a full-length novel.

THE HOUSE AND the people were new to her. They had given her a key, as most did. Angela had a cat to feed and a rubber plant to water. These tasks done, she went upstairs, feeling excited, and into the bedroom where she supposed they slept.

They had left it very tidy, the bed made with the covers drawn tight, everything on the dressing table neatly arranged. She opened the cupboards and had a look at their clothes. Then she examined the contents of the dressing-table drawers. A box of jewellery, scarves, handkerchiefs that no one used anymore. Another drawer was full of face creams and cosmetics. In the last one was a bundle of letters, tied up with pink ribbon. Angela untied the ribbon and read the letters which were from Nigel to Maria, the people who lived here, love letters written before they were married, full of endearments, pet names, and promises of what he would do to her next time they met and how he expected she would respond.

She read them again before tying the ribbon round them and putting them back. Letters were a treat; she rarely came upon any in her explorations of other people's houses. Letters, like so many other things, had gone out of fashion. She went downstairs again, repeating under her breath some of the phrases Nigel had written and savouring them.

In the street where she lived Angela was much in demand as babysitter, dog-walker, cat-feeder, and general carer. Her clients, as she called them, thought her absolutely reliable and trustworthy. No one had ever suspected that she explored their houses while alone in them. After all, it had never occurred to Peter and Louise to place hairs across drawer handles; Elizabeth would hardly have known how to examine objects for fingerprints; Miriam and George were not observant people. Besides, they trusted her.

Angela lived alone in the house that had been her parents' and spent one weekend a month staying with her aunt in the Cotswolds, and while there she went to the Methodist church on Sunday. She had a job in the bank half a mile away. Once a year she and another single woman she had met at work went to Torquay or Bournemouth for a fortnight's holiday. She had never been out with a man; she never met any men except the ones in her street who were married or living with a partner. She had no real friends. She knitted, she read a lot, she slept ten hours a night.

Sometimes she asked herself how she had come to this way of living, why had her life not followed the pattern of other women's, why had it been without adventure or even event, but she could only answer that this was the way it had happened. Gradually it had happened, without her seeing an alternative or knowing how to stop its inexorable progress to what it had become. Until, that is, Humphrey asked her to feed the cat while he was away, and from that beginning she built up her business.

She had keys to eleven houses. Caring for them, their owners' children, elderly parents, pets, and plants, had become her only paid employment, for, thankful to do so at last, she had given up her job. At first, performing these tasks punctually and efficiently had been enough—the gratitude she received and the payment. She liked her neighbours' dependence on her. She had become indispensable and that gave her pleasure. But after a time she had grown restless sitting in John and Julia's living room with a sleeping baby upstairs, she had felt frustrated as she locked Humphrey's door and went home after feeding the cat. There should be something more, though more what? One night, when Diana's baby cried and she had been in to quieten it, her footsteps, as if independently of her will, took her along the passage into its parents' bedroom. And so it began.

The contents of cupboards and drawers, the bank statements and bills, Louise's diary—that was her most prized find—Ken's certificates, Miriam's diplomas, Peter's prospectuses, Diana's holiday snapshots, all this showed her what life was. That it was the life of other people and not hers did not much trouble her. It educated her. Searching for it, finding new aspects of it, additions to what had been examined and learned before, was something to look forward to. There had not been much looking forward in her existence, or much looking back, come to that.

The neighbour who had written the love letters had recently moved into the house four doors down. Angela was recommended to him and his wife by Rose and Ken next door.

"If you'd like to let me have a key," Angela had said, "it will be quite safe with me." She made the little joke she always made. "I keep all the keys under lock and key."

"We're away quite a lot," said Maria, and Nigel said:

"It would be a load off our minds if we could rely on you to feed Absalom."

When her business first started Angela conducted her investigations of someone else's property only when legitimately there with a duty to perform. But after a while she became bolder and entered a house whenever the fancy took her. She would watch to see when her neighbours went out. Most of them were out at work all day anyway. It was true that all the keys were kept locked up. They were in a strongbox, each one labelled. Angela always asked for the back-door key. She said it was more convenient if there was a pet to be fed and perhaps exercised. What she didn't say was that you were less likely to be seen entering a house by the back door than the front.

The principal bedroom at Nigel and Maria's had been thoroughly explored on her first visit. But only that one bedroom. Once, greedy for sensation, during a single two-hour duty at John and Julia's she had searched every room, but since then she had learned restraint. It was something to dread, that the treasures in all the houses she had keys to might become exhausted, every secret laid bare, her goldmines overworked and left barren. So she had left the desk in Maria's living room for another time, though it had been almost more than she could bear, seeing it there, virgin so to speak, inviolate. She had left the desk untouched and all the cupboards and filing cabinets unplundered in the study they had made out of the third bedroom.

Maria went away one evening. Nigel told Angela she had gone and he would be joining her in a day or two. She noticed he stayed away from work, and she waited for him to call and ask her to feed Absalom in his absence. He never came. Angela was much occupied with babysitting for Peter and Louise, driving Elizabeth's mother to the hospital, letting in the meter man and the plumber for Miriam and George, and taking Humphrey's cat to the vet, but she had time to wonder why he hadn't asked.

Returning home from watering Julia's peperomias, she met Nigel unlocking his car. He had Absalom with him in a wicker basket.

"Going away tonight?" Angela said hopefully.

"I shall be joining Maria. We thought we'd try taking Absalom with us this time, so we shan't require your kind services. But I expect you've plenty to do, haven't you?"

Thinking of the evening ahead, Angela said she had. She was almost as excited as on the day she began reading Louise's diary. Angela gave it an hour after Nigel's car had gone. She took the key out of the strongbox and let herself into the house. A happy two hours were spent in a search of the desk, and although it uncovered no more love letters, it did disclose several final demands for payment of bills, an angry note from George complaining about Absalom's behaviour in his garden, and, best of all, an anonymous letter.

This letter was printed in ink and suggested that Maria had been having an affair with someone called William. Angela thought about this and wondered what it would be like, having an affair when you were married, that is, and she wondered what being married was like anyway, and whether it was William's wife or girlfriend who had written the letter. She put everything back in the desk just as she had found it, being careful not to tidy up.

The rooms upstairs she left for next day. It was a Friday and she was due to drive to Auntie Joan's for the weekend that evening, but first she had Elizabeth's dogs to walk morning and afternoon and Elizabeth's mother to fetch from the hospital, the electrician to let in for Rose and Ken, and Louise's little girl to meet from school. There were two hours to spare between coming back from the hospital and fetching Alexandra. Taking care not to be seen by the electrician, putting in a new point next-door in the back room, Angela let herself into Nigel and Maria's house.

Overnight, she had felt rather nervous about that desk and the first thing she did was check that everything was back in place. An examination quickly reassured her that she had accurately replicated its untidiness. Then she went upstairs and along the passage to the study. Louise's diary notwithstanding, Maria and Nigel's house promised to afford her the richest seam of treasure she had yet encountered. And who knew what would be behind this door in the cupboards and the filing cabinets? More love letters, perhaps, hers to him this time, more insinuations of Maria's infidelity, more unpaid bills, even something pointing to illegality or crime.

Angela opened the door. She took a step into the room, then a step backwards, uttering a small scream she would have suppressed if she could. Maria lay on the floor, wearing a nightdress, her long hair loose and spread out. There was a large brown stain that must have been blood on the front of her nightdress and unmistakable blood on the floor around her. Angela stood still for what seemed a very long time, holding her hand over her mouth. She forced herself to advance upon Maria and touch her. It was her forehead she touched, white as marble. Her fingertip encountered icy coldness and she pulled it away with a shudder. Maria's dead eyes looked at her, round and blue like marbles.

Angela went quickly downstairs. She was trembling all over. She let herself out of the back door, locked the door, and put the key through the letter box at the front. It somehow seemed essential to her not to have that key in her possession.

She went home and packed a bag, found her car keys. Fetching Alexandra was forgotten, and so were Elizabeth's dogs. Angela got into her car and drove off northwards, exceeding the speed limit within the first five minutes. She thought she would stay at least a fortnight with Auntie Joan. Perhaps she would never come back at all. If this was life, they could keep it. It was death, too.

THE SAFEST LITTLE TOWN IN TEXAS

Jeremiah Healy

Jeremiah Healy is one of those writers who discover at the very outset of their career a character appealing enough to be used in novel after novel. Knowing a good thing when he'd created it, Healy stuck exclusively to his debut character, private eye John Francis Cuddy, over the course of fifteen years and more than a dozen books, until the spring of 1999 when his non-series suspense thriller The Stalking of Sheilah Quinn *was released. The popular appeal and critical acclaim of the Cuddy tales, which have earned the author a Shamus Award and ten Shamus Award nominations, derives from their superb plotting, snappy prose and dialogue, and their depiction of a character who manages to be tough and sensitive at the same time. The author, a recently retired law professor, says he often uses his fiction to explore "legal issues that fall between the cracks of our justice system."*

ALONE IN THE stolen '92 Ford, Polk Greshen checked the rearview mirror. No cars behind him, period, much less one with bubble-lights on its roof. First good omen since he'd killed that gas-station attendant over the Oklahoma line.

"Damn-fool beaner," thought Polk, focusing back on the road in front of him. "I tell him, 'All right, I'll be needing your cash,' and he makes like, '*Señor, no hablo* the English.' Only the beaner'd have to be blind not to see the nine-millimeter in my hand, me waving it at the register. What'd he think I meant? But no, the man has to be a hero, try for the tire iron he had on a shelf behind some oil cans. Well, now he ain't never gonna '*hablo* the English.' Or anything else, far as that goes."

Polk had boosted the Ford from a movie-house parking lot five miles from the station, so he figured it was still a pretty safe vehicle in terms of being connected to the killing. Radio didn't work, but the air did—praise the Lord. Also, he'd found a set of keys under the driver's seat that fit.

"Damn-fool owner, might 's well leave them sticking in the ignition." Only thing was, the Oklahoma police could have the license plate on their hot list by now, and Polk was pretty sure those computer things could run the tags on any car they stopped.

So after killing the attendant, Polk had driven real conservative-like, getting on U.S. 283 south and crossing the Red River into Texas north of Vernon. Maybe an Oklahoma stolen car wouldn't get onto the hot list for Texas, and he could always hole up with a cousin lived just outside Hobbs, New Mexico, which should be due southwest from where he was right now. "About got enough money from the beaner's till to see me through gas and food, long's I don't go hog-wild on things." Polk also figured it was smart to stick to the smaller roads, and so far he'd been right.

Until the Ford's goddamn oil light came on.

Polk used the heel of his hand to wham at the light, but that didn't do any good. Pulling over to the side of the road, he got out. The heat was like standing on top of a griddle, but Polk didn't plan to be in it long. He went to the trunk of the car, using the key that didn't fit the ignition to open the lid. A rat-eared blanket, two wrenches, and . . . a bird cage? Would you look at that.

But no oil. Figures.

Polk slammed down the lid. "Should of stole some from that beaner back at the gas station. It was an omen, for sure, him having that tire iron by the cans there."

The air frying his lungs, Polk tried to guesstimate where he was at. Hour or more east of Lubbock, probably. But he hadn't seen a soul along the road, not a house, nothing for quite a while. Looking west, there seemed to be some kind of signpost only half a mile on.

Back behind the wheel, Polk drove toward the signpost. Sure enough, it marked a small intersection, the arrow aiming north with "Bibby, 2 miles." Better bet than taking a chance on civilization suddenly sprouting up in front of him.

Muttering under his breath at the oil light, Polk Greshen turned right.

"Well, well. Do you believe it?"

Polk expected Bibby to be no more than a crossroads, lucky to have a general store with a pump outside it. Instead, just about the time he could make out a clump of buildings in the distance, there was this real nice mini-billboard on the side of the road.

WELCOME TO BIBBY
THE SAFEST LITTLE TOWN IN TEXAS
POP. 327

Another favorable impression as he approached the first few buildings
along the main street. Old and mostly wood, except for the bank, which
was yellow brick. But everything all spruced up with new paint and bright
little signs like BIBBY CAFE and COLE'S HARDWARE and so on. Good
omen, for a change. All the way at the end of the street, Polk thought he
could see POLICE on a bigger sign with something else writ smaller beneath it, but it was too far away to read. "Don't think I'll be visiting that
end of town, anyway, no-thank-you-sir."

There was almost no vehicle traffic, only a couple of people walking
heat-slow past the storefronts. Fortunately, in the next block Polk spotted
a filling station—not a national company, just "GAS"—but it had a couple
of service bays. He pulled into the station near the pumps, and a mechanic
came out from one of the bays, wiping grease off his hands with a rag.

The man was dressed in a white T-shirt and denim overalls, all kinds of
things sagging in his pockets. Polk thought he must be just about dying
from the temperature, though the mechanic gave no notice of it walking
over to the Ford.

Polk glanced down at his own clothes. New, tooled boots; sharp, stone-
washed jeans; and a Led Zeppelin tank-top from that Tulsa rockshop, the
nine millimeter barely a lump where he'd stuck it in his belt under the top.
"I'll probably look mighty city to these folks."

The man's overalls had a name patch on the left breast. "Sid," was what
it said.

Without turning off the engine, Polk looked at him. "Sid, I'll be needing
some oil."

A nod. "What weight you got in her now?"

Polk could hot-wire a car, but he didn't ever have one long enough to
think of such things. "Not sure about that."

Another nod. "Your light come on, did it?"

"About three miles back, give or take."

Sid nodded again. "Let me take a look under her."

Polk had run some cons himself in the past, so he sure could see one
coming at him now. He got out of the Ford, trying not to breathe the heat
too deeply, and squatted down as Sid did about the sorriest push-up you've
ever seen, face staring under the chassis.

"See that there?"

Polk used his hand to brace himself, nearly burning the skin right off the palm on Sid's hot asphalt. Following the mechanic's pointing finger, he could see the kind of drip-drip-drip you get from an old faucet. Only it wasn't water.

"Oil, huh?"

"That's what they call it." Sid got to his feet like a lame bear. "I'm gonna have to put her up on the rack, try and plug the leak."

"How much?"

"Won't know that till I get her up there."

Polk figured he could kiss what was left of the beaner's money good-bye. "How long, then?"

A sweep of the hand toward the other cars in the lot. "Got four ahead of you."

Polk considered grabbing this hick by the straps on his overalls, shaking him till he thought some about changing his priorities. But Polk was a wanted man driving a stolen car, and the less attention he drew, the better.

"Any place to eat?"

"Cafe. You must've passed her a few blocks back, way you were driving."

"Thanks." Saying it kind of flat.

As Polk began to walk, he adjusted the gun in his belt for strolling instead of driving. Passing two of the cars ahead of him for servicing, he automatically glanced at their steering wheels. Both had their keys still in the ignition.

Despite the temperature, Polk smiled, talking softly to himself. "Well, well. Old Sid tries to hold me up, leastways I can get myself some substitute transportation."

Heading south toward the cafe, he noticed keys in the ignition of most every parked car on his side of the street and felt his smile getting wider. "My kind of town, Bibby is."

"Afternoon."

As the screened door slapped closed behind him, Polk looked at the woman who'd spoken. She was dressed in one of those old-fashioned waitress outfits and a bulky apron. Chubby, with brassy hair and too much makeup, her nametag read "Lurlene." Polk thought about how convenient it was, everybody sporting their names for him, but he wondered how come they needed to, since in a town of 327, you'd think everybody would know each other. "Maybe their way of remembering who they are themselves," thought Polk, and laughed.

"What's so funny," said Lurlene. Not sassy, just curious-like.

"Nothing." Polk slid onto one of the chrome stools, resting his elbows on the Formica counter under a ceiling fan that might have been put up there in the year one. He glanced around the cafe. Old skinny couple—wearing sweaters, dear Lord—in one of the booths, young momma and her yard-ape in another. Four stools away, the only other customer at the counter was a fat fart pushing sixty, his rump overhanging the seat cushion, a fraying straw Stetson angled back on his head.

"Get you something?"

Polk looked at Lurlene. "Coffee. And a menu."

She gave him a piece of orange paper, the items hand-writ on it, then poured some coffee from a pot into a white porcelain cup with a million little cracks on its surface, like a spider web.

"Lurlene, honey?" said the fat fart.

"Yes, Chief?"

Polk froze as she moved with the coffee pot to the other end of the counter. Then Polk, as casual as he could, kind of scoped out the man who might be a police.

Talking to Lurlene like she was a schoolgirl, but wanting to change a twenty. Polk noticed there was no gun on his belt. Maybe the fire chief? Un-unh. As the fat fart turned, Polk could see a peace officer's badge on the khaki shirt. Now what kind of damn fool wears a badge without toting something to back it up?

Lurlene came toward Polk, pawing under the counter for what turned out to be her pocketbook. Opening it, she shook her head. "Sorry, Chief. And I know there's not enough in the register yet."

Polk looked up at the clock on the wall. 1:15 in the P.M. Must do one hell of a business, not enough change in the drawer after lunchtime to so much as cash a twenty. Briefly, he thought about helping the lawman out, and almost laughed again.

"Well," said the chief, "I'll just ask Mary over to the bank. Be right back."

Polk watched the fat fart take about thirty seconds to make it off his stool and waddle out the door toward the yellow-brick building across the street.

Lurlene spoke to the back of Polk's head. "Decide on what you'll be having?"

He turned his face toward her. "Hamburger, medium. Fries."

"You got it."

Lurlene went through a swinging door, and he could hear her voice repeating his order. Left her pocketbook open on the counter, in plain view and an arm's reach from a total stranger.

When the waitress came back out, Polk said, "Hey, you forgot something here."

"What else you want?" Again not sassy, now just confused.

"It's not what I want." Polk gestured, feeling charitable. "Your pocket-book. Shouldn't be leaving it out like that."

Lurlene laughed and waved him off. "Oh, that's all right. Bibby's the safest little town in Texas."

Polk thought about the billboard he'd seen. "That why your police don't even carry a gun?"

"The chief? Well, he don't really need to."

"Kind of odd, don't you think?"

"Not for Bibby. The chief used to be the guard, over to our bank? At least until the bank realized it didn't really need a guard. Seemed a shame to have Harry—that's his name, 'Harry'—be out of a job, so we kind of voted him police chief. Only he don't have that much chiefing to do, since he don't have any officers under him. But somebody's got to process the paperwork those folks over to Austin make us file, and that keeps Harry just real busy."

Polk sipped his coffee, but he was really tasting all this information. A police chief without a gun or other officers, a bank without a guard. And himself, Polk Greshen, sitting here with a broke-down stolen car, a passing need for money, and a nine mil' under his tank-top. Omens. Omens just everywhere you looked.

He said, "Sounds like y'all don't have much crime around here."

"None, really. Not since we also voted to—"

At which point the cafe door slapped shut again, and fat-fart Harry the Chief returned to the counter, easing his haunches down on the stool he'd left and allowing as how he could use maybe one more cup of Lurlene's coffee before heading back to the office.

Which sounded to Polk like fine timing. Yes, fine timing indeed.

Polk was kind of clock-watching. Ten minutes since the chief left the cafe and started walking up the street toward his station. The hamburger and fries Lurlene had brought weren't half bad, though Polk realized his immediate prospects just might've brightened the meal some.

The young momma and her kid got up to leave their booth, the old skinny couple in their sweaters having teetered out a little before that. Polk decided he didn't really want to be Lurlene's only customer in the cafe. You spend too much time alone with a person, they tend to remember your face that much better.

What Polk figured: I finish up here, cross the street, and slip into the bank. With any luck at all, won't be no crowd there, given how dead old Bibby seems to be. I flash the nine mil' under some teller's nose, then take what they got in cash and run to Sid's garage. Only a few blocks, and either he's got the Ford ready, or I boost one of the others. Hell, this town, I could jump in practically any car parked along the street, find the keys still in the ignition.

"More coffee?"

He looked up at Lurlene, poised with the pot over his cup.

"Just the check."

After leaving a dollar tip—right generous, too—Polk got off his stool and ambled outside, not wanting to appear like he was in a hurry just yet. The young momma and her kid drove by in a Chevy pickup heavy on the primer, but the old skinny couple were sitting on a shaded bench a block toward the gas station. The woman jawing away, the man looking to be falling asleep. "Can't hardly blame him," thought Polk.

The rest of the street was almost deserted, Polk having to wait for only one car to go by before crossing to the bank. He entered the double doors, and it was dark enough inside that he had to let his eyes adjust some to the room.

High ceiling, with polished mahogany along the walls. The business counter was made of the same, three of those old-fashioned teller's cages like . . . like the bird-thing he'd found in the trunk of the Ford. Another omen.

One colored girl, maybe twenty or so, stood behind the cage closest to the doors. There was nobody else in the place, and no sound, either.

"Well, well," thought Polk. "All by herself for true, and not even bulletproof glass between us."

He walked up to the girl's cage, a little placard with "MARY" on the counter. Goddamn, but this is one well-identified town—Polk remembering Chief Harry saying that name back at the cafe.

"Help you, sir?"

Polk grinned, reaching under his tank-top. "You surely can, Miss Mary. I'll be needing some cash for my friend here."

The girl looked down at his side of the counter as Polk brought the gun's muzzle up, pointed dead center on her chest.

"You getting the picture, Miss Mary?"

"Yessir."

Said it real calm. Had to give her credit, didn't seem even a bitty-bit scared.

"All your money, now. And don't be pushing no alarm buttons, neither."

"We don't have none to push."

Polk couldn't believe this town. Wished he'd found it sooner in his life. "The money, Miss Mary."

He watched as she opened a cash drawer and started stacking bills in front of him. Polk wasn't the best at doing sums real quick, but he could see lots of twenties and even some fifties in with the others. Might not have to hole-up with his cousin in New Mexico after all.

The girl stopped, closing the drawer.

"That it?" said Polk.

"Less'n you want the coins, too."

He grinned. Genuine brave, this Miss Mary. "No, they'd just slow me down." He gathered the cash, stuffing it into the pockets of his jeans. "Now, I'm gonna walk through your door there, and if you just sit tight and don't do nothing stupid, my partner out front won't have to shoot you. Got all that?"

"Yessir."

"Good. Pleasure doing business with you, Miss Mary."

Polk backed up a few steps, then turned to open the door, sticking the nine mil' back under his shirt.

From behind him, Mary said, "Sir?"

Polk turned back to see her leveling a pistol at him.

He barely had time to duck before the first round went off, deafening him and grazing his upper left arm, the flesh feeling like it bumped into a branding iron. Yowling, Polk barged through the doors just as a second round from Mary's pistol lodged in the jamb next to his head.

Outside, Polk drew his own weapon, looking up to see Lurlene at the door of the cafe, the old skinny couple rousting themselves from their bench. No problem, once I . . .

Out of the corner of his eye, Polk saw Lurlene's hand come up from the bulging apron, a small black—Goddamn, no!

Her first bullet whistled past his shoulder as he broke into a loose-limbed jog, the boots not really made for it, his legs feeling like they were taking an awful long time to get the message from his brain. He'd gotten about abreast of the old skinny couple when—

No. No, this can't be.

The man was down on one knee, sighting a long-barreled revolver, while the woman had a cigarette lighter in her—Wait, a derringer?

They opened up on him, too, and Polk felt something like a hammer whack him in the right thigh. He nearly fell, afraid to look down and maybe see his own—No, can't think like that. Got to get the car.

After what seemed to Polk like a mile of running through sand, Sid was there, just ahead, by one of his gas pumps. Closing the driver's door of the Ford, as though he'd just rolled it out from the bay.

Already gasping for breath, Polk began waving to him with the nine mil'. "Sid, Sid . . ."

The mechanic waved back with one hand, dipping the other into one of the sagging pockets in his overalls and drawing a snub-nose belly-gun.

"No!" Polk knew he was screaming as he dived to the pavement, the bullets whining in ricochet around him.

Struggling back to his feet, the pain in his thigh growing bad—real bad—Polk willed himself up the street. He could hear the sound of people coming after him, different kinds of shoes making different kinds of noises. "The police . . ." he thought. "I make it . . . to the station . . . Chief Harry . . . stop this . . . crazy . . ."

Hobbling like a man in a three-legged race, Polk got to within fifty feet of sanctuary when he felt something hit him in the back. More like a baseball bat than a hammer this time, and he pitched forward hard, his weapon clattering a body-length away from his hand.

The shoe sounds behind him were getting closer.

With the last of his strength, Polk managed to lift his face off the pavement, see Chief Harry standing with fists on his hips in the station's doorway. The smaller lettering under "POLICE" arced above the peace officer's head.

The sign read:

Bibby, Texas
Where every citizen has a permit to carry.

Polk Greshen thought about all the paperwork that might cause, and why Chief Harry might be too busy to worry about toting a gun himself.

BECAUSE IT WAS THERE

Peter Lovesey

Gold and Silver Dagger Awards, an Ellery Queen's Mystery Magazine *Readers Award, an Anthony Award, and the Mystery Writers of America's Golden Mysteries Short Story Prize are just a few of the plaudits that come to mind with the name Peter Lovesey. Seldom has a writer been so consistently acclaimed, and it all began with his deciding to try his hand at a novel-writing contest carrying a thousand-pound prize. That was thirty years ago: Lovesey entered, won the prize, and soon saw his novel, the first in his Victorian series starring Sergeant Cribb, in print. The Cribb adventures have now come to an end, and the author is concentrating much of his effort on a series of contemporary police mysteries featuring Inspector Peter Diamond. By the time the Cribb series had completed its run, it had been adapted for television, with Lovesey writing many of the scripts, and had created for its author a worldwide reputation as a writer with wit, style, and the ability to carry off complex plots. Readers in search of more historical mysteries by Lovesey will be glad to know that he still writes about Victorian England in a series centered on Bertie, the Prince of Wales.*

THEY ARE DEAD now, all three. Professor Patrick Storm, the last of them, went in August, aged eighty-two. Of pneumonia. The obituary writers gave him the send-off he deserved, crediting him with the inspiration and the dynamism that got the new theatre built at Cambridge. The tributes were blessedly free of the snide remarks that are almost obligatory two-thirds of the way into most of the obits you read—"not over-concerned about the state of his dress" or "borrowing from friends was an art he brought to perfection." No such smears for Patrick Storm. He was a decent man, through and through. A murderer, yes, but decent.

The press knew nothing about the murder. I don't think anyone knew of it except me. Patrick amazed me with it over supper in his rooms a couple of years ago. He wanted the facts made public at the proper time, and asked me to take on the task. I promised to wait until six months after he was gone.

This is the story. About January, 1975, when he had turned sixty, he received a phone call. A voice he had not heard in almost forty years, so it was not surprising he was slow to cotton on. The words made a lasting impression; he gave me the conversation verbatim. I have it on tape, and I'll reproduce it here.

"Professor Storm?"

"Yes."

"Patrick Storm?"

"Yes."

"Pat, late of Caius College?"

" 'Late' is the operative word," said Patrick. "I was there as an undergraduate in the nineteen thirties."

"You don't have to tell me, old boy. Remember Simon Brown?"

"To be perfectly frank, no." He didn't care much for that over-familiar "old boy."

"Well, you wouldn't," the voice at the end of the line said in the same confident manner. "I had a nickname in those days. You would have known me as 'Cape'—short for 'Capability.' Does it ring a bell now?"

Patrick Storm had not cast his thoughts so far back in many years. So much had happened since, to the world, and to himself. The thirties were another age. Faintly a bell did chime in his brain. "Cape, you say. Are you a Caius man yourself?"

"The Alpine Club."

"Oh, that." Patrick had done some climbing in his second year at Cambridge. Not much. He hadn't got to the Alps. The Welsh Mountains on various weekends. He didn't remember much else. So "Cape" Brown had been one of the Alpine Club people. "It's coming back to me. Didn't you and I walk the Snowdon Horseshoe together, with another fellow, one Easter?"

"Climbed, old boy. Climbed. We weren't a walking club. The other chap was Ben Tattersall, who is now the Bishop of Westbury, would you believe?"

"Is he, by Jove?"

"You remember Ben, then?"

"Certainly, I remember Ben," said Patrick in a tone suggesting that some people had more right to be remembered than others.

Cape Brown said, "You wouldn't have thought he'd make it to bishop, not the Ben Tattersall I remember, telling his dirty joke about the parrot."

"I don't remember that."

"The parrot who worked for the bus conductor."

"Oh yes," said Patrick, pretending he remembered, not wanting to prolong this. "What prompted you to call me?"

"Old time's sake. It's coming up to forty years since we asked some stranger to take that black and white snapshot with Ben's box Brownie on the summit of Snowdon. April first, nineteen thirty-six."

"As long ago as that?"

"You, me, and Ben, bless him."

"If what you say is right, he can bless us," Patrick heard himself quip.

Cape Brown chuckled. "You haven't lost your sense of humour, Prof. Might have lost all your other faculties—"

"Hold on," said Patrick. "I'm not *that* decrepit."

"That's good, because I was taking a risk, calling you up after so long. You could have had a heart condition, or chronic asthma."

"I've been fortunate."

"Looked after yourself, I'm sure?"

"Tried to stay fit, yes."

"Excellent. And you're not planning a trip to the Antipodes this April? You're game for the climb?"

"The what?"

"The commemorative climb. 'Walk,' if you insist. Don't you remember? Standing on the top of Snowdon, we pledged to come back and do it again in another forty years. The first suggestion was fifty, but we modified it. Three old blokes of seventy might find it difficult slogging up four mountain peaks."

Patrick had no memory of such a pledge, and said so. He had only the faintest recollection of standing on Snowdon in a thick mist.

"Ben didn't remember either when I phoned him just now, but he doesn't disbelieve me."

"I'm not saying I disbelieve you. . . ."

"That's all right, then. Ben has all kinds of duties for the Church, but Easter is late this year, and April first happens to fall on a Thursday, so he thinks he can clear his diary that day. He's reasonably fit, he tells me. Does a fair bit of fell walking in the summer. You'll join us on the big day, won't you?"

It would have been churlish to refuse when the bishop was going to so much trouble. Patrick said he would consult his diary, knowing already that the first week in April was clear. "Where are you suggesting we meet—if I can get there?"

A less decent man would have made an excuse.

*   *   *

April first, 1976, in the car park at Pen-y-pass. The three sixty-year-olds faced each other, ready for the challenge. "*We* may have deteriorated in forty years, but the equipment has improved, thank God," Cape Brown remarked when the first handshakes were done.

Ben the bishop allowed the Almighty's name to pass without objection. "I think I was wearing army boots from one of those surplus stores," he said. He looked every inch the fell-walker in his bright blue padded jacket and trousers and red climbing boots. Patrick remembered him clearly now, and he hadn't altered much. More hair than any of them, and still more black than silver.

If the weather was favourable, the plan was to walk the entire Horseshoe, exactly as they had in 1936. A demanding route that each of them now felt committed to try. And a sky of Cambridge blue left them no last-minute get-out. There was snow on the heights, but most of the going would be safe enough.

"Just before we start, I'd like you to meet someone," Cape said. "She's waiting in the car."

"She?" said Patrick, surprised. He had no memory of women in the Alpine Club.

"Your wife?" said the bishop.

Patrick could not imagine why a wife should be on the trip. What was she going to do while they walked the Horseshoe? Sit in the car?

"A friend. Come and meet her."

She was introduced as Linda, and she was dressed for climbing, down to the gaiters and boots. However, she was far too young to have been at Cambridge before the war. "You don't mind if Linda films us doing bits of our epic?" Cape said. "She won't get in our way."

"She has a cine-camera with her?" said the bishop.

"You'll see."

Linda, dark-haired and with an air of competence that would have seemed brash in the young women of the nineteen thirties, opened the boot of the car and took out a professional-looking movie camera and folding tripod.

"I didn't know you had this in mind," Patrick said confidentially to Cape Brown.

"I thought it was just the three of us," the bishop chimed in. "Three men."

"Don't fret. She'll keep her distance, Ben. Just pretend she isn't there. How do you think they film those climbs on television? Someone is holding a camera, but you never see him. We're the stars, you see. Linda is just recording the event. And she's a bloody good climber, or she wouldn't be here."

In the circumstances it was difficult to object. Nobody wanted to start the walk with an argument. They set off on the first stage, up the Miners' Track towards Bwlch y Moch, with Cape Brown stepping out briskly between the blue-black slate rocks and over the slabs that bridged the streams. Linda, carrying her camera, followed some twenty yards behind, as if under instructions not to distract the threesome on their nostalgic trip.

They paused on Bwlch y Moch, the Pass of the Pigs. Below, Llyn Llydaw had a film of ice that the sun had yet to touch. They hadn't seen a soul until now, but there were two climbers on the coal-black cliff across the lake. "Lliwedd," said the bishop. "I remember scaling that with the Alpine Club."

"Me, too," said Cape. "Wouldn't want to try it at my age. Shall we move on, gentlemen?"

The path leading off to the right was the official start of the Horseshoe. Crib Goch, the first of the four peaks, was going to be demanding as they got closer to the snow line. Towards the top it would need some work with the hands, steadying and pulling.

Once or twice Patrick Storm looked back to see how Linda was coping. She had the camera slung on her back and was making light work of the steep ascent.

After twenty minutes, weaving upwards through the first patches of snow, breathing more rapidly, Pat Storm was beginning to wonder if he would complete this adventure. His legs ached, as he would have expected, but his chest ached as well and he felt colder than he should have. He glanced at his companions and drew some comfort from their appearance. The bishop was exhaling white plumes and wheezing a little, and Cape Brown seemed to be moving as if his feet hurt. He had given up making the pace. Patrick realised that he himself had become the leader. Aware of this, he stopped at the next reasonably level point. The others needed no persuading to stop as well. They all found rocks to sit on.

"In the old days, I'd have said this was a cigarette stop," Patrick said. "Time out to admire the view. I'm afraid it's necessity now."

The bishop nodded. He looked too puffed to speak.

Cape said, "We set off too fast. My fault."

They spent a few minutes recovering. Each knew that after they reached the summit of Crib Goch, the most challenging section of the whole walk lay ahead, a razor-edged ridge with a sheer drop either side, leading out to the second peak, Crib-y-Ddysgl.

Presently a cloud passed across and blotted out the sun. The cold began to be more of a problem than the fatigue, so they went on, with Patrick leading, thinking what an idiot he had been to agree to this.

Unexpectedly Cape said, "Tell us a joke, Ben. We need one of your jokes to lift morale."

The bishop managed an indulgent smile and said nothing.

Cape moved shoulder to shoulder with him. "Come on. Don't be coy. Nobody tells a dirty joke better than you."

Patrick called across, "We're not undergraduates, Cape. Ben is a bishop now."

"So what? He's a human being. You and I aren't going to think any the worse of him if he makes us smile. He isn't leading the congregation now. He's on a sentimental walk with his old oppos. Up here, he can say what he bloody well likes."

They toiled up the slope with their private thoughts. Climbing did encourage a feeling of comradeship, a sense that they were insulated from the real world, temporarily freed from the constraints of their jobs.

Cape would not leave it. "The one that always cracked me up was the bus conductor and the parrot. Remember that one, Ben?"

The bishop didn't answer.

Cape persisted, "I can't tell it like you can. I always get the punch line wrong. This bus conductor was on a route through London that took him to Peckham via St. Paul's and Turnham Green. He got fed up with calling out to people, 'This one for Peckham, St. Paul's and Turnham Green.' "

"No," said Ben unexpectedly. "You're telling it wrong. He was fed up with shouting, 'This one for St. Paul's, Turnham Green, and Peckham.' "

"Right," said Cape. "I can't tell them like you can. So what happened next? He bought a parrot."

The bishop said in a monotone, as if chanting the liturgy, "He bought a parrot and taught it to speak the words for him. And the parrot said the thing perfectly. Until one day it got in a muddle, and said, 'Bang your balls on St. Paul's, Turnham Green, and Peckham.' "

Cape Brown made the mountainside echo with laughter and Patrick felt compelled to laugh too, just so that it didn't appear he disapproved. The joke was at the level of a junior school of forty years ago. Odd, really, that a bishop should have retained it all this time, but then not many risqué jokes are told to bishops.

Ben Tattersall's face was already pink from the effort of the climb. Now it had turned puce. He took a quick glance over his shoulder. Fortunately Linda and her camera were well in the rear.

The cloud passed by them, giving a stunning view of the Glyders on their right.

Scrambling up the last steep stretch, they reached the summit of Crib Goch in sunshine. Ahead, the mighty expanse of Snowdon was revealed, much of it gleaming white. Cape Brown unwrapped some chocolate and divided it into three.

"Shouldn't we offer some to your friend Linda?" Patrick asked.

"She's not my friend, old boy. She's just doing a job."

And when Linda caught up, she did her job, circling them slowly with the camera, saying nothing.

"So what's the world of academia like?" Cape asked Patrick, when the filming was done and they were resting, trying not to be intimidated by the prospect of the next half-hour. "At each other's throats most of the time, are you?"

"It is competitive at times," Patrick confirmed.

"And is it still a fact that a pretty woman can get a first if she's willing to go to bed with the prof?"

"In my case, definitely not."

"A *clever* woman, then."

"A clever woman gets her first by right," Patrick pointed out.

"The clever ones don't always have the confidence in their ability," said Cape. "They can be looking for another guarantee."

"I won't say it hasn't happened."

"We're all ears, aren't we, Ben?" said Cape.

The bishop gave a shrug. He was staring out at the black cliffs of Lli-wedd. He'd looked increasingly unhappy since finishing the joke about the parrot.

Patrick sympathised. Out of support for the wretched man, he felt an urge to be indiscreet himself, to share in the impropriety up there on the mountain. "There *was* a student a few years ago," he said. "Quite a few years, I ought to say. She was very ambitious not merely to get a first, which was practically guaranteed because she was so brilliant, but to beat the other high flyers to a research scholarship."

"And she gave you the come-on?" said Cape.

"I knew what she was up to, naturally, but it still surprised me somewhat. This was in the nineteen fifties, before casual sex became commonplace. One summer afternoon in my rooms in college, I yielded to temptation."

"And she got her scholarship?"

"She did. She went on to get a doctorate, and she is now a government minister." He named her.

"That's hot news, Pat," said Cape. "What was she like in bed—playful?"

"All this is in confidence," said Patrick. He looked across at Linda, and she was filming the view, too far away to have heard. "It was terrific. She was incredibly eager."

"You heard that, Ben?" said Cape. "The minister bangs like the shithouse door in a gale. Don't go spreading it around the clergy."

Ben Tattersall was hunched in embarrassment.

Patrick felt a surge of anger. The whole point of his story had been to take the heat off Ben. "How about you, Cape? Ben and I have been very candid. We haven't heard much from you—about yourself, I mean."

"You want the dirt on me? That's rich."

"Why?"

"Ironic, then. Fine, I can be as frank as you fellows, if it keeps the party going. You may not have seen me in forty years, but I'll bet you've seen my work on television. Have you watched *The Disher?*"

"The what?"

"The Disher. The series that dishes the dirt on the rich and famous. It's mine. I'm the Disher. As you know if you watch it, my voice isn't used at all. You have to be so careful with the law. No, my subjects condemn themselves out of their own mouths, or the camera does it, or one of their so-called friends."

Patrick was too startled to comment.

The bishop said, "I don't get much time for television."

"Make some time about the end of February. You'll be on my programme telling the one about the parrot."

The bishop twitched and looked appalled.

"I mean it, Ben. That's my job."

Patrick said, "Remember what day it is. He's having us on, Ben. She didn't film us when you were telling the joke. I checked."

Cape said, "But you didn't check the sound equipment in my rucksack. It's all on tape. The parrot joke. And your sexy-minister story, Pat. We don't expect you to talk to the camera when you spill the beans. We tape it and use the voice-over. A long shot of us trekking up the mountain, and your voices dishing yourselves. Very effective."

"Let's see this tape recorder."

Cape shook his head. "At this minute, you don't know if I'm kidding or not. I'd be an idiot to confirm it, specially up here. But I warn you, gentlemen, if you try anything physical, Linda is under instructions to get it on film."

"He's bluffing," Patrick told the bishop. "He probably sells used cars for a living."

Ben Tattersall was on his feet. "There's a way of finding out. I'm going to ask the young woman. Where is she?"

Cape said, "She went ahead, to film us crossing the ridge."

It was becoming misty up there, with another cloud drifting in, and Linda was no longer in view.

"This will soon blow across," Cape said. "We can safely move on. Then you can ask Linda whatever you like." His calm manner was reassuring.

The others followed.

Curiously enough, the snow was not a handicap on this notorious ridge. It was of a soft consistency that provided good footholds and actually gave support. Had the night before been a few degrees colder, the frozen surface would have made the near-vertical edges a real hazard.

The mist obscured the view ahead, which was a pity, because the rock pinnacles and buttresses are spectacular, but Patrick was secretly relieved that he was unable to see how exposed this razor edge was. He kept his eyes on the footprints Cape had made, while his thoughts dwelt on his own foolishness. What had induced him to speak out as he had, he could not think. To a degree, certainly, it was out of sympathy for Ben Tattersall after that mortifyingly juvenile joke. There was also, he had to admit, some bravado, the chance to boast that a university professor's life was not without its moments. And there was the daft illusion that this expedition somehow recaptured lost youth, with its lusts and energy and aspirations.

I must be getting senile, he thought. If it really does get out, what I told the other two, the tabloid press will be onto her like jackals.

He had never heard of this television programme Cape claimed to work for. But in truth he didn't watch much television these days. He preferred listening to music. So it might conceivably exist. Some of the things he had seen from time to time were blatant invasions of people's privacy.

No, the balance of probability was that Cape was playing some puerile All Fools' Day joke. The man had a warped sense of humour, no question.

On the other hand, a programme as unpleasant as *The Disher*—if it existed—must have been devised by someone with a warped sense of humour.

"It goes out late at night on ITV," Ben Tattersall, close behind him, said, as if reading Patrick's thoughts. "I've never seen it, but a Master of Foxhounds I know was on it. He resigned because of it."

"It's real?"

Cape Brown, out ahead, turned and said, "Of course it's real, suckers. You don't think I was shooting a line?"

In turning, he lost balance for a moment and was forced to grab the edge of a rock while his feet flailed across the snow.

"Hold on, man," said Patrick, moving rapidly to give assistance. He grabbed the shoulder strap of Cape's rucksack. Ben Tattersall was at his side and between them they hauled him closer to the rock.

In doing so, they disturbed the flap of his rucksack. Out of the top fell a sponge-covered microphone attached to a lead. It swung against his thigh.

Patrick stared in horror and looked into Ben Tattersall's eyes. Despair was etched in them.

"Look away."

"What?" said the bishop.

"Look away."

Impulse it was not. These things always appear to happen in slow motion. Patrick had ample time to make his decision. He put a boot against Cape Brown's armpit and pushed with his leg. The fingers clutching the rock could not hold the grip. Cape let go and plunged downwards, out of sight, through the mist. He made no sound.

"He lost his grip," Patrick said to Ben Tattersall. "He lost his grip and fell."

Nobody else had witnessed the incident. Linda was far ahead, her view obscured by the mist.

Cape Brown's body was recovered the same afternoon. Multiple injuries had killed him. The sound equipment in his rucksack was smashed to pieces.

Each of them appeared as a witness at the inquest. Each said that Cape lost his grip before they could reach him. After giving evidence, they didn't speak to each other. They never met again. Ben Tattersall died prematurely of cancer two years later, and was given a funeral attended by more than twenty fellow bishops and presided over by an archbishop.

Patrick lived on until this year, having, as I explained, confessed to me that he had killed Cape Brown. He need not have spoken about it. How typical of him to want the truth made public.

And there is something else I must make clear. As Patrick explained it to me, his story about the minister offering to sleep with him to earn her scholarship was pure fabrication. Nothing of the sort happened. "I made it up," he said. "You see, I had to think of something worse than a bishop telling a dirty joke, just to spare him all that embarrassment. After I'd concocted the story, I knew if it went on television everyone would believe it was true. People *want* to believe in scandals. Her career would have been ruined, quite unjustifiably. So you can imagine how I felt when I saw that microphone fall out of the rucksack."

You must agree he was a decent man.

THE THIRD MANNY

Terence Faherty

Terence Faherty is hard to classify because his work runs counter to so many genre expectations. As Publishers Weekly *said in a review of one of his Owen Keane novels, Keane is "an odd bird in an equally odd series, but one that is consistently low-key, gently thoughtful, and enlightening." One of the things that makes Keane different from other sleuths is that he has no fixed occupation and drifts from place to place as the series progresses. A newspaper copy editor in one story, a bartender in another, Keane's disaffection allows him to make sharp observations, and the author's ability to sustain a thoughtful mood while unfolding a complicated plot is praiseworthy. A second series by the New Jersey–based author takes a look at 1940s Hollywood, where its protagonist, Scott Elliott, a WWII hero and failed writer, works as a security-guard-cum-sleuth. Faherty is a recipient of a Shamus Award for Best Novel, an additional nomination for the Shamus Award, and a nomination for the Edgar Allan Poe Award.*

1.

MANNY IS AN unusual name, but I've known three bearers of it. The first was a Brooklyn garage owner who once stored a car for me. The second was the supervisor of a sweatshop bar I'd briefly tended in Atlantic City. The third Manny, Manny Vu, very nearly killed me.

My name, incidentally, is Owen Keane. Manny Vu and I came together on Highway Nine in the southernmost tip of New Jersey one rainy afternoon. The rain was light but steady, just enough to disappoint the summer renters on the barrier islands to the east, the "shoobies," as the year-round residents derisively dubbed the tourists. I was no shoobie, having lived for years on the northern edge of Great Egg Bay. But as I headed south to visit an old friend who was renting a house in West Cape May, I was entering unfamiliar territory. Even so, I felt safe enough leaving the Garden State Parkway when I encountered a traffic backup near the Burleigh exit. I knew that wherever the parkway went, the older Route Nine eventually followed.

I was no sooner settled onto the two-lane than I came to a long break in the oncoming traffic. The gap let me see the car from some distance, a little blue Japanese coupe that passed three slower cars in a single bound. The coupe never recovered from that pass; it was already skidding when it reentered the northbound lane. I thought for a heartbeat that the car would hit a pole on its side of the road. But the driver corrected, then over-corrected, then came at me across the center line.

There was a picket fence to my right. I would have taken it in preference to the oncoming car if I'd had time to think. But I didn't have time. I hit the brakes hard, not remembering to pump them until I began to hydro-plane. By then the oncoming car was pirouetting, its front end turning away from me and toward the fence. I saw the coupe's left rear fender perpen-dicular to my Chevy's snub nose and a foot away. Then I closed my eyes.

When I opened them again, I was sitting at an angle in my seat. That is, the seat was at an angle, the Chevy having come to rest in a shallow ditch. Smoke was pouring from its sprung hood. Even after my brain had correctly reclassified it as steam coming from the smashed radiator, I stayed pan-icked. I fumbled with my seat belt, forced open my door against the resis-tance of the ditch bank, and tumbled out.

The blue coupe had gone through the fence and into the yard beyond. It was still upright, but it had skidded around to face the street. I could see the crumpled passenger side and the front end, which was wearing broken pickets like an obscene garland.

I stumbled to the wreck. The little car's windshield was starred. I couldn't see the driver until I reached his open window. Then I didn't see him clearly for the warm rain in my eyes. I could just make out a slight dark-haired figure slumped over a bloody steering wheel. Before I could reach out to touch it, someone touched me. She moved me aside without really looking at me, a young woman with clipped hair and sunglasses as narrow as swim-mer's goggles.

"Let me," she said. "I'm a nurse."

I tried to watch through the ruined windshield, but I was distracted by a slip of paper tucked behind the visor. It was a computer-printed receipt for the Cape May-Lewes ferry with a banner headline: "THIS IS NOT A BOARDING PASS."

There was more to read—something about the number of axles and a time and a date—but the rain was in my eyes again. I brushed at them with my hand. It came away bright red.

I tapped the nurse on the shoulder and showed her my hand. She looked past it to my face and then addressed someone behind me.

"Sit him down before he falls down."

2.

Two ambulances responded to calls placed on cell phones by rubberneckers on Nine. Before the driver of the coupe had been removed from his car, I was in the first ambulance, on my way to Cape May Memorial, strapped to a board as a precaution against neck injuries. I'd already decided that I'd live, having eavesdropped on an exchange between the rescue technician and the nurse with the narrow sunglasses. I'd heard: "Superficial scalp wound, the kind that bleeds like a son of a bitch." The second opinion had been a reassuring "Yep."

At the hospital, they took a more circumspect approach. It was one of the rare times when I had health insurance, and the emergency-room doctors made the most of it. After my wound had been sewn up and covered with a nearly invisible dressing, I was X-rayed from a number of angles, with and without my board. Then I was placed in a room whose only reading material was a chart of the human endocrine system. That was just as well, as my head was aching seriously by then. Also my chest, where the shoulder harness had caught me, and my left knee. I slumped in my chair, held a cold pack to my head, and thought of the motionless driver of the coupe.

Other than the receipt from the ferry, I'd noted only the car's New Jersey plates and its make and model: Nissan Sentra. I ran over this scant information again and again in between replays of the crash itself. Whenever a nurse came by to promise me the prompt attention of a radiologist, I asked about the Sentra's driver. Each time I was told he hadn't been admitted.

That mystery was finally explained to me by a Cape May County sheriff's deputy who arrived to take my statement. She was a blonde of no great height named Nelson whose belt—as crowded with equipment as Batman's—made her hips look incredibly wide.

I regretted that unkind observation when I got to know Deputy Nelson, a process that happened almost as fast as the accident had. Before she'd gotten my brief statement down, I'd seen pictures of her kids and heard her opinion of Route Nine—dangerous—and the hospital—first rate.

"Don't worry about your partner not showing up, Mr. Keane," she said, referring to the driver of the coupe. "He might have been taken to County General. That's the older hospital down south. They get the county business, by which I mean the people without health insurance. Could be the other driver—" She consulted her clipboard. "Could be Mr. Vu didn't have health insurance. A lot of people don't these days. I can call down there for you if you want. But it wasn't your fault, the accident. You did everything you could do."

She'd already assured me of that several times. I wondered if she considered all accident survivors to be sensitive on the point or if I was projecting a particularly guilty aura. "I could have turned into the fence," I said.

"Then he would have hit the car behind you. That was the nurse who stopped to help you. She had two kids in her car. If you'd crossed the center line, you would have hit the car behind Mr. Vu, a subcompact with two retired teachers in the front seat. So you see, it worked out about as well as it could have. God was directing things out there today."

Including the initial skid, I thought. It was a theological perspective that led a person to dwell on minor details, something I was inclined to by nature. At the moment, I was interested in the information the deputy had on her clipboard. I was straining my sore neck for a better view when Nelson surprised me by handing the board over.

"I wasn't able to interview him," she said. "He was still unconscious when they took him away. But I got some basic information from his driver's license."

I was reading it. Name: Manny Vu. Address: 52 McClelland Street, Jersey City. Age: eighteen.

"Feel free to make a note of that for your insurance company," Nelson said. "Or you can wait for your copy of my report. I'm not sure about Mr. Vu's auto insurance," she added, preparing me for the blow. "I called the number Information had for that Jersey City address, but the girl I spoke to was too upset to tell me much."

A doctor arrived then with a packet of X-rays. The deputy greeted him like a candidate for office and then took back her clipboard.

"I'll call County General," she told me. "I'll know something before you're through here."

She was back before the radiologist had even unpacked. "Something's wrong down there, Mr. Keane. I'm going to drive down and check it out. I'll call you at home."

"Did he die?" I asked.

"No," she said. "He walked away."

3.

My old friend, the temporary resident of West Cape May, came by the hospital to pick me up about four-thirty. Her name was Marilyn Tucci. She was a New York City office worker two weeks into a three-week vacation. A shoobie, therefore, although I'd never have actually called her that. She'd been my girlfriend, once upon a time, but I'd never dared to call her that, either.

When she arrived at the hospital, Marilyn hid her concern for me under a mask of irritation. She hid it so well that only someone as familiar with her as I was could even glimpse it.

"It took you a week to talk me into an afternoon visit," Marilyn said as she walked me to her car, a tiny station wagon. "Now I suppose you're expecting to stay over tonight."

"The doctors did suggest that I be kept under observation," I said.

"I've been suggesting that for years," Marilyn replied.

As she drove us south on Nine, I did a little discreet observing of my own, noting Marilyn's biohazard tan and her hair, a symphony of sun-lightened kinks and curls barely held in place by a deceptively girlish head-band. And I wondered whether, sore bones and all, there might be a possibility of progressing beyond observation to an actual physical exam.

Marilyn settled the matter a mile or so later. "You can stay. I've a second bedroom I'm not using."

I returned to a consideration of the outside world just in time to see the site of the accident coming up. I pointed it out to my driver. She slowed, but didn't stop.

"You're lucky to still be walking around, Keane. Come to think of it, I've been saying that for years, too."

I was thinking of using the crack as a segue to the subject of Manny Vu, the man who had walked away from County General. Before I could, I spotted a sign for Rio Grande. I asked Marilyn to take the next right.

"Why exactly?"

"My car was towed to a lot in Rio Grande. I want to check it out."

"Okay, but if there's an overnight bag in the trunk, you're walking home."

Rio Grande wasn't a big place, and I had the lot's address, given me by Deputy Nelson. But it still took us awhile to home in. J&S Towing was well outside of town, on a road that had almost petered out by the time it reached the salvage yard's sandy drive. The whole establishment consisted of a tin-roofed building and a quarter acre of rusting cars surrounded by a chain-link fence.

The entrance to the little building was guarded only by a screen door, unlatched. I could hear a phone ringing just inside. I'd been hearing it ever since Marilyn parked her car. I went in, calling "Hello" but not expecting an answer.

The customer area was a room with discount-store paneling and shag carpet that had enough sand in it to grow tomatoes. I tracked in a little more on my walk to a chest-high counter. It held the ringing phone and two business-card stands. Both displays contained J&S Towing cards. Those on the left belonged to someone named John Pardee, those on the right to a Stu Hunter.

Beyond the counter was a desk that supported a citizens-band radio and an obsolete computer. Behind the desk was the obligatory calendar featuring the more than obligatory woman. She was wearing only her underwear and carrying an assault rifle. The combination seemed incongruous to me, but she looked comfortable with it. While I was meditating on that, the radio came to life.

"Crabber to Clammer, come back. John, you there? Come back. Where the hell are you? Come back."

"Please do," I said.

I found Marilyn waiting next to her car. "Nobody home?"

"Looks that way. I'm going to find the Chevy."

"Be careful, Keane. Meaner than a junkyard dog is more than just a snappy lyric."

Despite that reservation, Marilyn walked with me around the shack to the fenced lot. The fence had a gate and the gate had a chain and a padlock. But the lock was open and the chain was hanging loose.

"They're a little slack on security," Marilyn observed. "Then again, who'd want to steal these beauties?"

The inventory consisted of a dozen wrecks in various stages of decay. The one I'd come to see was front and center, a red Chevrolet Cavalier, a foot or so shorter than it had been when it left the factory in 1986.

"Totaled," Marilyn said, peeking under the tented hood.

The Chevy was only the second car I'd ever owned. I'd never felt any real love for it, but we'd been through a lot together. I hated to see it squatting in the weeds.

Marilyn had circled around behind the car. "Someone's been in your trunk," she said.

"It must have popped open during the wreck."

"Your spare tire's been thrown out. And your jack."

It was true. Even the old blanket I kept on hand for emergency picnics was on the ground.

"You don't have a flat. Somebody's been searching for goodies. I don't suppose you had a CD changer in there."

"Never heard of such a thing," I said. I opened the passenger door and then the glove compartment. Its contents were untouched, as near as I could tell. I took the registration and the insurance papers and left the rest of the clutter.

Marilyn was calling to me. "This one's been rifled, too."

She was standing next to Manny Vu's Nissan Sentra. Its hatch-back had been popped open, and its spare tire and jack removed.

I looked inside the Sentra, avoiding the bloody steering wheel. The back-seat had been pulled apart. The bottom section now rested against the backs of the front buckets. The coupe's glove box had been opened and emptied. Forgetting my fear of dried blood, I checked the visor for the receipt from the ferry. It was gone.

"Think we scared away one of Rio Grande's notorious spare-tire thieves?" Marilyn asked.

"I hope so," I said.

4.

Marilyn's house was a toy Cape Cod a long way from any beach. "You can save a lot of money if you're willing to drive a little," she said as we parked.

She needn't have troubled to explain. I knew Marilyn. She wanted the ocean and the beach and even the restaurants and shops in moderation. But what she really prized after forty-nine weeks in New York City was privacy. She'd found it in West Cape May. Her little house had a deck that looked out on a flat yard bordered by crab trees. Neither the yard nor the trees seemed even to have noticed the afternoon's rain. Beyond the tree border was an even browner field.

We sat considering the view, Marilyn drinking Chablis and me iced tea. Instant iced tea, which my hostess had whipped up herself. She talked about her vacation to date and her job. I thought about Manny Vu.

After a time, Marilyn said, "What about dinner? I can make something or we can order a pizza."

I stole a glance at my glass. The ice cubes were brown with the residue of undissolved iced-tea mix. "Hold the anchovies," I said.

Before Marilyn could stir from her seat, her phone rang. She went to answer it and came back quickly and displeased.

"It's for you. A Deputy Nelson. You told her you'd be here?"

"I called it a remote possibility," I said and moved inside as fast as my sore knee would let me.

The deputy's friendly voice was comforting, but the feeling didn't last. "We've got a real mystery here, Mr. Keane. I don't know much more than I did the last time I saw you. They're telling me that Mr. Vu just got up and walked out of here."

"He was okay?"

"No, he was badly hurt. His condition was described to me as serious but not life-threatening. They had him stabilized, and they were going to do more tests. When they went to check on him, he was gone."

"When was this?"

"Around three-thirty is when they think he left. He was last checked about twenty after three."

"He wasn't hooked up to any medical monitors?"

"One. It was switched off. The nurse's station was busy and nobody noticed. He removed his own IV, too. And get this. He made his bed."

That interesting detail didn't jibe with the vision I'd been having of a bandaged Manny Vu trashing his wrecked car and mine.

"We're searching the area," Nelson was saying. "No one saw him walking around. None of the local cab companies called for him. We haven't gotten any reports of stolen cars. Like I said, I can't tell you much."

I wasn't sure why she was telling me anything. I decided that she needed to tell somebody and I was handy. I felt a similar temptation regarding what we'd found in Rio Grande, but I overcame it.

When the deputy finished with me, I dug out the two towing-company business cards. I noted that the office number was the same on both but the emergency number was different. I decided that each was the home number of the partner whose name appeared on the card.

I dialed the office number. It was picked up on the first ring by a man who said, "John?"

"Mr. Hunter?" I asked back, shuffling my two cards. "My name is Keane. My car was towed to your lot this afternoon. A red Cavalier."

"Right. Sorry. Things are a little messed up here. I don't have your paperwork in front of me. Let us know if you want the car moved someplace else. If your claims adjuster wants to inspect the car here, he should call first so someone can be here to unlock the gate."

"I was there an hour ago," I said. "The gate was wide open."

"Shit. Sorry. Didn't know you'd been here. My partner was supposed to be watching the store. He went off somewhere and left everything open. He's the one who towed your car, so he'll have to get your ticket ready. Your bill, I mean. You're probably not in a hurry for that."

"Somebody broke into my car after it got to your lot."

"Shit. I didn't go in there to look. I locked things up again, though."

"I'd like to talk to your partner about it."

"So would I," Hunter said with some feeling. "But I don't know where he's gotten off to."

"Is there any chance he'd be at his home number?"

"Not unless he just got there. I drove past his place on my way here and there was no sign of John or his truck. He does this every once in a while when the weather's nice. Takes off, I mean. One of us will call you tomorrow and straighten all this out."

He asked me for a phone number. I looked up at the number on Marilyn's rented wall phone but decided not to risk it. I gave him my number in Mystic Island and hung up.

5.

Before rejoining Marilyn on the porch, I checked the cabinet nearest the phone. The phone book was tucked inside it, a combination white and yellow pages rolled up like a sleeping bag. In it, I found a John Pardee with a Rio Grande address. The phone number was the same one given as the emergency number on his business card. The clincher, if I needed one, was that the address was on the same road as J&S Towing. Stu Hunter had just told me he'd passed by his partner's place on his way to the lot. I tried Pardee's number and got no answer.

Outside, Marilyn was mellower than I had any right to expect. I discreetly checked the level of the wine in her bottle and decided it was safe to proceed with the plan I'd hatched in her kitchen.

"I'd like to borrow your car for an hour or so," I said. "I can stop while I'm out and pick up dinner."

"Where do you think you're going?"

"Back to Rio Grande. I want to talk to the man who towed my car."

"About what? The trunk being opened?"

"That and other things."

"Let's have it, Keane. Don't stop until you're sure I won't say, 'Go on.' "

I told her the little I knew about Manny Vu's disappearance.

"What makes you think this Pardee knows anything about that?"

I shrugged.

"Call him."

"I tried. He's not at home, or he's not answering. He might be in for visitors."

"And if he's not, you can nose around," Marilyn said, reading me like the top line of an eye chart. She knew me that well. Well enough to know that I'd never been able to resist a mystery, despite having decades of good reasons for resisting them.

I could no longer surprise Marilyn, but she could still surprise me. "I'll go with you," she said.

It was still light and would be for a while. The drive back to Rio Grande felt shorter, as return trips always do. It helped that we stopped short of a full round trip to J&S Towing. About a mile short. I was driving, due to Marilyn's high Chablis content. Driving and navigating both, since I was the one who spotted the mailbox marked "Pardee" in faded script.

The box belonged to an old farmhouse, not recently painted, and a barn, never painted. I parked next to the open barn door, which made it a logical first stop on the walking tour. There were no vehicles inside, no tow trucks, no cars, no motorcycles. Just a pile of old junk ready for a trip to a garbage dump or a flea market. The walls were hung with hoses and ladders and a pair of rakes that were unlike any I'd ever seen, long-handled with light tines that curled up from a basketlike base.

I found Marilyn outside next to a tomato patch that lay between the barn and the house. A former patch, I should say, as it had been harvested in a very complete but unorthodox way. The dozen or so plants, heavy with green and red tomatoes, had been pulled out of the ground, stakes and all. The victims lay in neat rows on either side of the rectangular bed.

"What the hell?" Marilyn asked, summing up the situation.

By then I was stepping up onto the farmhouse's listing front porch. A bumper sticker had been pasted to the little gable above the porch. "Second Amendment Spoken Here." Beneath it, the front door was standing open, its job being done by a patched screen door. I had a flashback to the deserted office at J&S Towing. Nevertheless, I knocked before trying the screen door. It wasn't latched.

"You don't believe in signs?" Marilyn asked from down on the drive. "This Pardee is a gun nut. You go in there, you're giving him a free shot."

"Mr. Pardee?" I called out. Like my earlier knocking, the words seemed to live on for a long time inside the house. "Stay there," I told Marilyn. "If you see anyone, whistle."

The front room smelled of old cigarette smoke and sweat. The whole house probably did, but I stopped noticing fairly quickly. I was too busy trying to decide whether the house had been searched. Like the barn, it was a mess, things scattered everywhere, junk mail and back issues of hunting magazines mostly. But that might just have been Pardee's way of keeping house.

The question got black and white as soon as I entered the bedroom. There

I found a full-size bed completely disassembled. The footboard and headboard leaned against facing walls to my right and left. The mattress slumped against the wall facing me, blocking most of the light from the room's only window. The box spring stood next to the doorway, not leaning at all. I stepped into the gloom, tripping on the bed rails and slats, and confirmed what I'd glimpsed from the doorway: The mattress had been slit open from corner to corner.

Marilyn's whistle interrupted what might have been a very long reverie on the subject of the bed. I went out through a back door and found her standing near her station wagon, looking out toward the road. A man was looking back from the road's far side. He was big and dressed in a T-shirt as long as a nightshirt. He had shoulder-length hair that looked silvery in the last of the sunlight.

"Can we go, Keane?" Marilyn asked. "The greenheads are starting to bite."

"Where did he come from?"

"The last house we passed on the right. I saw him step out just as we were turning in here. He must watch the place for Pardee."

Watching was all he seemed interested in doing at the moment. "It's time for dinner, I think," I said.

A spigot poked through the brick foundation of the house on the driveway side. I turned it on and let it run for a moment, Marilyn and the man with the silver hair both watching me. Then I turned it off and scraped up two handfuls of sandy mud. I smeared one handful across the station wagon's front license plate and the other across the rear plate.

"What's going on?" Marilyn demanded, her earlier mellowness already halfway to a hangover.

"Whatever it is," I said, "I don't like it."

We drove out past the watching man. At the last second, I thought to put my hand over my bandage.

6.

Marilyn's displeasure lasted through dinner at a roadside hamburger stand named Doc's, through the uneventful night, and well into breakfast the next morning. She brightened somewhat toward the end of that meal, the thaw coinciding with my request that she drop me at the nearest rental-car agency.

Marilyn was so happy about the plan that she generously offered to drive me up to Atlantic City, much closer to my home. That would make dropping the car back off easier, she argued. And keep me from coming anywhere near Cape May again while she was there, I thought. Whatever her motive, Marilyn deposited me at a Budget Car Rental on Route Thirty. She was gone before the clerk had finished explaining the damage waiver.

For once, I was happy enough to be deserted, as I was feeling distinctly like a lightning rod. I rented the cheapest car on the lot—a Dodge Neon described by the clerk as green, but actually chartreuse—and drove to my little house in Mystic Island.

After I'd showered, I felt a little less stiff and sore but no easier. I paced through my few rooms until my knee started to ache, then went out to sit on the edge of the marina where my neighbors docked their boats. I left the sliding door on the back of the house open in case Deputy Nelson or John Pardee or my insurance agent called. No one did, not even Marilyn to see if I'd gotten home all right.

When the sun got too warm for sitting, I fished in my wallet for Nelson's phone number. I came up instead with Manny Vu's address in Jersey City. Before I could talk myself out of it, I was headed north on the Garden State Parkway, trying to hear the Neon's tinny radio over the whine of its transmission.

I hadn't thought to rescue my well-worn state map from the Cavalier, so I was navigating by a complimentary Budget map, which was far from detailed. In fact, it seemed to suggest that there were large parts of New Jersey that hadn't been explored, a feeling I'd sometimes had myself. Luckily, I'd thought to consult an old atlas before leaving my house. It had told me that Jersey City was situated on the Hudson at the western end of the Holland Tunnel, that it was a shipping and manufacturing center founded in 1630 by the Dutch, traces of whom could still be found, notably a statue of Peter Stuyvesant. More helpful was a street map that showed Manny Vu's street, McClelland Street. It was very near the river.

So I took the parkway to the New Jersey Turnpike and the turnpike north to the last exit before the Hudson. I'd seen the exit many times, the sign for the New York ferry always catching my eye. The ferry operation turned out to be bigger than I'd imagined. According to its signage, it catered to theater and museum goers as well as humble commuters. I passed a row of modern blue and white boats and block after block of fenced parking lots, occupying ground that must once have held warehouses.

At a private lot just outside the ferry company's chain-link fence, I asked for McClelland Street. The old man at the lot's gate—a rope between two oil drums—told me it was one block up the street I was on, Pike.

"But you'll never squeeze a car in there," he added. "Not even a mouse car like that."

I took the hint and left the Neon with him, paying the daily rate, the only rate he offered. The climb to McClelland Street was short but steep. Halfway there, Pike's asphalt paving ended in an irregular line that looked like a wave of spilled crude. From there up, the pavement was brick, so old Peter Stuyvesant might once have trod it.

McClelland Street seemed to be paved with people. Asian people. The street was an open-air produce market, crowded with shoppers at what my stomach told me was half-past lunchtime. In addition to fruits and vegetables, some of which I actually recognized, stands sold smoked and fresh fish, cooked and uncooked chickens—the cooked ones hanging by their feet—and dry goods, no can or box of which had a label I could read.

For that matter, I couldn't understand most of what was being said by the busy people around me. Even at the stand where I bought some grilled meat on a stick, the only two words of English I recognized were "three" and "dollars."

Fifty-two McClelland Street was on the far edge of the market block, a narrow brick building whose first floor was a jewelry shop. I asked there for Manny Vu. The proprietor directed me to a stairway in an alley between Fifty-two and its neighbor.

When I was halfway up the metal stairs, a door opened off the landing at the top and a young Asian woman stepped out. She was barefoot, dressed in jeans and a Knicks T-shirt, her black hair lying loose across her shoulders. When she saw me, her face fell. It was beautiful nonetheless.

"Yes?" she asked.

"Sorry for bothering you. I'm looking for Manny Vu."

"He's not here," she said, her only accent a north Jersey one. She'd held the door open behind her. Now she backed toward it.

"He and I were in an accident yesterday," I said, speaking quickly. "Down near Cape May. I was wondering if he was okay."

I was also wondering whether this was the girl Deputy Nelson had spoken to on the phone. I decided she was. She'd frozen in place the moment I'd mentioned the accident.

"Come in, please," she said.

7.

The doorway off the iron landing opened directly onto a living room, dark and warm and crowded with furniture. In one corner, a television played softly. I recognized the movie, the original *Ghostbusters*, but not the dialogue, which had been redubbed. Hunched next to the television on the end of a sofa was a hairless old man wrapped in a heavy robe. He was watching the screen with rapt, unsmiling attention.

The old man didn't notice me until the young woman switched off the VCR beneath the color set. Then he smiled, almost toothlessly. The woman spoke to him in something that sounded to me like Chinese, her words so fast and flat that I could barely spot the breaks between them. He replied briefly. Then she turned to me.

"I told my grandfather that you were in the accident with my brother. He said he'd noticed that you'd been hurt. I'm sorry I didn't myself."

"It's nothing," I said.

"Can you tell us what happened? The deputy who calls is too busy consoling us to give us much information. She frightens me."

I told them about the accident, laying the blame on the wet roads. The woman translated softly as I went. The old man nodded once, after I'd mentioned the Cape May ferry. I ended by repeating the question about Manny's condition. His sister hesitated for a long time, as though expecting the old man to answer. "We haven't heard," she finally said.

"But you know he walked away from the hospital," I said.

Her stricken look told me that she did. To relieve that look, I asked what I thought was an innocuous follow-up. "Was Manny down south on business?"

Now the sister looked stricken and frightened. This time, the old man did break the silence. The translation was: "Would you like some tea?"

She left to make it without switching back on the VCR. I was tempted to do it myself, to distract Manny's grandfather from his examination of me. Instead, I glanced around the room. I was looking for Manny. I found him on a small table that held only the photo and a votive candle in a green metal holder. The group was a small one: the old man, a younger man who might have represented the missing generation, and two teenagers. They were Manny and his sister, I guessed. Judging by her age in the photo, it had been taken three or four years earlier. In it, Manny Vu was a smiling kid with a broad face and bushy hair. I decided that the middle-aged man was Manny's father. The background of the shot was the Hudson River and a section of the New York skyline.

New York figured in the tea service the young woman carried from the kitchen. In my mug specifically, which bore the ubiquitous "I ♥ New York" slogan.

The old man used his mug as a hand warmer and began to speak. The young woman translated, sitting beside him on the couch.

"You noticed the picture of Manny and his father. We four escaped from Vietnam together in nineteen eighty-five. We were three weeks in an open boat and six months in a refugee camp in Thailand."

Listening to the sad-eyed woman, I got the sense that she knew the story so well and had heard her grandfather's version so often that she was summarizing as much as translating.

"Then we were allowed to come to this country. Manny's father, our father, still had American friends from the army. They helped him get a job here. Working on the ferry boats."

I looked at the group portrait again, noting for the first time the metal railing against which the four stood and the invisible breeze that blew strands of hair across the girl's face and stood Manny's up in front. The photograph had been taken on the deck of one of the ferries.

"My grandfather says that's why Manny took the ferry ride down south. He was visiting, in a way, with his father, who died two years ago in an accident on the river. Manny was reconciling with his father yesterday, Grandfather thinks. Reconciling with his death. Manny hasn't been the same since our father died. He couldn't accept it. He wouldn't go near the Hudson ferry boats. He wouldn't accept a job from the ferry company when they offered him one."

The old man talked on for a long time, but the woman was silent and, I thought, alarmed. When he finished, she said, "My brother was a good man. He was raised to be good always. Our father's death hurt him, opened him up to the many dark temptations of this country. Now my grandfather knows that Manny is safe. When he stepped onto that ferry, he turned his back on the darkness. My grandfather thanks you for bringing him word of this."

She looked considerably less grateful herself as she stood up expectantly. I set down my mug and stood, too. Manny's grandfather and I exchanged nods, then I was out on the iron landing, suspended between the sounds of the street market and the noise of the river traffic.

I turned to the girl, startling her. "I forgot to tell you my name. I want to give you my phone number, too."

She held up her hand. "It's better we don't know," she said.

8.

I got back to Mystic Island just in time to take a long, unpleasant call from my insurance agent. I'd run in from the carport to catch the ringing phone, certain it was Marilyn. When my doorbell rang later that evening, I jumped to the same hopeless conclusion.

The person I found on my doorstep was a woman. And she was about Marilyn's age: late thirty-something. She may even have been a New Yorker. She held herself like one: erect, head back, her slightly beaked nose sniffing the Mystic air critically. But she wasn't on vacation. I deduced that from her tailored tan slacks and a sleeveless white blouse of some soft matte material—and from the badge she flashed me.

"Mr. Keane? My name is Nancy Wildridge. I work for the ATF. The Bureau of Alcohol, Tobacco, and Firearms."

"I hope you're here about alcohol," I said. "I don't stock the other two."

Wildridge passed up the opportunity to display her smile. "Actually, I'm not. May I come in?"

She gave my living room a once-over and said, "This was built as a weekend getaway, right? The whole street was. How did you ever find this hole-in-the-wall?"

I wasn't sure whether she meant the house or Mystic Island. "It's my uncle's place. I'm watching it for him."

"What else do you do, Mr. Keane?"

"At the moment, I seem to be answering questions. I'm not sure why."

Wildridge gave off checking a dusty bookcase for fingerprints and considered me. "That alcohol you mentioned, what form does it take?"

"Beer."

"Sounds good."

By the time I'd collected two bottles, Wildridge had exited via the rear sliding door. I found her staring down into the lagoon. I handed her her beer and steeled myself for more by-play. But that part of the scene was over.

"I understand you were involved in a traffic accident with a man named Manny Vu."

"Yes," I said. "Do you know what happened to him?"

"Only in general terms." She picked up a pebble from my pebbled backyard and tossed it into the lagoon. "That happened to him."

"I don't understand."

"He disappeared, Mr. Keane. More precisely, he was made to disappear. Given all the water you folks have around here, I wouldn't be surprised if he's in some right now. Way over his head."

"You think he's dead?"

The agent was watching the ripples she'd caused on the glassy lagoon. "What do you know about John Pardee?" she finally asked.

"He towed my car to Rio Grande, where it was broken into. I tried to talk to him about it, but he'd . . ."

"Disappeared too?" Wildridge suggested. "So did his truck." She picked up two more pebbles but must have decided the business was too theatrical, because she dropped them at her feet.

"Neither one has turned up. We're trying to trace two people who stopped by Pardee's house last night. Man and a woman. Man looked something like you, although our witness, a nosy neighbor, didn't mention any-thing like that patch on your forehead. He didn't get their license-plate number, either. The man smeared the plates with mud. That's an odd thing to do, don't you think? An innocent man might stop by to discuss some-thing—to complain about his car being broken into, for instance—but why the mud? Only a man who was up to something would do that."

"Or a man who had stumbled into something, who had found something disturbing."

"Like a slashed mattress and a dozen disinterred tomato plants?"

"And a nosy neighbor."

Wildridge took a long drink from her sweating bottle. "Whatever spooked this guy, his instincts were sound. This is definitely something you don't want to be involved in."

"Seems like I already am."

"I don't know. You're still here, aren't you? I was half expecting to find your house open and empty tonight. Maybe it will be tomorrow night."

"You're wasting it," I said. "I'm as scared as I get right now. Why don't you just tell me why the ATF is interested in Manny Vu?"

"Because it's better that you don't know."

That reminded me of Manny's sister's parting remark. "Tell his family what happened to him, then. They're desperate to find out."

"You've talked with them?"

"I was up there this afternoon."

Up until that moment, I'd felt as though I'd been dealing with a sales-person who was sure I couldn't afford anything in her shop. Now I'd sud-denly produced a gold card.

"Buy me another beer," Wildridge said.

9.

We went inside for the second beer, since the mosquitoes were now si-phoning it off as fast as we could drink it. Wildridge chose the kitchen table for our talk. Under the table's dangling light fixture, her prematurely dyed hair looked more red than brown.

"What did you think of the Vus?" she asked.

"They seemed like nice people."

"You were especially taken with the sister, I'll bet. Sam."

"Sam?"

"Short for Samantha. Her American name. Her late father thought his kids needed them to fit in. I don't know where he got Manny. Maybe from a Pep Boys ad."

"What happened to the mother?"

"Died before they left Vietnam. That's the story. For all I know, they ate her during the boat trip."

"You don't think much of the family," I observed after we'd stared at each other for a time.

"What did they tell you about Manny?"

"That he was a good kid. A little shaken up over his father's death."

Wildridge was nodding and smirking at the same time. "A boy scout was Manny. A choir boy. Except you couldn't trust his singing. Did they happen to mention Shadow Street?"

"No, where's that?"

"How about a gang Manny might have belonged to?"

"No," I said again, but I was thinking of the old man's cryptic reference to dark temptations. "Is Shadow Street where this gang is located?"

"Originally. The real street is spelled S-H-A-D-O-E. Shadoe was a Civil War general, like McClelland. Jersey City liked to name streets for them, way back when. The gang members use the more conventional spelling to better reflect their method of operation, which is stealth itself. Know much about Vietnamese gangs?"

I shook my head.

"They haven't gotten the press they deserve. But they're a real problem. In New York's Chinatown, they're *the* problem. Their members are mostly young ex-refugees born into the mess we left over there after the war. They're extremely violent, ostentatiously violent, since a good bit of their income comes from protection rackets, which means it comes from fear.

"Shadow Street goes exactly the opposite way. No publicity. No public beatings or executions of uncooperative merchants. The unlucky party just disappears. It's ingenious in a way, since the gang gets the credit for any unexplained happening, whether they're involved or not. I'd congratulate their *Ank kai*, their leader, if I knew who he was. But the only gang members we know by name are the small fry."

"Like Manny Vu?"

"He was well on his way to becoming a member. Someone interrupted his initiation. Owen Keane. When Manny smacked into you yesterday, he was making his first trip as an official Shadow Street mule."

Wildridge paused to let me guess what Manny had been carrying for the gang. I considered the three options offered by the name of her bureau. "Guns?"

"Exactly. Twelve machine pistols purchased by legitimate buyers down in easygoing Virginia and passed to our boy Manny, part of a steady stream

of guns headed north to New York City. Uzis or Tech-9s; Manny wasn't
sure which they would be."

"Manny told you about them?" Now her earlier quip about a choir boy
made sense. A choir boy whose singing couldn't be trusted. "Manny was
an informant?"

"I thought so. I bought into his whole refugee-boy doe-eyed American-
dream act. He was supposed to drive north yesterday on I-95 and stop to
have coffee with me outside Philly."

"So you could take the guns?"

"We hadn't made a decision on that. Manny's potential as an informant
was golden. A source inside Shadow Street would be worth a lot more than
a dozen guns. But Manny took the decision away from us when he drove
east out of Baltimore, crossed Delaware, and took that ferry."

"What happened after the accident?"

Wildridge had been doing most of the talking, but she'd somehow also
finished her beer. She rolled the empty bottle back and forth between her
hands. On each roll, it clinked against a diamond engagement ring.

"I doubt we'll ever know for sure," she said. "We do know that Deputy
Nelson, one of Cape May's finest, called Sammy Vu around two-thirty, half
an hour after your accident. I think little Sammy called someone connected
with Shadow Street."

"I find that hard to believe."

"Most men would," Wildridge said dryly. "Nevertheless, at three-thirty
Manny was spirited out of the hospital."

"No one could have gotten down from Jersey City in an hour."

"I know. But the gang has branches, notably in Philadelphia. We've also
heard rumors of an operation in Atlantic City, which would be close
enough. Somehow the gang did it. The way Manny's bed was made up
was as good as a Shadow Street calling card."

"Why would they kill him?"

"To keep him from ever talking to us."

"Are you sure it wasn't because he'd already talked to you?"

Wildridge shrugged. "Meanwhile, back in Rio Grande, a tow-truck driver
named Pardee was finding the gun shipment hidden in Manny's car. Being
a public-spirited citizen, he decided to keep them. I figure he had maybe
an hour to stash them somewhere. Then the gang picked him up."

"And he told them where the guns were hidden?"

"That's the rub. Pardee had to know his life was at stake. So he had to
have told them. Unless he pulled a gun of his own and forced the issue.
But there were no reports of a gun battle around Rio Grande, and people
would notice something like that down there. So I'm thinking Pardee told

them, but they somehow misunderstood him. Either he tried to be cute with them, or there was some kind of language barrier or cultural barrier. None of these kids are English majors. They felt confident enough that they'd find the guns to kill Pardee. Then they didn't find them."

"How do you know that?"

Wildridge looked at her watch and stood up. "I don't know, Mr. Keane. I'm guessing. You do a lot of that with Shadow Street. Pardee's nosy neighbor was a Vietnam vet. Yesterday evening around six he heard something that froze his blood: someone cursing in Vietnamese. He snuck up on Pardee's house and saw men in black arguing. The vet was half convinced they were Vietcong. You're lucky he didn't shoot at you when you rolled in an hour later.

"The way they were yelling at each other and the way they left Pardee's place, it wasn't Shadow Street at its best. Discipline had broken down. That's what makes me think they didn't find the guns."

She led me to the front door. On the threshold, she turned and handed me two bits of paper. One was her business card. The other was the slip of hospital notepaper on which I'd written Marilyn's number for Deputy Nelson. "You might suggest to your lady friend that she cut her vacation short. I don't think the gang can trace her, but it's better to be safe."

"What do I cut short?" I asked.

"Good question. Since you've introduced yourself to Sammy Vu, I don't know what advice to give you."

"She wouldn't let me tell her my name."

Wildridge pondered that for a time in the darkness of the carport. Then she asked, "What were you looking for at Pardee's?"

"Answers, not guns."

"I'd settle for the guns. I'd take one up to Jersey City and wave it at the Vus to show them what a scumbag their darling Manny really was."

10.

After Nancy Wildridge left me, I drove to a convenience mart and called Marilyn, afraid to use my own phone in case some all-powerful gang had tapped the line. I blurted out a not very coherent warning. Marilyn laughed at me and hung up. When I fell asleep hours later, I was still wondering how I would convince her, how I would convince myself that what Wildridge had told me was true. When I woke late the next morning, the answer was my first thought: Find the guns.

If the ATF agent was right, there'd been some miscommunication between Pardee and his captors. She'd offered two explanations. Either Pardee had given a false answer, or the gang members had misinterpreted what he'd said. If Pardee had lied, the guns could be anywhere. If he'd told the truth, the places Shadow Street had searched were clues to what he'd told them. To find the guns, I only had to identify Pardee's answer and interpret it correctly.

That and risk my life. I spent the morning trying to whittle the risk down mentally. The gang had already written off the guns, I told myself. Probably they'd already replaced them. And they hadn't connected me with their disappearance. If they had, I'd have disappeared myself.

Then I thought of something that made all my rationalizing obsolete. I figured out what Pardee's slashed mattress, ruined garden, and missing truck had in common. Ten minutes after that, I was headed south in my chartreuse Neon, clashing with every tree I passed.

I stopped at a parkway phone to try Marilyn again. This time she hung up between the initial and terminal syllables of my first name. With my next quarter, I called Stu Hunter of J&S Towing. My insurance agent had promised me that he'd deal with Hunter, but I was hoping he hadn't called him yet. He evidently hadn't, because Hunter didn't seem surprised to be hearing from me. I asked him to wait in his office until I got there.

As I drove through little Rio Grande, I wondered about Hunter's frame of mind, which I hadn't been able to gauge over the phone. If Agent Wildridge had told him about Shadow Street, he might greet me with a shotgun. He'd certainly be leery of any questions from me.

As it turned out, Hunter, a short man with a backwoodsman's beard, was friendly and relaxed. I decided that Wildridge had questioned him but not briefed him. He seemed genuinely confident that his partner, "Old John," would turn up soon, probably hungover.

I went through the pretense of scheduling a showing of the wrecked Chevy for my claims adjuster. Then I steered the conversation back to Pardee. "I was here in the waiting room when you tried to radio him the afternoon of the accident," I said. "You called him something odd. Was it Clammer?"

"Right," Hunter said. "His CB handle. John's Clammer and I'm Crabber on account of he clams all the time and I prefer to catch crabs. There's at least a little art to netting a crab off a piling or trapping one. Doesn't take any brains to rake up a clam. Edible rock collecting, that's what I call it."

That confirmed the guess I'd made about the strange basket rakes I'd found in Pardee's barn. "Where do you clam around here?"

"More places all the time, since the water's gotten cleaner. Almost any water that's shallow enough to walk around in or work from a skiff at low tide. For old John, though, there's only one place. His ancestral clam bed, he calls it. Claims it's belonged to his family since the Revolution, which is bullshit. It's a swampy little inlet off Jarvis Sound."

I looked blank and pointed west. Hunter patiently pointed east. "It's out at the end of Sanderling Road, past the bird sanctuary."

"Can you catch crabs there?" I asked, having learned all I'd hoped to learn.

"Hell no," Hunter said, and launched into an exhaustive description of blue-shell crabs. I listened for half an hour, until I was certain my clam questions had been safely buried. As I left, I casually mentioned that my insurance agent would call to finalize the details.

At a Route Nine filling station I asked for Sanderling Road and was told to follow the signs for the famous bird sanctuary. I passed this landmark a few minutes later, after a lonely drive through weedy mud flats on a narrow two-lane. The road continued past the sanctuary entrance but seemed uncertain about the decision. As was I.

Half a mile later the road ended at a metal barricade. I got out, kicking beer cans left by local romantics. Their tire tracks marked the sandy berm. I looked for and found a set of heavier, broader tracks, the kind a tow truck might leave. So far, so good.

I stood between the tracks and stared out at Jarvis Sound, a quiet expanse of dark blue water bordered by reeds so uniform in height they might have been regularly mowed. Running up to a muddy little beach before me was a narrow finger of the sound. John Pardee's ancestral clam bed, I hoped.

Bed was the key word, the answer to the riddle posed by Shadow Street's erratic search. Pardee's bed was the epicenter of their work in his house. A garden plot might be called a bed. A truck has a bed. Whatever Pardee had told his captors, it had had something to do with a bed. "The guns are under my bed." They'd killed him, thinking his information too simple to misconstrue. And they'd been wrong.

If my nose was any judge, it was low water. I took off my sneakers and socks, rolled up the legs of my shorts, and waded in, armed with a driftwood branch. The bottom was a sandy muck. I moved forward slowly, probing on every side with the branch and doubting furiously. How would Pardee have waterproofed the guns? He'd only had an hour to work with, less driving time. What kind of container would both keep the guns dry and not float?

I couldn't think of one. I found that I couldn't think of anything except an image Wildridge had left with me, a picture of Manny Vu's body, lying weighted down in some lonely body of water. Perhaps this water. In no time I had myself convinced that I was as likely to find Vu and Pardee as the guns. More likely.

Just as I had that thought, I scared up a snowy egret that had been crouching on a reedy bar near the mouth of the inlet. When my heart stopped racing, I found I was staring at the little island. As far as I could tell, it was dry even at high tide. I waded toward it, forgetting to prod with my stick, imagining new last words for Pardee: "The guns are behind my bed."

The bar was half the size of a tennis court. To search it, all I had to do was climb the bank and stare. Near the center of the driest land was a pile of driftwood and uprooted reeds, some of them still green. At the bottom of the pile I found a nylon duffel bag.

11.

At two the following afternoon I stood on the observation deck of the car ferry Cape Haloran as it droned across a placid Delaware Bay. I stood at the forward railing, which overlooked the lines of parked cars and the open bow with its webbing gate. Out on the horizon, Cape May was only a flat line of blue gray, its lighthouse still a speck.

I was staring toward the cape, but I was seeing a different horizon, an island so crowded with buildings that it looked like a mountain range pushed up from the seabed. Manhattan. That was the view Manny Vu's father had had on every outbound trip of his ferry. A prospect that had symbolized opportunity for generations. And on every return trip, he'd seen what? Jersey City, with its Saigon market and its streets named for forgotten heroes of a civil war. The past.

I wondered how often Mr. Vu had thought of his voyage from Vietnam to Thailand as he'd worked on his ferry. Every day? Every trip? Never? Had he seen his round trips on the Hudson as an ironic commentary on his voyage of escape, or a constant celebration of it?

And how had Manny seen them? Did he turn down a job on the Hudson ferry because the link to his father's life and death was too strong or because the job was too small-time for him? What had he seen when he'd stood where I was now standing on the last day of his life? The promised land, or the first stop in an endless series of round trips?

The answer depended on which view of Manny was correct. Was he the good but troubled kid, or the refugee on the make? Had he ridden the ferry on that last afternoon to reestablish some link to his past, or to outsmart the law?

Or both. The more I thought about Manny, the more I saw him as somewhere between the two extremes. Not a bad kid or a good one, just a kid in a bad spot. A stranger in a very strange land, despite his American name, all of whose choices were hard ones. The hardest was the deal Wildridge had offered him: Trade your friends for a pat on the back from your new country. Trade your past for your future. That was a deal I'd never been able to go through with myself.

I hadn't believed Wildridge when she'd said the ATF hadn't made a decision regarding Manny's guns. I doubted Manny had believed her either. Had he still been trying to make his own decision as he'd crossed on this ferry? I opened my mind to the moment—to the sun on the water, to the fishing boats bobbing on the horizon, to the gulls keeping station in the stiff breeze—and waited for an answer, as Manny Vu might have done.

My answer came in the form of a woman in huge sunglasses, a jogging bra, and biker's shorts who poked my shoulder. Marilyn Tucci.

I'd shown up on her doorstep the evening before disguised as a pizza deliveryman, one of the Uzis hidden in my white cardboard box. Being Marilyn, she'd had to reach out and touch the thing before she'd finally believed me. Then I'd made the mistake of telling her what I intended to do with the guns, and she'd insisted on coming along. We'd taken a morning ferry to Delaware and killed an hour in colonial Lewes. Now we were on our way back.

"This is it," Marilyn said. "The water isn't going to get any deeper. There are a couple of smokers out back, but I think I can distract them."

I hadn't explained the symbolism of the ferry ride to Marilyn, so there was no point in telling her I needed more time to work on my composite picture of Manny. "Lead the way," I said.

We walked around to the rear of the ship, where Marilyn prepared to sunbathe for the enjoyment of the fantail smokers. I descended a steep metal stairway to the car deck. The deck was open on the rear of the ferry, just as it was on the front. And the stern was as open as the bow, the gap through which the cars had been driven on protected only by a net woven of broad straps.

The Neon was parked three cars from the end of the leftmost row. I walked to it casually, on the lookout for jaded commuters napping in their cars. I took a very heavy nylon duffel bag from the backseat of the compact and walked to the open stern. Once there I removed a camera from the bag and pretended to photograph the Lewes breakwater as it faded in the distance. Then I looked up at the observation deck. No one was watching me. I wondered if Marilyn was sunbathing topless. However she'd done it, she'd given me my chance.

I crouched behind a van and unzipped the bag completely. The guns were all there, boxy and ugly, wrapped in some oily toweling. They would never be used by any gang members. But they'd never be turned over to the ATF, either. I was afraid Wildridge would make good on her threat and wave one of the guns under the nose of the old man on the sofa. I'd unwittingly brought him the message that his grandson was safe. I wanted him to go on believing that. For some reason, I wanted to believe it myself.

Beyond the crash net, the ferry's wake boiled white. I tossed the guns into the wake, one by one.

DETAILS

Kristine Kathryn Rusch

A former editor of The Magazine of Fantasy and Science Fiction, *Kristine Kathryn Rusch wrote nearly two dozen science-fiction novels before trying her hand at mystery fiction. In 1998, with only one mystery novel to her credit, the versatile author rocketed to the top of the* Ellery Queen's Mystery Magazine *Readers Award list for the story reprinted here. That same year, she was also the Readers Award winner for* Asimov's Science Fiction, *proving that it's possible, if still uncommon, for an author to cross genres and write at an equally high level in each. Rusch is the recipient of a score of fiction awards and nominations, most for her science fiction; they include the Locus Award for Best Short Fiction, the John W. Campbell Award, and the Hugo Award.*

No MORE ALCOHOL, no more steak. In the end, it's the little things that go, and you miss them like you miss a lover at odd times, at comfort times, at times when you need something small that means a whole lot more.

I've been thinking about the little things a lot since my granddaughter drove me to the glass and chrome hospital they built on the south side of town. Maybe it was the look the doctor gave me, the one that meant *You should've listened to me, George.* Maybe it was the sight of Flaherty's, all made over into a diner.

Or maybe it's the fact that I'm seventy-seven years old and not getting any younger. Every second becomes a detail then. An important one, and I can hear the details ticking away quicker than I would like.

It gets a man to thinking, all those details. I mentioned it to Sarah on the way back, and she said, in that dry way of hers, "Maybe you should write some of those details down."

So I am.

*   *   *

227

I know Sarah wanted me to start with what she considers the beginning: my courting—and winning—of her grandmother. Then she'd want me to cover the early marriage, and of course the politics, all the way to the White House years.

But Flaherty's got me thinking—details again—and Flaherty's got me remembering.

They don't make gas stations like that anymore. You know the kind: the round-headed pumps, the Coke machine outside—the kind that dispenses bottles and has a bottle opener built in—and the concrete floor covered with gum and cigarette butts and oil so old it looks like it came out of the ground.

But Flaherty's hasn't been a gas station for a long time. For years it was closed up, the pumps gone, plywood over the windows. Then just last summer some kids from Vegas came in, bought the land, filled the pits, and made the place into a diner. For old folks like me, it looks strange— kind of like people being invited to eat in a service station—but everyone else thinks it looks authentic.

It isn't.

The authentic Flaherty's exists only in my mind now, and it won't leave me alone. It never has. And so I'm starting with my most important memory of Flaherty's—maybe my most important memory, period—not because it's the prettiest or the best, but because it's the one my brain sticks on, the one I see when I close my eyes at night and when I wake bleary-eyed in the morning. It's the one I mull over on sunny mornings, or catch myself daydreaming about as I take those walks the doctor has talked me into.

You'd think instead I'd focus on the look in Sally Anne's eyes the first time I kissed her, or the way that pimply-faced German boy moaned when he sank to his knees with my knife in his belly outside of Argentan.

But I don't.

Instead, I think about Flaherty's in the summer of 1946, and me fresh home from the war.

I got home from the war later than most.

Part of that was because of my age, and part of it was that I'd signed up for a second tour of duty, WWII being that kind of war, the kind where a man was expected to fight until the death, not like that police action in Korea, that strange mire we called Vietnam, or that video war those little boys fought in the Gulf.

I came back to McCardle in my uniform. I'd left a scrawny teenager, allowed to sign up because old Doc Elliot wanted to go himself and didn't want to deny anyone anything, and I'd come back a twenty-five-year-old who'd killed his share of men, had his share of drunken nights, and slept with women who didn't even know his name, let alone speak his language. I'd seen Europe, even if much of it'd been bombed, and I knew how its food tasted, its people smelled, and its women smiled.

I was somebody different and I wanted the whole world to know.

The whole world, in those days, was McCardle, Nevada. My grandfather'd come West for the Comstock Lode, but made his money selling dry goods, and when the Lode petered, came to McCardle. He survived the resulting depression, and when the boom hit again around the turn of the century, he doubled his money. My father got into government early on, using the family fortune to control the town, and expected me to do the same.

When I came home, I wasn't about to spend my whole life in Nevada. I had the GI Bill and a promise of a future, a future I planned on taking.

I had the summer free, and then in September, I'd be allowed to go East. I'd been accepted to Harvard, but I'd met some of those boys and decided a pricey, snobby school like that wasn't a place for me. Instead, I went to Boston College, because I'd heard of it and because it wasn't as snobby and because it was far away.

It turned out to be an okay choice, but not the one I'd dreamed of. Nothing ever quite turns out the way you dream.

I should've known that the day I drove into McCardle in '46, but I didn't. For years, I'd imagined myself coming back all spit-polished and shiny, the conquering hero. Instead, I was covered in the dust that rolled into the windows of my ancient Ford truck, and the sweat that made my uniform cling to my skinny shoulders. The distance from Reno to McCardle seemed twice as long as it should have, and when I hit Clark County, I realized those short European distances had worked their way into my soul.

Back then, Clark County was so different as to be another country. Gambling had been legal since I was a boy, but it hadn't become the business it is now. Bugsy Siegel's dream in the desert, the Flamingo, wouldn't be completed for another year, and while Vegas was going through a population boom the likes of which Nevadans hadn't seen since the turn of the century, it wasn't anywhere near Nevada's biggest city.

McCardle got its share of soldiers and drifters and cons looking for a great break. Since gambling was in the hands of local and regional folks, its effects were different around the state.

McCardle's powers that be, including my father, took one look at Siegel and his ilk and knew them for what they were. Those boys couldn't buy land, they couldn't even get anyone to talk to them, and they moved on to Vegas, which was farther from California, but much more willing to be bought. Years later, my father would brag that he stared down gangsters, but the truth of it was that the gangsters were looking for a quick buck, and they knew that they'd be fighting unfriendliness in McCardle for generations, when Vegas would have them for a song.

Nope. We had our casino, but our biggest business was divorces. For a short period after the war, McCardle was the divorce capital of the U.S. of A.

You sure could recognize the divorce folks. They'd come into town in their fancy cars, wearing too many or too few clothes, and then they'd go to McCardle's only hotel, built by my grandfather's dry-goods money long about 1902, and they'd cart in enough luggage to last most people a year. Then they'd visit the casino, look for the local watering holes, and attempt to chat up a local or two for the requisite two weeks, and then they'd drive off, marriage irretrievably broken. Some would go back to Reno, where they'd sign a new marriage license. Others would go about their business, never to be thought of again.

In those days, Flaherty's was on the northeastern side of town, just at the edge of the buildings where the highway started its long trek toward forever. Now Flaherty's is dead center, but in those days, it was the first sign you were coming into civilization, that and the way the city spread before you like a vision. You had about five minutes of steady driving after you left Flaherty's before you hit the main part of McCardle, and I decided, on that hot afternoon, that five minutes was five too many.

I pulled into Flaherty's and used one thin dime to buy myself an ice-cold Coca-Cola.

I remember it as if it happened an hour ago: getting out of that Ford, my uniform sticking to my legs, the sweat pouring down my chest and back, the grit of sand in my eyes. I walked past several cars to get to the concrete slab they'd built Flaherty's on. A bell ting-tinged near me as someone's tank got filled, and in the cool darkness of the station proper a little bell pinged before the cash register popped open. Flaherty himself stood behind the register in those days, although like as not by '46, you'd find him drunk.

The place smelled of gasoline and motor oil. A greasy Philco perched on a metal filing cabinet near the cash register, and it was broadcasting teen idol Frankie Sinatra live, a pack of screaming girls ruining the song. In the bay, a green car was half disassembled, the legs of some poor kid sticking out from under its side as he worked underneath. Another mechanic, a guy named Jed, a tough who'd been a few years behind me in school, leaned into the hood. I remembered Jed real well. Rumor had it he'd knifed an Indian near a roadside stand. I'd stopped him from hitting one of the girls in my class when she'd laughed at him for asking her on a date. After that, Jed and I avoided each other when we could and were coldly polite when we couldn't.

The Coke bottle—one of the small ones that they don't make anymore—popped out of the machine. I grabbed its cold wet sides and used the built-in bottle opener to pop the lid. Brown fizz streamed out the top, and I bent to catch as much of it as I could without getting it on my uniform.

The Coke was ice cold and delicious, even if I was drinking foam. In those days, Coke was sweet and lemony and just about the best nonalcoholic drink money could buy. I finished the bottle in several long gulps, then dug in my pocket for another dime. I hadn't realized how thirsty I was, or how tired; being this close to home brought out every little ache, even the ones I had no idea I had. I stuck the dime in the machine and took my second bottle, this time waiting until the contents settled before opening it.

"Hey, soldier. Mind if I have a sip?"

The voice was sultry and sexy and very female. I jumped just a little at the sound. I hadn't seen anyone besides Flaherty and the grease monkeys inside, even though I had known, on some level, that other folks were around me. I kept a two-fingered grip on the chilly bottle as I looked up.

A woman was leaning against the building. She wore a checked blouse tied beneath her breasts, tight pants that gathered around her calves, and Keds. She finished off an unfiltered cigarette and flicked it with her thumb and forefinger into the sand on the building's far side. Her hair was a brownish red, her skin so dark it made me wonder if she were a devotee of that crazy new fad that had women lying in the sun all hours trying to get tan. Her eyes were coal black, but her features were delicate, almost as if someone had taken the image from a Dresden doll and changed its coloring to something else entirely.

"Well?" she said. "I'm outta dimes."

I opened the bottle and handed it to her. She put its mouth between those lips and sucked. I felt a shiver run down my back. For a moment, it felt as if I hadn't left Italy.

Then she pulled the bottle down, handed it back to me, and wiped the condensation on her thighs. "Thanks," she said. "I was getting thirsty."

"That your car in there?" I managed.

She nodded. "It made lots of pretty blue smoke and a helluva groan when I tried to start it up. And here I thought it only needed gas."

Her laugh was deep and self-deprecating, but beneath it I thought I heard fear.

"How long they been working on it?"

"Most of the day," she said. "God knows how much it's going to cost."
"Have you asked?"

"Sure." She held out her hand, and I gave the bottle back to her, even though I hadn't yet taken a drink. "They don't know either."

She tipped the bottle back and took another swig. I watched her drink and so did most of the men in the place. Jed was leaning on the car, his face half hidden in the shadows. I could sense rather than see his expression. It was that same flatness I'd seen just before he lit into the girl outside school. I didn't know if I was causing the look just by being there, or if he'd already made a pass at this woman and failed.

"You're not from McCardle," I said.

She wiped her mouth with the back of her hand and gave the bottle back to me. "Does it show?" she asked, grinning.

The grin transformed all her strange features, making her into one of the most beautiful women I'd ever seen. I took a sip from the bottle simply to buy myself some time, and tasted her on the glass rim. Suddenly, it seemed as if the heat of the day had grown more intense. I drank more than I intended, and pulled the bottle away only when my body threatened to burp the liquid back up.

"You just visiting?" I asked, which was the only way I could get the answer I really wanted. She wasn't wearing a ring; I suspected she was here for a quickie divorce.

"Taking in the sights, starting with Flaherty's here," she said. "Anything else I shouldn't miss?"

I almost answered her seriously before I caught that grin again. "There's not much to the place," I said.

"Except a soldier boy, going home," she said.

"Does it show?" I asked, and we both laughed. Then I finished the second bottle, put it in the wooden crate with the first, and flipped her a dime.

"The next one's on me," I said as I made my way back to the Ford.

"You're the first hospitable person I've met here," she said and I should've heard it then, that plea, that subtle request for help.

Instead, I smiled. "I'm sure you'll meet others," I said, and left.

Kinda strange I can remember it detail for detail, word for word. If I close my eyes and concentrate, the taste of her mingled with Coke comes back as if I had just experienced it; the way her laugh rasped and the sultry warmth of her voice are just outside my earshot.

Only now the memory has layers: the way I felt it, the way I remembered it at various times in my life, and the understanding I have now.

None of it changes anything.

It can't.

No matter what, she's still dead.

I was asleep when Sheriff Conner showed up at the door at ten A.M. two mornings later. I was usually up with the dawn, but after two nights in my childhood bed, I'd finally found a way to be comfortable. Seems the bed was child-sized, and I had grown several inches in my four years away. The bed was a sign to me that I didn't have long in my parents' home, and I knew it. I didn't belong here anyway. I was an adult, full grown, a man who'd spent his time away from home. Trying to fit in around these people was like trying to sleep in my old bed: Every time I moved I realized I had grown beyond them.

When Sheriff Conner arrived, my mother woke me with a sharp shake of the shoulder. She frowned at me, as if I had embarrassed her, and then she vanished from my room. I pulled on a pair of khakis that were wrinkled from my overnight case, and combed my hair with my fingers. I grabbed a shirt as I wandered barefoot into the living room.

Sheriff Conner was a big man with skin that turned beet red in the Nevada sun. His blond hair was cropped so short that the top of his head sunburned. He hadn't changed since I was a boy. He was still too large for his uniform, and his watch dug red lines into the flesh of his wrist. I always wondered how he could be comfortable in those tight clothes in that heat, but, except for the dots of perspiration around his face, he never seemed to notice.

"You grew some," he said as the screen door slammed behind my mother.

"Yep," I said.

"Your folks say you saw action."

"A bit."

He grunted and his bright blue eyes skittered away from mine. In that moment, I realized he had been too young for WWI, and too old for this war, and he was one of those men who wanted to serve, no matter what the cause. I wasn't that kind of man, only I learned it later when I contemplated Korea and the mess we were making there.

"I guess you just got to town," he said.

"Two days ago."

"And when you drove in, you stopped at Flaherty's first, but didn't get no gas." His tone had gotten sharper. He was easing into the questions he felt he needed to ask me.

"I was thirsty. It's a long drive across that desert."

He smiled then, revealing a missing tooth on his upper left side. "You bought a soda."

"Two," I said.

"And shared one."

So that was it. Something to do with the girl. I stiffened, waiting. Sometimes girls who came on to a man like that didn't like the rejection. I hadn't gone looking for her over to the hotel. Maybe she had taken offense and told a lie or two about me. Or maybe her soon-to-be ex-husband had finally arrived and had taken an instant dislike to me. Maybe Sheriff Conner had come to warn me about that.

"You make it your policy to share your drinks with a nigra?"

"Excuse me?" I asked. I could lie now and say I was shocked at his word choice, but this was 1946, long before political correctness came into vogue, almost a decade before the official start of the Civil Rights Movement, although the seeds of it were in the air.

No. I wasn't shocked because of his language. I was shocked at myself. I was shocked that I had shared a drink with a black woman—although in those days, I probably would have called her colored so as not to give too much offense.

"A whole buncha people saw you talk to her, share a Coke with her, and buy her another one. A few said it looked like there was an attraction. Couple others coulda sworn you was flirting."

I had been flirting. I hadn't seen her as black—and yes, back then, it would have made a difference to me. I've learned a lot about racial tolerance since, and a lot more about intolerance. I wasn't an offensive racist in those days, just a passive one. A man who kept to his own side of the street and didn't mingle, just as he was supposed to do.

I would never have flirted if I had known. No matter how beautiful she was. But that hair, those features all belied what I had been taught. I had thought the darkness of her skin due to tanning not to heredity.

I had seen what I had wanted to see.

Sheriff Conner was watching me think. God knows what kind of expressions had crossed my face, but whatever they were, they weren't good.

"Well?" he asked.

"Is it against the law now to buy a woman a drink on a hot summer day?" I asked.

"Might be," he said, "if that woman shows up dead the next day."

"Dead?" I whispered.

He nodded.

"I never saw her before," I said.

"So you usually just go up and share a drink with a nigra woman you never met."

"I didn't know she was colored," I said.

He raised his eyebrows at me.

"She was in the shade," I said, and realized how weak that sounded.

The sheriff laughed. "And it's all the same in the dark, ain't it?" he said, and slapped my leg. I'd heard worse, much worse, in the army but it didn't shock me like he just had. I'd never heard Sheriff Conner be crude before, although my father always said he was. Apparently the sheriff was only crude to adults. To children he was the model of decorum.

I wasn't a child any longer.

"How'd she die?" I asked.

"Blow to the head."

"At the station?"

"In the desert. Her pants was gone, and that scrap of fabric that passed for a blouse was underneath her."

The desert. Someone had to take her there. I felt myself go cold.

"I didn't know her," I said, and if she had been a white woman, he might have believed me. But in McCardle, in those years and before, a man like me didn't flirt with—hell, a man like me didn't talk to—a woman like her.

"Then what was she doing here?" he asked.

"Getting a divorce?"

"Girls like her don't get a divorce."

That rankled me, even then. "So what do they do?"

He didn't answer. "She wasn't here for no divorce."

"Have you investigated it?"

"Hell, no. Can't even find her purse."

"Well, did you trace the license on the car."

He frowned at me then. "What car?"

"The one the guys were fixing, the green car. They had it nearly taken apart."

"And it was hers?"

"That's what she said." At least, that was what I thought she said. I suddenly couldn't remember her exact words, although they would come to me later.

The whole scene would come to me later, like it was something I made up, like a dream that was only half there upon waking and then came, full-blown and unbidden, into the mind.

That your car? I said to her, and she didn't answer, at least not directly. She didn't say yes or no.

"Did you check with the boys at the station?" I asked.

"They didn't say nothing about a car."

"Did you ask Jed?"

The sheriff frowned at me. I'd forgotten until then that he and Jed were drinking buddies. "Yeah, of course I did."

"Well, I can't be the only one to remember it," I said. "They had it torn apart."

"Izzat so?" he asked, stroking his chin. "You think that's important?"

"If it tells you who she is, it is," I said, a bit stunned at his denseness.

"Maybe," he said, but he didn't seem to be thinking of that. He seemed focused on something else altogether. The look that crossed his face was half sad, half worried. Then he heaved himself out of the chair and left without even a goodbye.

I sat on the sofa, wondering what, exactly, that all meant. I was still shaken by my own blindness, and by the sheriff's willingness to accuse me of a crime that seemed impossible to me.

It seemed impossible that a woman that vibrant could be dead.

It seemed impossible that a woman that vibrant had been black.

It seemed impossible, but there it was. It startled me.

I was more shocked at her color than at her death.

And that was the hell of it.

I tried not to think of it.

I'd learned how to do that during the war—it's what helped me survive Normandy—and it had been effective during my tour.

But it stopped working about a week later when her family showed up.

They came for the body, and they seemed a lot more out of place than she had. Her father was a big man, the kind most folks in McCardle would have crossed the street to avoid or would have bullied out of fear. Her mother was delicate, with the same Dresden features as her daughter but on much darker skin. The auburn hair didn't seem to come from either of them.

And with them was her husband. He wore a uniform, like I did, and his eyes were red, as if he'd been crying for a long, long time. I saw them come out of the mortuary, the parents with their arms around each other, the husband walking alone.

The husband threw me, and made me even more uncomfortable than I had already been.

I thought she had flirted with me.

I usually didn't mistake those things.

But, it seemed, I made a whole lot of mistakes in that short half-hour I had known her.

They drove out that night with her body in the back of their truck. I knew that because my conscience forced me over to the hotel to talk to them, to ask them about the green car, and to tell them I was sorry.

When I got there, I learned that the only hotel in McCardle—my family's hotel—didn't take their kind. Maybe that, more than an assumption, explained the sheriff's remark: Girls like her didn't get a divorce.

Maybe they didn't, at least not in McCardle, because the town made sure they couldn't, unless they had some place to stay.

And there weren't blacks in McCardle then. The blacks didn't start arriving for another year.

The next day, I moved, over my mother's protests, into my own apartment. It was a single room with a hot plate and a small icebox, over the town's only restaurant. I shared a bathroom with three other tenants and counted myself fortunate to have two windows. The place came furnished, and the Murphy bed was long enough for me, although even with fans I had trouble sleeping. The building kept the heat of the day, and not even the temperature drop after sunset could ease it. On those unbearable summer nights, I lay in tangled sheets, the smell of greasy hamburgers and chicken-fried steak carried on the breeze. I counted it better than being at home.

Especially after the nightmares started.

Strangely, they weren't about her. Nor were they about the war. I didn't have nightmares about that war for twenty years, not until I started seeing images from Vietnam on television. Then a different set of nightmares came, and I went to the V.A. where I was diagnosed with a delayed stress reaction and given a whole passel of drugs that I eventually pitched.

No. Those early nightmares were about him. Her husband. The man with the olive green uniform and the red eyes. I knew guys like him. They walked with their backs straight, their faces impassive. They didn't move unless they had to, and they never talked back, and if they showed emotion, it was because they thought guys like me weren't looking.

He hadn't cared about hiding it anymore. His emotion had been too deep.

And once Sheriff Conner figured out I had nothing to do with it, he'd declared the case closed. Over dinner the night before I left, my father speculated that Conner'd just shown up to show my father who was boss. Mother'd ventured that Conner hoped I was guilty, so it'd bring down the whole power structure of the town.

Instead, I think, it just brought Conner down. He was out of office by the following year, and the year after that he was dead, a victim of a slow-speed, single-vehicle, drunken car crash in the days before seat belts.

I think no one would have known what happened if it hadn't been for those nightmares. I'd dream in that dry, dry heat of him just standing there, looking at me, eyes red, face impassive. Her body was in the green car beside us, and he would stare at me, as if I knew something, as if I were keeping something from him.

But how could I have known anything? I'd shared a Coke with her and gone on.

I hadn't even bothered to learn her name.

In the sixties they called what I was feeling white liberal guilt. Not that I had done anything wrong, mind you, but if I had known what she was— who she was—I would have acted differently. I knew it, and it bothered me.

It almost bothered me more than the fact that she was dead.

Although that bothered me too. That, and the dreams. And the green car.

I went to Flaherty's soon after the dreams started and filled up my tank. I got myself another Coke and I stared at the spot where I had seen her. The shadows were dark there, but not that dark. The air was cool, but not that cool, and only someone who was waiting for a car would choose to wait in that spot, on that day, with a real town nearby. She must have been real thirsty to ask me for a drink.

Real thirsty and real scared.

And maybe she took one look at my uniform and thought I'd be able to help her.

She even tried to ask.

You're the first hospitable person I've met here, she'd said.

I'm sure you'll meet others.

What she must have thought of that sentence.

How wrong I'd been.

I took my Coke and walked around the place, seeing lots of cars half finished, and even more car parts, but nothing of that particular shade of green.

Her family had taken her home in a truck.

The car was missing.

And as I leaned on the back of that brick building, the bottle cold in my hand, I wondered. Had the mechanics started working on the car because they too hadn't realized who she was? Had she gotten all the way to Nevada traveling white highways and hiding her darker-than-expected skin under a trail of moxie?

I went into the mechanic's bay, and Jed was there, putting oil into a 1937 Ford truck that had seen better days. A younger man stood beside him, and I wagered from the cut of his pants and the constant movement of his feet that he'd been the guy under the car that day.

I leaned against the wall, sipping my Coke, and watched them.

They got quiet when they saw me. I grinned at them. I wasn't wearing my uniform that day, just a pair of grimy dungarees and a T-shirt. Even so, I was hot and miserable, and probably looked it.

I tilted my bottle toward them in a kind of salute. The younger man, the one I didn't recognize, nodded back.

"You see that girl the other day?" I asked. I might have said more. I try not to remember. I can't believe the language we used then: Japs and niggers and wops; the way we got gypped or jewed down; laughing at the pansies and whistling at the dames. And we didn't think anything of it, at least I didn't. Each word had to be unlearned, just as—I guess—it had to be learned.

Jed put a hand on his friend's arm, a small subtle movement I almost didn't see. "Why're you askin'?" And I could feel it, that old antipathy between us. Every word we'd ever exchanged, every look we had was buried in those words.

He wouldn't talk to me, not really. He wouldn't tell me what I needed to know. But his friend might. I had to play that at least.

"I was wondering if she's living around here," I said with an intentional leer.

"You don't know?" the younger asked.

My heart triple-hammered. I knew then that the sheriff hadn't told anyone he'd come after me. "Know what?"

"They found her in the desert with her face bashed in."

"Jesus," I said softly, then whistled for good measure. "What happened?"

"Dunno," Jed said, his hand squeezing the other boy's arm. Jed saw my gaze drop to his fingers, and then go back to his face. He grinned, like we were sharing a secret. And I didn't like what I was thinking.

It seemed simple. Too simple. Impossibly simple. A man couldn't just sense that another man had done something wrong. He needed proof.

"Too damn bad," I said, taking another swig of my Coke. "I woulda liked a piece of that."

"You and half the town," the younger one said, and laughed nervously.

Jed didn't laugh with him, but stared at me with narrowed green eyes. "I can't believe you didn't hear of it," he said. "The whole town's been talking."

I shrugged. "Maybe I wasn't listening." I set the Coke down beside the radio and scanned the bay. "What're they gonna do with that car of hers? Sell it?"

"Ain't no one found it," the younger boy said.

"She drove it outta here?" I asked. "She said it seemed hopeless."

Finally Jed grinned. He actually looked merry, as if we were talking about the weather instead of a murder. "Women always say that."

I didn't smile back. "What was wrong with it?"

"You name it," the younger one said. "She'd driven that thing to death."

I knew one more question would be too many, but I couldn't stop myself. "She say why?"

"You got a reason for all this interest, George?" Jed asked. "You can't get nothing from her now."

"Guess not," I said. "Just seems curious somehow. Woman comes here, to this town, and ends up dead."

"Don't seem curious to me," Jed said. "She didn't belong here."

I stared at him a moment. "People don't belong a lotta places but that doesn't mean they need to die."

He shrugged and turned away, ending the conversation. I picked up my Coke bottle. It had gotten warm already. I took another sip, letting the sweet lemony taste and the carbonation make up for the lack of coolness.

Then I went outside.

What did I want with all this? To get rid of some guilt? To make the dreams go away?

I didn't know, and it angered me.

"Hey." It was the younger one. He'd come out into the sun, ostensibly to smoke. He lit up a Chesterfield and offered me one. I took it to be companionable, and we lit off the same match.

Jed peeked out of the bay and watched for a moment, then disappeared, apparently satisfied that nothing was going to be said, probably thinking he had the kid under his thumb. Only Jed was wrong.

The younger one spoke softly, so softly I had to strain to hear, and I was standing next to him. "She said she was driving from Mississippi to California to join her husband. Said he'd got back from Europe and got a job in some plant in Los Angeles. Said they'd make good money there, but they didn't have it now, and could we do as little as possible on the car, so that it'd be cheap."

"Did you?" I asked. And when he looked confused, I added for clarification, "Keep it cheap?"

He took a long drag off the cigarette, and let the smoke out his nose. "We didn't finish," he said.

I felt that triple-hammer again. A little bit of adrenaline, something to let me know that I was going somewhere. "So where's the car?"

"We left it in the bay. Next morning, we come back and it's gone. Jed, there, he cusses her out, says all them people are like that, you can't trust 'em for nothing, and that was that. Till the sheriff showed up, saying she was dead."

The car I saw couldn't have been driven, and the woman I saw couldn't have fixed it. She would not have stopped here if she could.

"You left the car in pieces?" I asked. "And it was gone the next day? Someone drove it out of here?"

He shrugged. "Guess they finished it."

"That would've taken some know-how, wouldn't it?"

"Some," he said. He flicked his cigarette butt onto the sandy gravel. I glanced up. Jed was staring at us from the bay. I felt the hair on the back of my neck rise.

I took another drag off my cigarette and watched a heat shimmer work its way down the highway. The boy started walking away from me.

"Where was she?" I asked. "When you left? Where was she?"

And I think he knew then that my interest wasn't really casual. Up until that point, he could have pretended it was. But at that moment, he knew.

"I dunno," he said, and his voice was flat.

"Sure you do," I said. I spoke softly so Jed couldn't overhear me.

The man looked at my face. His had turned bright red, and beads of sweat I hadn't noticed earlier were dotting his skin. "I—left her outside. Near the Coke machine."

With a car that didn't run, and no place to take her in for the night.

"Did you offer to give her a lift somewhere?"

He shook his head.

"Was the station still open when you left?"

"For another hour," he said.

"Did you tell the sheriff this?"

He shook his head again.

"Why not?"

He glanced at Jed, who had crossed his arms and was leaning against the bay doors. "I didn't think it was none of his business," the boy whispered.

"You didn't think, or Jed there, he didn't think?"

"Neither of us," the boy said. "Jed told her she could sleep in there by the car. But it woulda been an oven, even during the night. I think she knew that."

"Is that where she slept?"

"I dunno." This time the boy did not meet my gaze. Sweat ran off his forehead, onto his chin, and dripped on his shirt. He didn't know, and he was sorry.

And so was I.

If I was going to pursue this logically, then I had to think logically. And it seemed to me that whoever killed the girl had known about the car. I couldn't believe she would have talked to anyone else—I suspected she only spoke to me because I was in uniform. And if I made that assumption, then the only other people who would have known about her, about the car, about the entire business were the people who worked the station.

"Who was working that night?" I asked.

"Mr. Flaherty," he said.

Mr. Flaherty. Mac Flaherty, whom I'd known since I was a boy. He was a hard, decent man who expected work out of his employees, payment from his customers, and good money for a job well done. I'd seen Mac Flaherty in his station, at church, and at school getting his son, and I couldn't believe he had killed someone.

But then, I had. I had killed a lot of boys overseas, and I would have killed more if Hitler hadn't proved he was a coward and did the world a favor by dying by his own hand.

And the Mac Flaherty who ran the station now wasn't the same man as the one I'd known. I'd learned that much in my few short days in McCardle.

A shiver ran down my back. Then I headed inside, looking for Mac Flaherty, and finding him.

Mac Flaherty was drunk. Not falling-down, noticeable drunk, but his daily drunk, the kind that made a man a bit blurry around the edges, kept him from feeling the pain of day-to-day living, and kept him working a job he no longer liked.

Once Flaherty'd loved his work. It had been obvious in the booming way he'd greet new customers, in the smile he wore every day whether going or coming from work.

But then he left for the war, like I did, only he came back in '43 minus three fingers on his left hand to find his wife shacking up with the local undertaker, and a half-sibling for his son baking in the oven. The wife, not he, took advantage of the McCardle divorce laws, and Flaherty was never the same. She and the undertaker left that week, and apparently, Flaherty never saw his kid again.

I went inside the service station's main area, and the smell of beer mixed with the stench of gasoline. Flaherty was clutching a can, staring at me.

"You harassing the kid?" he asked.

"No," I said, even though I felt that wasn't entirely true. "I was just curious about the woman who died."

"She something to you?" Flaherty asked.

"Only met her the once," I said.

"Then what's the interest?"

"I don't know," I said, and we both seemed surprised by my honesty. "Your boy says he left her sitting outside. That true?"

Flaherty shrugged. "I never saw her. Not when I locked up."

"What about her car?"

"Her car," he repeated dully. "Her car. I had it towed."

"At night?"

"That morning," he said. "When it became clear she skipped out on me."

"Towed where?" I asked.

"My place," he said. "For parts."

And those parts had probably already been taken, along with anything incriminating. I didn't say that aloud, though.

"You have any idea who killed her?" I asked.

"What do you care?" he asked, gaze suddenly back on me, and sharper than I would have expected.

I thought of Jed then, Jed as I'd seen him that day, staring at me, that flat look on his face. "If Jed killed her—"

"I didn't see Jed touch nobody," Flaherty said. "And I wouldn't say if I did."

I froze. "Why not?"

Flaherty frowned, his eyes small and bloodshot. "He's the best mechanic I got."

"But if he killed someone—"

"He didn't kill no one."

"How can you be so sure?"

"What happened, happened," Flaherty said. "Let's not go wrecking more lives." Then he grabbed the bottle of beer he'd been nursing and took a sip, his crippled hand looking unbalanced in the grimy afternoon light.

By the time I got back with the sheriff, Jed was gone. Not that it mattered. The case went down on the books as unsolved. What else could it have been with the other kid denying he'd even talked to me, and Mac Flaherty swearing that the girl'd been fine when he drove by at midnight, fine and unwilling to leave her post near the Coke machine. He'd winked at the sheriff when he'd told that story, and the sheriff seemed to accept it all.

I went to Jed's apartment and found the door open, all his clothes missing, and a neighbor who said that Jed had run in, not even bothering to change, and packed a bag, then took some money from a jam jar he'd had under his bed and disappeared down the highway, never to be seen again.

He'd been driving one of Flaherty's rebuilds.

When I found out, I told the sheriff, and the sheriff'd been unimpressed. "Man can leave town if'n he wants," the sheriff said. "Don't mean he killed nobody."

No, I suppose it didn't. But it seemed like a huge coincidence to me, the girl getting beaten to death, Jed watching us talk, and then, when he knew I'd left for the law, disappearing like he did.

It was just that the sheriff saw no percentage in pursuing the case. It'd been interesting when he could come after me because of my family, because of the power we had, but it soon lost its appeal when the girl's family took her away. Took her away and pointed the finger at a good local boy, a mechanic who could down some beers and tell great jokes, who'd gone off to serve his country same as the rest of us. Jed had had worth to the sheriff; the girl had had none.

I don't know why he killed her. We'll never know now. Jed disappeared but good, and wasn't heard from until five years ago, when what was left of his family got an obituary mailed to them from somewhere in Canada. He'd died not saying a word—

Sorry. Got interrupted there. Was going to come back to it this afternoon, but things changed this morning.

About nine A.M., I walked into my front room, buttoning one of my best shirts in preparation for yet another meeting with that pretty doctor down at the glass and chrome white elephant, when I saw Sarah sitting in my best chair, feet on the footstool my granny hand-stitched, and all forty handwritten pages of this memory in her hands. She was reading raptly, which I found flattering for the half-second it took to realize what she was doing. I didn't want anyone to read this stuff until I was dead, and here was my granddaughter staring at the pages as if they were something outta Stephen King.

She looked up at me, her heart-shaped face so like Sally Anne's at that age that it made my breath catch, and said, "So you think you're some bad guy for failing this woman."

I shook my head, but the movement didn't stop her.

"You," she says, "who've done more for people—black, white, or purple—than anyone else in this town. You, who opened that civil-rights law practice back East, who fought every racist law and every racist politician you could find. For God's sake, Gramps, you marched with Dr. King, and you were a presidential advisor on civil rights. You're the kinda man who shows the rest of us how to live our lives, and you're feeling like this? You're being silly."

"You don't understand," I said.

"Damn straight," she said, and I winced, as I always do, at the sailor language she uses. "You shouldn't be mulling over this anymore. You did what you could, and more, it seems, than anyone else."

"And even that wasn't enough."

"Sometimes," she said, "that happens, Gramps. You know that. Hell, you taught it to me."

Seems I did. But that wasn't the point either, and I didn't know how to tell her. So I didn't. I took the papers from her, put them back on my desk where they belonged, and let her drive me to the doctor so that they both could feel useful.

And all the way there and all the way back, I thought about how to make my point so that girls like her would understand. You see, the world is so different now, and yet it's still the same. Just the faces change, and a few of the rules.

These days, Jed would've been arrested, or the sheriff would've been bounced out of office, or the press'd make some huge scandal over the whole thing.

But it wouldn't be that simple, because pretty women don't approach strange men anymore, especially if the strange men are in uniform, and pretty women certainly don't wait alone in gas stations while their cars are being repaired.

But they're still dying, because they're women or because they're black or because they're in the wrong place at the wrong time, and there's so damn many of them we just shrug and move on, shaking our heads as we go.

But that isn't my point. My point is this:

I wouldn't have marched with Dr. King if it weren't for that poor girl, and I wouldn't have made it my life's work to stamp out all the things that cause the condition I found myself in that hot afternoon, the condition that would have led me to ignore a girl if I'd noticed the true color of her skin.

Because I think I know why she died that day. I think she died because she'd flirted with me.

And that just wasn't done between girls like her and men like me.

Jed wouldn't have taken her to the desert if she'd been white. He would've thought she had family, someone who'd miss her. He might have roughed her up for talking to me. He might have had a few words with me.

But he didn't. I did something unspeakable to people of our generation, and he saw a way to get back at me. If I'd talked to her, then I'd want to do what was probably done to her before she died. And if she'd fought, then I'd have bashed her. That's what the sheriff was thinking. That's what Jed wanted him to think.

And all because of who she was, and who I was, and who Jed was.

The sad irony is that if I'd kept my place, she'd be alive, and because I didn't, she was dead. That had bothered me then, and bothers me now. Seems a man—any man—should be able to talk to whomever he wants. But what bothered me more was the fact that when I learned, on the same morning, that she was black and that she was dead, it bothered me more that she was black and that I had talked to her.

It just wasn't done.

And I was more worried about my own blindness than I was about one woman's life.

Since that day, hers is the face I see every morning when I wake up, and every night when I doze. And if God gave me the chance to relive any day in my life, it'd be that one, not, strangely, the day I enlisted or the day I deliberately misunderstood that German kid asking for clemency, but the day I inadvertently led a pretty girl to her death.

White liberal guilt maybe.

Or maybe it was the last straw, somehow.

Or maybe it was the fact that I had so much trouble learning her name.

Learning her name was harder than learning the identity of the man who killed her. It took me three more weeks and a bribe to the twelve-year-old son of the owner of the funeral home.

Not that her name really mattered. To me or to anyone else.

But it mattered to her, and to that man in uniform with the red, red eyes. Because it was the only bit of her that couldn't be sold for parts. The only bit she could call completely hers.

Lucille Johnson.

Not quite as exotic as I would have thought, or as fitting to a woman as beautiful as she was. But it was hers. And in the end, it was all she had.

It was a detail.

An important detail.

And one I'll never forget.

ONE BAG OF COCONUTS

Edward D. Hoch

For more than thirty years Edward D. Hoch has made his living almost entirely on the sale of his short stories: For twenty-seven years he's had a story in every issue of the monthly Ellery Queen's Mystery Magazine. *It doesn't take much skill at addition to see that this adds up to a very large number of stories. In fact, the author now has more than 820 short stories in print, and he shows no sign of slowing down. Early in his fiction-writing career, which began in 1955 with the publication of a short story featuring an occult character by the name of Simon Ark, Hoch wrote several novels, three of them science fiction. He is one of a few trusted authors enlisted by Ellery Queen to ghostwrite, and he produced one of the Queen team's full-length novels and one of the short stories that bear the Queen byline. Hoch's fans are especially keen followers of his series characters. The half-dozen different series he has running, as of this printing, in* Ellery Queen's Mystery Magazine *all include characters who work in the traditional detective mold. The stories are almost all miniature novels, with a full cast of characters and clues fairly given. Hoch has won both the Edgar Allan Poe Award and the Anthony Award for entries in series that are still running in* Ellery Queen's Mystery Magazine. *In fact, his Anthony Award was earned by the story you are about to read.*

THE SUNTANNED MAN with the wild hair passed through customs at Heathrow Airport without difficulty, carrying a single suitcase and a burlap sack clearly marked "Coconuts." Both had been checked in Madagascar to avoid having them pass through gate security points. After glancing in the suitcase and feeling a few of the coconuts through the burlap, the inspector waved the traveler on. After all, he had come from a place where coconut palms were commonplace. Hurrying through the waiting crowd, knowing no one would be meeting him, the man headed outdoors toward the line of London taxis in the covered loading area. A driver stepped out to take his suitcase and the man was just opening the back door to enter the cab when his body seemed to jerk and tumble forward. A blossom of blood grew suddenly in the center of his back.

The bag of coconuts landed on the pavement next to the taxi. That bag of coconuts was to summon Jeffrey Rand out of retirement.

Rand had visited the American Embassy in Grosvenor Square before, but this was his first meeting with Mr. Ralph Coir of the United States Fish and Wildlife Service, Division of Law Enforcement. "I'm retired, you know," he said after the amenities had been dealt with.

Coir was a bald man running to overweight. He wore thick glasses and must have been near retirement age himself. "Mr. Rand, you were recommended by a high government official as being the perfect man for this job. You would be paid on a per diem basis, plus expenses. I understand that you did a good bit of intelligence work during the Cold War, and in recent years you've been invaluable in certain African matters."

Rand laughed at the suggestion. "I'm hardly an African expert."

Ralph Coir flipped through the pages of a report on the desk in front of him. "It says here you met your future wife in nineteen seventy-one while on assignment in Egypt. You returned there in seventy-two, seventy-four, ninety-four, and ninety-six. In nineteen ninety-three, you were on a ship in the Red Sea, and in ninety-four you performed an invaluable service on an island off the east coast of Africa."

Rand smiled slightly. There was no point in growing angry about this combing through of his life. "I believe you missed some of the Egyptian visits. My wife is from Cairo and we return there frequently."

Coir folded his hands on the papers, signifying they had served their purpose. "I'm especially interested in your visits to the East African islands because this present business concerns Madagascar. I stopped there myself recently, on my way back from South Africa. The flora and fauna of that island are fantastic. It's a thousand miles long and a nation all by itself since the French granted independence in nineteen sixty. The people are more Malayan-Indonesian than African or Arab."

Rand shrugged. "How does all this concern me?"

Coir showed him a head-and-shoulders photograph of a man with a deep tan and unruly hair. His eyes were closed. "This is Telga Toliara. He was killed at Heathrow Airport two days ago."

"Killed? How?"

"Shot. Scotland Yard thinks it was a silenced weapon which may have been concealed in a cane. At least no one heard or saw it happen. He was just entering a taxi, carrying this." He reached beneath the desk and brought up a burlap bag marked "Coconuts."

Rand felt them through the bag and then untied the top, reaching inside. He gave a yelp of pain and surprise as something alive nipped at his finger. "What in hell—?"

"I'm sorry," the American said. "I should have warned you." He tipped the bag and emptied a dozen medium-sized turtles onto the desktop. "We cleaned and fed them, of course. I only returned them to the burlap to give you some idea of how they slipped through customs."

"Turtles?" Rand stared at them in amazement, clutching his bitten finger.

"To be exact, they're radiated tortoises, very rare. Females are worth about ten thousand dollars each on the black market when they're fully grown. They were being smuggled from Madagascar to Florida by way of London. The dead man was changing planes at Heathrow. They ended up on my desk, as do all smuggled animals bound for America." He smiled slightly. "Of course, with the coconut label on the bag the embassy people thought they were being funny presenting it to me."

"You want me to investigate a case of animal smuggling?" Rand asked in a sceptical tone of voice.

"That, and murder. You know the east coast of Africa, even if not Madagascar itself. More than that, you've had a lifetime of intelligence work."

"Certainly there must be Americans who—"

"An American in this area would arouse too much suspicion. That's why we asked for your government's help. It's an illegal ten-billion-dollar business, Mr. Rand."

"What do you want from me?"

He indicated the tortoises. "Trace these back to their source, find us the people behind the smuggling operation and Toliara's murder, and we might be able to shut down at least the Madagascar part of this operation."

That was how Rand came to arrive in Antananarivo, called Tana, the centrally located capital city where more than a million and a half people suffered daily in the tropical heat. The city itself sprawled over the sides of a dozen red-dirt hills, and the slanted roofs on many of its low native and French colonial buildings hinted at heavy seasonal rains. At this time of the year, late spring, it was merely hot.

Why Rand had taken on the contract work for the United States Fish and Wildlife Service was something he had a hard time explaining to Leila, his wife of more than twenty years. But she was still teaching at Reading University and would be for another few weeks until semester's end. At least the trip to Madagascar should keep him from growing bored.

Someone once called Tana a city of dusty beauty. It was all of that, but Rand soon determined that the dust which filled the air was really smoke, drifting in from burning forests and grasslands far away. The roads were cluttered with carts drawn by zebu, Indian beasts of burden that resembled oxen. As he passed a man carrying a live chicken over his shoulder, no doubt for an evening meal, he decided it was not a city he would like to call home.

On the lengthy plane trip Rand had read about the island's unique wild-life in a government report Coir had given him. Madagascar was the only place on earth where lemurs lived in the wild. There were three-foot-long chameleons and various other unique reptiles, including the valuable radi-ated tortoise. The free-market democracy that had replaced the country's Communist dictatorship in 1993 was still working out its kinks, and smug-glers had found that the illegal trade in exotic pets was one of the few dependable businesses around. It was also one of the safer ones. Customs officials, on the lookout for cocaine, often missed a smuggled supply of cockatoo eggs from Australia or radiated tortoises from Madagascar. Even if the smugglers were caught and convicted, a first offense might not bring prison time.

Rand had been given the address of Toliara's house near the downtown area. Hiring a taxi to take him there, he found a square two-story building with a gated passageway leading to an interior courtyard. It was one of the better sections of the city and he was surprised that the gate was unlocked. He asked the driver to wait and stepped inside. The first thing he saw in the courtyard was a large shade tree with a bright green lizard scurrying toward him along one branch. He drew back in alarm and heard gentle laughter from somewhere behind him.

"Don't worry. Max won't hurt you," a woman's voice reassured him.

For a moment he still could not see her. Then a flash of red on an upstairs balcony caught his eye and he observed a young woman with blond hair descending an iron staircase from the second floor. She wore a long house-coat and as she drew nearer he saw that she was barefoot. "My name is Adelaide Toliara, and you are Mr.—?"

"Rand. I'm British."

"I could tell," she said with a smile. Her accent was British colonial and it took him a moment to place it.

"And you're Australian."

"Very good, Mr. Rand."

"Adelaide. Named after the city."

"Of course." She'd come up to him now and even without shoes she was almost his height. "What do you want? Have you brought home my husband's ashes?"

"I'm sorry, no. I imagine his death was a great shock to you."

"Not especially. The only shock was that he died at the London airport rather than in a Tana brothel."

Rand glanced uncomfortably at the lizard, which hung from a branch directly over his head. "Might we go inside for a chat?"

"It's too hot in there. Come over in the shade. We have a table and chairs."

He followed her across the courtyard to a green wrought-iron table with four matching chairs. The lizard made no attempt to follow. Adelaide picked up a small bell on the table and rang it. A native servant appeared and she asked Rand what he'd like to drink.

"Something cool would be nice," he admitted.

"The water isn't fit to drink, but I have some Tusker from the mainland."

He'd drunk the African beer before. "That'll be fine."

"Two Tuskers," she told the servant, who retreated in silence.

"Do you live here alone?" Rand asked.

"When my husband is away. I guess now he's away permanently." She thought about that, then added, "But I have a great many friends. Sometimes they stay overnight. And my servant Janje has a room downstairs."

"I wanted to talk to you about Telga's business," he said as the servant returned with glasses and two bottles of Tusker.

"The animal business."

"Yes."

She sighed and poured herself a beer. "I came here from Australia three years ago to work as a teacher. Telga was virtually the first person I met on the island. I knew he was in the export business but I didn't learn about the animal trade until after we were married. It seemed harmless enough." For the first time she allowed her pale blue eyes to meet Rand's.

"The smuggling and selling of exotic animals is big business these days. Those tortoises your husband was carrying could be worth ten thousand dollars each when grown."

"That much?"

"I need to know where he obtained them, Mrs. Toliara."

She tilted her head slightly, as if thinking about the question and how to answer it. Finally she said, "I'm told the jungles of Madagascar are full of exotic animals. As our population increases, more and more of those jungles are being burnt away, not unlike the rain forests of the Amazon. Telga told me that if the animals weren't captured and exported they'd die."

"I suppose there's some truth to that," Rand agreed. "But the fact remains that this animal trade is illegal, and a great many people are profiting from it. Was your husband capturing the animals himself?"

"No, no!" She scoffed at the idea. "He bought them from a middleman, someone named Frier at the Ice Cream Bar. It used to sell ice cream, now it sells whiskey and women."

"Do you know Frier? Could you introduce me?"

She hesitated only a moment. "I could, but what's in it for me?"

"You might help find your husband's killer."

A slow smile curled her lips. "I could do that, yes. Finish your beer and we'll go for a walk. The Ice Cream Bar is only a half-mile down the road."

Rand sent the waiting taxi on its way and walked with her. She had not bothered with shoes, and he realized now that the red housecoat was really some sort of native dress. "Don't your feet get dusty?" he asked, watching the sand gradually coat her red toenails.

"I don't like shoes. My feet sweat in this climate."

The Ice Cream Bar no longer catered to children. Though it was still midafternoon, a half-dozen men loitered at the bar and a few others sat at a table playing some sort of gambling game with matchsticks. They seemed to be Malaysians, though Rand couldn't be certain. A couple of dusky women sat together at one end of the bar, ignored by the men.

Adelaide spoke quietly to one of the men at the bar and he glanced over at Rand. He was dressed better than the others; in a shirt with epaulets that might have indicated a ship's officer, but his thin body and sallow complexion hinted at some recent illness. He sauntered over and joined them at a table. "This is Captain Frier," Adelaide said. "Mr. Rand."

Frier smiled, showing a gold tooth, and shook hands. "You're interested in animals?"

"At the moment, radiated tortoises."

"Very rare. Each one is different, you know."

"Mrs. Toliara's husband was killed smuggling them into Heathrow Airport."

"I was sorry to hear that. Such things are rare. It's not a violent game."

"What do you deal in?" Rand asked.

"Reptiles. Snakes and tortoises. They're the best because they can survive long trips without food or water. Birds and monkeys are tough. Only ten percent of the birds survive."

"Aren't the customs agents on this end watching for them?"

Frier raised a hand and signaled the bartender. "Another rum here. You want anything?" Rand and Adelaide both ordered Tuskers. "When things are tight we take the animals off the island in speedboats. Madagascar has no coast guard."

"But Telga left from here, planning to change planes in London for a flight to Orlando, Florida."

Captain Frier shrugged. "That means he paid someone at the airport. It's often done. A safer way these days is to transport the animals by boat to the French island of Réunion, east of here, or to South Africa. There the animals are supplied with fake documents indicating they've been bred in captivity, making their shipment legal."

"Do you have a boat for this?" Rand asked.

Frier squinted at him and grinned. "I could find you one."

Adelaide was getting nervous. "He's an investigator, Frier, not a customer."

"I'm trying to learn about the business," Rand admitted. "For example, which is easier to smuggle, snakes or tortoises?"

"Snakes," Frier answered at once. "They can fit into almost any shape of cavity and stay there. I can introduce you to a couple of the boys, if you're looking for a boa."

"I want to know where the tortoises come from."

"One good place is Tulear, on the southwest coast. Ask around for a woman named Gin. She is known as the tortoise merchant."

When Rand and Adelaide left the Ice Cream Bar he asked if she'd be staying on now that her husband was dead. "Of course," she answered. "Where else would I go?"

"But what is there for you here?"

She shrugged. "I like the animals."

The plane that took Rand from the capital to Tulear was a small propeller craft that seemed to cruise along barely above the treetops. He saw a great deal of the country during the two hours of the flight, passing over burning grasslands and once flying straight through a cloud of smoke rising from a jungle river basin. The airport at Tulear was smaller than Tana's, but flying over the town's harbor he was impressed by the blueness of the water. As soon as he stepped from the plane he felt a cool breeze that offered welcome relief from the oppressive heat of the capital city.

It was a poor town, with a sense of desperation about it. Along the beach fishermen caught what they could, and tropic winds sent eddies of sand into the air. Still, there was a beach hotel for tourists and Rand took a room there. The first man he asked about Gin, the tortoise merchant, spit on the ground and walked away. He had better luck with a teenage boy, offering him money before asking the question. "Gin Gin," the boy answered with a grin, grabbing at the folded bill. "She lives with the tortoises. Down that street to the end, a small house with a tin roof." Then he was gone.

Rand walked quickly down the street, careful to avoid the occasional groups of young men who stood watching him. It was not a place he'd like to be after dark. There was only one house with a tin roof, and he knocked at the rickety door. After a moment a native woman appeared. "I am interested in tortoises," he told her.

"Come in," she answered in French. It was a language Rand knew moderately well. He was surprised to hear it spoken here until he remembered the island's former ties with France.

"You are Gin?"

"Yes. I will show you tortoises."

She was slim and moderately attractive, with dark hair and eyes. Her age was impossible to guess. It might have been thirty or fifty. He followed her into the tin-roofed shack and she showed him a pen piled two and three deep with radiated tortoises. There were easily two dozen of them, a fortune to this woman if she were halfway around the world in Florida. Rand reached out to touch their shells, marveling at the grooved black lines broken by designs of white and beige, no two alike.

"What do you sell these for?" he asked.

She mentioned a figure in Malagasy francs about equal to one pound, far from the ten thousand American dollars these would bring at their final destination. "That is for local people, for food. Three times that much for others like yourself."

At three pounds they were still a fantastic bargain. "Do you know a man named Telga Toliara? Is he a customer?"

"He comes in a boat, buys many tortoises at a time. I have not seen him in a few weeks."

"He's dead," Rand told her, "killed in London."

"A dangerous city."

Rand glanced out the door where the young men loitered. "It's not exactly safe around here."

"They protect me," she said simply.

"Where do these tortoises come from? I'm seeking the source."

"Up the coast. The natives catch them and bring them to me in outrigger canoes."

"When is the next shipment due?"

Gin shrugged. "Maybe tonight. But they will not trust you. Your clothes are too new. They always expect the gendarmes."

"I needed something to wear in the jungle," Rand explained. "The rest of my things are at the hotel."

"Why bother with a hotel when you can sleep on the sand under the stars?"

"My aging bones cry out for a mattress," he told her. "I will come back after dark."

"Perhaps around ten," she suggested as he handed her some francs.

The town seemed to take on a new life after dark, with the sound of an Indian sitar being played somewhere in the distance. There were bonfires along the beach, and groups of people Rand could barely make out, some kneeling for rites he could only imagine. Somewhere far out over the water the glowing trail of a skyrocket streaked across the heavens and then arced into the sea. He moved cautiously, aware of the possibilities for trouble. Once he passed a man in a white suit carrying a furled umbrella, looking completely out of place. But then he no doubt looked out of place himself.

The woman Gin was waiting for him. "They are coming tonight, soon," she told him. She carried a large woven basket, as if for shopping.

"How do you know?"

"Did you see the rocket a few minutes ago? That is Kriter's signal. His canoe will be here soon."

They walked down to the water together, watching the waves dash against the sand. He loved seeing it, remembering his boyhood visits to Brighton beach where there was nothing but pebbles waiting for another ten thousand years of erosion to grind them into sand.

The outrigger canoe was on them before Rand realized it, and a bare-chested young Malaysian leapt out to pull it onto shore. "Only nine tonight, Gin," he said in French. "They're all busy mating."

She flipped back the burlap covering and shined a small flashlight on them. Rand could see the radiating lines of the tortoise shells, as different as fingerprints. "I'll take them," she said quickly.

Kriter motioned toward Rand. "You got a buyer here already?"

"Maybe." She hoisted the sack full of tortoises onto the sand and took several Malagasy franc notes from her pocket.

"There'll be more next time," he promised, pushing off in the outrigger. The entire transaction had taken only a few minutes.

Gin shook her head in disgust. "He usually has seventy or eighty for me. I think he's selling to someone else up the beach."

Rand remembered the man in the white suit. "Is this the rainy season here?"

"No rain until next month," she told him.

"Have you seen any strangers lately? A man in a white suit with an umbrella?"

"There are always tourists."

He took the bag full of radiated tortoises from her, careful not to put his fingers in it. "I may want to buy these from you later. First I'm going to take a walk up the beach. If Kriter landed somewhere else first, where might it have been?"

"Perhaps Ankil Cove, two miles north of here."

"Can I walk along the beach?"

"At night?"

"Right now."

She shrugged. "It is safer than through the jungle. There is a small village there, but the natives are friendly." He wondered if she was mocking him.

After carrying the sack of turtles back to her shack, he returned to the beach and set off up the coast. The stars seemed different from those he saw in London, brighter and more numerous without the glare of city lights. In spots the beach narrowed as the jungle reached out, but for the most part it was an easy, pleasant walk, his way lit by a full moon. Finally, ahead, he saw more bonfires on the beach and knew he'd reached the village at Ankil Cove. That was when he saw the man in the white suit again.

He turned as Rand approached, almost in slow motion, and raised his furled umbrella. Rand dove sideways into the sand, but not quite quickly enough. The silenced bullet creased the side of his head, and everything went black.

When he awakened it was morning, and by the light from the sun he could see small octopuses hung out to dry on racks, already caught by the dawn fishermen. Crouched next to him on the sand, staring into his face, was a lizard he'd seen before.

"Back among the living, Mr. Rand?" a voice asked, and he turned his head slightly to see Adelaide Toliara standing there in a short beach jacket, her legs bare beneath it. She put her arm down to Max and the lizard ran up to her shoulder, its long tail swishing from side to side.

"What happened to me?" he managed to ask. The side of his head hurt a bit, but otherwise he seemed all right.

"You were shot. Luckily the bullet only grazed your skull. I bathed it with some palm oil."

"It was the man in the white suit. Where is he?"

"I don't know. He thinks you're dead."

"He's the one who killed your husband."

Her eyes closed for just an instant and then she opened them and asked, "Why do you say that?"

"Scotland Yard suspected Toliara was killed with a silenced gun hidden inside a cane, because no one heard or saw it. It isn't the rainy season here, yet this man was carrying a furled umbrella. He was certainly out of place, and when I saw him point that umbrella at me I dove for the sand. You know him, don't you?"

"I know him, yes."

Rand tried to sit up. It made his head hurt. For just an instant he was seeing double and it seemed as if the lizard's head were on Adelaide's body. "What are you doing here, anyway? And what's that lizard doing around your neck?"

"Max is a Madagascan day gecko. Very rare. Most geckos found elsewhere are nocturnal. As for what I'm doing here, I'm completing my husband's work."

"You bought the tortoises from Kriter last night."

"Is there anything wrong with that?"

"A woman called Gin was waiting for them on the beach in Tulear."

Adelaide snorted. "She is nothing. She swindled Telga out of a whole shipment once."

"Where is the man in the white suit now?"

"Stop calling him that! His name is Sidney Moullion. He's South African."

"Why did he kill your husband?"

"He had no reason to kill him," she said, reaching back to stroke Max's head.

"But he came here to help you smuggle tortoises."

"One last time. Telga had another trip on his contract."

"What's Moullion's part in all this?"

"Ask him yourself. He'll be coming back for me soon."

"Back here? What for?" Rand was immediately on alert.

"He has some work to do. Then we'll leave together. I've got sixty-five radiated tortoises in sacks."

"Are you going to carry those through customs? More bags of coconuts?" He stood up, shakily, and surveyed the area in all directions. If Sidney Moullion was coming back, he wanted to be ready this time.

"I'll get them through," she assured him.

Off in the distance Rand heard the sound of an approaching speedboat. Adelaide's smile vanished. "You should take cover somewhere. I don't want any more shooting."

"It's him, isn't it?"

"Might be." She dropped the gecko to the ground and motioned Rand into the jungle.

"If you're taking the tortoises, what's he coming back for?"

"I don't know." She seemed distracted. "He does something to them."

"Does something?"

The boat came into view, heading directly for the beach. Rand quickly retreated from view, taking cover at the edge of the trees. He could see Moullion at the wheel of the sleek craft, killing the engine and gliding to a gentle halt in the surf. Adelaide Toliara ran to meet him. The South African waded through the shallow water, looking a bit foolish as he clutched his umbrella.

The woman was speaking to him, carrying on a conversation perhaps meant to distract him from questions about Rand. But as they came closer he heard Moullion ask, "Where is the body?"

"I dragged it into the jungle," she answered.

He studied the sand for a moment and then grabbed her by the arm. "The truth! There are no drag marks in the sand!"

"I—"

"He's alive, isn't he?"

All her pent-up fury seemed to explode then. "Damn it, Sidney, why did you have to kill Telga?"

"That's none of your business." He dropped his umbrella and swung his fist at her.

Prudence might have told Rand to flee deeper into the underbrush, but there was the woman to be considered. He burst from his hiding place and shouted, "Here I am!"

Before Moullion could reach for the umbrella, Rand was on him, toppling him, tussling in the sand. They rolled over once, and Rand already knew he was no match for the younger man. The South African was on top, closing his hands around Rand's throat, when there came a gentle cough behind him. Rand recognized the sound of a silenced gunshot even before the man's hands loosened on his throat.

"I had to do it," Adelaide said, holding the smoking umbrella.

Moullion had rolled over on his back, gasping for breath. Rand leaned close and said, "You're dying. Tell me what's behind this."

He opened his mouth but at first no words came out. Then he patted the breast pocket of his white jacket and mumbled something. Rand strained to hear it. "Diamonds to coconut," Moullion said, and then he was gone.

"Did I kill him?" Adelaide asked.

"You did, and saved my life in the process." He reached into the dead man's breast pocket and took out a folded envelope sealed with tape. "Do you know about this?" he asked her.

"What is it?"

Rand tore a corner off the envelope and poured the contents into the palm of his hand. "Diamonds, and fair-sized ones at that. There must be fifty of them, at least."

She nodded. "From South Africa. I should have known."

"His dying words were 'Diamonds to coconuts.' But how was he smuggling them?"

"Inside the tortoises," she said. "Telga told me once that he seemed to be force-feeding them with some sort of baster. We never knew exactly what he was doing."

"Smuggling diamonds inside of smuggled tortoises. That's a new one on me," Rand admitted. "But it still doesn't tell us why he killed your husband."

"What will I do now?" Adelaide asked, more to herself than to Rand.

"I'd suggest you leave the body here. Turn the tortoises loose and go home. I'll take care of things in London." He picked up the fallen umbrella gun from where she'd dropped it.

"It's over, then?"

"For you. I have one more bit of business."

It had suddenly occurred to him what Moullion's dying words meant.

Ralph Coir welcomed Rand like some nineteenth-century explorer who'd located the source of the Nile. "I read your report, Rand. That was a magnificent piece of work. With Moullion's death this entire smuggling operation seems to have been closed down. I know it's only one of many, but an important one."

"The umbrella gun?"

The bald man nodded. "Ballistics says it's the weapon that killed Telga Toliara, just as you suspected. And the diamonds were a great surprise to everyone." He smiled at Rand. "Your report says Moullion was shot accidentally as you struggled over the weapon."

"That's more or less how it happened."

"Did he ever say why he shot Toliara at Heathrow Airport?"

"No, but I think I can answer that question," Rand said. "You see, there was something staring me in the face from the very beginning and I didn't see it."

"What was that?" Coir asked.

"If Toliara was changing planes at Heathrow for a flight to Florida with the tortoises, why had he passed through customs? Why was he outside the building entering a taxi?"

"Perhaps he had a layover of several hours."

"Even if he had, why double his risk by passing through customs twice, here and in Florida? He could have remained in the transit lounge and allowed his checked luggage and sack of coconuts to be loaded directly onto the Florida plane. The truth was, he never intended to continue on to Florida. He was going to find a buyer on his own in London. Moullion must have been at Heathrow to guard against just such a possibility, and when he saw it happening he killed Toliara."

Ralph Coir shifted uneasily at his desk. "What did he accomplish by that? The coconuts—the tortoises—were still lost to him, along with their hidden cargo of diamonds."

"I asked myself the same question. He might have acted instinctively, without weighing the consequences of his act, but that seemed highly unlikely. There was another possibility. He may have known that by killing Toliara he wasn't abandoning the prize but actually saving it. This could only be true if he knew that the sack of smuggled tortoises, once found by the police, would eventually end up on the desk of his partner in crime—yourself, Mr. Coir."

"That's ridiculous!" the bald man sputtered. "What are you trying to do, Rand?"

"Just get at the truth. You hired me, remember? I suppose you needed some sort of investigation for the record, and never thought I'd get as far as I did. You told me yourself that seized animals bound for America ended up here. If you couldn't arrange somehow to keep them yourself, you could still remove the shipment of South African diamonds they'd been fed. I remember you told me you'd visited South Africa recently."

Coir stared at Rand with fiery eyes. "It's too bad Sidney Moullion isn't alive to back up your assertions."

"He talked about it before he died," Rand said blandly.

"Talked? What did he say?"

"His exact words were 'Diamonds to coconuts.' It meant nothing to me at first, but then I remembered you mentioning that the embassy staff thought they were being funny presenting you with a bag of coconuts. It's your name, Mr. Coir. Coconut fiber, used in rope and matting, is called *coir*. To Moullion 'coconuts' was a code name for Ralph Coir, and it was the word he spoke as he was dying."

The American actually snickered. "Wow! I'd like to see that one get laughed out of court!"

"Oh, I doubt if it will come to court. I have filed a report on my suspicions with your superiors, however. I think it's time you got out of the exotic pet business and the diamond business too, Mr. Coir."

Ralph Coir stood up. "I believe we've talked long enough, Mr. Rand. Good day, sir."

"Good day," Rand said with a smile. "I'll submit a bill for my expenses."

THE SKY-BLUE BALL

Joyce Carol Oates

There was a time when mystery and other genres were considered inferior forms of fiction by the literary-minded. That attitude has changed over the past couple of decades, thanks partly to the efforts of literary writers such as Joyce Carol Oates who have made it an avowed aim to blur the boundaries between genre and literary fiction. Said Publishers Weekly *of one of this author's suspense novels penned under the name Rosamund Smith, "Nobody walks the dark side with a more menacing gait than Oates/Smith." And yet this master of heart-stopping suspense also writes the kind of mainstream fiction that claims the nation's most prestigious awards: a National Book Award, nominations for the Pulitzer Prize and the PEN/Faulkner Award, the National Book Critics Award, the Rea Award for the Short Story, the O. Henry Prize, the O. Henry Special Award for Continuing Achievement, the PEN/Malamud Award for Lifetime Achievement, the Lilia Fish Rand Fiction Prize, and more. Joyce Carol Oates's style is unmistakable. Her tales for* Ellery Queen's Mystery Magazine *usually take us deep within the mind of a central character, allowing us to think the story's dark thoughts in precisely the way her character would think them.*

IN A LONG-AGO time when I didn't know *Yes I was happy, I was myself and I was happy.* In a long-ago time when I wasn't a child any longer yet wasn't entirely not-a-child. In a long-ago time when I seemed often to be alone, and imagined myself lonely. *Yet this is your truest self: alone, lonely.*

One day I found myself walking beside a high brick wall the color of dried blood, the aged bricks loose and moldering, and over the wall came flying a spherical object so brightly blue I thought it was a bird!—until it dropped a few yards in front of me, bouncing at a crooked angle off the broken sidewalk, and I saw that it was a rubber ball. A child had thrown a rubber ball over the wall, and I was expected to throw it back.

Hurriedly I let my things fall into the weeds, ran to snatch up the ball, which looked new, smelled new, spongy and resilient in my hand like a rubber ball I'd played with years before as a little girl; a ball I'd loved and had long ago misplaced; a ball I'd loved and had forgotten. "Here it comes!" I called, and tossed the ball back over the wall; I would have walked on except, a few seconds later, there came the ball again, flying back.

A game, I thought. *You can't quit a game.*

So I ran after the ball as it rolled in the road, in the gravelly dirt, and again snatched it up, squeezing it with pleasure, how spongy, how resilient a rubber ball, and again I tossed it over the wall; feeling happiness in swinging my arm as I hadn't done for years since I'd lost interest in such childish games. And this time I waited expectantly, and again it came!— the most beautiful sky-blue rubber ball rising high, high into the air above my head and pausing for a heartbeat before it began to fall, to sink, like an object possessed of its own willful volition; so there was plenty of time for me to position myself beneath it and catch it firmly with both hands.

"Got it!"

I was fourteen years old and did not live in this neighborhood, nor anywhere in the town of Strykersville, New York (population 5,600). I lived on a small farm eleven miles to the north and I was brought to Strykersville by school bus, and consequently I was often alone; for this year, ninth grade, was my first at the school and I hadn't made many friends. And though I had relatives in Strykersville these were not relatives close to my family; they were not relatives eager to acknowledge me; for we who still lived in the country, hadn't yet made the inevitable move into town, were perceived inferior to those who lived in town. And, in fact, my family was poorer than our relatives who lived in Strykersville.

At our school teachers referred to the nine farm children bused there as "North Country children." We were allowed to understand that "North Country children" differed significantly from Strykersville children.

I was not thinking of such things now, I was smiling thinking it must be a particularly playful child on the other side of the wall, a little girl like me; like the little girl I'd been; though the wall was ugly and forbidding with rusted signs EMPIRE MACHINE PARTS and PRIVATE PROPERTY NO TRESPASSING. On the other side of the Chautauqua & Buffalo railroad yard was a street of small, wood-frame houses; it must have been in one of these that the little girl, my invisible playmate, lived. She must be much younger than I was; for fourteen-year-old girls didn't play such heedless games with strangers, we grew up swiftly if our families were not well-to-do.

I threw the ball back over the wall, calling, "Hi! Hi, there!" But there was no reply. I waited; I was standing in broken concrete, amid a scrubby patch of weeds. Insects buzzed and droned around me as if in curiosity, yellow butterflies no larger than my smallest fingernail fluttered and caught in my hair, tickling me. The sun was bright as a nova in a pebbled-white soiled sky that was like a thin chamois cloth about to be lifted away and I thought, *This is the surprise I've been waiting for.* For somehow I had acquired the belief that a surprise, a nice surprise, was waiting for me. I had only to merit it, and it would happen. (And if I did not merit it, it would not happen.) Such a surprise could not come from God but only from strangers, by chance.

Another time the sky-blue ball sailed over the wall, after a longer interval of perhaps thirty seconds; and at an unexpected angle as if it had been thrown away from me, from my voice, purposefully. Yet there it came, as if it could not not come: My invisible playmate was obliged to continue the game. I had no hope of catching it but ran blindly into the road (which was partly asphalt and partly gravel and not much traveled except by trucks) and there came a dump truck headed at me, I heard the ugly shriek of brakes and a deafening angry horn and I'd fallen onto my knees, I'd cut my knees that were bare, probably I'd torn my skirt, scrambling quickly to my feet, my cheeks smarting with shame, for wasn't I too grown a girl for such behavior? "Get the hell out of the road!" a man's voice was furious in rectitude, the voice of so many adult men of my acquaintance, you did not question such voices, you did not doubt them, you ran quickly to get out of their way; already I'd snatched up the ball, panting like a dog, trying to hide the ball in my skirt as I turned, shrinking and ducking so the truck driver couldn't see my face, for what if he was someone who knew my father, what if he recognized me, knew my name. But already the truck was thundering past, already I'd been forgotten.

Back then I ran to the wall, though both my knees throbbed with pain, and I was shaking as if shivering, the air had grown cold, a shaft of cloud had pierced the sun. I threw the ball back over the wall again, underhand, so that it rose high, high—so that my invisible playmate would have plenty of time to run and catch it. And so it disappeared behind the wall and I waited, I was breathing hard and did not investigate my bleeding knees, my torn skirt. More clouds pierced the sun and shadows moved swift and certain across the earth like predator fish. After a while I called out hesitantly, "Hi? Hello?" It was like a ringing telephone you answer but no one is there. You wait, you inquire again, shyly, "Hello?" A vein throbbed in my forehead, a tinge of pain glimmered behind my eyes, that warning of pain, of punishment, following excitement. The child had drifted away, I supposed; she'd lost interest in our game, if it was a game. And suddenly it seemed silly and contemptible to me, and sad: There I stood, fourteen years old, a long-limbed weed of a girl, no longer a child yet panting and bleeding from the knees, the palms of my hands, too, chafed and scraped and dirty; there I stood alone in front of a moldering brick wall waiting for—what?

It was my school notebook, my several textbooks I'd let fall into the grass and I would afterward discover that my math textbook was muddy, many pages damp and torn; my spiral notebook in which I kept careful notes of the intransigent rules of English grammar and sample sentences diagrammed was soaked in a virulent-smelling chemical and my teacher's laudatory comments in red and my grades of A (for all my grades at Stry-kersville Junior High were A, of that I was obsessively proud) had become illegible as if they were grades of C, D, F. I should have taken up my books and walked hurriedly away and put the sky-blue ball out of my mind entirely but I was not so free, through my life I've been made to realize that I am not free, as others appear to be free, at all. For the "nice" surprise carries with it the "bad" surprise and the two are so intricately entwined they cannot be separated, nor even defined as separate. So though my head pounded I felt obliged to look for a way over the wall. Though my knees were scraped and bleeding I located a filthy oil drum and shoved it against the wall and climbed shakily up on it, dirtying my hands and arms, my legs, my clothes, even more. And I hauled myself over the wall, and jumped down, a drop of about ten feet, the breath knocked out of me as I landed, the shock of the impact reverberating through me, along my spine, as if I'd been struck a sledgehammer blow to the soles of my feet. At once I saw that there could be no little girl here, the factory yard was surely deserted, about the size of a baseball diamond totally walled in and over-grown with weeds pushing through cracked asphalt, thistles, stunted trees, and clouds of tiny yellow butterflies clustered here in such profusion I was made to see that they were not beautiful creatures, but mere insects, hor-rible. And rushing at me as if my very breath sucked them at me, sticking against my sweaty face, and in my snarled hair.

Yet stubbornly I searched for the ball. I would not leave without the ball. I seemed to know that the ball must be there, somewhere on the other side of the wall, though the wall would have been insurmountable for a little girl. And at last, after long minutes of searching, in a heat of indignation I discovered the ball in a patch of chicory. It was no longer sky blue but faded and cracked; its dun-colored rubber showed through the venous-cracked surface, like my own ball, years ago. Yet I snatched it up in tri-umph, and squeezed it, and smelled it—it smelled of nothing: of the earth: of the sweating palm of my own hand.

THE WRONG HANDS

Peter Robinson

A good sense of place is a strong asset in a crime writer and Yorkshire-born Peter Robinson is eminently gifted with it. His books featuring Detective Chief Inspector Alan Banks take place in a fictional Yorkshire dale, but it is a place that combines the features and atmosphere of several of the real dales in a masterful way. Robinson, who has resided in Canada since finishing his undergraduate degree in England in the mid-1970s, saw his Inspector Banks series get off to a brilliant start when the first novel received award nominations from both the Crime Writers of Canada and Britain's Crime Writers' Association. The series has since received acclaim in the United States as well, and it is well-earned praise, for Robinson, like the living authors in the field he most admires, Ruth Rendell and P. D. James, has succeeded in the difficult task of bringing to the police novel elements of the psychological thriller. His unusual talents have earned him an Edgar Allan Poe Award nomination from the Mystery Writers of America and three Arthur Ellis Awards from the Crime Writers of Canada.

"IS EVERYTHING IN order?" the old man asked, his scrawny fingers clutching the comforter like talons.

"Seems to be," said Mitch.

Drawing up the will had been a simple enough task. Mr. Garibaldi and his wife had the dubious distinction of outliving both their children, and there wasn't much to leave.

"Would you like to sign it now?" he asked, holding out his Mont Blanc.

The old man clutched the pen the way a child holds a crayon and scribbled his illegible signature on the documents.

"There . . . that's done," said Mitch. And he placed the papers in his briefcase.

Mr. Garibaldi nodded. The movement brought on a spasm and such a coughing fit that Mitch thought the old man was going to die right there and then.

But he recovered. "Will you do me a favour?" he croaked when he'd got his breath back.

Mitch frowned. "If I can."

With one bent, shrivelled finger, Mr. Garibaldi pointed to the floor under the window. "Pull the carpet back," he said.

Mitch stood up and looked.

"Please," said Mr. Garibaldi. "The carpet."

Mitch walked over to the window and rolled back the carpet. Underneath was nothing but floorboards.

"One of the boards is loose," said the old man. "The one directly in line with the wall socket. Lift it up."

Mitch felt and, sure enough, part of the floorboard was loose. He lifted it easily with his fingernails. Underneath, wedged between the joists, lay a package wrapped in old newspaper.

"That's it," said the old man. "Take it out."

Mitch did. It was heavier than he had expected.

"Now put the board back and replace the carpet."

After he had done as he was asked, Mitch carried the package over to the bed.

"Open it," said Mr. Garibaldi. "Go on, it won't bite you."

Slowly, Mitch unwrapped the newspaper. It was from December 18, 1947, he noticed, and the headline reported a blizzard dumping twenty-eight inches of snow on New York City the day before. Inside, he found a layer of oilcloth wrapped around the object. When he had folded back that too, the gun gleamed up at him. It was old, he could tell that, but it looked in superb condition. He hefted it into his hand, felt its weight and balance, pointed it towards the wall as if to shoot.

"Be careful," said the old man. "It's loaded."

Mitch looked at the gun again, then put it back on the oilcloth. His fingers were smudged with oil or grease, so he took a tissue from the bedside table and wiped them off as best he could.

"What the hell are you doing with a loaded gun?" he asked.

Mr. Garibaldi sighed. "It's a Luger," he said. "First World War, probably. Old, anyway. A friend gave it to me many years ago. A German friend. I've kept it ever since. Partly as a memento of him and partly for protection. You know what this city's been getting like these past few years. I've maintained it, cleaned it, kept it loaded. Now I'm gonna die I want to hand it in. I don't want it to fall into the wrong hands."

Mitch set the Luger down on the bed. "Why tell me?" he asked.

"Because it's unregistered and I'd like you to hand it over for me." He shook his head and coughed again. "I haven't got long left. I don't want no cops coming round here and giving me a hard time."

"They won't give you a hard time." More like give you a medal for handing over an unregistered firearm, Mitch thought.

"Maybe not. But . . ." Mr. Garibaldi grabbed Mitch's wrist with his talon. The fingers felt cold and dry, like a reptile's skin. Mitch tried to pull back a little, but the old man held on, pulled him closer, and croaked, "Sophie doesn't know. It would make her real angry to know we had a gun in the house the last fifty years and I kept it from her. I don't want to end my days with my wife mad at me. Please, Mr. Mitchell. It's a small favor I ask."

Mitch scratched the side of his eye. True enough, he thought, it *was* a small favour. And it might prove a profitable one, too. Old firearms were worth something to collectors, and Mitch knew a cop who had connections. All he had to say was that he had been entrusted this gun by a client, who had brought it to his office, that he had put it in the safe and called the police immediately. What could be wrong with that?

"Okay," he said, rewrapping the gun and slipping it in his briefcase along with the will. "I'll do as you ask. Don't worry. You rest now. Everything will be okay."

Mr. Garibaldi smiled and seemed to sink into a deep sleep.

Mitch stood on the porch of the Garibaldi house and pulled on his sheepskin-lined gloves, glad to be out of the cloying atmosphere of the sickroom, even if it was minus ninety or something outside.

He was already wearing his heaviest overcoat over a suit and a wool scarf, but still he was freezing. It was one of those clear winter nights when the ice splinters underfoot and the breeze off the lake seems to numb you right to the bone. Reflected street lamps splintered in the broken mirror of the sidewalk, the colour of Mr. Garibaldi's jaundiced eyes.

Mitch pulled his coat tighter around his scarf and set off, cracking the iced-over puddles as he went. Here and there, the remains of last week's snow had frozen into ruts, and he almost slipped and fell a couple of times on the uneven surface.

As he walked, he thought of old Garibaldi, with no more than a few days left to live. The old man must have been in pain sometimes, but he never complained. And he surely must have been afraid of death? Maybe dying put things in perspective, Mitch thought. Maybe the mind, facing the eternal, icy darkness of death, had ways of dealing with its impending extinction, of discarding the dross, the petty and the useless.

Or perhaps not. Maybe the old man just lay there day after day running baseball statistics through his mind; or wishing he'd gone to bed with his neighbour's wife when he had the chance.

As Mitch walked up the short hill he cursed the fact that you could never get a decent parking spot in these residential streets. He'd had to park in the lot behind the drugstore, the next street over, and the quickest way there was through a dirt alley just about wide enough for a garbage truck to pass through.

It happened as he cut through the alley. And it happened so fast that, afterwards, he couldn't be quite sure whether he felt the sharp blow to the back of his head before his feet slipped out from under him, or after.

When Mitch opened his eyes again, the first thing he saw was the night sky. It looked like a black satin bedsheet with some rich woman's diamonds spilled all over it. There was no moon.

He felt frozen to the marrow. He didn't know how long he had been lying there in the alley—long enough to die of exposure, it felt like—but when he checked his watch, he saw he had only been out a little over five minutes. Not surprising no one had found him yet. Not here, on a night like this.

He lay on the frozen mud and took stock. Despite the cold, everything hurt—his elbow, which he had cracked trying to break his fall; his tailbone; his right shoulder; and, most of all, his head—and the pain was sharp and spiky, not at all numb like the rest of him. He reached around and touched the sore spot on the back of his head. His fingers came away sticky with blood.

He took a deep breath and tried to get to his feet, but he could only manage to slip and skitter around like a newborn lamb, making himself even more dizzy. There was no purchase, nothing to grip. Snail-like, he slid himself along the ice towards the rickety fence. There, by reaching out and grabbing the wooden rails carefully, he was able to drag himself to his feet.

At first, he wished he hadn't. His head started to spin and he thought it was going to split open with pain. For a moment, he was sure he was going to fall again. He held on to the fence for dear life and vomited, the world swimming around his head. After that, he felt a little better. Maybe he wasn't going to die.

The only light shone from a street lamp at the end of the alley, not really enough to search by, so Mitch used the plastic penlight attached to his key ring to look for his briefcase. But it wasn't there. Stepping carefully on the ribbed ice, still in pain and unsure of his balance, Mitch extended the area of his search in case the briefcase had skidded off somewhere on the ice when he fell. It was nowhere to be found.

Almost as an afterthought, as the horrible truth was beginning to dawn on him, he felt for his wallet. Gone. So he'd been mugged. The blow had come *before* the fall. And they'd taken his briefcase.

Then Mitch remembered the gun.

The next morning was a nightmare. Mitch had managed to get himself home from the alley without crashing the car, and after a long, hot bath, a glass of scotch, and four extra-strength Tylenol, he began to feel a little better. He seemed to remember his mother once saying you shouldn't go to sleep after a bump on the head—he didn't know why—but it didn't stop him that night.

In the morning he awoke aching all over.

When he had showered, taken more Tylenol, and forced himself to eat some bran flakes, he poured a second cup of strong black coffee and sat down to think things out. None of his thoughts brought any comfort.

He hadn't gone to the cops. How could he, given what he had been carrying? Whichever way you looked at it, he had been in possession of an illegal, unregistered firearm when he was mugged. Even if the cops had been lenient, there was the Law Society to reckon with, and like most lawyers, Mitch feared the Law Society far more than he feared the cops.

Maybe he could have sort of skipped over the gun in his account of the mugging. After all, he was pretty sure that it couldn't be traced either to him or to Garibaldi. But what if the cops found the briefcase, and the gun was still inside it? How could he explain that?

Would that be worse than if the briefcase turned up and the gun was gone? If the muggers took it, then chances were someone might get shot with it. Either way, it was a bad scenario for Mitch, and it was all his fault. Well, maybe *fault* was too strong a word—he couldn't help getting mugged—but he still felt somehow responsible.

All he could do was hope that whoever took the gun would get rid of it, throw it in the lake, before anyone came to any harm.

Some hope.

Later that morning, Mitch remembered Garibaldi's will. That had gone, too, along with the briefcase and the gun. And it would have to be replaced.

There's only one true will—copies have no legal standing—and if you lose it you could have a hell of a mess on your hands. Luckily, he had Garibaldi's will on his computer. All he had to do was print it out again and hope to hell the old guy hadn't died during the night.

He hadn't. Puzzled, but accepting Mitch's excuse of a minor error he'd come across when proofreading the document, Garibaldi signed again with a shaking hand.

"Is the gun safe?" he asked afterwards. "You've got it locked away in your safe?"

"Yes," Mitch lied. "Yes, don't worry, the gun's perfectly safe."

Every day Mitch scanned the paper from cover to cover for news of a shooting or a gun found abandoned somewhere. He even took to buying the *Sun*, which he normally wouldn't even use to light a fire at the cottage, because it covered far more local crime than the *Globe and Mail* or the *Toronto Star*. Anything to do with a gun was sure to make it into the *Sun*.

But it wasn't until three weeks and three days after the mugging—and two weeks after Mr. Garibaldi's death "peacefully, at home"—that the item appeared. And it was big enough news to make the *Globe and Mail*.

> Mr. Charles McVie was shot dead in his home last night during the course of an apparent burglary. A police spokesperson says Mr. McVie was shot twice, once in the chest and once in the groin, while interrupting a burglar at his Beaches mansion shortly after midnight last night. He died of his wounds three hours later at Toronto East General Hospital. Detective Greg Hollins, who has been assigned the case, declined to comment on whether the police are following any significant leads at the moment, but he did inform our reporter that preliminary tests indicate the bullet was most likely fired from an old 9mm semiautomatic weapon, such as a Luger, unusual and fairly rare these days. As yet, police have not been able to locate the gun. Mr. McVie, 62, made his fortune in the construction business. His wife, Laura, who was staying overnight with friends in Windsor when the shooting occurred, had no comment when she was reached early this morning.

The newspaper shook in Mitch's hands. It had happened. Somebody had died because of him. But while he felt guilt, he also felt fear. Was there really no way the police could tie the gun to him or Mr. Garibaldi? Thank God the old man was dead, or he might hear about the shooting and his conscience might oblige him to come forward. Luckily, his widow, Sophie, knew nothing.

With luck, the old Luger was in the deepest part of the lake for sure by now. Whether anyone else had touched it or not, Mitch knew damn well that he had, and that his greasy fingerprints weren't only all over the handle and the barrel, but they were on the wrapping paper, too. The muggers had probably been wearing gloves when they robbed him—it was a cold night—and maybe they'd had the sense to keep them on when they saw what was in the briefcase.

Calm down, he told himself. Even if the cops did find his fingerprints on the gun, they had no way of knowing whose they were. He had never been fingerprinted in his life, and the cops would have no reason to subject him to it now.

They couldn't connect Charles McVie to either Mr. Garibaldi or to Mitch.

Except for one thing.

Mitch had done McVie's will two years ago, after his marriage to Laura, his second wife.

Mitch had known that Laura McVie was younger than her husband, but even that knowledge hadn't prepared him for the woman who opened the door to him three days after Charles McVie's funeral.

Black became her. Really became her, the way it set off her creamy complexion, long blond hair, Kim Basinger lips, and eyes the colour of a bluejay's wing.

"Yes?" she said, frowning slightly.

Mitch had put on his very best, most expensive suit, and he knew he looked sharp. He didn't want her to think he was some ambulance chaser come after her husband's money.

As executor, Laura McVie was under no obligation to use the same lawyer who had prepared her husband's will to handle his estate. Laura might have a lawyer of her own in mind. But Mitch *did* have the will, so there was every chance that if he presented himself well she would choose him to handle the estate too.

And there was much more money in estates—especially those as big as McVie's—than there was in wills.

At least, Mitch thought, he wasn't so hypocritical as to deny that he had mixed motives for visiting the widow. Didn't everyone have mixed motives? He felt partly responsible for McVie's death, of course, and a part of him genuinely wanted to offer the widow help.

After Mitch had introduced himself, Laura looked him over, plump lower lip fetchingly nipped between two sharp white teeth, then she flashed him a smile and said, "Please come in, Mr. Mitchell. I was wondering what to do about all that stuff. I really could use some help." Her voice was husky and low-pitched, with just a subtle hint of that submissive tone that can drive certain men wild.

Mitch followed her into the high-ceilinged hallway, watching the way her hips swayed under the mourning dress.

He was in. All right! He almost executed a little jig on the parquet floor.

The house was an enormous heap of stone overlooking the ravine. It had always reminded Mitch of an English vicarage, or what he assumed an English vicarage looked like from watching PBS. Inside, though, it was bright and spacious and filled with modern furniture—not an antimacassar in sight. The paintings that hung on the white walls were all contemporary abstracts and geometric designs, no doubt originals and worth a small fortune in themselves. The stereo equipment was state of the art, as were the large-screen TV, VCR, and laser-disc player.

Laura McVie sat on a white sofa and crossed her legs. The dress she wore was rather short for mourning, Mitch thought, though he wasn't likely to complain about the four or five inches of smooth thigh it revealed. Especially as the lower part was sheathed in black silk stockings and the upper was bare and white.

She took a cigarette from a carved wooden box on the coffee table and lit it with a lighter that looked like a baseball. Mitch declined the offer to join her.

"I hope you don't mind," she said, lowering her eyes. "It's my only vice."

"Of course not." Mitch cleared his throat. "I just wanted to come and tell you how sorry I was to hear about the . . . the tragic accident. Your husband was—"

"It wasn't an accident, Mr. Mitchell," she said calmly. "My husband was murdered. I believe we should face the truth clearly and not hide behind euphemisms, don't you?"

"Well, if you put it like that. . . ."

She nodded. "You were saying about my husband?"

"Well, I didn't know him well, but I *have* done some legal work for him—specifically his will—and I am aware of his circumstances."

"My husband was very rich, Mr. Mitchell."

"Exactly. I thought . . . well . . . there are some unscrupulous people out there, Mrs. McVie."

"Please, call me Laura."

"Laura. There are some unscrupulous people out there, and I thought if there was anything I could do to help, perhaps give advice, take the burden off your hands . . . ?"

"What burden would that be, Mr. Mitchell?"

Mitch sat forward and clasped his hands on his knees. "When someone dies, Mrs.—Laura—there are always problems, legal wrangling and the like. Your husband's affairs seem to be in good order, judging from his will, but that was made two years ago. I'd hate to see someone come and take advantage of you."

"Thank you," Laura said. "You're so sweet. And why shouldn't you handle the estate? Someone has to do it. I can't."

Mitch had the strangest feeling that something was going awry here. Laura McVie didn't seem at all the person to be taken advantage of, yet she seemed to be swallowing his line of patter. That could only be, he decided, because it suited her, too. And why not? It would take a load off her mind.

"That wasn't the main reason I came, though," Mitch pressed on, feeling an irrational desire to explain himself. "I genuinely wanted to see if I could help in any way."

"Why?" she asked, blue eyes open wide. "Why should you? Mr. Mitchell, I've come to learn that people do things for selfish motives. Self-interest rules. Always. I don't believe in altruism. Nor did my husband. At least we were agreed on that." She turned aside, flicked some ash at the ashtray, and missed. In contrast to everything else in the place, the tin ashtray looked as if it had been stolen from a lowlife bar. "So you want to help me?" she said. "For a fee, of course."

Mitch felt embarrassed and uncomfortable. The part of him that had desperately wanted to make amends for his part in Charles McVie's death was being thwarted by the frankness and openness of the widow. Yes, he could use the money—of course he could—but that really *wasn't* his only reason for being there, and he wanted her to know that. How could he explain that he really wasn't such a bad guy?

"There are expenses involved in settling an estate," Mitch went on. "Of course there are. But I'm not here to cheat you."

She smiled at him indulgently. "Of course not."

Which definitely came across as, *"As if you could."*

"But if you'll allow me to—"

She shifted her legs, showing more thigh. "Mr. Mitchell," she said. "I'm getting the feeling that you really do have another reason for coming to see me. If it's not that you're after my husband's money, then what are you after?"

Mitch swallowed. "I . . . I feel . . . You see, I—"

"Come on, Mr. Mitchell. You can tell me. You'll feel better."

The voice that had seemed so submissive when Mitch first heard it now became hypnotic, so warm, so trustworthy, so easy to answer. And he had to tell someone.

"I feel partly responsible for your husband's death," he said, looking into her eyes. "Oh, I'm not the burglar, I'm not the killer. But I think I inadvertently supplied the gun."

Laura McVie looked puzzled. Now he had begun, Mitch saw no point in stopping. If he could only tell this woman the full story, he thought, then she would understand. Perhaps she would even be sympathetic towards him. So he told her.

When he had finished, Laura stood up abruptly and walked over to the picture window with its view of a back garden as big as High Park. Mitch sat where he was and looked at her from behind. Her legs were close together and her arms were crossed. She seemed to be turned in on herself. He couldn't tell whether she was crying or not, but her shoulders seemed to be moving.

"Well?" he asked, after a while. "What do you think?"

She let the silence stretch a moment, then dropped her arms and turned around slowly. Her eyes did look moist with tears. "What do I think?" she said. "I don't know. I don't know what to think. I think that maybe if you'd reported the gun stolen, the police would have searched for it and my husband wouldn't have been murdered."

"But I would have been charged, disbarred."

"Mr. Mitchell, surely that's a small price to pay for someone's life? I'm sorry. I think you'd better go. I can't think straight right now."

"But I—"

"Please, Mr. Mitchell. Leave." She turned back to the window again and folded her arms, shaking.

Mitch got up off the sofa and headed for the door. He felt defeated, as if he had left something important unfinished, but there was nothing he could do about it. Only slink off with his tail between his legs feeling worse than when he had come. Why hadn't he just told her he was after handling McVie's estate. Money, pure and simple. Self-interest like that she would have understood.

Two days later, and still no developments reported in the McVie investigation, Laura phoned.

"Mr. Mitchell?"

"Yes."

"I'm sorry about my behaviour the other day. I was upset, as you can imagine."

"I can understand that," Mitch said. "I don't blame you. I don't even know why I told you."

"I'm glad you did. I've had time to think about it since then, and I'm beginning to realize how terrible you must feel. I want you to realize that I don't blame you. It's not the gun that commits the crime, after all, is it? It's the person who pulls the trigger. I'm sure if the burglar hadn't got that one, he'd have got one somewhere else. Look, this is very awkward over the telephone; do you think you could come to the house?"

"When?"

"How about this evening. For dinner?"

"Fine," said Mitch. "I'm really glad you can find it in your heart to forgive me."

"Eight o'clock?"

"Eight it is."

When he put down the phone, Mitch jumped to his feet, punched the air, shouted, "Yes!"

"Dinner" was catered by a local Italian restaurant, Laura McVie not being, in her own words, "much of a cook." Two waiters delivered the food, served it discreetly, and took away the dirty dishes.

Mostly, Mitch and Laura made small talk in the candlelight over the pasta and wine, and it wasn't until the waiters had left and they were alone, relaxing on the sofa, each cradling a snifter of Courvoisier XO cognac, with mellow jazz playing in the background, that the conversation became more intimate.

Laura was still funereally clad, but tonight her dress, made of semi-transparent layers of black chiffon—more than enough for decency—fell well below knee-height. There was still no disguising the curves, and the rustling sounds as she crossed her legs made Mitch more than a little hot under the collar.

Laura puckered her lips to light a cigarette. When she had blown the smoke out, she asked, "Are you married?"

Mitch shook his head.

"Ever been?"

"Nope."

"Just didn't meet the right girl, is that it?"

"Something like that."

"You're not gay, are you?"

He laughed. "What on earth made you think that?"

She rested her free hand on his and smiled. "Don't worry. Nothing made me think it. Nothing in particular. Just checking, that's all."

"No," Mitch said. "I'm not gay."

"More cognac?"

"Sure." Mitch was already feeling a little tipsy, but he didn't want to spoil the mood.

She fetched the bottle and poured them each a generous measure. "I didn't really *love* Charles, you know," she said when she had settled down and smoothed her dress again. "I mean, I respected him, I even liked him, I just didn't love him."

"Why did you marry him?"

Laura shrugged. "I don't know, really. He asked me. He was rich and seemed to live an exciting life. Travel. Parties. I got to meet all kinds of celebrities. We'd only been married two years, you know. And we'd only known one another a few weeks before we got married. We hadn't even . . . you know. Anyway, I'm sorry he's dead . . . in a way."

"What do you mean?"

Laura leaned forward and stubbed out her cigarette. Then she brushed back a long blond tress and took another sip of cognac before answering. "Well," she said, "now that he's dead, it's all mine, isn't it? I'd be a hypocrite and a fool if I said that didn't appeal to me. All this wealth and no strings attached. No responsibilities."

"What responsibilities were there before?"

"Oh, you know. The usual wifely kind. Charles was never, well . . . let's say he wasn't a very passionate lover. He wanted me more as a showpiece than anything else. Something to hang on his arm that looked good. Don't get me wrong, I didn't mind. It was a small price to pay. And then we were forever having to entertain the most boring people. Business acquaintances. You know the sort of thing. Well, now that Charles is gone, I won't have to do that anymore, will I? I'll be able to do what I want. Exactly what I want."

Almost without Mitch knowing it, Laura had edged nearer towards him as she was speaking, and now she was so close he could smell the warm, acrid smoke on her breath. He found it curiously intoxicating. Soon she was close enough to kiss.

She took hold of his hand and rested it on her breast. "It's been a week since the funeral," she said. "Don't you think it's time I took off my widow's weeds?"

When Mitch left Laura McVie's house the following morning, he was beginning to think he might be onto a good thing. Why stop at being estate executor? he asked himself. He already knew that, under the terms of the will, Laura got everything—McVie had no children or other living relatives—and *everything* was somewhere in the region of five million dollars.

Even if he didn't love her—and how could you tell if you loved someone after just one night?—he certainly felt passionately drawn to her. They got on well together, thought alike, and she was a wonderful lover. Mitch was no slouch, either. He could certainly make up for her late husband in that department.

He mustn't rush it, though. Take things easy, see what develops. . . . Maybe they could go away together for a while. Somewhere warm. And then . . . well . . . five million dollars.

Such were his thoughts as he turned the corner, just before the heavy hand settled on his shoulder and a deep voice whispered in his ear, "Detective Greg Hollins, Mr. Mitchell. Homicide. I think it's about time you and I had a long talk."

Relieved to be let off with little more than a warning for cooperating with the police, Mitch turned up at Laura's the next evening as arranged. This time, they skipped the dinner and drinks preliminaries and headed straight for her bedroom.

Afterwards, she lay with her head resting on his shoulder, smoking a cigarette.

"My God," she said. "I missed this when I was married to Charles."

"Didn't you have any lovers?" Mitch asked.

"Of course I didn't."

"Oh, come on. I won't be jealous. I promise. Tell me."

She jerked away, stubbed out the cigarette on the bedside ashtray, and said, "You're just like the police. Do you know that? You've got a filthy mind."

"Hey," said Mitch. "It's me. Mitch. Okay?"

"Still . . . They think I did it, you know."

"Did what?"

"Killed Charles."

"I thought you had an alibi."

"I do, idiot. They think the burglary was just a cover. They think I hired someone to kill him."

"Did you?"

"See what I mean? Just like the cops, with your filthy, suspicious mind."

"What makes you think they suspect you?"

"The way they talked, the way they questioned me. I think they're watching me."

"You're just being paranoid, Laura. You're upset. They always suspect someone in the family at first. It's routine. Most killings are family affairs. You'll see, pretty soon they'll drop it."

"Do you really think so?"

"Sure I do. Just you wait and see."

And moments later they were making love again.

Laura seemed a little distracted when she let him in the next night. At first, he thought she had something on the stove, but then he remembered she didn't cook.

She was on the telephone, as it turned out. And she hung up the receiver just as he walked into the living room.

"Who was that?" he asked. "Not reporters, I hope?"

"No," she said, arms crossed, facing him, an unreadable expression on her face.

"Who, then?"

Laura just stood there. "They've found the gun," she said finally.

"They've what? Where?"

"In your garage, under an old tarpaulin."

"I don't understand. What are you talking about? When?"

She looked at her watch. "About now."

"How?"

Laura shrugged. "Anonymous tip. You'd better sit down, Mitch."

Mitch collapsed on the sofa.

"Drink?"

"A large one."

Laura brought him a large tumbler of scotch and sat in the armchair opposite him.

"What's all this about?" he asked, after the whiskey had warmed his insides. "I don't understand what you're saying. How could they find the gun in my garage? I told you what happened to it."

"I know you did," said Laura. "And I'm telling you where it ended up. You're really not that bright, are you, Mitch? How do *you* think it got there?"

"Someone must have put it there."

"Right."

"One of the muggers? But . . . ?"

"What does it matter? What matters is that it will probably have your fingerprints on it. Or the wrapping will. All those greasy smudges. And even if it doesn't, how are you going to explain its presence in your garage?"

"But why would the cops think I killed Charles?"

"We had a relationship. We were lovers. Like I told you, I'm certain they've been watching me, and they can't fail to have noticed that you've stayed overnight on more than one occasion."

"But that's absurd. I hadn't even met you before your husband's death."

"Hadn't you?" She raised her eyebrows. "Don't you remember, honey, all those times we met in secret, made love cramped in the back of your car because we didn't even dare be seen signing in under false names in the Have-a-Nap Motel or wherever? We had to keep our relationship very, very secret. Don't you remember?"

"You'd tell them that?"

"The way they'll see it is that the relationship was more important to you than to me. You became obsessed by jealousy because I was married to someone else. You couldn't stand it anymore. And you thought by killing my husband you could get both me and my money. After all, you did prepare his will, didn't you? You knew all about his finances."

Mitch shook his head.

"I *would* like to thank you, though," Laura went on. "Without you, we had a good plan—a very good one—but *with* you we've got a perfect one."

"What do you mean?"

"I mean you were right when you suggested I had a lover. I do. Oh, not you, not the one I'm handing over to the police, the one who became so obsessed with me that it unhinged him and he murdered my husband. No. I've been very careful with Jake. I met him on the Yucatán Peninsula when Charles and I were on holiday there six months ago and Charles went down with Montezuma's revenge. I know it sounds like a cliché, but it was love at first sight. We hatched the plan very quickly and we knew we had to keep our relationship a total secret. Nobody must suspect a thing. So we never met after that vacation. There were no letters or postcards. The only contact we had was through public telephones."

"And what happens now?"

"After a decent interval—after you've been tried and convicted of my husband's murder—Jake and I will meet and eventually get married. We'll sell up here, of course, and live abroad. Live in luxury. Oh, please don't look so crestfallen, Mitch. Believe me, I *am* sorry. I didn't know you were going to walk into my life with that irresistible little confession, now, did I? I figured I'd just ride it out, the cops' suspicions and all. I mean, they might suspect me, but they couldn't prove anything. I *was* in Windsor staying with an old university friend. They've checked. And now they've got you in the bargain. . . ." She shrugged. "Why would they bother with little old me? I just couldn't look a gift horse in the mouth. You'll make a wonderful fall guy. But because I like you, Mitch, I'm at least giving you a little advance warning, aren't I? The police will be looking for you, but you've still got time to make a break, leave town."

"What if I go to them, tell them everything you've told me?"

"They'll think you're crazy. Which you are. Obsession does that to people. Makes them crazy."

Mitch licked his lips. "Look, I'd have to leave everything behind. I don't even have any cash on me. Laura, you don't think you could—"

She shook her head. "Sorry, honey. No can do. Nothing personal."

Mitch slumped back in the chair. "At least tell me one more thing. The gun. I still don't understand how it came to be the one that killed your husband."

She laughed, showing the sharp white teeth. "Pure coincidence. It was beautiful. Jake happens to be . . .

". . . a burglar by profession, and a very good one. He has worked all over the States and Canada, and he's never been caught. We thought that if I told him about the security system at the house, he could get around it cleverly and . . . Of course, he couldn't bring his own gun here from Mexico, not by air, so he had to get one. He said that's not too difficult when you move in the circles he does. The kind of bars where you can buy guns and other stolen goods are much the same anywhere, in much the same sort of neighborhoods. And he's done jobs in Toronto before.

"As luck would have it, he bought an old Luger off two inexperienced muggers. For a hundred bucks. I just couldn't believe it when you came around with your story. There couldn't be two old Lugers kicking around the neighborhood at the same time, could there? I had to turn away from you and hold my sides, I was laughing so much. It made my eyes water. What unbelievable luck!"

"I'm so glad you think so," said Mitch.

"Anyway, when I told Jake, he agreed it was too good an opportunity to miss, so he came back up here, dug the gun up from where he had buried it, safe in its wrapping, and planted it in your garage. He hadn't handled it without gloves on and he thought the two young punks he bought it from had been too scared to touch it, so the odds were, after you told me your story, that your fingerprints would still be on it. As I said, even if they aren't . . . It's still perfect."

Only tape hiss followed, and Detective Hollins flipped off the machine. "That it?" he asked.

Mitch nodded. "I left. I thought I'd got enough."

"You did a good job. Jesus, you got more than enough. I was hoping she'd let something slip, but I didn't expect a full confession and her accomplice's name in the bargain."

"Thanks. I didn't have a lot of choice, did I?"

The last two times Mitch had been to see Laura, he had been wearing a tiny but powerful voice-activated tape recorder sewn into the lining of his suit jacket. It had lain on the chair beside the bed when they made love, and he had tried to get her to admit she had a boyfriend, as Hollins had suspected. He had also been wearing it the night she told him the police were about to find the Luger in his garage.

The recorder was part of the deal. Why he got off with only a warning for not reporting the theft of an unregistered firearm.

"What'll happen to her now?" he asked Hollins.

"With any luck, both her and her boyfriend will do life," said Hollins. "But what do you care, after the way she treated you? She's a user. She chewed you up and spat you out."

Mitch sighed. "Yeah, I know . . ." he said. "But it could have been worse, couldn't it?"

"How?"

"I could've ended up married to her."

Hollins stared at him for a moment, then he burst out laughing. "I'm glad you've got a sense of humor, Mitchell. You'll need it, what's coming your way next."

Mitch shifted uneasily in his chair. "Hey, just a minute, Hollins. We made a deal. You assured me there'd be no charges over the gun."

Hollins nodded. "That's right. We did make a deal. And I never go back on my word."

Mitch shook his head. "Then I don't understand. What are you talking about?"

"Well, there's this woman from the Law Society waiting outside, Mitchell. And she'd *really* like to talk to you."

NOT ENOUGH MONKEYS

Benjamin M. Schutz

Benjamin M. Schutz's work exemplifies perfectly the tradition in which specialized scientific knowledge is brought into the making of a mystery plot. A clinical and forensic psychologist, Schutz skillfully weaves his scientific knowledge of the criminal mind into the stories and novels he writes—primarily in the hard-boiled vein. With his series character private eye Leo Haggerty taking the lead in most of his tales, the author has won a Shamus Award for best novel from the Private Eye Writers of America and an Edgar Allan Poe Award for best short story from the Mystery Writers of America.

"DR. TRIPLETT, DR. Ransom Triplett?"

I looked up from my exam-covered desk. A young woman hugging a fat file stood in the doorway. I guess just looking up was enough for her, because she entered arm outstretched, hand aimed at the middle of my chest, and said, "I'm Monica Chao, I have a project I'd like to interest you in."

I rose from my chair, intercepted her hand mid-desk, and nodded to the empty chair on her right.

"I've just come from the state penitentiary. I've been talking with some of the staff there and we believe that a terrible miscarriage of justice is going to happen." She hoisted the file onto the desk, where it landed with a thud and lay still as a corpse.

"Actually, the miscarriage is ongoing. Dr. Triplett, they have an innocent man on death row there. He is going to be executed the first of next month."

"And?" I asked.

"And I want you, no, I hope you'll be willing to help me prove this. They're going to execute an innocent man."

"Excuse me, Miss Chao, how old are you?"

"I beg your pardon." She stiffened in her seat.

"What are you, twenty-four, twenty-five—twenty-six at the most? Am I correct?"

"I fail to see the relevance of my age."

"Humor me. Am I correct?"

She thought about it for a minute. "Close enough. Let's just leave it at that."

"First time to the penitentiary, yes?"

She nodded.

"And lo and behold, you found an innocent man there. Ms. Chao, the prisons are full of innocent men; in fact, they are filled with nothing but innocent men. I have been practicing forensic psychology for almost twenty years; I have yet to meet a man in prison who did the crime. One million innocent men behind bars. Amazing. No wonder crime is on the rise. All the villains are still on the streets. Please, Ms. Chao, no innocent-men stories. I don't know what brought you to the prison, but the innocent-man story gets the inmate an hour, maybe two, alone with a lawyer. An attractive woman like yourself, they probably had a raffle to see who'd get to look up your skirt."

She slid one hand down from her lap to smooth her hem across her thigh. Satisfied that I was merely rude, she was about to fire a response.

I put up my hands in surrender. "Please, Ms. Chao. I get calls or visits like this all the time. If you want to interest me in a project, bring me something truly rare, a culpable convict, a man who says he did it, or better yet, the rarest of all—a remorseful man, a man tortured by guilt over the horrors he inflicted on other people. For that you have my undivided time and attention."

I looked down at the exam I had been grading. Her chair didn't move.

"I don't know what else you have going on in your life, Dr. Triplett, that could be more important than saving an innocent man's life, but I'm not going to let you run me off with your cynicism." She pushed the file toward me. "Don't read it. It's on your head. If they execute an innocent man how will you explain that you didn't have time even to look at the file?" Her jaw was determined but her eyes glistened with oncoming defeat.

"I'm going to do everything I can for my client. He is not going to die because I didn't turn over every rock or look into every corner."

"And what rock am I under, Ms. Chao? Who sent you to me?"

"Mr. Talaverde did."

"Paul Talaverde? My old friend?" I smiled at the memory.

"Yes. I work in the pro bono section of the firm."

"What did he say?"

"I'd really rather Mr. Talaverde talk to you. It was his idea."

"No, no, no. You're going to do whatever it takes for your client, re-member? This is what it takes; if you want me to read this file you tell me what Paul Talaverde said."

She smiled at me. "And if I do, you'll agree to read the file?"

I shook my head sadly. "No, you have no leverage here. I'm mildly curious, you're desperate." I pushed the file back at her.

"Okay, you asked for it. He said you used to be the best forensic psy-chologist around, but that you were burned out now. Actually, he said you pretended to be burned out, but that you could still be seduced if the case was interesting enough. He said that if that didn't work, I should try to shame you into it. You had always been vulnerable to that, and probably still were."

"Anything else?"

She looked away and pursed her mouth in distaste. "He said I should start with you because your contract at the university forbids you from doing private-practice work for a fee. So, if you took the case . . ."

"The price was right. Paul say anything else?"

"No, that was it."

"Then we're still friends. Tell him he was right on two counts. Now, I have a couple of questions for you, Ms. Chao."

She brushed an eave of lustrous black hair out of her face and clasped her hands around her knee, a perfect impression of the earnest student eager to please.

"Who did you talk to at the prison? You said 'we' believe there is a terrible miscarriage? Truth or seduction, Ms. Chao?"

"Truth, Dr. Triplett. Our firm got a call from Otis Weems, he was original counsel on this case, saying that one of the doctors at the prison had called him very concerned about Earl, that's Earl Munsey, the defendant." She pointed to the case file.

"Mr. Weems didn't want to get into it, you know the ineffective-counsel issues, so it was assigned to me. I went up to the prison to talk to the doctor. Then I talked to Earl Munsey. Obviously you think I'm a naive fool, but I'm convinced that Earl Munsey didn't do it and they are going to execute an innocent man."

"What did the doctor say?"

"He said Earl was deteriorating as the execution date approached."

"Deteriorating how?"

"You name it. He paced his cell at all hours. He wouldn't leave for exercise. He was convinced that they would move up the date and take him right off the yard. He stopped eating. Then last week he started crying all the time, calling for his mother. He started banging his head against the walls of his cell, he tore off his fingernails digging at the brick."

"You've never been on death row, have you?"

"No. Don't ever want to, either."

"It's ugly, very ugly. It's cases like this that make people question what we're doing. We destroy another human being's sense of dignity, reduce them to a gibbering gobbet of fear. Why? Then you remember what they did to some other human being and it gets real complicated. At least it does for me."

"Are you in favor of the death penalty?"

"I think in some cases it's just. There are some people who do things for which they should forfeit their lives. But then I don't believe in the sanctity of life. Suicide makes sense to me, so does abortion. What I think is neither here nor there. What you are describing happens all the time. The law prohibits the execution of a mentally ill person. But then, who wouldn't be mentally ill at the prospect of death by electrocution? The prison hospitals routinely medicate prisoners to near-comas as their dates approach so they won't act in such a way as to appear mentally ill and avoid execution. It's a hell of a choice for the doctors. Do nothing and watch your patients shit themselves like crazed rats and then get executed anyway, or trank them to the eyeballs so they're easier to kill. So far you haven't told me anything unusual to warrant looking into this case. It's interesting that the doctor called his attorney, most of the time they wouldn't bother. What's got you so convinced this guy is innocent, not just terrified?"

"When I got there to see him he was curled up on the floor, rocking back and forth, crying for his mother, saying, 'I didn't do it, I didn't do it,' over and over again. I just watched him through the window of his cell. When I went in he didn't even know I was in the room. Nothing changed. I told him who I was. Nothing. No new evidence, no claims that someone else did it or he was framed. He didn't ask me to represent him. Just rocking and crying."

"Did he know you were coming?"

"No. It was on the spur of the moment. The prison doctor had called his attorney, who called us. Mr. Talaverde asked me to go up right away. I didn't tell the doctor I was coming, neither did Mr. Talaverde. We didn't even agree to look into it, so his attorney couldn't have told him anything. I checked with the doctor. Weems hadn't gotten back to him."

"All right. Leave me the file. I'll read it tonight and call you tomorrow." She was right, I didn't have anything more important to do.

"Here's my home number," she said as she wrote on the back of a business card. "My son's been sick. I may not be in the office tomorrow." She slid the card over to me. I put it in the file.

I finished my workout, showered, changed, made a pitcher of gin and tonic, and set it on the patio table next to the file. I put a fresh, clean legal pad and pen on the other side. I poured a drink, sat down, and opened the Earl Munsey file.

Earl Munsey had been nineteen when he was arrested for the murders of Joleen Pennybacker, Martha Dombrowski, and Eleanor Gelman. Pennybacker was found in a model home by a real-estate agent, Dombrowski in an empty house by the residents when they returned from a trip, and Gelman in a rental condo, by the next occupants. At first the three women appeared to have been murdered where they were found, with the murder weapons at the scene: Pennybacker's skull crushed by a blood-covered wooden stick; Dombrowski shot in the head by the .32 caliber gun found next to her body; and Gelman bludgeoned by the fifteen-pound dumbbell near her.

Medical examination revealed that these were postmortem wounds and that each woman had been strangled by a soft ligature, perhaps rubber tubing. They had all been sexually assaulted before death, with bruising of the genital area but no penetration. There were no hair samples or bodily fluids at the scene of the crime. In addition, each victim had been bled, probably by syringe, and splashes of their blood were found at the next crime scene. They had been murdered elsewhere and placed at the scenes.

I picked up the crime-scene psychological profile. The profiler had been Warren Schuster, trained at Quantico, now a consultant in private practice.

All three crime scenes had a number of similarities. The women were partially clothed and appeared to have been killed by surprise, in the middle of an activity: Pennybacker sitting in front of a makeup mirror; Dombrowski in the kitchen, in front of an open refrigerator; and Gelman in the foyer with money in her hand, perhaps making change for a delivery. The reality of the murders was quite the opposite. All three endured multiple, near-death strangulations along with repeated, unsuccessful attempts at penetration both anal and vaginal.

Schuster concluded that the crimes represented two levels of reality. One, the final scenes of partially clad women, surprised and quickly killed, was based on an actual event, probably from the killer's adolescence. The killer had been, perhaps, a peeping Tom who had been caught by a woman, maybe even reported to the police, hence the undress, the surprise, their being in the middle of ordinary activities. The postmortem wounds were the revenge of the discovered voyeur for her reporting him to the authorities, or laughing at him when she discovered him. The actual murders were the enactments of his fantasies. What he wanted to do to the women as he watched them. What he hadn't done the first time.

Schuster suggested they look for a white male, early twenties, with a history of sexual offenses such as obscene phone calls, exposing himself, peeping into houses. He would have an extensive collection of pornography, probably emphasizing sadomasochistic themes, and have at least one camera with telephoto lenses. I'd have said the same thing.

The police put that together with the commonalities of the locations and began to look at delivery men, cable installers, cleaning services, utility repairmen, mailmen. They were linking the profile to those who had the opportunity to get into the locations with the bodies. They also videotaped the crowds that showed up at each crime scene.

There at the intersection of history, opportunity, and obsession stood Earl Munsey, a vocational-school work-study employee of Beauty Kleen Restorations, Inc., a cleaning service with contracts that included all three locations. At fifteen, Earl had been arrested on a charge that he had spied on a neighbor going from her bedroom to her shower. That charge brought forth three other complainants. He was convicted and given a suspended sentence and placed in a residential facility for a year. He continued with outpatient counseling and community-service hours cleaning the bathrooms at the city park. That led to his employment with Beauty Kleen. A search warrant of his parents' home turned up dozens of bondage magazines and videos, but no cameras. He also had a file about all the crimes sealed in a plastic bag and suspended from the floor vent in his bedroom into the ductwork. Earl had keys to all the locations, and although he was not assigned to the crews that were cleaning them, he could have easily gained access with the bodies. He was in the videotapes of the crowds at all three crime scenes. The neighbors all described Earl as a "strange duck," a "lurker," not a stalker, but always in the background, watching women, then scurrying off when their eyes met his.

I flipped over to the counseling notes from the residential facility. Psychological testing showed that Earl had an IQ of 82, was dyslexic, learning disabled by a sequential processing disorder, and attention deficit disordered. He had poor impulse controls, was often flooded by his feelings, used fantasy to excess to relieve chronic feelings of depression and emptiness. He was passive, easily suggestible, quite concrete in his thinking and rigid in his judgments. The therapist noted that Earl was unable to articulate why he had been watching the women and denied doing it even though there had been numerous witnesses. Therapy was eventually terminated as unproductive, and he was recommended for a job that was structured and did not involve contact with the public. That was the last anyone heard of Earl Munsey for three years.

The police had all they needed for an arrest. Earl was Mirandized and waived having an attorney present. Prosecutors would later argue that his psychological evaluation was not known to them at the time and that the standard error of the measure of an IQ of 82 could place it in the average range and his consent should have been considered competent. He was questioned by Detectives Ermentraut and Bigelow for almost forty-eight straight hours. At the end of which Earl Munsey signed a confession to the three murders.

I read the confession. There was no mention of how Earl Munsey lured the women into his van, which was presumed to be where the killings took place, or managed to keep from leaving a single piece of forensic evidence tying him to the crime. Earl claimed to have been in a fog and that it "wasn't him" who had picked up the women. The murders, however, were described in gruesome detail.

The prosecution charged Earl with capital murder while committing felony sexual assault, attempted rape, and sodomy and asked for the death penalty. Without too much protest from Otis Weems, they got it.

Clipped to the back of the file was a bag of photographs from the crime scenes. I looked at the backs and arranged them in order. There was no identification of who took the photos, Ermentraut or Bigelow.

First was Joleen Pennybacker on the floor in front of a makeup mirror. Perfumes and potpourri were spilled on the floor. She was nude except for a pair of fur wraps around her neck. Next to her was a bloody wooden stick matted with her hair and brains.

Martha Dombrowski lay on the kitchen floor clad only in a college T-shirt. Food from the open refrigerator lay around her, a can, ground meat, donuts, and a .32-caliber pistol that had left her with a small round hole in the middle of her forehead.

Eleanor Gelman was in the entrance foyer, also clad only in a college T-shirt. She had a twenty-dollar bill in her right hand, and there were some coins around her left hand. Next to her was a bloody, crusted dumbbell with five-pound plates.

I closed the file. Monica Chao had things to work with, especially the confession, but I didn't see how I could help her. The profile and crime-scene analysis made sense to me. I could see Earl Munsey doing this crime. Maybe the confession was coerced and there were gaps in it. Maybe they shouldn't have convicted him. Maybe she could parlay that into a new trial. That didn't mean he didn't do it. Not in the post-O. J. world.

I called Monica Chao and told her I had no ideas and that I would return the file to her. She asked if I could come by tonight. She had some more information that she had received by court order and she didn't want to waste time. I got directions to her place and drove over.

She opened the door and motioned me inside. Monica wore running shoes, jean skirt, and a cream-colored blouse knotted at the midriff. Her hair was pulled back into a glossy ponytail. A young boy, perhaps five, stood in the center of the living room.

"This is my son, Justin. Justin, say hello to Dr. Triplett." Justin approached with his hand out but a somber look on his face. We shook hands and he turned back to his game on the floor.

"Listen, I just wanted to drop this off. I'll let you get back to whatever . . ."

She ushered me into the kitchen. "Justin's upset right now. His father and I separated a couple of months ago. He keeps hoping we'll get back together again. Whenever somebody comes over, he's hoping it's his dad. When it's not, he's disappointed."

"Listen, I don't have anything to tell you. Not from a psychological point of view. You have the confession to work with. . . ."

"No, I don't. Weems argued that on the first appeal. That and the consent. He lost. I don't have anything. Before you give up on this, look at what I got today at the office. It's the photos from Ermentraut and Bigelow. Along with their notes. The photos you saw were from the first officers on the scene, the patrolmen."

"Okay, I'll look at them," I said resentfully, ready to be out from under one of her rocks. "How late are you going to be up tonight? I'll drop them back when I'm done."

"You can do it here. I've got an office set up next to the living room. Justin and I were about to eat. Why don't you look at the stuff, stay for dinner, and tell me what you think. I'm making hot-and-sour soup and Dan Dan noodles, it's Justin's favorite."

"What's Dan Dan noodles?"

"It's a spicy chili peanut sauce over noodles. Very good."

"Okay. Where are the photos?" The sooner I started, the sooner I was done.

"In my office, on the desk. I'll let you know when we're ready to eat."

I walked out of the kitchen and across the living room. Justin was on his elbows and knees, staring down at a board on the floor before him. His chin rested in the cup of his palms.

I turned into the first door on the left, sat down at Monica's desk, and put the file next to her printer. I picked up the photographs. They were larger than the ones the patrolmen had taken. I propped them up side by side in front of the computer screen. I flipped up Ermentraut's notebook and read his notes.

Joleen Pennybacker: four bloodstains on floor; furs not part of house decor; potpourri?: lab says it's dried thyme leaves; perfumes: Escada and Opium, from the house; wooden stick: solid maple—look at local cabinet-makers, furniture repair shops.

I looked at Joleen Pennybacker: young, slim, ghostly pale in the harsh flash light. The pool of blood under her head black, not red. Lying on her back, eyes wide, hands up, fingers spread as if startled by someone standing in front of her. Had she been sitting? Why no chair? The two furs draped over her shoulder and around her neck. Trying them on before she got dressed? A gift? The sensuous feel of fur on skin? The potpourri and per-fume spilled on the floor. As if she'd pulled them over in a struggle or standing up to flee. Someone she'd seen in the mirror. The bloody stick that stopped her.

I picked up Martha Dombrowski's picture. I tilted it under the light then reached over and turned on Monica's desk lamp. In the corners, four dark stains. Just like the first scene. Repetition becomes ritual. Another indicator that these tableaux had symbolic meaning to the killer. He was putting order on his chaos. Shaping it to give him release from his hungers. For the moment.

Martha was older, softer. Again on her back. Nude except for the T-shirt. A college. I brought the photo closer: University of California. She, too, had her hands up as if startled and a pool of black blood under her head. There was food strewn around her and the refrigerator door was open. The dropped gun. She hears someone, has food in her hands, a midnight snack perhaps, turns, sees the killer. Only he is not a killer yet. She sees him watching her. She's going to report him, like the first one did. He can't let that happen. He shoots her. He drops the gun and runs. Ritual reenact-ments of his trauma, his shame, only he's rewritten the end. They don't tell, they die. He escapes to watch them again. Better yet, he does what he only dreamed of the first time. But he can't. Even with them subdued, restrained, he can't get it up, can't put it in. A level of inhibition even this degree of control and power can't conquer. Twisted religious upbringing? What did Munsey's parents do to him?

Thank God they caught this guy. He'd have kept doing this until he was able to penetrate his victims. And then he'd have kept on anyway, just hyphenating his career: serial killer-rapist.

I looked at the notes. Food: can of baked beans, open with lid; package of ground meat; box of donuts. The food belonged to the owners of the house. T-shirt: University of California. Neither the victim nor the residents attended the school. Boyfriend? Killer? Blood not the victim's. Match for #1. The gun was a .32-caliber H & R. No serial number. A later note said ballistics couldn't match it with any other killings and they hadn't been able to trace its owner.

The last picture was Eleanor Gelman. Again the four bloodstains. Again the body nude except for a college T-shirt. This time it's the University of Richmond. Was Munsey's first victim, the one who reported him, a college student? She's on her back in the foyer. This time her hands have money in them. Coins all around the left one, dropped when she's startled, a twenty in her right. For whom? Where's her purse? I scanned the corners of the photo to see if it was on the floor or hanging from a doorknob. Why get it out to give to someone? She's only half dressed. So many questions but the answer is always the same—silence. Her head sits in a pool of blood. Satan's halo, viscous, sickly sweet, the light shining off bits of bone and brain. I looked at the dumbbell. There was a difference with this one. Her ankles were tied. With what?

I looked at Ermentraut's notes. Bloodstains not the victim's. Same as victim #2. T-shirt—victim did not go to University of Richmond. Her son? Money: 7 cents—all pennies. Ankles: rubber tubing. Chemistry supplies? M.E. says consistent with ligatures on all three victims.

I stared at all three pictures. A triptych from Earl Munsey's unconscious. The same scene over and over again, unchanging forever. That's one definition of hell.

"Are you staying for dinner?"

I looked down. Justin stood there just as somber as before. Dark eyes peering up from under his bowl-cut black hair.

"I was going to. Your mom offered since I'm helping her with her work. Is that okay with you?"

Justin put his hand on my arm. "Do you know my dad?"

"No, I don't," I said gently.

"Oh." He turned away, then back. "Can you play with me? Just until Mom calls me to eat?"

I looked at the photos. Nothing there. I might as well play with the little guy. His dad would if he were here.

"Sure. Just until your mom calls."

I pushed away from the console and followed him into the living room. A sliding-glass door and surrounding windows let plenty of light into the room and it bounced off the dark parquet floor. A large-screen TV sat in the center of the far wall surrounded by a built-in bookcase. I scanned the books: cookbooks, exercise books, books on divorce and child-rearing, romances, mysteries, arts and crafts, everything but law books. A low, cream-colored leather sofa and chair set encircled a wood and glass coffee table. A free-form cypress base with bronze claws gripping a palette-shaped glass top.

Justin sat down in between the table and the sofa and picked up a plastic frame. I thought about squeezing in next to him but chose an adjoining side of the table. His mother poked her head around the corner.

"We'll eat in just a couple of minutes." Then she lifted her head up towards me.

"Anything?"

"Where do you stand on feeding the messenger?"

"We feed them in these parts. Good news or bad."

"I still don't see anything."

"Okay."

Justin scooted over towards me and handed me the frame. It was covered with numbered plastic shingles.

"How do you play, Justin?"

"It's a memory game. You have to remember where the matching pictures are. When they match you take them off the board."

"Show me. We'll do this one for practice. It won't count, okay?"

"Okay. See, here is a pony, and this one is a pony. So I take them off." He lifted two numbered shingles, revealing the ponies. Off they came, revealing another layer underneath.

"What's this, Justin?" I asked, noticing that he was sitting right up next to my leg and starting to list to starboard. I hoped that he wouldn't climb into my lap, so I called out for help.

"How's dinner coming?"

"Couple more minutes, that's all." And so the *Titanic* was lost.

"This is the next part," he said, now looking up at me from the space between the board and my chest.

"Once you uncover the board, you have to guess the puzzle. That's hard. I have a good memory, but my mom gets the puzzles right. That's how she wins. She's really smart. She's a lawyer."

"I'm sure she is, Justin. Since this is just practice, I'm going to look at the puzzle. Maybe I can show you some tricks. Help you beat your mom."

"Cool," he said and clapped his hands.

I pulled the backing up and looked at it. "You know, Justin, if your memory is good, you might try to uncover the corners first. That puts a frame on the puzzle. It's a lot easier to figure out from the edges in instead of the middle out."

A chill went down my back and out my arms as the picture in my head disappeared and a great white shape rushed to breach into recognition on the vast empty sea of my mind.

I stood up, handed Justin the board, and hurried back to the office. Sliding into the chair, I pulled an empty legal pad in front of me and stared at the pictures.

"Aren't we going to play anymore?" Justin asked forlornly, from the doorway.

I looked over my shoulder. "I'm sorry, Justin. This is very important. I'll play with you when I'm done. I promise. Okay?"

"You promise?"

"Yes. I promise, Justin."

He stood there trying to decide the worth of my word, weighing it against the collection of promises he already held. He turned and walked away. I heard the shingles spill onto the wooden floor.

His mother appeared in the doorway. "What happened? He just ran into his room. Dinner's on."

"I'm sorry. I was playing with him when I got this idea about Munsey and the murders. I bolted over here to try it out and I told him I couldn't play with him now. I'll just scoop this stuff up and take it back to my place. Let you and him get on with dinner."

She came towards me. "Do you have something?"

"No, no. I have an idea. I need to try it out. It's probably nothing. I really need to get on it while it's fresh, before I lose it." I started to take the pictures down.

"No, no," she said, palms up in retreat. "Stay here. I'll close the door. We'll be quiet. Do what you have to. We don't have any time to spare. If you've got an idea, run with it. Do you want any food?"

"No, thank you. How about a cup of coffee? You might want to put on a pot. This could take awhile."

"Sure. Coming right up." She shook her fists in excitement and disappeared.

I wondered if this scene had been played out before, with her husband. The disappointed child, the abandoned dinner, work demands taking priority. Eventually sliding from a separation that was impromptu and random to one that was formalized and permanent.

I didn't need food. I was burning up excitement as fuel, the same excitement I felt every time I had panned golden nuggets of meaning out of the onrushing blur of life. So far, that had turned out to be the one enduring passion of my life.

I drew diagrams and schematics, scribbled translations and made lists and erased them all. The hours wore on. The refills of coffee told me so.

The trash can filled, then overflowed. I kept drawing and writing. Eventually, the tide of erasures receded and I was left with a single page of work. The clock said two A.M. when Monica knocked on the doorframe.

"How's it going?"

"Gone as far as I can. I'm done."

"Want something to eat?"

"No, thanks. I'm caffeinated to the eyeballs. I can't eat when I'm wired like this."

She slid down along the wall until she sat cross-legged on the floor. She sipped from a steamy mug. "So?" she said, dipping her head in anticipation, her eyes as somber as her son's had been.

I took off my glasses, rubbed my eyes for a minute, put the glasses back on, and turned to the pictures.

"I was playing that game with Justin and telling him how frames help solve puzzles, when it occurred to me. There were frames on these murder scenes. See here." I pointed to the bloodstains around each body. "They aren't from the victims. Ermentraut's notes say that, or I think they do. They're unnecessary to the scene. There's plenty of blood all over the place from the head injuries. Why the frame? What does a frame do?"

Monica shrugged. "I don't know. I've never actually been at a crime scene."

"A frame tells you what the field of information is. What's inside is important, what's outside is not. Serial killers don't frame their work. They know what's important. They arrange it just so. They remove what's irrelevant. When it's just right, when it's satisfying, they stop. That's the 'art,' if you want, in the composition.

"If Schuster's right, then this is Earl Munsey's ritual reenactment of his shame, changed to include his fantasized torture and rape and revenge. Very satisfying. This is a scene by Earl for Earl. There's no need for a frame. Suppose, just suppose, this isn't a construction for the killer's own use, own pleasure. Who is it for? It's a construction. There's no question about that. He brought the bodies, the weapons, the blood, the props. Who's going to see this? The police. It's a message to them. They need a frame. They have ignorant eyes. They don't know what to attend to, what to ignore. He's helping us poor dumb bastards along. He's jumping up and down, waving his arms, saying Here I am, here I am."

"Did you figure out the messages?" A tentative, hopeful smile emerged across her narrow oval face.

"I think so."

"What do they say?"

"Bear with me. I have to explain this step by step. The logic seemed inescapable to me when I was doing it. But delusions can be quite logical, too. You have to understand it and believe it. If I can't convince you, you can't convince anyone else."

"The typical way of interpreting a crime scene for clues to the killer's personality is actuarial and symbolic. What do most serial killers have in common? What are the significant correlates? What needs do certain acts satisfy? For example, why mutilate the face? Why take souvenirs? And so on. We're talking about translating their hidden, obscure inner language because they're talking to themselves, not us.

"Suppose this guy is talking to us. He speaks our language. How do we read? Left to right. Top to bottom. So I looked at what was inside the frames. Here is Joleen Pennybacker."

I picked up the photo and used my hands to frame her body. "Left to right: furs, body, potpourri. Top to bottom: perfume, bloody stick. Gibberish, right? That's what I've been doing all night. Trying every different category that might describe each element, trying to make sentences out of them."

"Have you?"

"Yes."

"What do they say?"

"First, there are rules to the messages. All languages have grammar and syntax. Ignore the bodies. They're irrelevant, zeros, place-holders. Without them there is no crime scene. No crime. He killed these women as bait. To draw us in as an audience. That's why there's no penetration. His driving need isn't sexual, it's narcissism. He demonstrates his power by leaving an abundance of clues that nobody gets. He's diddling us, not them. He's been laughing at us for two years now."

"Those poor women. You're saying he killed them just to show us how smart he is, that he could get away with it. This is incredible." She shuddered.

"Don't say that. It has to be credible. Otherwise Earl Munsey fries for this. His eyes explode, his blood boils, his hair bursts into flame. And this bastard laughs all the way to hell.

"This is Joleen Pennybacker. Furs; thyme, not potpourri. It was all dried thyme; scents, not perfumes. The murder weapon, a blood-covered stick, a red stick. Furs, thyme, scents, red stick. *First time since Redstick.* He's announcing his appearance. He's telling us where he came from. I did this one and I said, Triplett, you're crazy. You've tortured the data beyond recognition. You're the infinite number of monkeys. *Voilà!* Random hammering on the keys and we get *Hamlet*. Once, perhaps. What if they're all meaningful and related? God couldn't make enough monkeys to pull that off."

I picked up the next picture. "This is Martha Dombrowski. Remember, ignore her body. Left to right: can, not food, not beans; look at the T-shirt: University of California, UC is visible, the rest needs a magnifying glass; and meat. Then: a donut and a gun. Can UC meat. Donut a gun. *Can you see me? Done it again.* Again. Number two. It only makes sense as the second of a series. They either both make sense or neither of them does."

I exchanged photos. "Here's Eleanor Gelman. These coins, I counted them. All pennies. Copper. Coppers. The shirt: University of Richmond, same maker. UR, then a dumbbell. The twenty, that stumped me. Money, greenbacks, dollars, currency, a bill, Bill, his name? It's Jackson's face on the bill. See how her thumb is pressed over it. Then her ankles. Tied? Knot? Tube? Hose? Bound." I stopped to see if she was convinced. She looked like she was trying to suppress a grimace. Her plum-colored lips darkened.

"Cops, you are dumbbells, Jackson bound." He's going to Jackson. That's where his next victims will be found. Some town named Jackson."

I leaned back. Monica looked into her cup. No help there.

"I know: A tale told by an idiot, full of sound and fury, signifying nothing. Perhaps, but I know one thing for certain. A demonstrable scientific fact."

"What's that?"

"If I'm right, Earl Munsey couldn't have killed those women."

"Why?"

"He's dyslexic, and he has a sequencing disorder. He reverses letters and words. He couldn't put a rebus together."

"A rebus?"

"That's what I think they are. It's a kind of puzzle where images stand for the syllables of words.

"We're halfway home. If I'm right, then Earl Munsey is indeed innocent. Now we have to prove that I'm right. But that's for tomorrow," I looked at the clock, "or later, whichever comes first."

"You can crash here if you want. I made up the bed in the guest room."

"No, I don't think so. Besides, wouldn't that get you in hot water with your ex? Most custody orders forbid overnight guests of the opposite sex."

"Yeah, well, John isn't in any position to dictate terms to me. Not with him out every night being true to his new gay identity. I may have been just a treatment plan for John when we were married, but I'm a whole lot more trouble now." She nodded, agreeing with herself.

I remembered why I quit doing custody work and switched to criminal. Too much violence in the custody work.

"I just think it'd be confusing for Justin to find me here when he wakes up. Tell him I haven't forgotten my promise. I'll play with him next time I'm over." I wondered if she'd remember to do that. If not, I'd call him myself. If you couldn't keep your word to a child your priorities were in serious disarray.

I put my work in the file, took my mug to the kitchen pass-through and wished Monica good night.

"Thank you for everything. Even if you can't prove your theory, I appreciate how hard you've worked, and I'll tell Earl you did all you could. But I have faith in you. If it's there, you'll find it, that's what Paul Talaverde said about you."

"Yeah, well, even a stopped clock is right twice a day. I'll call you when I know something." I waved and turned down the steps.

"Good night, Dr. Triplett. And good luck."

She was still outlined in the doorway, her head resting against the frame, when I drove away.

The first thing I did the next day was call Ermentraut. He was in court, so I left a message. Then I tried Bigelow.

"Homicide, Detective Bigelow."

"Detective, this is Dr. Ransom Triplett. I wonder if I could have a couple of minutes of your time."

"Couple of minutes, sure. What about?"

"Earl Munsey."

"Oh Christ. Are you one of those bleeding hearts that thinks we shouldn't execute this bastard? Let me tell you something. I was there. At the scene. At the morgue. I saw what he did. I'll sleep like a baby the day they serve him up the juice of justice. Goodbye . . ."

"Whoa, whoa, just a second, please. This is not about whether he should be executed. I've been going over the file as a consultant to his attorney. Personally, I think you guys have the right man."

"Damn straight we do. And another thing, that confession was pristine. Clean all through. We never touched him. We read him his rights. What were we supposed to do? Talk him out of it? Oh no, Mr. Munsey, that would be unwise, here, let us call a lawyer for you. Why don't we just stop trying to catch anybody? He freaking confessed. What do these people want?"

"Well, detective, I just want to ask you a couple of small questions, so I can explain them to his attorney. It just might put this whole thing to rest."

"Okay, what is it?"

"The things that were around the body. That Munsey planted at the scene . . ."

"You mean like the gun, the tubing, that stuff?"

"Yeah. Did any of that lead anywhere?"

"No. The stuff at the first scene came from the model home. Except the herbs that he spilled. We took his picture to local groceries. Nothing. The food was from the owners. The gun was a Saturday-night special, cold, no serial numbers. We hit all the gun shops, the known dealers. No one could ID Munsey. Same thing for the tubing, the dumbbell. He could have gotten them anywhere. Yard sales—hell, he could have stolen them out of a garage. None of that stuff went anywhere."

"Last question. The blood spatters on the floor. Detective Ermentraut's notes aren't clear. The blood spatters at the scenes aren't the victims'. Whose were they?"

"Uh, let me remember. I think it was victim number one's blood at the second scene and number two's at the next one. Yeah, that's right."

"Could you tell me the victims' blood types?"

"Yeah, hold on. We pulled that jacket on account of people like you. This one is not gonna get away."

I doodled on my pad. Zeros, large ones, small ones. Then I linked them. All the little naughts going nowhere. Earl Munsey was moving slowly, inexorably towards eternity.

"Okay. Here's the lab report. You want the DNA markers and everything, or just the type?"

"Blood type is fine."

"Girl number one was O positive. Girl number two was AB. Girl number three was B positive. No, that's the stains. The girls were AB, B positive, and A."

"You ever find the third girl's blood?"

"No. He must have stashed it somewhere. We figure he'd have used it at the next scene. But then there wasn't a next scene."

"Thanks, detective."

"No problem. Six days and it won't matter anymore."

"Yeah," I said and hung up. Unless you're wrong. Then six days from now it'll matter forever.

I spent the next two days pursuing my theory without any success, although my geographical knowledge was enormously enriched. I learned that there were eighteen Jacksons in the United States, strung from California to New Jersey and from Minnesota to Louisiana. Almost all were small towns with few homicides and not one that looked at all like my rebus killer.

Then I tried Red Stick. Make no mistake about it. There is not one Redstick, U.S.A. There are six Red Oaks and five Redwoods and I called them all. No murders at all like mine.

I sat on the porch, watching one of Earl Munsey's last four sunsets. A gin and tonic slowly diluted on the table next to me. I had nothing. A theory that tortured me with its plausibility, that I refused to accept as a statistical chimera, a product of just enough monkeys scribbling associations to three pictures. Maybe it was data rape, me forcing myself all over the pictures. They yielded up a facsimile of meaning, enough to get me to roll off, grunting in satisfaction, while they lay there, mute in the darkness, their secrets still unknown.

Well, it hadn't been good for me, either. We were running out of time and I had no ideas, bright or otherwise. The phone rang.

"Dr. Triplett. This is Monica Chao. I was wondering how you were doing. We're running out of time."

"I know. How am I doing? Not well at all. I've called every Jackson, every Redwood, every Red Oak in the country. Nothing. I don't know what else to do. Maybe it's all a mirage, an illusion. They aren't rebuses at all. The fact that I've created these sentences is a monument to human inventiveness in the face of complexity and ambiguity. Or I'm right. They are rebuses and I'm just not good enough to translate them correctly. Maybe we need more monkeys. I don't know. Whoever the killer is, he and I don't seem to speak the same language."

I forgot all about Monica. I felt an avalanche slowing, turning on itself, turning into a kaleidoscope, slowing further, settling, stopping, halted. The pattern blazed through my mind. I began to laugh, a cleansing cackle of satisfaction. Had I seen the truth or only applied even finer filigree to my delusion? One call would tell all. I heard someone calling my name in the distance.

"Monica, I have to go. I'll call you right back. I think I've solved it. I hope I have."

I dialed the operator, got the area code I wanted, and then dialed information for the police department's central phone number. I was shuttled through departments toward Homicide.

A voice answered, "Thibault."

"Baton Rouge Homicide?" I said, savoring each syllable.

"Yeah. Who is this?"

I gave my name. "Detective Thibault, I'm working on a case here in Virginia. A man's going to be executed in four days for a series of murders up here. Some last-minute evidence has emerged that may link him to murders elsewhere. Baton Rouge in particular. If so, they would have been at least three years ago. Were you in Homicide then?"

"Doctor, I investigated Cain. I've been twenty-seven years in Homicide in this city. There ain't hardly a murder here I don't know something about, but they're also startin' to run together. I'm due to retire end of the year. I hope this one had a flourish, or four days won't do it."

"Our killer," I said, glad to relinquish ownership, "had an unusual MO. He only killed women and then he placed the bodies in conspicuous locations, where they were sure to be found."

"Got to do better than that, Doc. That's half of our murders. How'd he do 'em?"

"He strangled them after an attempted sexual assault. But at the crime scenes there were weapons found, or rather planted, so that it looked like the victims had been killed where they were found. Clubs, guns, that sort of thing."

"That doesn't ring any bells. Anything else?"

"He took some blood from each victim and he'd spatter it around the next crime scene."

Thibault was silent for a minute. When he spoke his voice was strangely hoarse. "Your boy's gonna go when, four days, you said?"

"Yeah, why?"

"Let me ask you a question. Your first victim, what kind of blood type?"

"AB, but—"

We finished the sentence in harmony. "The bloodstains were O positive."

"Yes," I said, flooded with elation. "When did these killings occur?"

"They started five years ago. There were four of them over the course of a year. Then they stopped."

"That's great. Do you have the lab work on these stains?"

"Yeah. They're in the file. I'd have to go dig it out, but I could fax it to you. Take an hour or so."

"If the blood's a match, our guy couldn't have done it. He was in a residential facility that whole year. This is great. Listen, I don't want to be rude, but I've got to call the lawyer with this news."

Thibault's voice was thick and weary when he spoke.

"As soon as you know, Doc, call me right back. You see, if your boy didn't do it, and that's our blood at the scene, then I've got a call to make. 'Cause our guy didn't do it, either. And his next of kin aren't going to like that one little bit."

* * *

AUTHOR'S NOTE: I would like to thank the following people for their help with this story: noted defense attorney Peter Greenspun; Dr. Jane Greenstein; Constance Knott; Officer Adam K. Schutz; Dr. Mark E. Schutz; and my son, Jakob Lindenberger-Schutz, who solved it in a flash.

BIG SISTER

Andrew Vachss

Readers in search of true hard-boiled fiction need look no further than Andrew Vachss. His novels featuring series character Burke, an unlicensed private eye who walks the meanest of mean streets, often involve child abuse and they are told with uncompromisingly gritty detail. Vachss has a purpose in writing these books: For nearly twenty-five years he's been a lawyer and advocate for children. He began writing fiction as a way of making a large audience aware of the plight of the kinds of children he encountered in his law practice. The books have become bestsellers, and they are so well written that they have also received considerable critical acclaim. The author is the winner of the Grand Prix de Littérature Policière and other distinguished prizes.

WHEN SHE DIDN'T come on Visiting Day, I knew what it meant. There's only one thing that would make Margaret miss coming to see me.

It's always been like that, my big sister looking out for me. She's only nine years older, but it was like she was my mother. I guess she was, when I think about it. My mother died when I was born. Died giving birth to me, my father always said when he was mad. Or drunk. Which is pretty much how he was all the time.

My sister is the only one I can ever remember taking care of me. I mean, my father worked, so I guess he did some of it too. Paying the rent and buying food. But it was Margaret who did everything else.

She even went to the Catholic school when they kicked me out the first time. The nuns were so impressed with her, only fifteen years old and all, they let me stay. But it didn't matter. My father said that's what he expected. He couldn't beat any sense into me, so what made Margaret think the nuns could? Margaret told him that hitting me wasn't the way to teach me anything, and my father hit her. By the time I got the knife from the kitchen, he had stopped, but Margaret was still crying so I tried to stab him anyway.

Everybody came to the house. The police and the social workers and people from the church and neighbors. It was like a zoo. And I was the animal. Finally, they said it was up to my father. He went into the bedroom with Margaret and closed the door so they could talk. When they came out, my father said he wanted me to stay. So I didn't have to go away.

I went to public school. It was a lot better. They didn't pay so much attention to you.

The first time I got arrested, it was Margaret who came to the station. She was all grown by then. The cops let me go back with her.

The first time I went to juvenile court, Margaret went with me too. And the judge let me go home with her.

Margaret was good at that stuff.

But when I got to be around thirteen, fourteen, I don't remember exactly, it didn't do any good. I went away. It was only for a short time. But then it happened again, and I went away for longer. When I came back, I was seventeen. Margaret was living with a man. He was an old man. Almost like my father. Margaret told me I could stay with them until I got a job and my own place.

What happened was, I *did* jobs. But Margaret didn't know anything about that. Everything would have been okay, maybe, if that man hadn't hit her. I don't even remember his name.

Margaret went to court with me again. She told the jury how the man had beat her all the time. She said some of the things he made her do. I started crying when I heard it. I couldn't help it.

The jury let me go home with her.

I was out for almost five years before they got me. I wasn't so surprised. I was very good at doing people, but I was never slick.

The cops knew it wasn't personal. They knew I didn't know the men who died. They knew I was in O'Donnell's crew too. But that was all they knew, and I didn't tell them anything. The D.A. said they could give me some deal. I was a young man. I could be out in ten years at the most if I told them who ordered the hits. If I didn't talk, I was going away forever.

I didn't tell them anything. After a while, they could see I was never going to.

Margaret visited me in the jail, before the trial. I told her the truth like I always do. I told her what I did. The different jobs, all of them. I told her I wasn't going to get off. Not this time. But I promised her I would work real hard and try to do good wherever they sent me.

O'Donnell got me a lawyer. He wasn't too bad, but I knew what his real job was. So I told the lawyer to tell O'Donnell I'd never rat him out so long as he did this one thing for me. The lawyer, he said that would never be a problem. O'Donnell's name never came up at the trial I got life.

The first time Margaret visited me, when I was upstate, she was a mess. She looked so old, I almost didn't recognize her.

She told me about it, finally.

And O'Donnell kept his word.

It didn't happen again for almost three years. Margaret tried to explain it to me. She had been in therapy to understand herself, why she kept going back to the same kind of guys. She told me that she had low self-esteem. From not being pretty and not dating when she was a girl and being too fat and. . . . something she had to do with my father to keep him from sending me away. There was nothing I could do about that. He was already dead. His liver.

I told her she was a real pretty girl, and she could get any guy she wanted. She told me her youth was gone. She wasn't a girl. She was too old to do anything except work and live with guys who beat her up and took her money now.

O'Donnell got that one done too.

I didn't feel bad about it. He owed me. Anyway, there was a guy in here who was maybe a problem, and I took care of him for O'Donnell. Fair is fair.

Anyway, after a while, Margaret must have figured out what was going on—she knew I could tell when one of those men was hurting her. Margaret never missed a visit, so when she didn't come this time, I knew what the reason was. She was afraid I'd be able to tell.

I knew the name of the guy she was living with, and the place where they lived, too. Margaret wrote me letters. She was the only one who did. So when she didn't come, I didn't need to talk to her. I knew what to do.

Margaret missed three more visits, then she came. She looked better. We didn't say anything about the guy. She told me she was still in therapy, but she was worried that she'd fall back into old habits. Patterns, she called them. Over the next few years, she fell back into that pattern four more times. Then the cops came to see me.

"We know you're the one getting these guys done," the younger one said.

I didn't say anything.

"Ah, Mickey's too smart to go for that," the older cop told his partner. "He knows another few life sentences won't matter—you can only do one of them, and Mickey's never getting out anyway."

I didn't say anything.

"You're working O'Donnell's boys pretty hard," the older one told me. "Must be averaging a hit a year, just keeping you quiet."

I didn't say anything.

"I got something to show you," he said.

I took a look at the papers he had. There were photographs of Margaret. She looked good in the pictures. Young and happy. One of them, she was getting into a new Cadillac. There were bank statements and other stuff too. And a picture of a house. Margaret was standing in front of it, smiling. Her arm was around another woman, a smaller woman, nice-looking, with short hair.

"Your sister's real smart," the older cop said. "You know she's the most reliable hitter in the city now? A contract killer. And the beauty part is, she gets O'Donnell's crew to do all the work."

I didn't say anything. I didn't look at him.

"She hasn't lived with a man in a long time, kid," the older cop said to me. Real soft and gentle. "She's gay, your sister Margaret. Those addresses where she tells you she lives? Those aren't her addresses. They're the addresses of guys who got contracts out on them. That's some big sister you got, Mickey."

"She sure is," I told him. Proud.

POPPY AND THE POISONED CAKE

Steven Saylor

Many writers of historical mysteries say their preference for historical settings arises from a desire not to have to use modern science and forensics in the evaluation of clues, as one must almost always do in a contemporary whodunit. Steven Saylor, one of the genre's leading historical novelists, chose ancient Rome as his setting not because it allowed him to simplify the detailing of the plot but because, as he says, "The final years of the Roman republic offer a treasure trove of all the stuff that makes for a good read: political intrigue, courtroom drama, sex scandals, extremes of splendor and squalor, and no shortage of real-life murder mysteries." His series stars Gordianus, a "Finder"—a career the author invented but which is somewhat comparable to a modern private eye—and it got off to an auspicious start when the very first tale, a short story for Ellery Queen's Mystery Magazine, *won the Robert L. Fish Award for best short by a new author. Since then, Saylor has gone on to publish four novels in the Gordianus series, one of which is currently optioned for film. His latest novel-length work is also historical, set in Texas in the nineteenth century.*

"Young Cicero tells me that you can be discreet. Is that true, Gordianus? Can you keep a confidence?"

Considering that the question was being put to me by the magistrate in charge of maintaining Roman morals, I weighed my answer carefully. "If Rome's finest orator says a thing, who am I to contradict him?"

The censor snorted. "Your friend Cicero said you were clever, too. Answer a question with a question, will you? I suppose you picked that up from listening to him defend thieves and murderers in the law courts."

Cicero was my occasional employer, but I had never counted him as a friend, exactly. Would it be indiscreet to say as much to the censor? I kept my mouth shut and nodded vaguely.

307

Lucius Gellius Poplicola—Poppy to his friends, as I would later find out—looked to be a robust seventy or so. In an age wracked by civil war, political assassinations, and slave rebellions, to reach such a rare and venerable age was proof of Fortune's favor. But Fortune must have stopped smiling on Poplicola—else why summon Gordianus the Finder?

The room in which we sat, in Poplicola's house on the Palatine Hill, was sparsely appointed, but the few furnishings were of the highest quality. The rug was Greek, with a simple geometric design in blue and yellow. The antique chairs and the matching tripod table were of ebony with silver hinges. The heavy drapery drawn over the doorway for privacy was of some plush green fabric shot through with golden threads. The walls were stained a somber red. The iron lamp in the middle of the room stood on three griffin's feet and breathed steady flames from three gaping griffin mouths. By its light, while waiting for Poplicola, I had perused the little yellow tags that dangled from the scrolls which filled the pigeonhole bookcase in the corner. The censor's library consisted entirely of serious works by philosophers and historians, without a lurid poet or frivolous playwright among them. Everything about the room bespoke a man of impeccable taste and high standards—just the sort of fellow whom public opinion would deem worthy of wearing the purple toga, a man qualified to keep the sacred rolls of citizenship and pass judgment on the moral conduct of senators.

"It was Cicero who recommended me, then?" In the ten years since I had met him, Cicero had sent quite a bit of business my way.

Poplicola nodded. "I told him I needed an agent to investigate . . . a private matter. A man from outside my own household, and yet someone I could rely upon to be thorough, truthful, and absolutely discreet. He seemed to think that you would do."

"I'm honored that Cicero would recommend me to a man of your exalted position and—"

"Discretion!" he insisted, cutting me off. "That matters most of all. Everything you discover while in my employ—*everything*—must be held in the strictest confidence. You will reveal your discoveries to me and to no one else."

From beneath his wrinkled brow he peered at me with an intensity that was unsettling. I nodded and said slowly, "So long as such discretion does not conflict with more sacred obligations to the gods, then yes, Censor, I promise you my absolute discretion."

"Upon your honor as a Roman? Upon the shades of your ancestors?"

I sighed. Why must these nobles always take themselves and their problems so seriously? Why must every transaction require the invocation of dead relatives? Poplicola's earth-shattering dilemma was probably nothing more than an errant wife or a bit of blackmail over a pretty slaveboy. I chafed at his demand for an oath and considered refusing; but the fact was that my daughter Diana had just been born, the household coffers were perilously depleted, and I needed work. I gave him my word, upon my honor and my ancestors.

He produced something from the folds of his purple toga and placed it on the little table between us. I saw it was a small silver bowl, and in the bowl there appeared to be a delicacy of some sort. I caught a whiff of almonds.

"What do you make of that?" he said.

"It appears to be a sweet cake," I ventured. I picked up the little bowl and sniffed. Almonds, yes; and something else . . .

"By Hercules, don't eat any of it!" He snatched the bowl from me. "I have reason to believe it's been poisoned." Poplicola shuddered. He suddenly looked much older.

"Poisoned?"

"The slave who brought me the cake this afternoon, here in my study— one of my oldest slaves, more than a servant, a companion really—well, the fellow always had a sweet tooth . . . like his master, that way. If he shaved off a bit of my delicacies every now and then, thinking I wouldn't notice, where was the harm in that? It was a bit of a game between us. I used to tease him; I'd say, 'The only thing that keeps me from growing fat is the fact that you serve my food!' Poor Chrestus . . ." His face became ashen.

"I see. This Chrestus brought you the cake. And then?"

"I dismissed Chrestus and put the bowl aside while I finished reading a document. I came to the end, rolled up the scroll, and put it aside. I was just about to take a bite of the cake when another slave, my doorkeeper, ran into the room, terribly alarmed. He said that Chrestus was having a seizure. I went to him as quickly as I could. He was lying on the floor, convulsing. 'The cake!' he said. 'The cake!' And then he was dead. As quickly as that! The look on his face—horrible!" Poplicola gazed at the little cake and curled his lip, as if an adder were coiled in the silver bowl. "My favorite," he said in a hollow voice. "Cinnamon and almonds, sweetened with honey and wine, with just a hint of aniseed. An old man's pleasure, one of the few I have left. Now I shall never be able to eat it again!"

And neither shall Chrestus, I thought. "Where did the cake come from?"

"There's a little alley just north of the Forum, with bakery shops on either side."

"I know the street."

"The place on the corner makes these cakes every other day. I have a standing order—a little treat I give myself. Chrestus goes down to fetch one for me, and I have it in the early afternoon."

"And was it Chrestus who fetched the cake for you today?"

For a long moment he stared silently at the cake. "No."

"Who, then?"

He hunched his thin shoulders up and pursed his lips. "My son, Lucius. He came by this afternoon. So the doorkeeper tells me; I didn't see him myself. Lucius told the doorkeeper not to disturb me, that he couldn't stay; he'd only stopped by to drop off a sweet cake for me. Lucius knows of my habit of indulging in this particular sweet, you see, and some business in the Forum took him by the street of the bakers, and as my house was on his way to another errand, he brought me a cake. The doorkeeper fetched Chrestus, Lucius gave Chrestus the sweet cake wrapped up in a bit of parchment, and then Lucius left. A little later, Chrestus brought the cake to me. . . ."

Now I understood why Poplicola had demanded an oath upon my ancestors. The matter was delicate indeed. "Do you suspect your son of tampering with the cake?"

Poplicola shook his head. "I don't know what to think."

"Is there any reason to suspect that he might wish to do you harm?"

"Of course not!" The denial was a little too vehement, a little too quick. "What is it you want from me, Censor?"

"To find the truth of the matter! They call you Finder, don't they? Find out if the cake is poisoned. Find out who poisoned it. Find out how it came about that my son . . ."

"I understand, Censor. Tell me, who in your household knows of what happened today?"

"Only the doorkeeper."

"No one else?"

"No one. The rest of the household has been told that Chrestus collapsed from a heart attack. I've told no one else of Lucius's visit, or about the cake."

I nodded. "To begin, I shall need to see the dead man, and to question your doorkeeper."

"Of course. And the cake? Shall I feed a bit to some stray cat, to make sure . . ."

"I don't think that will be necessary, Censor." I picked up the little bowl and sniffed at the cake again. Most definitely, blended with the wholesome scent of baked almonds was the sharper odor of the substance called bitter-almond, one of the strongest of all poisons. Only a few drops would suffice to kill a man in minutes. How fiendishly clever, to sprinkle it onto a sweet almond-flavored confection, from which a hungry man with a sweet tooth might take a bite without noticing the bitter taste until too late.

Poplicola took me to see the body. Chrestus looked to have been fit for his age. His hands were soft; his master had not overworked him. His waxy flesh had a pinkish flush, further evidence that the poison had been bitter-almond.

Poplicola summoned the doorkeeper, whom I questioned in his master's presence. He proved to be a tight-lipped fellow (as doorkeepers should be), and added nothing to what Poplicola had already told me.

Visibly shaken, Poplicola withdrew, with instructions to the doorkeeper to see me out. I was in the foyer, about to leave, when a woman crossed the atrium. She wore an elegant blue stola and her hair was fashionably arranged with combs and pins into a towering configuration that defied logic. Her hair was jet black, except for a narrow streak of white above her left temple that spiraled upward like a ribbon into the convoluted vortex. She glanced at me as she passed but registered no reaction. No doubt the censor received many visitors.

"Is that the censor's daughter?" I asked the doorkeeper.

"No."

I raised an eyebrow, but the tight-lipped slave did not elaborate. "His wife, then?"

"Yes. My mistress Palla."

"A striking woman." In the wake of her passing, a kind of aura seemed to linger in the empty atrium. Hers was a haughty beauty that gave little indication of her age. I suspected she must be older than she looked, but she could hardly have been past forty.

"Is Palla the mother of the censor's son, Lucius?"

"No."

"His stepmother, then?"

"Yes."

"I see." I nodded and took my leave.

I wanted to know more about Poplicola and his household, so that night I paid a visit to my patrician friend Lucius Claudius, who knows everything worth knowing about anyone who counts in the higher circles of Roman society. I intended to be discreet, honoring my oath to the censor, and so, after dinner, relaxing on our couches and sharing more wine, in a round-about way I got onto the topic of elections and voting, and thence to the subject of census rolls. "I understand the recent census shows something like eight hundred thousand Roman citizens," I noted.

"Indeed!" Lucius Claudius popped his pudgy fingers into his mouth one by one, savoring the grease from the roasted quail. With his other hand he brushed a ringlet of frizzled red hair from his forehead. "If this keeps up, one of these days citizens shall outnumber slaves! The censors really should do something about restricting citizenship."

My friend's politics tend to be conservative; the Claudii are patricians, after all. I nodded thoughtfully. "Who are the censors nowadays, anyway?"

"Lentulus Clodianus . . ." he said, popping a final finger into his mouth, ". . . and old Lucius Gellius Poplicola."

"Poplicola," I murmured innocently. "Now why does that name sound familiar?"

"Really, Gordianus, where is your head? Poplicola was consul two years ago. Surely you recall that bit of unpleasantness with Spartacus? It was Poplicola's job as consul to take the field against the rebel slaves, who gave him a sound whipping—not once, but twice! The disgrace of it, farm slaves led by a rogue gladiator, thrashing trained legionnaires led by a Roman consul! People said it was because Poppy was just too old to lead an army. He's lucky it wasn't the end of his career! But here it is two years later, and Poppy's a censor. It's a big job. But safe—no military commands! Just right for a fellow like Poppy—been around forever, honest as a stick."

"Just what do the censors do?"

"Census and censure, their two main duties. Keep the roll of voters, assign the voters to tribes, make sure the patrician tribes carry the most weight in the elections—that's the way of it. Well, we can hardly allow those seven hundred and ninety-nine thousand common citizens out there to have as much say in electing magistrates as the thousand of us whose families have been running this place since the days of Romulus and Remus; wouldn't make sense. That's the census part."

I nodded. "And censure?"

"The censors don't just say who's a citizen and who's not; they also say what a citizen should be. The privilege of citizenship implies certain moral standards, even in these dissolute days. If the censors put a black mark for immoral conduct by a man's name in the rolls, it's serious business. They can expel a fellow from the Senate. In fact . . ." He leaned forward and lowered his voice to emphasize the gravity of what he was about to say. "In fact, word has it that the censors are about to publish a list of *over sixty men* they're throwing out of the Senate for breach of moral character— taking bribes, falsifying documents, embezzling. Sixty! A veritable purge! You can imagine the mood in the Senate House. Everyone suspicious of everyone else, all of us wondering who's on the list."

"So Poplicola is not exactly the most popular man in the Forum these days?"

"To put it mildly. Don't misunderstand, there's plenty of support for the purge. I support it myself, wholeheartedly. The Senate needs a thorough housecleaning! But Poppy's about to make some serious enemies. Which is ironic, because he's always been such a peacemaker." Lucius laughed. "Back when he was governor of Greece in his younger days, they say Poppy called together all the bickering philosophers in Athens and practically pleaded with them to come to some sort of consensus about the nature of the universe. 'If we cannot have harmony in the heavens, how can we hope for anything but discord here on Earth?' " His mimicry of the censor's reedy voice was uncanny.

"Census and censure," I murmured, sipping my wine. "I don't suppose ordinary citizens have all that much to fear from the censors."

"Oh, a black mark from the censor is trouble for any man. Ties up voting rights, cancels state contracts, revokes licenses to keep a shop in the city. That could ruin a man, drive him into poverty. And if a censor really wants to make trouble for a fellow, he can call him before a special Senate committee to investigate charges of immorality. Once that sort of investigation starts, it never ends—just the idea is enough to give even an honest man a heart attack! Oh yes, the censorship is a powerful office. That's why it has to be filled with men of absolutely irreproachable character, completely untainted by scandal—like Poppy." Lucius Claudius suddenly frowned and wrinkled his fleshy brow. "Of course, there's that terrible rumor I heard only this afternoon—so outrageous I dismissed it out of hand. Put it out of my mind so completely that I actually forgot about it until just now . . ."

"Rumor?"

"Probably nothing—a vicious bit of slander put about by one of Poppy's enemies . . ."

"Slander?"

"Oh, some nonsense about Poppy's son, Lucius, trying to poison the old man—using a sweet cake, if you can believe it!" I raised my eyebrows and tried to look surprised. "But these kinds of stories always get started, don't they, when a fellow as old as Poppy marries a woman young enough to be his daughter, and beautiful as well. Palla is her name. She and her stepson Lucius get along well—what of it? People see them out together now and again without Poppy, at a chariot race or a play, laughing and having a good time, and the next thing you know, these nasty rumors get started. Lucius, trying to poison his father so he can marry his stepmother—now that would be a scandal! And I'm sure there are those who'd like to think it's true, who'd love nothing better than to see Poppy pulled down into the muck right along with them."

The attempted poisoning had taken place that afternoon—and yet Lucius

Claudius had already heard about it. How could the rumor have spread so swiftly? Who could have started it? Not Poplicola's son, surely, if he were the poisoner. But what if Poplicola's son were innocent of any wrongdoing? What if he had been somehow duped into passing the deadly cake by his father's enemies, who had then gone spreading the tale prematurely . . .

Or might the speed of the rumor have a simpler explanation? It could be that Poplicola's doorkeeper was not nearly as tight-lipped as his terse answers had led me to think. If the doorkeeper told another slave in the household about the poison cake, who then told a slave in a neighbor's house, who then told his master . . .

I tried to keep my face a blank, but Lucius Claudius saw the wheels spinning in my head. He narrowed his eyes. "Gordianus—what are you up to? How did we get onto the subject of Poplicola, anyway? Do you know something about this rumor?"

I was trying to think of some way to honor my oath to the censor without lying to my friend, when I was saved by the arrival of Lucius Claudius's beloved Momo. The tiny Melitaean terrier scampered into the room, as white as a snowball and almost as round; lately she had grown as plump as her master. She scampered and yapped at Lucius's feet, too earthbound to leap onto the couch. Lucius summoned a slave, who lifted the dog up and placed it on his lap. "My darling, my sweet, my adorable little Momo!" he cooed, and in an instant seemed to forget all about Poplicola, to my relief.

Bitter-almond is a difficult poison to obtain. I am told that it is extracted from the pits of common fruits, but the stuff is so lethal—a man can die simply from having it touch his skin, or inhaling its fumes—that most of the shady dealers in such goods refuse to handle it. The rare customer looking for bitter-almond is usually steered into purchasing something else for his purpose, "Just as good," the dealer will say, though few poisons are as quick and certain as bitter-almond.

My peculiar line of work has acquainted me with all sorts of people, from the highest of the high, like Poplicola, to the lowest of the low—like a certain unsavory dealer in poisons and potions named Quintus Fugax. Fugax claimed to be immune to every poison known to man, and even boasted that on occasion he tested new ones on himself, just to see if they would make him sick. To be sure, no poison had yet killed him, but his fingers were stained permanently black, there was a constant twitch at the corner of his mouth, his skin was covered with strange splotches, his head was covered with scabs and bald spots, and one of his eyes was covered with a rheumy yellow film. If anyone in Rome was unafraid to deal in bitter-almond, it was Quintus Fugax.

I found him the next day at his usual haunt, a squalid little tavern on the riverfront. I told him I wanted to ask some general questions about certain poisons and how they acted, for my own edification. So long as I kept his wine cup full, he agreed to talk with me.

Several cups later, when I judged that his tongue was sufficiently loosened by the wine, I asked him if he knew anything about bitter-almond. He laughed. "It's the best! I always tell people so, and not just because I'm about the only dealer who handles it. But hardly anybody wants it. Bitter-almond carries a curse, some say. People are afraid it'll turn on them, and they'll end up the dead one. Could happen; stuff can practically kill you just by you looking at it."

"Not much call for bitter-almond, then?"

"Not much." He smiled. "But I did sell a bit of it, just yesterday."

I swirled my wine and pretended to study the dregs. "Really? Some fishmonger wanting to do in his wife, I suppose."

He grinned, showing more gaps than teeth. "You know I never talk about my customers."

I frowned. "Still, it can't have been anyone very important. I'd have heard if some senator or wealthy merchant died from sudden convulsions after eating a hearty meal."

Fugax barked out a laugh. "Ha! Try a piece of cake!"

I caught my breath and kept my eyes on the swirling dregs. "I beg your pardon?"

"Customer wanted to know if you could use bitter-almond in an almond sweet cake. I said, 'Just the thing!'"

"What was he, a cook? Or a cook's slave, I suppose. Your customers usually send a go-between, don't they? They never deal with you face-to-face."

"This one did."

"Really?"

"Said she couldn't trust any of her slaves to make such a sensitive purchase."

"*She?*"

He raised his eyebrows and covered his mouth, like a little boy caught tattling, then threw back his head and cackled. "Gave that much away, didn't I? But I can't say who she was, because I don't know. Not poor, though. Came and went in a covered litter, all blue like her stola. Made her bearers stop a couple of streets away so they couldn't see where she went and I wouldn't see where she came from, but I sneaked after her when she left. Watched her climb into that fancy litter—hair so tall she had to stoop to get in!"

I summoned up a laugh and nodded. "These crazy new hairstyles!"

His ravaged face suddenly took on a wistful look. "Hers was pretty, though. All shiny and black—with a white streak running through it, like a stripe on a cat! Pretty woman. But pity the poor man who's crossed her!"

I nodded. "Pity him indeed . . ."

The enviable corner spot on the street of the bakers was occupied by a family named Baebius; so declared a handsomely painted sign above the serving counter that fronted the street. A short young blonde, a bit on the far side of pleasingly plump but with a sunshiny smile, stepped up to serve me. "What'll you have today, citizen? Sweet or savory?"

"Sweet, I think. A friend tells me you make the most delicious little almond cakes."

"Oh, you're thinking of Papa's special. We're famous for it. Been selling it from this shop for three generations. But I'm afraid we don't have any today. We only make those every other day. However, I can sell you a wonderful cheese and honey torte—very rich."

I pretended to hem and haw and finally nodded. "Yes, give me one of those. No, make it three—hungry mouths at home! But it's too bad you don't have the almond cakes. My friend raves about them. He was by here just yesterday, I think. A fellow named Lucius Gellius."

"Oh yes, we know him. But it's not he who craves the almond cakes, it's his father, the censor. Old Poplicola buys one from every batch Papa bakes!"

"But his son Lucius *was* here yesterday?"

She nodded. "So he was. I sold him the sweet cake myself and wrapped it up in parchment for him to take to his father. For himself and the lady he bought a couple of little savory custards. Would you care to try—"

"The lady?"

"The lady who was waiting for him in the blue litter."

"Is she a regular customer, too?"

The girl shrugged. "I didn't actually see her; only got a glimpse as Lucius was handing her the custard, and then they were off toward the Forum. There, taste that and tell me it's not fit for the gods."

I bit into the cheese and honey torte and feigned an enthusiastic nod. At that moment, it could have been ambrosia and I would have taken no pleasure in it.

*   *   *

I made my report to Poplicola that afternoon. He was surprised that I could have concluded my investigation so swiftly, and insisted on knowing each step in my progress and every person I had talked to. He stood, turned his back to me, and stared at the somber red wall as I explained how I came to suspect the use of bitter-almond; how I questioned one of the few men who dealt in that particular poison, plied him with wine, and obtained a description that was almost certainly of Palla; how the girl at the bakery shop not only confirmed that Lucius had purchased the cake the previous day, but saw him leave in a blue litter with a female companion.

"None of this amounts to absolute proof, I admit. But it seems reasonably evident that Palla purchased the bitter-almond in the morning, that Lucius was either with her at that time, and stayed in the litter, or else joined her later, and then the two of them went to the bakery shop, where Lucius purchased the cake. Then one or both of them together sprinkled the poison onto the cake—"

Poplicola hunched his gaunt shoulders and produced a stifled cry, a sound of such despair that I was stunned into silence. When he turned to face me, he appeared to have aged ten years in an instant.

"All this is circumstantial evidence," he said, "not legal proof."

I spoke slowly and carefully. "Legal proof is narrowly defined. To satisfy a court of law, all the slaves involved would be called upon to testify—the litter bearers, your doorkeeper, perhaps the personal attendants of Palla and Lucius. Slaves see everything, and they usually know more than their masters think. They would be tortured, of course; the testimony of slaves is inadmissible unless obtained by torture. Acquiring that degree of proof is beyond my means, Censor."

He shook his head. "Never mind. We both know the truth. I knew it all along, of course. Lucius and Palla, behind my back—but I never thought it would come to this!"

"What will you do, Censor?" It was within Poplicola's legal rights, as *paterfamilias*, to put his son to death without a trial or any other formality. He could strangle Lucius with his own hands or have a slave do it for him, and no one would question his right to do so, especially in the circumstances. He could do the same thing to his wife.

Poplicola made no answer. He had turned to face the wall again, and stood so stiff and motionless that I feared for him. "Censor . . . ?"

"What will I do?" he snapped. "Don't be impertinent, Finder! I hired you to find out a thing. You did so, and that's the end of your concern. You'll leave here with some gold in your purse, never fear."

"Censor, I meant no—"

"You swore an oath, on your ancestors, to speak of this affair to no one but me. I shall hold you to it. If you're any sort of Roman—"

"There's no need to remind me, Censor," I said sharply. "I don't make oaths lightly."

He reached into a pouch within his purple toga, counted out some coins, laid them on the little table before me, and left the room without saying another word.

I was left to show myself out. On my way to the foyer, addled by anger, I took a wrong turn and didn't realize it until I found myself in a large garden surrounded by a peristyle. I cursed and turned to retrace my steps, then glimpsed the couple who stood beneath the colonnade at the far corner of the garden, their heads together as if engaged in some grave conversation. The woman was Palla. Her arms were crossed and her head was held high. The man, from his manner toward her, I would have taken to be her husband had I not known better. Lucius Gellius looked very much like a younger replica of his father, even to the chilly stare he gave me as I hastily withdrew.

In the days that followed, I kept my ears perked for any news of developments at the house of Poplicola, but there was only silence. Was the old man plotting some horrible revenge on his son and wife? Were they still plotting against him? Or had the three of them somehow come together, with confessions of guilt and forgiveness all around? I hardly saw how such a reconciliation could be possible after such a total breach of trust.

Then one morning I received a note from my friend Lucius Claudius:

Dear Friend, Dinner Companion, and Fellow Connoisseur of Gossip,

We never quite finished our discussion about Poplicola the other day, did we? The latest gossip (horrible stuff): On the very eve of the great purge in the Senate, one hears that certain members are planning to mount a prosecution against the censor's son, Lucius Gellius, accusing him of *sleeping with his stepmother* and *plotting to kill Poppy*. Such a trial will stir up a huge scandal—what will people think of a magistrate in charge of morals who can't stop his own son and wife from fornicating and scheming to do him in? Opponents (and likely targets) of the purge will say, "Clean up your own house, Poplicola, before you presume to clean ours!"

Who knows how such a trial might turn out? The whole family

will be dragged through the mud—if there's any dirt on any of them, the prosecutors will dig it up. And if Lucius is found guilty (I still can't believe it), they won't allow him exile—he'll be put to death along with Palla, and to save face Poplicola will have to play stern *paterfamilias* and watch while it's done! That would be the death of Poppy, I fear. Certainly, it would be the end of his political career. He'd be utterly humiliated, his moral authority a joke. He couldn't possibly continue as censor. No purge of the Senate, then, and politics can go on as usual! What an age we live in.

Ah well, come dine with me tonight. I shall be having fresh pheasant, and Cook promises to do something divine with the sauce. . . .

The pheasant that night was succulent. The sauce had an intriguing insinuation of mint that lingered teasingly on the tongue. But the food was not what I had come for.

Eventually we got around to the subject of the censor and his woes.

"There's to be a trial, then," I said.

"Actually . . . no," said Lucius Claudius.

"But your note this morning—"

"Invalidated by fresh gossip this afternoon."

"And?"

Lucius leaned back on his couch, stroked Momo, and looked at me shrewdly. "I don't suppose, Gordianus, that you know more about this affair than you're letting on?"

I looked him in the eye. "Nothing that I could discuss, even with you, my friend, without violating an oath."

He nodded. "I thought it must be something like that. Even so, I don't suppose you could let me know, simply yes or no, whether Lucius Gellius and Palla really—Gordianus, you look as if the pheasant suddenly turned on you! Well, let no one say that I ever gave a dinner guest indigestion from pressing an improper question. I shall simply have to live not knowing. Though in that case, why I should tell *you* the latest news from the Forum, I'm sure I don't know."

He pouted and fussed over Momo. I sipped my wine. Lucius began to fidget. Eventually his urge to share the latest gossip got the better of him. I tried not to smile.

"Very well, since you must know: Poppy, acting in his capacity as censor, has convoked a special Senate committee to investigate his own son on a charge of gross immorality—namely this rumor about adultery and attempted parricide. The committee will take up the investigation at once, and Poppy himself will preside over it."

"But how will this affect the upcoming trial?"

"There won't be a trial. The investigation supersedes it. It's rather clever of Poppy, I suppose, and rather brave. This way he heads off his enemies, who would have made a public trial into a spectacle. Instead, he'll see to the question of his son's guilt or innocence himself, behind closed doors. The Senate committee will make the final vote, but Poppy will oversee the proceedings. Of course, the whole thing could spin out of his control. If the investigating committee finds Lucius Gellius guilty, the scandal will still be the ruin of Poppy." He shook his head. "Surely that won't happen. For Poppy to take charge of the matter himself, that must mean that his son is innocent, and Poppy knows it—doesn't it?" Lucius raised an eyebrow and peered at me expectantly.

"I'm not sure what it means," I said, and meant it.

The investigation into the moral conduct of Lucius Gellius lasted two days, and took place behind the closed doors of the Senate House, where none but scribes and witnesses and the senators themselves were allowed. Fortunately for me, Lucius Claudius was among the senators on the investigating committee, and when the investigation was done he invited me once again to dine with him.

He greeted me at the door himself, and even before he spoke I could tell from his round, beaming face that he was pleased with the outcome.

"The committee reached a conclusion?" I said.

"Yes, and what a relief!"

"Lucius Gellius was cleared of the charges?" I tried not to sound sceptical.

"Completely! The whole business was an absurd fabrication! Nothing to it but vicious rumors and unfounded suspicions."

I thought of the dead slave, Chrestus. "There was no evidence at all of Lucius Gellius's guilt?"

"No such evidence was presented. Oh, so-and-so once saw Palla and Lucius Gellius sitting with their legs pressed together at the Circus Maximus, and another so-and-so saw them holding hands in a market-place one day, and someone else claims to have seen them kiss beneath some trees on the Palatine Hill. Nothing but hearsay and rubbish. Palla and Lucius Gellius were called upon to defend themselves, and they both swore they had done nothing improper. Poplicola himself vouched for them."

"No slaves were called to testify?"

"This was an investigation, Gordianus, not a trial. We had no authority to extract testimony under torture."

"And were there no other witnesses? No depositions? Nothing regarding the poisoned cake that was rumored?"

"No. If there *had* been anyone capable of producing truly damning evidence, they'd have been found, surely; there were plenty of senators on the committee hostile to Poppy, and believe me, since the rumors first began, they've been scouring the city looking for evidence. It simply wasn't there."

I thought of the poison dealer, and of the blond girl who had waited on me at the bakery shop. I had tracked them down with little enough trouble; Poplicola's enemies would have started out with less to go on, but surely they had dispatched their own finders to search out the truth. Why had the girl not been called to testify, at least? Had no one made even the simple connection between the rumor of the poisoned cake and the bakery shop which produced Poplicola's favorite treat? Could the forces against the censor have been so inept?

Lucius laughed. "And to think of the meals I left untouched, fretting over Poppy! Well, now that he and his household have been vindicated, he can get on with his work as censor. Tomorrow Poppy will post his list of senators who've earned a black mark for immoral conduct. Good riddance, I say. More elbow room for the rest of us in the Senate chambers!" He sighed and shook his head. "Really, all that grief, and the whole thing was a farce."

Yes, I thought warily, so it had ended up—a farce. But what role had I played in it?

The next day I went to the street of the bakers, thinking to finally taste for myself one of the famous almond sweet cakes baked by the Baebius family—and also to find out if, indeed, no one from the Senate committee had called upon the blond girl.

I strolled up the narrow, winding little street and arrived at the corner with a shock. Instead of the blond girl's smiling face behind the serving counter, I saw a boarded-up storefront. The sign bearing the family name, there for three generations, had been obliterated with crude daubs of paint.

A shopkeeper down the street saw me gaping and called to me from behind his counter.

"Looking for the Baebu?"

"Yes."

"Gone."

"Where?"

"No idea."

"When?"

He shrugged. "A while back. Just up and left overnight, the whole lot of them. Baebius, his wife and daughter, the slaves—here one day, all gone the next. Poff! Like actors falling through a trapdoor on a stage."

"But why?"

He gestured that I should step closer, and lowered his voice. "I suspect that Baebius must have gotten himself into serious trouble with the authorities."

"What authorities?"

"The Senate itself!"

"Why do you say that?"

"Just a day or two after he vanished, some pretty rough-looking strangers came snooping up and down the block, asking for Baebius and wanting to know where he'd gone. They even offered money, but nobody could tell them. And then, a few days after that, here come more strangers asking questions, only these were better dressed and carried fancy-looking scrolls; claimed they were conducting some sort of official investigation, and had 'senatorial authority.' Not that it mattered; people around here still didn't know what had become of Baebius. It's a mystery, isn't it?"

"Yes . . ."

"I figure Baebius must have done something pretty bad, to get out of town that sudden and not leave a trace behind." He shook his head. "Sad, though; his family had been in that shop a long time. And you'd think he might have given me his recipe for those almond cakes before he disappeared! People come by here day and night asking for those cakes. Say, could I interest you in something sweet? These honey-glazed buns are fresh out of the oven. Just smell that aroma. . . ."

Is it better to visit a poison dealer on a full stomach or an empty one? Empty, I decided, and so I declined the baker's bun and made my way across the Forum and the cattle market to the riverfront, and thence to the seedy little tavern frequented by Quintus Fugax.

The interior seemed pitch-dark after the bright sunshine. I had to squint as I stumbled from bench to bench, searching among the derelicts. Only the most hardened drinkers were in such a place at that time of day. The place stank of spilled wine and river rot.

"Looking for someone?" asked the tavern keeper.

"A fellow called Fugax."

"The scarecrow with the rheumy eye and the bad breath?"

"That's him."

"You're out of luck, then, but not as out of luck as your friend."

"What do you mean?"

"They dragged him out of the river a couple of days ago."

"What?"

"Drowned. Poor sod must have fallen in; not my fault if a man leaves here too drunk to walk straight. Or maybe . . ." He gave me a significant look. "Maybe somebody pushed him in."

"Why do you say that?"

"Fugax had been strutting around here lately, claiming he was about to come into a big sum of money. Crazy fool! Saying a thing like that in this neighborhood is asking for trouble."

"Where was he going to get this money?"

"That's what I wondered. I asked him, 'What, are you planning to sell your garden villa on the Tiber?' He laughed and said he had something to sell, all right—information, important information that powerful people would pay a lot for; pay to get it, or pay to keep others from getting it. Not likely, I thought! 'What could a river rat like you know that anybody would give a fig to find out?' He just laughed. The fellow was half crazy, you know. But I figure maybe somebody heard him bragging, tried to rob him, got angry when they didn't find much, and threw him in the river. The dock workers that found him say it looked like he might have hit his head on something—hard to tell with all those scabs and rashes. Did you know him well?"

I sighed. "Well enough not to mourn too much over his death."

The tavern keeper looked at me oddly. "You need something to drink, citizen."

I had declined the baker's bun, but I accepted the tavern keeper's wine.

The doorkeeper at Poplicola's house tersely informed me that his master was not receiving visitors. I pushed past him and told him I would wait in the red study. I waited for quite a while, long enough to peruse a few of the scrolls in Poplicola's little library: Aristotle on ethics, Plato on the examined life. There was a movement at the green curtain drawn over the doorway. It was not Poplicola who entered, but Palla.

She was shorter than I had thought; her elaborate turret of hair gave an illusion of height. But she was actually more beautiful than I had realized. By the reflected light of the red walls her skin took on a smooth, creamy luster. The bland youthfulness of her face was at odds with the worldliness in her eyes. Seeing her so close, it was harder than ever to calculate her age.

"You must be Gordianus," she said.

"Yes."

"My husband is physically and emotionally exhausted by the events of the last few days. He can't possibly see you."

"I think he should."

"Has he not paid you yet?"

I gritted my teeth. "I'm not an instrument to be used and then disposed of. I helped him discover the truth. I brought him certain information. Now I find that an innocent family has been driven into hiding, and another man is dead, very likely murdered to keep him quiet."

"If you're talking about that wretch Fugax, surely the whole city is better off being rid of such a creature."

"What do you know about his death?"

She made no answer.

"I insist that your husband see me," I said.

She looked at me steadily. "Anything you might wish to say to Poppy, you may say to me. We have no secrets from each other—not anymore. Everything has come out into the open between us."

"And your stepson?"

"Father and son are reconciled."

"The three of you have worked it all out?"

"Yes. But that's really none of your business, Finder. As you say, you were hired to find out a thing, and you did. There's an end of it."

"An end of Chrestus, and of Fugax, you mean. And who knows what's become of the baker and his family."

She drew a deep breath and gave me a bemused look. "The slave Chrestus belonged to my husband. His death was an injury to my husband's property. Chrestus was old and slow, he pilfered from his master's food and might not have survived another winter; his market value was nil. It's for Poppy and Poppy alone to seek recompense for the loss, and if he chooses to overlook it, then neither you nor anybody else has any business poking further into the matter."

She crossed her arms and paced slowly across the room. "As for Fugax, as I say, his death is no loss to anyone. A public service, I should think! When the trial began to loom, and then the investigation, he tried to blackmail us. He was a stupid, vile, treacherous little man, and now he's dead. That, too, is none of your business."

She reached the far corner and turned around. "As for the baker and his family, they were paid a more than adequate compensation for their trouble."

"The man's family had been in that shop for generations! I can't believe he left of his own free will."

She stiffened her jaw. "True, Baebius was not completely cooperative, at first. A certain amount of pressure was required to make him see reason."

"Pressure?"

"A black mark from a censor could have made a great deal of trouble for Baebius. Once that was explained to him, Baebius saw that it would be best if he and his family left Rome altogether and set up shop elsewhere. I'm sure his almond cakes will be just as popular in Spain as they were here in Rome. Poppy shall miss them, alas." She spoke without a shred of irony.

"And what about me?"

"You, Gordianus?"

"I knew more than anyone."

"Yes, that's true. To be candid, I thought we should do something about you; so did my stepson. But Poppy said that you had sworn an oath of secrecy upon your ancestors, that you gave him your word, Roman to Roman. That sort of thing counts for a great deal with Poppy. He insisted that we leave you alone. And he was right; you kept silent. He expects you to remain silent. I'm sure you won't let him down."

She flashed a serene smile, without the least hint of remorse. It struck me that Palla resembled a bit of poisoned cake herself. "So you see," she said, "it's all worked out for the best, for everyone concerned."

Legally and politically, the affair of Poplicola and the poisoned cake was at an end. The court of public opinion, however, would continue to try and retry the case for years to come.

There were those who insisted that the Senate investigation had been rigged by Poplicola himself; that vital witnesses had been intimidated, driven off, even killed; that the censor was morally bankrupt, unfit for his office, and that his happy household was a sham.

Others defended Poplicola, saying that all the talk against him originated with a few morally depraved, bitter ex-senators. There were even those who argued that the episode was proof of Poplicola's wisdom and profound sense of judgment. Upon hearing such shocking charges against his son and wife, many a man would have rushed to avenge himself on them, taking their punishment into his own hands; but Poplicola had exercised almost superhuman restraint, called for an official inquiry, and ultimately saw his loved ones vindicated. For his patience and cool-headed perseverance, Poplicola was held up as a model of Roman sagacity, and his loyal wife Palla was admired as a woman who held her head high even when enduring the cruelest slanders.

As for his son, Lucius Gellius's political career advanced more or less unimpeded by the scandal. He became more active than ever in the courts and in the Senate House, and openly expressed his ambition to someday be censor, following in his father's footsteps. Only rarely did his unproved crimes come back to haunt him, as on the occasion when he sparred with Cicero in a rancorous debate and threatened to give the great orator a piece of his mind—to which Cicero replied, "Better that, Lucius Gellius, than a piece of your cake!"

RUMPOLE AND THE ABSENCE OF BODY

John Mortimer

Whether they know it or not, nearly everyone is familiar with the work of John Mortimer, for Mortimer is the creator of the unforgettable Rumpole, barrister-at-law at London's Old Bailey. The Rumpole TV series ran on PBS and the BBC for many years, and most of the Rumpole stories to be found in anthologies and in Ellery Queen's Mystery Magazine first saw life as scripts for the TV series. Mortimer, a barrister himself since 1948, has said that Rumpole is based loosely on the character of his father, who also practiced law. The Rumpole series has already acquired the status of classic mystery fiction, but most of Mortimer's other fictional work is so truly mainstream that it cannot be considered to fall within the mystery genre.

"WHAT'S BETTER THAN the presence of mind in an accident? Absence of body." So far as I recall, this was my old father's only joke, if you can flatter it by calling it a joke. But when it comes to a trial for murder, the failure of the corpse to put in an appearance can be a considerable embarrassment to all concerned. So it was when the possibly late Charley Twineham failed to turn up, even in phantom form, at Number One Court in the Old Bailey, where his wife, Pauline, commonly known as "Poppy" Twineham, was on trial for his murder.

"Rumpole," my wife Hilda, known to me only as She Who Must Be Obeyed, trumpeted like the recording angel uttering a hostile verdict on the Day of Judgement. "How can you possibly defend that appalling Poppy woman?"

"Perfectly easy," I told her. "You put on the crumpled gown, perch the yellowing wig on your head, stand up, and try to make the prosecution witnesses look silly. Call me old-fashioned, but that's the way it's always worked for me in the past. And in her case the prosecution have completely failed to produce a corpse."

"She did away with him, quite obviously. He's undoubtedly at the bottom of the sea. I can't think how she got you to defend her. Fluttered her eyelashes at you, I suppose. You're such a fool, Rumpole. Where women are concerned."

In fact she was wrong. Poppy's eyelashes were not of the fluttering variety. She was a big, fair-haired, blue-eyed, you might say "beefy" woman who would have been naturally cheerful if she hadn't suffered the handicap of marriage to a smaller, crinkly-haired, devious businessman with protruding teeth who looked, in the photographs we had of him, like one of the smaller and less attractive rodents. The Twinehams had a six-year-old daughter named Charlotte, whom her father always called "Charlie," fondly believing that this child, to whom he gave all the love he denied her mother, was some perfected, far more attractive, and considerably more honest edition of himself.

Occasionally flush with money, often teetering on the verge of bankruptcy, the Twinehams kept a boat in the marina, handy for their cottage in Devon. This "twenty-six footer," as it came to be known among the landlubbers in the Old Bailey, was christened—inappropriately, if it was indeed the setting for a violent marital murder—*Love's Young Dream*. In it Poppy and her husband, unaccompanied by Charlotte, who was staying with a grandmother in Ealing, set sail, one winter morning, to practise for a local regatta. When *Love's Young Dream* returned to port, Poppy was the sole surviving member of the crew. Charley's body was never found and was presumed to be drifting away towards America, feeding fishes in unplumbable depths. Subsequent enquiries led to the arrest of Poppy on the charge of murder and landed me, ten days before Christmas, in the Ludgate Circus Palais de Justice, listening to that opera enthusiast and indifferent advocate, Claude Erskine-Brown, as he opened the prosecution against Hilda's least favourite woman. He presented a case which had every possible evidence of guilt about it except for that one essential—a dead person.

"I am distinctly worried," Claude confided in me as we sat in the Old Bailey canteen, drinking the black and watery brew which came out of the machine that dispensed indistinguishable tea, coffee, or soup. "I can't find enough Humpy Camels." Christmas was coming and that year it wasn't turtles or action men, Teletubbies or Barbie dolls, but a lugubrious family of ruminant quadrupeds who came inappropriately dressed as pop stars, space travelers, or members of famous football teams. Tristram and Isolde, the operatically named offspring of Claude and his wife Phillida, the Portia of our chambers, were then of an age to appreciate such toys. Sadly, Claude had searched some ten shops in vain; in that hectic week before Christmas, Humpies seemed to be all sold out, and Phillida was far too busy to join in the hunt.

"What can I do, Rumpole?" There was a note of desperation in my opponent's voice.

"Forget Humpy for the moment," I advised that stricken fellow. "Seek relief in some less taxing diversion. Such as the Twineham murder case."

I suppose, in the circumstances, it was not surprising that Claude's opening speech should have been a little distracted, at times incoherent, but the strength of the case against Poppy emerged strongly. Love had clearly died between her and Charley on the morning they took the boat out. When she returned alone, fellow members of the yacht club remembered shouting matches between the couple in which an irate Poppy had often wished her husband dead and had told him that she'd kill him if he got into another financial or amorous scrape, because Charley's ratlike appearance didn't stop him pursuing, and sometimes even catching, other women. She discussed, with various "friends," cases in which wives who had done in their husbands escaped because of extreme provocation. Further police searches revealed Poppy's diaries, to which she had confided her frequent temptations to enter a happy state of premature widowhood. Charley had left a sample of blood during the checkup at the doctor's, and his group was found to correspond to bloodstains on a heavy winch handle on board the good ship *Love's Young Dream*, and on the life jacket Poppy was wearing at the time of her husband's disappearance. It was the prosecution case that Poppy, taller and beefier than her husband, had stunned him with the winch handle and pushed him overboard. The boat wasn't far out when he vanished, and if he had fallen in by accident he might well have been able to swim ashore.

Poppy's account was rather different. It was true that she had quarrelled with her husband on the high seas, some dispute about an alien pair of knickers found in the washing machine after Poppy had been away for a weekend in Ealing, but she had gone down to the galley to make herself a cup of tea to calm her fury. When she returned to the deck, Charley had vanished into the ocean mists. After calling for a long time, she had steered *Love's Young Dream* back to harbour. She could think of no explanation for the blood on the winch handle and her life jacket.

"At the time he vanished from the deck of *Love's Young Dream*, Inspector, was not Charley Twineham in serious trouble with the police?"

"Do you mean at the time of the murder, Mr. Rumpole?" The deep and melancholy voice of Mr. Injustice Graves seemed to come from the bottom of the seas, or from an area inhabited by the dead.

"No, my Lord. I do not mean 'after the murder.' The prosecution still has to prove that any murder took place. May I remind your Lordship that this is a case of notable absence of body."

"The jury are no doubt aware," the old Gravestone intoned, "that there have been convictions for murder of a *corpus delicti.*"

"Oh, I'm sure, my Lord, that in the particular area of Bermondsey from which this jury are drawn, they talk of little but *'corpus delicti.'* What my Lord means," I translated for the benefit of twelve honest citizens, "is absence of body. Now, Inspector." I returned to the officer in charge of the case. "Wasn't Charley Twineham in trouble for taking orders by post for a huge number of nonexistent shoes, as well as trying to sell a number of empty houses he didn't own?"

"We were pursuing our enquiries, my Lord."

"Which might end up in charges of fraud, false pretences, and possibly forgery?"

"They might have, Mr. Rumpole, had Mr. Twineham still been alive," the inspector told me.

"Isn't that the point the jury have to decide?"

"I suppose it is," the officer conceded, and I gave a look of modest triumph at the jury, a pleasant moment interrupted by the rumble of the judge's graveyard voice.

"Assume that the deceased Twineham was thoroughly dishonest as you suggest, Mr. Rumpole. Does that justify anyone stunning him with a winch handle and pushing him into the sea?" My heart sank as the friendly faces of the Bermondsey twelve seemed to turn to stone at the judge's interruption.

Poppy's trial, which seemed to be heading remorselessly towards a verdict of "Guilty, my Lord," was interrupted by the great religious festival. The lights went on in Regent Street, the shops were crammed with the sort of presents you only buy as a final act of desperation, there were streamers in the Old Bailey canteen and limp holly decorated the screw's office down in the cells. The universal demand for Humpy Camels was such that, Claude told me in despair, he could find none available, even for ready money. Poppy was sent on a brief holiday to Holloway Prison until the second week in January.

It was there I visited her two days before Christmas, and did my best to cheer her up without offering false hopes. It was then she gave me some rather curious news.

"I heard from Mother," she said. "Little Charlotte—well, all right, we always call her Charlie—has been getting anonymous letters."

"What sort of letters?"

Poppy showed me one that her mother had sent on to her. The message was simple, even conventional—"Hope you get your heart's desire for Christmas." What was odd was that this document was constructed along the lines of poison pen letters, when the writer wants to hide his or her identity. The words had been cut out of newspapers and gummed onto a sheet of bright red cardboard.

"Did you get the envelope?"

"I talked to Mummy on the telephone. She said she threw it away. It's not important, is it?"

"I'm not sure. It might be."

And then Poppy, a large blond woman who had once been pretty and was now watery-eyed and pale from prison, said, in a matter-of-fact sort of way, "He's won now, hasn't he? He's got me locked up for life."

"I'm not altogether sure. The case isn't over until the fat foreman of the jury comes back with a verdict. It all depends on one person."

"You or me?"

"Neither of us. At the moment I'm thinking of a rather shadowy private dick. A person with a crumpled mac and a hat that saw better days. His name's Fig Newton."

Ferdinand Isaac George Newton, always known in the trade as "Fig" Newton, ace private eye and sleuth extraordinaire, had a rotten Christmas. He spent it keeping watch on Poppy's mother's house in Ealing, not in seasonal snow but in relentless rain which saturated his macintosh and penetrated his hat. Standing on the edge of the dark garden at tea time, he was rewarded. He became conscious of another shadowy figure in the garden, a shortish man with a long upper lip and protruding teeth, who approached the French windows, walking delicately, and stood peering into a bright room. Under a glittering tree he saw his daughter Charlotte, also known as Charlie, open her presents. He was so engrossed in this spectacle and delighted with his daughter's joy as she discovered a whole family of Humpy Camels, complete with spare costumes, that he didn't hear Fig Newton mutter into his mobile. He was unpleasantly surprised when, on leaving the garden ten minutes later, he saw a car with a blue light coming rapidly towards him, containing one of Fig's friends from the local force. In no time at all he was assisting the police with their enquiries.

*　　*　　*

"Charley Twineham was up to his neck in trouble and about to be arrested for fraud. He wanted to disappear, but to do it in a way which would be a revenge on his wife, whom he had grown to hate as passionately as he loved his small daughter. He knew his doctor had a specimen of his blood, and must have cut his finger to bleed a little more on the winch handle and his wife's life jacket. On that misty morning it wasn't hard to swim ashore. He must have had his line of retreat well planned."

"But there was so much evidence against that wretched woman." Hilda was still not sure, in spite of acquittal, that Poppy hadn't got away with murder. Later, finding we were short of cream for the reheat of the Christmas pudding, she said, "I know I ordered it. He never listens. Sometimes I could kill that milkman."

"Careful. Saying she could kill people was one of the strongest pieces of evidence against Poppy Twineham," I reminded her.

"Don't be silly, Rumpole. That woman obviously domineered over her unfortunate husband. You know I'm not like that, am I?"

I thought it was wiser not to answer. Instead I wondered how a man who could commit fraud and do his best to get his wife falsely convicted of murder still found it impossible not to watch his child open his presents at Christmas.

KILLING THE SIXTIES

Melodie Johnson Howe

Many people come to writing as a second career, but few from a first career as glamorous as Melodie Johnson Howe's. Self-described as "one of the last of the starlets," Howe starred in many movies, including Coogan's Bluff *with Clint Eastwood and* The Moonshine War *with Alan Alda, before turning seriously to writing. The first book in her Claire Conrad–Maggie Hill series of novels, which she describes as the female answer to Nero Wolf and Archie Goodwin, was nominated for three awards: the Edgar, the Anthony, and the Agatha. The critical acceptance her work has received is well-deserved; though her output is small, Howe is one of the genre's best short-story writers and novelists.*

WHAT DO YOU wear to meet an ex-lover who is now an aging rock star with a new liver? Well, a used liver, but new to him.

I decided on my blood-red linen dress.

The last time I saw Leon Ashe was in Chasen's about ten years ago, just before the restaurant closed for good. He was drunk and in a fight with the maître d' over the location of his table. As the waiters dragged Leon unceremoniously out of the restaurant he spotted me sitting on the banquette with my husband. "Diana!" he yelled. Then in his plaintive drunken voice he began singing the song he had written about me in the sixties; it was appropriately named "Diana," and its success had made him a giant rock star.

I didn't see him or hear from him again until last week, when he called to announce that he had a new liver. He asked if I'd come up to Oak Point, where he now lived, and spend the day with him. He suggested I meet him at a restaurant called Avanti. I was between movies, as most middle-aged actresses are, and with some coaxing on his part I agreed to drive up the coast to see him.

333

The reason I needed coaxing was because I never trusted Leon Ashe, even when I was madly in love with him back in the sixties. Leon thought of women the way he thought of the songs he wrote: the next one was always going to be Number One. The trouble with Leon is that "Diana" was the best song he ever wrote. You can hear it today in elevators and if you're holding on the phone. Funny how time equalizes everything. After all these years, the significance, the genius of Leon Ashe is reduced to muzak. An outcome he never anticipated in the sixties.

There was another reason I hesitated to see Leon: He always had an ulterior motive. Leon wanted something. I knew one thing he wouldn't want—to be lovers again. I'm too old for Leon now, even though I'm ten years younger than he is. His current and fifth wife is twenty-two. But, as I said, I had time on my hands, and despite everything, I always had a soft spot for Leon. After all, he wrote a beautiful love song for me when I was a tearful eighteen-year-old girl.

Oak Point is an expensive little village, nestled between the San Ysidro Mountains and the Pacific Ocean, just south of Santa Barbara. From my home in Malibu, it took me about an hour and a half to get there. The village consists of small shops, four or five Italian restaurants, and homes worth millions and millions of dollars. Many Hollywood people have moved up to Oak Point to get away. But I've been around long enough to know that you can't get away from Hollywood. Like smog, Hollywood moves and settles wherever it wants to. You can't shake it off like water, or sand from the beach. And it doesn't matter if you're a success or a failure, you're always breathing it, living it, hoping for just one more chance from it. In other words, while the Hollywood people were retreating to Oak Point, they were still waiting for the phone to ring.

Avanti is a small, comfortably chic outdoor restaurant. I parked the car, smoothed my blood-red dress, combed my determinedly blond hair, put on some fresh lipstick, and went into the patio area. Shadowed from the sun by market umbrellas, the Oak Pointers were busy eating. The women, mostly middle-aged, were lean, taut, and as determinedly blond as I. The men had an air of robustness about them that comes more from money than fitness. Behind them the San Ysidro Mountains rose in jagged grandeur. Clouds carved ragged white holes into a brilliant blue sky.

"Diana? Diana Poole!" Leon stood when he saw me.

"Hello, Leon."

We embraced. Then, holding me at arm's length, he leaned his head back, squinted as if I were a newspaper he was trying to read without glasses, and said, "You look great."

It's the one compliment that fits all middle-aged women, and because of that it irritates the hell out of me.

"So does the Grand Canyon, Leon," I laughed.

"What?" he muttered, distractedly, eyeing a lone man sitting at a table, reading a newspaper.

"You're looking well," I said.

"Feel wonderful. Sit down. Sit down."

His once shoulder-length black hair was now gray and shaggy. His dark beard was only a memory, but his eyes were still the color of glistening oil. His deeply lined face was thinner, causing his aquiline nose to appear larger. He wore a perfectly pressed blue work shirt and jeans. His black sports jacket was cashmere.

"God, I can't tell you how good it is to see you, Diana." He smiled his charmingly crooked smile.

"It's been a long time." I smiled back.

"But that's going to change."

"What is?"

"Now that your husband is dead. Oh, I'm sorry to hear about that, by the way. I should have written you. When did it happen?" He talked fast. His dark, furtive eyes roamed the patio. He wanted to get the subject of death over with.

"More than a year ago." Again the feeling of being set adrift from everything I knew and loved swept through me. Waiting for it to pass, I looked up at the mountains; the clouds had lowered and were trying to drape themselves over its peaks and ridges. The feeling of loss ebbed and I let my gaze drift back to Leon. For the first time I noticed the half-empty bottle of white wine.

"I saw you in that movie," he announced, "where you played Uma Thurman's mother. Kind of a small role for you, wasn't it?"

"It gets tougher the older you get."

"It doesn't have to." He poured himself a glass of wine. "Is Uma seeing anyone?"

"You asked me to come all the way up here to find out if Uma Thurman is seeing someone?" I joked.

"I just wondered, that's all." His voice was serious. "Possibilities, you know what I mean?"

The waiter swooped by, tossed menus on the table, and poured me a glass of wine.

"We'll have another bottle," Leon ordered.

"Should you be drinking?" I asked when the waiter left.

"I have a second chance at life, Diana," he said excitedly.

"That's wonderful. But I thought that drinking and drugs is what got to your liver in the first place. I remember when you were on stage and told everybody in the audience to drop acid."

"But that's just it. I'm gonna do it all over again, Diana. Well, not acid. Though I think for a short period it did make me more creative. Back then I would've tried anything to be more creative."

"Do what all over again?"

"I'm going to live my life over. How many people get that chance?" He downed his wine. "It took me thirty-some years to need a transplant, so I figure I have another thirty years before this one gives out. Then it won't matter. Who wants to live past eighty?" he asked, sounding like the young Leon I had once loved.

"I remember when we didn't want to live past thirty. I don't think that's the way it works, Leon. Do your doctors know you're drinking?"

With a suspicious glance he leaned close and whispered, "Is that guy staring at me?"

"What guy?" I looked around.

"Jesus, Diana, don't be so obvious. He's sitting alone. Pretending to read his newspaper." He sneaked a peek. "He's not watching me now. You can look."

I peered at a man who was about Leon's age sitting at a table for two. He had a slight belly, thinning grayish-blond hair, and was dressed in khakis and a baby-blue polo shirt. After sipping his beer he patted his neatly trimmed moustache and seemed to be thoroughly engrossed in the *Wall Street Journal*.

"He *is* reading his newspaper, Leon."

"The doctors say this happens with a transplant. It's a kind of temporary paranoia. You know, you feel guilty for getting to live while the others . . ." He paused, shifting restlessly in his chair.

"Others what?"

"Others on the list. The ones that didn't get the liver, the ones who've been waiting a long time." He tossed back some more wine. "Let's face it, it helps to have a name, it helps to have money. I took advantage of that. Why shouldn't I? I was dying. People wanted me to live. I wrote some great songs, man. They still love me for that. I was part of their youth. No, I helped create their youth, their memories. That's why I want to start writing again. I owe it to them." He slammed his hand on the table. A sparrow scavenging for bread crumbs flew away. A few heads turned. The man reading the *Journal* never looked up.

"That's why I wanted to see you, Diana. You were there when it all started for me. Remember?" He grinned charmingly and poured the rest of the bottle into his glass.

"Of course I do."

"I was sitting at the bar in Martoni's."

Martoni's was a restaurant located near the recording studios in Hollywood. In the sixties it became a hangout for the music people.

"You were with some guy," he said. "You were crying."

"Yes, I'd just broken up with him. God, what was his name? I can't even remember why we were angry at one another."

"He wanted to marry you, Diana."

"That's right. And I wanted to be an actress. I was only eighteen, the last thing I wanted was marriage. What was his name?"

"His name doesn't matter."

"John! John . . . something. God, I thought I would never forget him. What was his last name?"

"He's not important," Leon said testily. "It's what happened that's important, Diana. I had been watching you from the bar."

"John. John . . . God, I almost had it."

"Forget the last name. You got up and went to the restroom. He got up and left the restaurant. I couldn't believe a guy could leave anyone so beautiful as you. You looked like Marianne Faithful."

"Even Marianne Faithful looked like Marianne Faithful in those days. When I returned to the table you were sitting in John's place. I was still crying. And without saying anything you handed me your handkerchief. No, your bandanna. It was a very touching gesture."

"And then I asked you your name, remember?"

"And I told it to you."

"And while you cried I wrote the lyrics for a song on the back of a cocktail napkin. I wanted to cheer you up."

"Very sad words for a very sad young woman."

"I want to do it again," he declared.

"Do what again?"

"Your husband is dead, which is similar to that guy walking out on you," he attempted to explain.

"It's not similar at all, Leon."

He leaned back in his chair and asked, "Why did you marry Colin anyway?"

"I loved him." What an inadequate phrase. Why does it always sound defensive?

"You loved me. And?"

"And what?"

"What other reason?"

"He never cheated on me," I teased.

"How do you know?" He smiled.

"I know."

"I cheated on you. And?"

"And I loved the way he wrote. I loved his words." Colin was a screenwriter and novelist. I have his two Oscars on the mantel. They are cold and heavy.

"And you never loved my words except for that one song. In fact, you stopped loving me when it became a hit. Left me just when I needed you the most," Leon complained.

"After you wrote 'Diana' you became terribly self-destructive."

"We were all self-destructive in the sixties."

"Not all of us. Just what do you want to do again, Leon?"

"I want to write you a song, Diana. Like I did in Martoni's."

We stared at one another. He was grinning, eager. I wasn't. I was feeling uncomfortable.

"Well, that's very sweet, Leon, but . . ."

"Sweet? Sweet! It's not sweet. All my other songs were never as good, were they? I mean, it was my voice that made all those stupid lyrics I wrote sound meaningful. My whole career, I kept trying to equal that one damn song. Every time I had a new album out it was compared to 'Diana.'"

"It happens."

"It didn't happen to the Beatles," he barked.

"Let me get this straight. You want to write me a new song. A song as good as the old one so you can have a number-one record again. You don't need me for that. Go do it."

Abruptly his mood shifted. "Every time I saw you up on the screen you reminded me of that song, and that you left me," he accused, furious.

"You left me. For another woman."

"I thought she would spark something in me the way you had. Only better. What was her name?"

"It doesn't matter." It was my turn to be testy.

"We always argued, didn't we?" he said sadly.

"Yes." I sighed.

"I just want to write one more great song. Is that such a terrible thing? And I want to do it with you, because you were there." Excited, he grabbed my arm. "I know I can have another hit." His jacket fell open, and I could see a gun in a holster attached to the side of his waistband.

"A gun?" I blurted.

"WHERE!" Leon jerked around in his chair. Another bird flew. A few more heads turned.

Lowering my voice, I said, "Attached to your waistband, Leon."

"Jesus Christ, don't do that, Diana. You scared the hell out of me." Hand shaking, he emptied his glass. Then he added, defensively, "I have a permit."

"To own a gun? Or to carry it on you?"

"How the hell do I know? Who reads the small print?"

"What are you afraid of, Leon?" I tried to keep my voice calm.

"I'm not paranoid," he protested. "I know that's what the doctors think. Temporary paranoia. But it's not true. Look around you. This isn't the world you and I grew up in. It's changed."

I looked around. Their stomachs filled with pasta and wine, the Oak Pointers leaned comfortably back in their deck chairs. The sun had lowered, the clouds had turned an unexplainable pink. The mountains were becoming a soft purple.

"Leon, you're living in one of the wealthiest, safest communities there is. That's what's changed."

"Someone wants me dead," he said flatly, reaching into his pocket for a crumpled piece of paper.

He handed it to me. Large letters, cut from a glossy magazine, were glued to the paper forming the sentence: YOU TOOK MY LIFE.

"When did you get this?"

"Soon after I moved up here. It was just left in the mailbox. Someone knows where I live."

"Were there other messages?"

"Two more over the last six months saying the same thing." His gaze darted to the lone man, who was now eating a bowl of Santa Barbara mussels.

"Why isn't that guy with somebody?"

"Maybe he's waiting for someone."

"But he's already eating. Nobody eats alone in this town. You can drink alone, but you can't eat alone. Don't you see?"

"See what?"

"Maybe it's him."

"Leon, he's just a man having lunch. Settle down, please."

"I can't. What if I took his wife, or daughter or son? Maybe he had a loved one on the list. Maybe I got the organ that was to go to someone he loved."

"That's all kept private. They don't tell people those things. No one could know. . . ."

"You can find out anything you want to in this world, Diana, if you have the money and the need."

"Hey, Leon, my man!" A short round man in his twenties, wearing a black coat, black silk shirt with no collar, black slacks, black woven slippers, and earrings, patted Leon's back. "How ya doing? I just came up from L.A."

"Steve!" Leon leapt to his feet and began pumping Steve's hand.

Steve turned to his companion and gushed, "Leon Ashe. The legend." His companion nodded vaguely, watching their waiting table.

"How come you didn't return my phone call?" Leon demanded.

"We'll talk, Leon." Steve edged quickly away. He and his friend sat down near the man who was eating alone.

"Do you know who that is?" Leon settled back in his chair. I shook my head.

"Steve Tinker. The number-one record producer. He's got three records in the top ten. I remember when I had two. He called me when he heard I was dying. Said how much I'd formed his views on music. Said he wished that he'd had a chance to work with me. Said he wouldn't be where he was today if I hadn't made the records I'd made. Especially, 'Diana.' " Leon stopped talking and lapsed into an uneasy silence. The lines deepened around his mouth, and he began to nod his head as if he'd just figured out something.

"I didn't die, Diana," he said harshly. "I lived. I called Steve Tinker back to see when he wanted to work with me. But he never returned my phone calls. Not one. I'm tired of being a freaking legend, Diana. I'm gonna show them. I'm gonna do it again. But I need you." He was pleading now.

"What do I have to do with any of this, Leon?"

"You were, you *are* 'Diana.' Don't you see? You were better than acid."

"How's your wife?"

"Young. She doesn't even know who Three Dog Night is. You don't think I can do it again, do you?"

"I think you don't *have* to do it again, Leon."

"I gotta take a leak." He jumped up and loped a wide circle around the lone man, who was busy plucking a mussel from its shell.

I took a sip of wine and for a brief moment wondered what my life would have been like if I had married John what's-his-name. He didn't want me to be an actress. I remembered that. So I would've ended up the wife of an insurance salesman? A banker? To me, John had represented what we were all afraid of in the sixties. Stability. He was hard-working. Earnest. But there was something about him, something I had responded to. What? I couldn't remember. And what were we doing in Martoni's? I must've taken him there. I was young and wanted to be a part of The Scene. And then I met Leon. Now, Leon wants to go back to that time, that moment. Or does he just want to be young again, and not afraid of death?

The number-one record producer got up and came toward me. "You a friend of Leon's?" he asked urgently.

"Yes."

"I did a good deed and called a dying man expecting . . ." He paused, dabbing at his small lips with his napkin, trying to find the right words.

"Expecting him to die?" I helped.

"Yes. So tell him to stop calling me. Or I'm going to start taking those calls of his as threats, as a form of stalking." He made an attempt at looking thoughtful and asked, "Didn't I just see you in something? You played Uma Thurman's mother in *Like Daughter*. You were great."

"Bette Davis was great."

"Is she seeing anybody?" he asked.

"Bette Davis?"

"Uma Thurman."

"Yes."

"Tell Leon to lay off." He clamped shut his small petty lips, stopped to shake someone else's hand, and returned to his table.

Leon did his unintentionally funny lope around the lone man, who was now dipping bread in his broth, and sat down opposite me.

"Where's the other bottle of wine?" he asked, rubbing his hands together. "I'm hungry. Let's eat."

We got the waiter's attention, ordered lunch, and Leon got his new bottle. Whispering, he asked, "Did you see the way he was looking at me?"

"The record producer?"

"The guy eating alone."

"He's not looking at you, Leon."

"He was."

"Maybe he knows who you are. Have you ever thought of that?"

"Why would he know?"

"Because you're a legend. Remember?"

"It's not that kind of look. He doesn't admire me. I can tell. I think I'm being followed."

"Did you go to the police with the messages?"

"What good are the police?" Not waiting for an answer, he quickly changed the subject back to us. "You and I may have argued, but we were magical together, Diana."

"We were miserable together, Leon. The minute your record came out and went to number one you changed. You lost your sense of humor, your wit. You spent your entire time, no, your entire career, trying to recreate that one record."

"I was an artist."

"Stravinsky was an artist. Picasso was an artist."

"Are you saying I wasn't? Are you saying I didn't know what I was doing?" he exploded. A wild look appeared in his dark eyes. A few people turned.

I lowered my voice and tried to reassure him. "I'm saying you wrote one hell of a song. But you were a better performer. Your best hits were with other people's songs. You didn't need to write another 'Diana.' You still don't need to do that. Find some rock standards, record them. That's what you need to do. Go out and perform. Rock-and-roll, now, is middle-aged and sober. Stop drinking."

"You've never understood me, have you? It was the singer-song-writers who were the freaking artists. I didn't want to be some parrot mouthing other people's words. I forgot what kind of shrew you are. Even at eighteen you had a tongue dipped in venom."

"Pen."

"What?"

"Never mind."

"I didn't ask you to come here to give me reality checks. When I was dying all I could think of was you. Thank God I lived so I could remember you as you really are. You haven't aged that well, Diana," he observed spitefully.

"At least I have my own liver," I snapped back.

"What do you mean by that?"

"It was a stupid reply to your attempt at a hurtful remark."

"No, you meant you're free from guilt. You meant you haven't taken something that really belongs to someone else. That's what you meant."

"I can't carry on this conversation anymore, Leon. I'm sorry, but we always end up hurting each other. I never should've come."

"No, you hurt me. I never hurt you," he persisted dangerously.

The lone man at the table stood. Holding his paper, he walked toward us.

"Excuse me, are you Leon Ashe?" he asked, slightly embarrassed.

Leon blanched. Trembling, he reached inside his sport coat, fumbling for his gun.

"Leon, don't." I grabbed hold of his arm. He shoved me away.

The man looked confused. "I just wanted to say that you wrote one of the greatest songs. You are Leon Ashe, aren't you?"

Leon pulled his gun out. But somehow he'd got it by the barrel. Attempting to get it pointed at the man, he knocked over the wine bottle: It shattered on the pavers. The man took a quick step back. The Oak Pointers began to move nervously in their chairs. Leon got the barrel pointed in the right direction. The man retreated some more.

"Leon, don't!" I screamed.

The sound of the gun cracked through the alfresco dining. Patrons ducked under their tables. Sunglasses flew, birds flew, wine glasses toppled.

"Leon!" I breathed in.

Still aiming the gun, Leon stood. The man froze. Then Leon dropped his gun, clutched his chest, and fell to the ground. The man let his newspaper fall, displaying his own gun. We looked briefly at one another as he placed it on the table and walked out to the parking lot.

"Call for help," I screamed, kneeling by Leon.

Blood ran from his mouth. His eyes were half open. I felt for a pulse. Leon Ashe was dead. The record producer was on his knees, waving his napkin as if he were surrendering. The customers, most of them flattened on the floor, began reaching for their wives, husbands, lovers, friends, sunglasses. I hurried out to the parking lot.

Eyes closed, the man leaned against a Range Rover. He clasped his hands tightly in front of him in a desperate kind of prayer. Sensing my presence, he slowly looked at me.

"Hello, Diana."

"John Hartford." I'd finally remembered the last name of the man who had left me in Martoni's all those years ago.

"I wrote you a poem on the back of a cocktail napkin." He spoke in a calm, quiet voice. "I left it for you on the table to let you know how much I loved you. I thought it would bring you back to me. That it would show you that I had more in me than just wanting to be a banker."

"You wrote the words to 'Diana'?"

"I was the romantic. Leon was a thief."

"But why kill him?"

"Leon got away with everything. Even my words. Even you. The day I read he was dying was one of the happiest days of my life. But then he got a liver transplant and moved to Oak Point. I put messages in his mailbox to scare him. But I knew he wasn't going to leave. He destroyed my youth; I wasn't going to let him destroy my retirement. I read about your husband's death. I'm sorry."

"Thank you."

"My wife died recently."

"I'm sorry."

"Thank you."

"You grew a moustache."

"Yes. Lost most of my hair." He flushed. "I wanted to call you, Diana. Tell you I was really the romantic."

"Why didn't you?"

"Would you have believed me?"

"Not when I was eighteen. But now? Yes."

"He shot Leon Ash. A rock'n'roll legend," the record producer chanted to a group forming around us. "A freakin' legend!" He still clutched his napkin, which was covered with marinara sauce or Leon's blood.

"I saw you play Uma Thurman's mother," John Hartford said, taking me in. "You are beautiful, Diana."

I put my hand on his cheek. He covered my hand with his.

"If only you'd called me," I said.

The police pulled up and got out of their cars. Without being commanded, John Hartford threw his arms in the air. It was a gesture worthy of the movies. Like leaving a poem on a table for a tearful young woman to discover.

TRADE WARS

Brendan DuBois

A writer who made his debut in Ellery Queen's Mystery Magazine's *Department of First Stories, Brendan DuBois has expanded his range to include stories for other national magazines such as* Playboy, *and novels in both the hard-boiled and thriller category. Even in his short stories, DuBois has always been inclined toward big, thrillerish themes, often involving organized crime, conspiracy, hit men and references to controversial past or present political issues. After completing three novels in his Lewis Cole mystery series, he decided to throw himself wholeheartedly into the thriller arena. The result was the recently published* Resurrection Day, *a what-if thriller that envisions what the world might have been like had John Kennedy not died. A two-time Edgar Award nominee, a finalist in the* Ellery Queen's Mystery Magazine *Readers Award competition, and a winner of the PWA's Shamus Award, DuBois is a writer to watch in the coming decade.*

JUST BEFORE HE landed at Logan in Boston, Sam Cullen looked at the seat pocket before him and saw a crumpled-up peanut bag left from a previous flight. It figured. His flight had been late, the carpeting inside threadbare, and the service halfhearted. He remembered trips he had been on years ago, even the ones from New York to Boston, where substantial service had been provided by friendly and competent flight attendants. This time around, it had been a warm beer—four dollars, thank you very much—and a plastic bag that had taken him almost ten minutes to open and contained exactly five peanuts. Two minutes per crunch. How satisfying. And throughout the food and beverage service, a female flight attendant had been complaining to her male helper about a burglary the previous week at her apartment.

He closed his eyes as the jet stumbled through its landing, feeling his fists clench at the bumpy approach in. He didn't open his eyes until the

345

plane had made it to the gate and the rest of the passengers had trooped off. After unbuckling his seatbelt he made his way forward and past the flight attendants, just nodding at their plastic "bye-byes," and went up the jetway and into the terminal.

Walking to baggage claim was slow going, for his right leg was acting up again. People in a hurry flowed about him as if they were a fast-moving stream and he a rock, cold and unmoving. The leg ached something fierce, right in the upper thigh, where a bullet had once torn through. The aching leg usually predicted rain but the cool May sky had been clear of clouds, so Sam figured it was his body again, unhappy at traveling, unhappy at another job in a foreign town, and letting him know about it. Tough. His body should talk to Raymo Keeley; it was Raymo's fault that he limped almost every day, for it was Raymo who'd shot him during that bungled liquor-store job on Seventh and 23rd, almost ten years ago.

So what. Raymo had gone to his reward, though not so soon as old Gus.

At the baggage claim his overnight black duffel bag was slowly going around the carousel. He had his claim check in hand but there was no one around to check him. Sloppy. All of this luggage right by a busy street filled with cars, buses, and taxicabs. So easy to race through and rip off a half-dozen pieces, with nobody seeing or caring.

The bag was heavy but comfortable in his hand, and he made it outside to a concrete island that had a sign that said COURTESY VEHICLES—LIMOUSINES. Horns blared and traffic was choked through the narrow lanes. There was a beefy man in a black suit, white shirt, and black tie, holding up a cardboard sign that had a single name scrawled on it: HANRATTY. He was leaning against a dark blue Town Car.

Sam went up to him. "Fenway Limo Service?"

"You got it," the man said.

"I'm Hanratty."

"Climb right in," the man said, opening the rear door and extending a hand for Sam's bag.

Sam held tight to the bag and got into the rear seat. The driver just shrugged and got into the front, and within seconds they were moving out of the terminal area and heading to an exit. Sam leaned back, bag at his side, and all the way into the city proper he and the driver exchanged not a single word, which was just fine.

The driver took him to a Sheraton Hotel in the downtown area, near the Prudential Center on Boylston Street. The ride had been slow and painful. Sam always had a hell of a time in Boston, for the damn city streets made no sense. Back home, you had to work to get lost, with everything set out in a pattern and in such perfect order. But in this crazy place, streets went one-way, two-way, and then one-way again, and one single street could have three or four names in the space of a half-dozen blocks. He also wasn't impressed with what he saw through the car window, but he knew his own hometown wasn't doing so great either. There were abandoned cars at the side of the street, great drifts of litter and trash along the sidewalks, and trembling men with plastic squeegees and buckets at the intersections. All the way in, too, he saw not a single cop.

After the driver dropped him off, he went through registration and check-in with a minimum of fuss and went up to his room. It was getting dark and he looked out at the lights of the city, feeling the pressure of a job that was due within twenty-four hours. He used the bathroom and went to the tiny desk by the side of his bed. Someone had been here before him, for in the top drawer was a nine-by-twelve brown envelope with "Hanratty" neatly typed in the center, and on top of the desk there was a small bottle of Jameson's Irish whiskey next to a full ice bucket. He filled a glass with ice cubes and splashed some whiskey over the cubes, and then stretched his aching leg out on the bed. He sipped at the whiskey and opened the envelope and got to work. Inside was a set of eight-by-ten photographs, color, showing a young man, maybe in his late twenties or early thirties. Stickers on the rear of each photo identified him: Sprague Coleman. He was dressed well, with expensive-looking suits, wrist jewelry, and hair that looked like it had only been touched by somebody calling him or herself a hair stylist. No barbers for Sprague Coleman. Behind the photos was a six-page biography of Sprague that was depressing and familiar reading, and a short note that said every Wednesday night, Sprague stopped for a fancy coffee at a restaurant on Newbury Street called the Appian Sway. How bloody cute. The note also said that Hanratty had a window of opportunity from 7 P.M. to 7:30 P.M., and that the cops wouldn't be a problem during that time period. Clipped to the sheaf of papers was a white square of cardboard about the size of a business card. On it was typed a phone number and a man's name. Underneath the name, in bold letters, was: FOR AN EMERGENCY ONLY.

Sam put the stuff back on the desk and stood up, feeling his back and knees creak. How many years had he spent doing this, and how many more remained? And what would good old Gus think?

"We're brooding," he announced to the empty room. "And brooding is bad. Time to focus."

He went over to the bed, where his overnight bag remained. It would have been easy enough to carry it onto the jet and store it in one of the overhead compartments, but he was more relaxed letting the baggage handlers take care of it. Less chance for mistakes, for things being learned about his business.

The zipper was fastened by a small combination lock, which he quickly undid. After emptying the bag of his shaving kit, change of clothes, and a couple of paperback books, he raised up a false bottom that had a special and quite illegal shielding material built in. He felt around the foam rubber fittings in the base of the bag and pulled up a shoulder holster, two full clips of 9mm. ammunition, his Smith & Wesson Model 12, 9mm. automatic pistol, and a tube silencer. He laid out his tools on the floral bedspread and scratched at his chin.

His instructions had said that Sprague Coleman enjoyed a restaurant visit every Wednesday night. Today was Tuesday. He had less than twenty-four hours to plan the very public execution of one Sprague Coleman.

Again, an announcement to an empty room: "Piece of cake."

After putting his tools back in the bag and putting the bag away in a closet, he took a long shower, enjoying the sensation of cleaning up after the flight in from New York City, but also enjoying the chance to relax and decompress a bit before going out for some night work. When he got out, he decided on a quick shave, and looked at the tired blue eyes and thin, wet brown hair about his head as he drew the disposable razor across his skin. It was an all-right face, one that didn't drive the women crazy, but was at least nondescript and easily forgettable, which suited him just fine.

He dressed in new jeans and a green pullover sweater, and in a few minutes he was a block away from the Sheraton, walking down Newbury Street. He knew from his research and reading that this was one of the priciest pieces of real estate in Boston, and the storefronts told him that his research was correct. All of the buildings were two-or three-story brownstones, most remodeled into restaurants, gift shops, and specialty stores. Handbags gave way to shoes and then to imported coffee and medieval art. For May it was a warm night, and the sidewalks were crowded with people. The two-lane, one-way traffic was bumper to bumper.

For all the wealth and contented crowds of people, however, Sam saw little signs of rot, little indications of distress. Men and women in cast off clothes, with thousand-yard stares, shuffled along the street and the sidewalks, shaking empty coffee cups, begging for change. A few of the stores were dark, plywood boarding up empty windows, the cracked wood marked with spray paint. Trash was still ankle deep, and there was the occasional bleeping howl of a car alarm. A blue and white Boston police cruiser inched along in the traffic, one headlight out, the right fender crumpled from an old accident. Both cops in the front seat looked exhausted.

Sam shrugged and kept on working. He saw the neon sign for the Appian Sway and crossed the street. Out of everything, he supposed he enjoyed the prep work the most, setting the scene, looking at the angles and possibilities, being the planner, knowing with sweet ecstasy that in less than a day someone would be meeting the fate that he had planned for him.

But there would be trouble ahead, that was for sure.

The place was too damn crowded.

He took a seat at a place next door called the Brass Cannon and had an iced tea, watching the Appian Sway at work. It would be too dangerous to spend extra time there. He didn't want any chance of later identification. The Appian Sway was mostly an outdoor cafe, with wrought-iron tables and chairs, sealed off from the street by a waist-high black metal fence. Each table had a blue and white umbrella overhead with the Appian Sway logo, and a corridor led into the restaurant proper. Not an empty table was to be seen, and there were easily twenty or thirty people within fifteen feet of the place.

What a mess.

He got up and ignored an outstretched coffee cup from a passing man with a garbage bag on his head, fastened by rubber bands, and went into the restaurant, thinking that a quick reconnoiter wouldn't hurt, and his mood was improved a bit. The damn place had another entrance, which was good. There was a counter where one could place an order and pick up some pastries, and a few tables inside in front of a door that led out to the next street over, Commonwealth Avenue. Not bad. Maybe it could work after all.

Still, all those people. He went back through the restaurant and out to Newbury Street, and after another thirty minutes found what he was looking for at a store that sold old science-fiction magazines and books. It was called Pulp Planet, and he was sorely tempted to buy some *Astoundings* from the early 1940s, but he refused to give in to temptation. No witnesses, no paper trails.

After all, he was a professional.

On his second day in Boston he visited the Museum of Fine Arts, enjoying walking through the cool corridors, looking at the hundreds of years of history at his fingertips. He found himself spending most of his time in the sections that had Roman and Egyptian art, where he was drawn to the dusty and shattered remains of those civilizations. They had endured for thousands of years before they fell apart, before the outsiders or barbarians or horsemen came and unseated them. He looked in vain for displays on the soldiers and centurions who had defended the empires, but there was nothing to remember them by. Just mementos of their governments, their ruling classes, their priests. And even they existed now only in books and museums, making a livelihood for a handful of professors throughout the world.

Not much of a legacy.

He checked the bright red numerals of the bedside clock. It was time. He'd spent the last hour in his hotel room, staring at the pictures of Sprague Coleman, committing each feature, every wrinkle and every smooth expanse of the man's skin to memory.

He got up and put on the shoulder holster, which was now holding his 9mm. Instead of a spare clip, he put the silencer in the leather holder that would have held the spare clip. No need for extra ammo tonight. Once he was satisfied that the holster was on right and wouldn't slip, he put on a heavy white cardigan, and over that a bright green nylon shell parka. Warm clothing, but it would do the job. He turned off the lights and left his room, and after going through the lobby he bought a copy of the day's *Globe* from the gift shop. He folded it in half and held it under his arm and walked outside. A light breeze had picked up and the weather had cooled, which was good. He didn't want to sweat, going to work.

Halfway to Newbury Street, he found that he was smiling. Not too tired yet, he thought, and he made his way along the sidewalk.

He walked the length of Newbury Street twice before the appointed time, and the thumping in his chest seemed to ooze and slow right down as he saw Sprague Coleman, smiling and happy and better looking than his photographs, sitting at an outdoor table in the Appian Sway. A muscular-looking man was sitting next to him, and they were joined by two young ladies who didn't seem to talk much but made up for it by laughing with bright eyes and stroking the arms of the men beside them. They were dressed almost identically, in short black dresses and leather jackets.

Sprague laughed along with them, but even at this distance, across the street, Sam could feel the tension in that face. Sprague had been in some dark rooms and had wet his hands many times, and Sam doubted there was much true humor behind those laughing eyes. Sprague had on a heavy black sweater and jeans, and his hair was perfect, not even a strand out of place.

Sure. Time to move on.

Sam crossed the street to the Appian Sway, and then swung away, heading over to the magazine and book shop, Pulp Planet. The store was small, with lots of shelves and old magazines and paperback books in plastic bags. Most of the people in the store were young men, maybe from MIT or

Harvard, computer types, looking at the literary ancestors of their current science-fiction reading. Sam let them browse and made his way to the rear of the store, which had a single restroom and a fire-alarm pull box on the wall. He took out a handkerchief, wrapped it around his hand, and pulled down the handle.

Instantly a loud hooting noise echoed through the store. Sam ducked into the restroom, splashed water on the crotch of his pants, and then came out swearing and pulling at his zipper. The store manager, a young man with a stringy beard and a ring looped through a pierced eyebrow, came back, scowling.

"Did you see the jerk who pulled it?" he asked, his eyes darting around.

"Hell no," Sam said. "I was in the middle of a leak and nearly passed out."

"Well, you better get out, the firefighters are on their way," the manager said. "Damn it, this is the second time this month."

He went outside and joined the throng that was gathering around the outside of the store, and then came the far-off sound of sirens. He pushed his way through the crowd and sat on the steps of an abandoned brownstone and got to work. Hunched over, acting like he wasn't feeling well, Sam pulled his pistol free and worked the action, holding the open newspaper over his lap. He then threaded in the silencer and folded up the *Globe*, concealing his weapon in the newspaper. Not a bad paper as papers go, he thought, going back onto the sidewalk. Editorial page was too damn liberal, but it had the best sports page in the country.

By the time he reached the Appian Sway, the fire trucks had arrived at Pulp Planet. They blocked traffic, their lights bounding in great red beams off the buildings. Horns blared and people clapped and laughed as the firefighters trudged into the building in their heavy gear. The sound of their truck radios was punctuated by great bursts of static. As Sam entered the Appian Sway, he was smiling again, for most of the people around him weren't looking at the middle-aged man in the bright green parka shell.

They were looking at the show outside of the magazine store.

Nice.

He worked quickly. At a dirty table he swiftly picked up an empty coffee cup and saucer, and shoving the newspaper and pistol under his arm, he whistled as he went through the maze of tables, passing the one containing Sprague Coleman and his friends. Sam didn't bother looking at them as he went by, even though he was close enough to smell the scents and colognes that the foursome were wearing.

He took a deep breath, and then another. Good old Gus.

He put the coffee cup and saucer down, shifted the paper and 9mm. into his right hand. He turned, now holding the paper in his left hand. A step, and then another.

The pistol and the silencer were now about six inches from the back of Sprague's head.

He fired. There was a coughing sound, and he fired again and again. Sprague pitched forward, causing the table to shake, dishes to rattle, and the young women gasped and screamed, and the other man was frozen in shock, but Sam was moving, moving quite quickly, and didn't care what any of them did.

He got out of the maze of tables and into the restaurant, heading for the other exit. Again using the *Globe* as cover, he put the 9mm. back into the shoulder holster, deftly unscrewing the silencer in the process.

Shouts and another scream back there.

Out on Commonwealth Avenue, he took off the parka shell, rolled it up in a ball with the newspaper, and shoved them both into a trash can. He kept on walking, now wearing the cardigan sweater, buttoned over the shoulder holster. A few more yards, and then he bent down as if to tie his shoe and dumped the silencer into a sewer. No regrets. It was now useless, having only been good for one job. Nothing like the movies and the TV shows, where the cool-blooded assassin used the same silencer over and over again. Typical fast-food media rubbish.

Another deep breath, sweeter than the one before. Job done. Just a matter of walking two or three more blocks and he'd be back at the hotel, and this time tomorrow, he'd be safe at home in his apartment.

So close.

He rounded the corner and a Boston police cruiser was heading past him, going barrel-ass, lights flashing.

Okay, just ignore it.

A sharp squeal of brakes.

Nothing to do with you. They just made the corner, that's all.

A racing engine, coming back in reverse.

Keep on going, just keep on going.

A door opening. A voice: "Hey, hey you!"

Ignore, ignore, ignore

"Hey, I'm talking to you! The guy in the white sweater! Hold up!"

He found that his hands were trembling. Not good, not good.

Sam turned, a hesitant smile on his face. "Who, me?"

The cruiser was at an angle, both doors open. One of the officers, a black man, was talking into a radio microphone. His white partner was coming up on the sidewalk, moving slow and easy, but his hand was on his holster. Nine millimeter Glocks. That's what the Boston cops now carried.

"Yeah, you," the cop said. His nametag said GRADY. "Where've you been the past few minutes?"

"I was up at the Common, and now I'm walking back to the hotel," Sam said. "I'm staying at the Sheraton."

"You stop at a coffee shop along the way, huh?"

"No, I didn't," Sam said. The other cop was now away from the cruiser, and was coming at him from another angle. Very good. These guys were young but they were good.

Grady smiled some more, but by now his weapon was out and at his side. "How come I don't believe you, then?"

"I don't really know," Sam said, knowing it was done, it was going down in flames and no parachutes were visible. Damn, to end it here in a town he didn't particularly like.

"Ken," Grady called out, and he didn't have to say any more, as his partner got closer. He then said, "All right, mister, are you right-handed or left-handed?"

"Right-handed."

"Okay, using your left hand, start unbuttoning your sweater, will you?"

Sam swallowed. His throat was quite dry. He raised up his hands and put them behind his head, interlocking his fingers. "I'm afraid I can't do that."

The two cops had him bracketed, weapons now up and pointing at him. People were stopping and standing on the sidewalk, staring, and even in all of this, Sam felt the flush of shame.

"And why not?" the cop called Ken demanded.

"Because I'm carrying, and I'm afraid you'll panic and shoot me."

The cops glanced at each other and then Grady said, "I want you to kneel down very slowly. Do it now."

Sam closed his eyes "Yes, Officer."

They yelled at him, they threatened him, they pleaded with him, and through it all Sam had just one answer to their demands: "I'd like to make a phone call, please." After a while they gave up on their threats and shouts, and he made his phone call, using the number provided to him back at the hotel. Then, as the cops in the precinct house went at him again, he waited.

But of course, this was Boston, and they didn't use precinct houses. They used districts. Like the one he was in now, District 4, on Warren Street. Not much charm or soul with that. Sam was put in an interrogation room

similar to ones he had seen over the years. The battered and stained furniture. The stale smell of sweat and cigarette smoke. The mirror on one
side that announced itself as one-way glass to anyone with an IQ above
that of a squirrel. The mirror was flanked by open curtains. He sat there
and folded his hands and waited.

Eventually the door opened and a black cop came in, but one dressed in
a white shirt with gold braid. In his dark hands he held a coffee cup, which
he passed over, and which Sam sipped at. The cop went over to the one-
way glass and drew the dark green curtains shut. He sat down heavily in
the chair across from Sam and Sam said, "What's the rank?"

"Deputy superintendent. The name is Paxton, Theo Paxton. You're Cullen, right?"

"Yes sir, I am."

"Hell of a mess."

"It certainly is."

"You tell anybody anything?"

"Not a word," Sam said.

"Good," Paxton said. He leaned forward, folding his hands. "It's going
to be tough, that's what I can say. The thing is, we got a quick ID of an
older guy doing the business. You were the only older guy out and about
on that block when the unit went by. Just tough luck, I guess."

Sam said, "I was told that I would have a window of opportunity for
about a half-hour. No cops. What happened?"

"Something about a false fire alarm just down the street, and these guys
tonight, they were real cowboys," Paxton said, almost apologetically. "They
were supposed to be on a traffic detail, but they decided to roll over and
take a look at the fire trucks. Then the call came in about what happened
at the Appian Sway."

"I don't care much about luck," Sam said. "I just care about getting out
of here."

"We're working on it, but it's going to be tough. You were carrying an
unregistered firearm right in the area of a homicide and your clip is missing
three rounds. A couple of witnesses were able to describe an older guy
going through the restaurant right after the action. Hard to let that one
squiggle through."

Sam stared straight into the other man's eyes. "I'm sure you'll do what
it takes."

A quick nod. "Jesus, yes, of course we will, but you realize that you're
burned in this city. You can't ever come back."

"That's the least of my worries."

Paxton took out a handkerchief and wiped at the back of his neck. "Man, this goddamn job . . . You want to talk about worries. Same story every year. Crime rates keep on going up, police budgets keep on getting cut, and the revolving doors at the court-houses get a fresh lubricating. Most nights, the collars we get, our guys are still doing the paperwork when the perps are rotated through and make bail and are back out on asphalt. Newspaper writers like to talk about thin blue lines. Hell, it ain't a line anymore. It's a picket fence."

Sam took another sip of his coffee, letting the other man speak.

"Thing is, too," Paxton said, "we always know who the bad guys are. Always. But you get tired trying to prove that, and the attorney general's office is swamped, and it's pick and choose time when it comes to the cases, and, well, you see a lot of stuff slide through."

"I'm sure," Sam said. "Like Sprague Coleman, right?"

Paxton looked embarrassed. "You read the file, right?"

"Yeah."

"One rotten guy, nasty right to the center," Paxton said. "Connected to a good portion of the coke trade in this city. We know he's responsible for a couple of homicides, and we're pretty sure he gunned down a state trooper out on the Mass Pike last winter, just for the hell of it. Likes pretty girls, and when he's done with them, he ensures they're pretty no more, and then he lets his boys have a piece before they get dumped. A real charmer, Sprague, and you know how much time he ever did?"

"No, but I'm sure you'll tell me."

"Eighteen months," Paxton said, pausing for effect. "Eighteen months, and in a juvie facility! Eighteen months for boosting cars and attempted murder when he was sixteen, and that was it."

"Until tonight."

Paxton gave a slow nod, picked up his uniform cap. "Yeah, that's for damn sure." The cop got up and looked over and said, "What got you in, if you don't mind me asking?"

Sam shrugged. He had told this story many times before. "Liquor-store robbery. It went bad real quick. Best friend of mine, guy named Gus, he got torn in half by a shotgun. The guy who was the trigger man, he got off with manslaughter."

The cop frowned. "His defense?"

"Urban post-traumatic stress disorder. The pressures of living in the city and being an underprivileged youth made him predisposed to a life of crime. The assistant AG on the case was still in his first post-college suit-coat and tie, and the defense was a sharp one. The jury bought. Didn't even serve two years."

Paxton put his cap on. "At least he didn't blame it on his mother."

"Give them time, they'll get back to that soon enough."

"Stay tight, we'll get you out."

Sam finished his coffee. "I'm sure you will."

The deputy superintendent was true to his word, and within an hour Sam was out in the police station's parking lot, ready to be driven back to his hotel and then to Logan. Just as Paxton was leading him to the car, however, the young cop Grady appeared, dressed in civvies.

"What the hell is going on?" Grady demanded, his face red with barely contained fury. "This was a good collar, a great pinch, and we're letting him go?"

"Not your business, Officer," Paxton said, using his best command voice. "There wasn't enough evidence to hold him, so off he goes."

Sam tried not to look at the young man as he got into the front seat of the car. Grady yelled and slapped his hands on the car's fender. "That's bullshit and you know it! What the hell is going on here? Is he the mayor's brother? The commissioner's cousin?"

Paxton started the car and backed out of the lot and within a minute or two they were on the street. "Sorry," he said, steering past a double-parked car.

"No problem."

"We'll talk to him some more, straighten him out. Don't want him going to the *Globe* or to the *Herald*."

Sam looked out at the passing buildings with no regret, knowing he would never be back in Boston again. "Give him a few more years, then he'll understand."

The next day he was back home and in the office of his boss. The man looked out on the streets below through a filthy window and said, "Are you sure they're all right in Boston?"

"Yes," Sam said, standing in front of the man's desk. "I can't ever go back, but they're pleased with the job."

"I'm sure they are. You do good work, ever since you took care of that character who killed Gus. Ray what's-his-name."

Sam nodded. "Raymo Keeley."

His boss turned in his chair and said, "What's it like in Boston?"

"Similar to here. Money being cut back, courts crowded, bad guys being set loose every day, nobody taking responsibility, nobody caring what's going on out there. Like that poet said: Things fall apart and the center can't hold."

"Some people care, you know that."

"Not enough."

His boss seemed to consider that. "True, but at least I can sleep at night, knowing we're trying."

"I'm glad you can, sir."

"Not being smart with me, Sam, are you?"

"No, not at all," he said. "Guess I'm just being tired."

His boss smiled up at him and said, "Feel like a trip west in a month?"

"Where to?"

"California. Los Angeles has agreed to join in our trade program. Thought you'd like to go out there to set things up, show them what we've been doing on the East Coast. Tell them that it makes more sense this way. If the bad guys start disappearing for no apparent reason, the domestic forces will be suspected. But if the talent is imported, then all the bases are covered. I'm sure even the LAPD could figure that one out."

"Fine, sir."

"Anything else?"

Sam wanted to speak, wanted to say something about the museum he had been in yesterday, seeing the dusty exhibits of empires past. He wanted to tell his boss that he sometimes felt like the last Egyptian soldier or last Roman centurion on the ramparts, defending an empire that was collapsing from rot and decay, wondering if his efforts meant anything at all.

Instead, he said, "No, nothing."

Another smile. "Then why don't you get to work, Sam."

Outside his boss's office the din was almost deafening: phones ringing, keyboards clattering, voices rising in anger or despair. Sam was amazed at the tiny bit of duty that still burned inside him. He tugged at his sergeant's uniform and went behind the great wooden desk, just inside from the front entrance, and a woman was there, waiting, her eyes red-rimmed with tears. She was dressed in a nurse's uniform and as Sam picked up a blank report she said, "I just got off shift and got home and my apartment's been broken into. Everything's gone! And it's the second time this year!"

"Sorry to hear that, ma'am," he said, sliding a pen and a blank form over to her. "If you could just start by filling out this report."

She swore and grabbed the pen and said, "I wonder when in hell you cops are going to start doing something about the crime out there. Jesus, I also had my purse snatched last week. What are you guys doing anyway?"

Sam smiled at her. "We're working on it."

UNDER THE KNIFE

Phil Lovesey

Son of mystery writer Peter Lovesey, whose work is also included in this volume, Phil Lovesey placed with the finalists in the Mystery Writers of America's Golden Mysteries Short Story Contest with his second published piece of fiction—the first had appeared in Ellery Queen's Mystery Magazine's *Department of First Stories during the previous year, 1994. His showing in the contest, which pitted him against many of the profession's most honored pros, boded well for his future and he has made good on his early promise by selling three full-length mystery novels and a score of short stories over the past six years. Phil Lovesey's cleverness in devising multiple twist endings is comparable with that of writers such as Peter Lovesey and Jeffery Deaver. He's a rising star in England and it is to be hoped that his work will soon be more available in the United States.*

"AND NOW," ANNOUNCED the contented surgeon, moving to the CD player, "for a spot of Viv . . ."

The opening bars of *The Four Seasons* drifted through the sumptuous lakeland cottage. The elderly surgeon smiled, watching the swell of his cognac as it circled inside the crystal brandy balloon. Then he downed it, completely satisfied, before pouring another.

He raised the glass to the luxurious empty room. "To weekends," he said. "Solitude and quiet. Far from the madding crowd. Cheers!" The second glass followed the first. He settled on the leather sofa, dipped into a bowl of dry-roasted peanuts, kicked off his shoes, and began the latest Dick Francis, while the wind howled outside. How he adored Friday nights . . .

He hadn't got three pages past the first murder when a sharp rap on the thick wooden front door disturbed him from the absorbing narrative.

He looked up astonished, completely unprepared for the sudden interruption. There it was again. Another knock, louder than the first. Cursing, he crossed the room to stand by the door.

"Yes?" he barked, frowning at the darkened wood.

The reply was urgent, unfamiliar. "Please help! There's been an accident. Someone's hurt!"

The surgeon cursed again. Accident? On a Friday night? Here? Bloody typical! Reluctantly, he opened the door, allowing a cold gust of night and a rain-lashed young man into his warm, hallowed sanctuary. He shut the door quickly, turning to the unexpected visitor, who stood in his water-proofs, dripping onto the lush Chinese rug.

"Jesus, it's pouring out there!"

"The accident?" the surgeon asked irritably, resigning himself to a disturbed night.

The young man smiled. "It hasn't happened yet, Granddad."

"I'm not sure I . . . ?"

But the young man had already pounced, throwing the elderly surgeon to the floor, straddling him easily. "Just so we both understand," he hissed. "I'm here to talk. Give me the answers and I'll go."

The old man struggled under the younger's rain-sodden bulk. "If it's money you want—"

The youth struck the surgeon's face with a cold hand. "Not listening, are we?" he teased, watching a spreading red patch on the puffy cheek. God, he was going to enjoy this! "I suggest we start again." He climbed off the old man. "Mr. Cedric Pinkerton."

The surgeon struggled to find his feet, fear now showing on his smarting face. The maniac knew his name! He thought fast. "I'm expecting friends at any minute," he croaked. "Just leave me now, and I won't say a word. Please."

The young man slumped in a red leather Chesterfield. "You can do better than that," he moaned. "I've followed you for weeks. Every Friday night, the same. You head out of Harley Street straight up here. No visitors. Ever."

Pinkerton lunged for the phone, swiftly pressing nine-nine-nine with shaking fingers.

"I've already cut the line, Granddad. Not outside the cottage, mind. Further down, where it runs into the woods. The police will just think a tree blew against it during the night." He smiled again, baring yellowing teeth. "A cruel coincidence."

Pinkerton replaced the useless receiver, studying his assailant's face in more detail. Gaunt, unshaven, wild-eyed. A drug addict, perhaps? Escapee from the local asylum? And why on earth had he been singled out for the deranged man's pleasure?

He took two deep breaths, trying to steady his nerves. "Do I know you?"

The young man clapped sarcastically as Nigel Kennedy stuck rigidly to Vivaldi in the background. "Now we're getting somewhere, Granddad!"

"Well?"

"You certainly used to. Had an intimate knowledge, I'd say."

Pinkerton racked his brains. Nothing about the man seemed familiar. He stared blankly back. "An ex-patient?" he offered, knowing he couldn't have treated the fellow since going private.

"Keep going."

"From the early days?"

The young man nodded.

"The very early days?"

He nodded again, this time adding a patronizing frown. "I made your reputation, old boy." He looked around him at the opulent trappings. "Feathered your goddamned nest."

Pinkerton gasped. The memories flooded back. Flash bulbs, questions, and the crying child in his arms. Surely it couldn't be . . . ?

The youth nodded again, reading the old man's mind.

"Ben?" Pinkerton whispered. "You?"

He was up on his feet, arms outstretched in the centre of the room. "At your service, Mr. Pinkerton." He extended a hand. "Ben Hopkins. Or as I used to be known—Ben, the Miracle Baby!"

"Ben?" Pinkerton repeated in sheer bewilderment, trying to reconcile distant memories of a tiny ball of gurgling flesh with the ranting figure pacing the floor.

The words fell quickly from Hopkins's pale lips. "Ben Hopkins. Born seventh May, nineteen seventy-three, with a collapsed lung and a hole in the heart. Enter suave, good-looking children's surgeon Cedric Pinkerton, whose mission, should he choose to accept it, to save the tiny tot and enhance his reputation considerably."

"That's not fair!" Pinkerton protested. "I'd taken the Hippocratic oath. It was my duty to save life, whenever possible."

Hopkins dismissed the suggestion, pressing on. "Six hours under the knife, as the nation held its breath. The life-saving operation is a complete success! The press arrive in droves for a stitch-by-stitch account. The legend of Ben the Miracle Baby is born."

"All this because I saved your life?"

Hopkins turned angrily, pointing a bony finger. "Saved?" he shouted. "*J'accuse*, Cedric Pinkerton, of destroying me, my family, and any chance I had of a normal life, while you reaped the profits from my rotten insides!" He unzipped his waterproofed jacket and pulled up a stained T-shirt to reveal a large pink scar running from his abdomen to his chest. "Your stitches in time must have saved you about nine million, eh?"

Pinkerton shook his throbbing head. "You would have died, Ben. I couldn't allow that. No one else was prepared to take the risks and perform the surgery. Your parents were desperate. . . ."

"My parents?" Hopkins exploded. "Want to know what happened to them?"

Pinkerton sighed heavily, his mind still frantically working to resolve the crisis. Whatever happened, Hopkins was younger and stronger. He might even be armed. Conversation seemed the best way to placate the man. "They divorced," he said slowly. "I do read the papers, you know. I did take an interest."

"From your flash Harley Street offices?" Hopkins hit back. "That must have been distasteful, reading about our grubby little world!"

"Look," Pinkerton tried to control his temper. "Your parents did their own deals with the press. . . ."

"And the advertising agencies," Hopkins replied bitterly. "Christ!" They had me posing in different brands of nappies before you could say, 'Thank you, the cheque's in the post!' All tastefully done, though. They even airbrushed out the scar."

"I'm sorry, Ben," Pinkerton replied. "I truly am. But I can't be held responsible for what happened after you left my care. I saved you, but I couldn't save you from the world."

Hopkins laughed out loud, a hollow bark ringing round the plush interior. "Of course, I was a bloody laughingstock at school. Imagine, a young boy struggling to make his way, always remembered as 'that miracle kid.' And all I saw was everyone else creaming off the profits. I grew to despise them all. But most of all"—he went and sat by Pinkerton, reclining on the sofa— "I completely despise you."

"Like I said, I wasn't to—"

"Shut it!" Another smack on the old man's face. More pleasure for Hopkins. "I dropped out of school, college, life. Got in with a new crowd, those who couldn't give a damn who I was, providing we could score some crack."

Pinkerton closed his eyes. "And that's what you want now, Ben? Money for drugs? Twisted revenge, is it? Go and see the man who toiled so desperately to save your life, then force him to give you the money to destroy it?"

Hopkins helped himself to a large brandy. "Not at all, Granddad. I'm off the gear now. One hell of an effort, believe me. But I'm clean. Want to know what saw me through the dark days?"

Pinkerton nodded slowly.

"The thought of this," Hopkins beamed. "You and me, here, right now. Our cosy little chat, miles from anywhere. Anyone."

Pinkerton made his second move, rising from the sofa. "I need the toilet."

Hopkins shoved him down. "And nip out so you can call the Old Bill on your mobile? Do me a favour. I do so hate your repeated assumption that I'm incredibly stupid. I've had a long time to think about this."

"But I need a pee!" Pinkerton protested.

Hopkins pointed to the roaring fire. "Put that out if you're desperate. You ain't leaving my sight."

Pinkerton had had enough. "Listen, Ben," he threatened. "I come here at the weekends to relax. I do not intend to have my privacy invaded by damn junkies with chips on their shoulders. I gave you life. If it spat back at you, then though. Those are the breaks."

"You destroyed my life the moment you saved it!"

"I had no choice!"

"The Hippocratic oath?"

Pinkerton nodded furiously. "Now what do you want, eh? I'm sick of all this!"

Hopkins sat quietly on the floor, considering the old man's argument. "Maybe you're right," he conceded. "After all, here you are, with all your wealth and reputation, and your life hasn't exactly been a bowl of cherries, has it?"

Pinkerton said nothing, wondering what Hopkins had planned.

"Take, for example, the good Mrs. Pinkerton. Quite a catch for the middle-aged surgeon."

"What are you driving at?"

"That made the papers, too, didn't it? The wedding, and the divorce." He poured himself another brandy. "As you'll appreciate, I take more than a passing interest in your affairs."

Pinkerton's eyes narrowed. "We were unlucky. It didn't work out."

Hopkins shook his head and smiled. "How we kid ourselves, eh? She dumped you, Pinkerton. Ran off with another bloke. Real goodlooking type. What was the name, now? Fines, yes, that's it, Steve Fines. A builder, I believe, who even helped dig your swimming pool. What was that headline again?" Hopkins scratched his head thoughtfully. " 'Builder Has Dip with Miracle Baby Doc's Missus!' Crude, but effective."

"Which goes to prove my point," Pinkerton replied through gritted teeth. "I've had plenty of knocks, too, but I don't turn up on my mother's doorstep blaming her for having me in the first place."

Hopkins smiled, then reached for a peanut, tossing it high into the air and catching it in his mouth. He nodded, munching on the nut. "I'm sorry," he said. "You're quite right. It was your duty to save me, and so you did. Anything which has happened since is simply the unpredictable machinations of the Hand of Fate. Or—I've made a dog's dinner out of my life and really shouldn't hold you to task over it." He rose to leave.

Pinkerton regarded him suspiciously. The manner was too patronising, the exit too sudden. There was more, he sensed it.

Hopkins turned at the door. "This, um, Hippocratic oath?"

"Yes, Ben?" The fear began to return.

"Well, just say, hypothetically, of course, that a young Adolf Hitler walks into your surgery one day. Would you treat him?"

The first bead of perspiration broke from Pinkerton's brow. Why wouldn't the bastard simply go, leave him to pack and head straight back for London? "If the condition was immediately life-threatening, Ben, then I'd have no alternative. As doctors, we aren't empowered to make moral judgements. Anyway, it's been . . . strange to see you again."

Hopkins smiled once more, extending a hand and shaking Pinkerton's enthusiastically. "Likewise," he said. "And I'm sorry for all the . . ."

"Don't be," Pinkerton gladly replied, opening the door.

"I just needed answers, you know? Needed to know you'd acted for my good, not yours."

Pinkerton's heart raced as he watched Hopkins step through the door and make his way to a large saloon car parked outside. Relief flooded through him. He was going, the bastard was going!

"Go inside," Hopkins shouted above the wind. "You'll catch your death!"

Pinkerton closed the door smartly behind him, leaning against the warm wood, shaking with gratitude.

Something was wrong. Why didn't the idiot start the car? Maybe he had, maybe Pinkerton just hadn't heard. Maybe Hopkins was already driving down the lane, taking his insane ramblings back through the deep, dark woods.

Pinkerton nearly jumped through his skin as Hopkins hammered on the door once more. Too late to slide the locking bolt, Pinkerton was pushed backwards as Hopkins burst in, struggling under the weight of a large canvas sack over his shoulder. A large, moving canvas sack.

"Just couldn't leave it at that," Hopkins gasped, moving unsteadily to the centre of the room and throwing the sack onto the floor. "I mean, you could have been lying, couldn't you?"

Pinkerton's eyes were rooted to the moving sack. It was struggling, definitely struggling. Muted cries competed with Vivaldi's final movement. Fear gripped Pinkerton's throat, and he watched in sheer terror as Hopkins unwrapped the wriggling bundle.

There, trussed with rope and tape, lay the sweat-sodden, gagged body of Steve Fines.

Hopkins turned to his infant saviour. "Thought we'd ask for a second opinion," he grinned.

"What the hell's going on?" Pinkerton asked, bottom jaw wobbling.

"Kitchen?" Hopkins demanded.

Pinkerton dumbly pointed, watching him disappear for a few seconds then return with a wicked-looking carving knife and a steel-tipped wooden tenderising mallet.

Fines struggled with even more fervour once Hopkins began to cut the ropes.

"Some anaesthetic required, wouldn't you say, Doctor?" Hopkins casually announced, bringing the mallet swiftly down on Fines's skull with a hideous crushing blow. "There, out cold. Now the game begins."

Pinkerton struggled for breath. "You're bloody mad!" he gasped.

Hopkins waved an admonishing finger. "I'd call it thorough." He rolled Fines's unconscious head in his hands, tenderly. "Good-looking sod. No wonder your wife dropped her drawers for him."

Pinkerton raised himself, strength returning, adrenalin coursing through his elderly veins. He lunged at Hopkins's squatting figure, but was easily pushed aside.

"Sit down, old man!" Hopkins bellowed, brandishing the knife before turning his attention to the stretched white neck in his lap. "I'd say," he said slowly, "it's about here!"

Pinkerton cried in terror as Hopkins deliberately stuck the knife into Fines's throat. A hiss of air preceded the first gurgling spurt of crimson blood.

Hopkins stepped back smartly. "Over to you, Mr. Surgeon," he grinned evilly, sitting back on the sofa surveying his handiwork. "Jesus, it really spurts up, doesn't it?"

Pinkerton raced to the punctured body, groping at the neck wound, trying to stem the flow. "What have you done?" he cried in total desperation.

Hopkins picked at his fingernails with the bloodied knife. "Essentially," he said brightly, "it's an ethical conundrum. Do you stick to your Hippocratic oath and save the man you detest more than anyone else in the world, or let him die so he'll never share your ex-wife's bed again?"

"You bloody maniac!"

Hopkins pulled a silly face. "Not as bloody as you are at the moment, Doctor. Shouldn't you be doing something a little more life-saving? That is, if you want me to really believe all this oath nonsense."

"A tourniquet!" Pinkerton pleaded as Fines's body wriggled beneath him. "A tea towel, anything!"

Hopkins poured himself another brandy, tossed another nut. "I swear by Apollo the physician, and Asclepius and Health, and to all the gods and goddesses . . . That's how it starts, isn't it?"

"The tea towel, now!" Blood was seeping through Pinkerton's fingers, loosening his grip on the wound.

". . . to reckon him who taught me this Art equally dear to me as my parents, to share my substance with him . . ."

"The kitchen! Please!"

Hopkins slowly wandered towards the kitchen. ". . . and relieve his necessities if required . . . blah, blah, blah . . . and abstain from whatever is deleterious and mischievous . . ." He returned with a neatly folded tea towel, dangling it inches from Pinkerton's desperate grasp.

"For God's sake!"

Hopkins dropped the towel. "Funny to think," he mused. "Last time we worked together all those years ago, it was me that was under the knife."

"Call an ambulance!"

Hopkins shrugged his shoulders. "Phone don't work," he sang teasingly.

"My mobile, upstairs! In my case. Hurry!"

Hopkins bowed and left the room once more, leaving Pinkerton to tie the white towel around Fines's spurting neck. In seconds a crimson blood spot burst from the cloth like a flowering rose.

Hopkins returned with the portable phone. "Oh no," he sighed, dropping it on the floor and crushing it with his boot. "Now it's broken."

"You stupid fool!" Pinkerton exploded. "What the hell are we going to do now?"

Hopkins ambled to the front door, cheekily waving goodbye with the carving knife, before reappearing several moments later. "Fortunately for Mr. Fines," he said, "he has an enduring love affair with the fresh-water trout." He placed a small plastic box by Pinkerton's side. "He's an angler. Spends most days by the river when he's not . . . you know, with your ex. It's where I bumped into him earlier today. I've been following Mr. Fines for some time, also." Hopkins flipped open the lid to reveal a selection of barbed fishing flies and coiled lines. "Perfect do-it-yourself suturing kit, wouldn't you say, Doc?"

Pinkerton was appalled. "Surely you're not . . . ?"

"Sew away, Doc!" Hopkins merrily replied. "That tea towel's going to be drenched in a minute." He picked up the tenderising mallet. "Some more anaesthetic before the big op?"

The professional in Pinkerton took over. "Put that down," he hissed. "Give me some twine. Thread it."

Hopkins whistled. "I'm impressed. Really, I am. But are you actually going to do it? Save the man who stole your woman. Stitch him up so he can slide back into bed with her, picking up where he left off?" He leaned closer, whispering in Pinkerton's ear. "I know all about you, Cedric. Made it my mission. You hate this man. You want him dead, don't you?"

"Give me the thread!"

"Why not let him die? Who's to know? He just simply disappeared on a fishing trip. That's his car, you know, outside."

"The thread!"

"Follow your heart, Cedric," Hopkins teased. "Let him bleed to death. No one knows he's here. Stuff the corpse in the boot, bury the car in the woods, clean up, and bingo, he's just another missing person. Who knows, you might be the first one your old lady turns to for comfort."

Pinkerton grabbed the proffered twine and barb, looking Hopkins squarely in the eye. "This is what you wanted, was it? What you planned for?" He unwrapped the towel, pressing on the gaping wound once more before commencing the first closing stitch. "I'll try to save him, exactly like I tried to save you. There's no difference!" A geyser of blood spurted high into the air. "Scissors!" he barked.

Hopkins stared blankly back.

"To cut the stitch, man!"

Hopkins shrugged his shoulders.

"The kitchen drawer! Now! Or he's going to die!"

Hopkins lazily fetched the scissors, leaning down and cutting the nylon fishing line himself. "I'd love to believe you. It all sounds so pure, so noble."

"What?" Pinkerton replied sharply, already working feverishly on the next stitch.

Hopkins leant forward and cut the next stitch obligingly. "You see, I maintain that your decision to save me was an entirely calculating one. You took a big risk with my life in order to enhance your own."

"Never!"

"Come on, Cedric," Hopkins replied, taking another handful of nuts. "It was a career move, with no thoughts for the consequences to me."

"You're wrong!"

"What? You're denying your riches?"

The next stitch was in, barely stemming the flow. "The money came later," Pinkerton replied quietly. "I haven't got a bloody crystal ball, man!"

"You used me! An innocent baby!"

"I saved a dying one!"

Hopkins settled back on the sofa and poured himself another brandy. "I didn't come here to argue," he said calmly. "That's why I devised this little test." He pointed to Fines's blood-soaked body. "You save him, and I'll believe all your ethical nonsense. Save the man you most despise, and I'll know you put my tiny body, my life, ahead of the money."

"You're sick!" Pinkerton was frantically trying to control the bleeding. "It's no good," he moaned. "He's going to die!"

"But what about the oath, Doc?"

"I've done all I can, for Christ's sake! He needs hospital attention, now!"

Hopkins pulled a mock face of astonishment. "You really want him to live, don't you?"

"I have no choice." Pinkerton made one last appeal. "Ben," he whispered, "if you have any humanity in you, we have to get him to hospital, now. If we could get him into the car, we could still save him."

"We? This is your problem, Doc. Your test."

Pinkerton screamed at the seated, grinning figure. "I can't do any more for him!"

"Well, you'd better take him to hospital then. Wrap him up and stick him in the car. Come on, you can do it!"

Pinkerton struggled to shift the barely living body.

"More effort, Doc!"

"You have to help!" Pinkerton gasped, sliding Fines on the blood-soaked floorboards towards the door.

"Tell you what," Hopkins offered brightly. "I'll open the car for you." He stood from the sofa, tossing another nut nonchalantly into the air.

Pinkerton struggled on, reaching the door, dragging Fines outside and laying him on the cold, wet grass by the side of the car. He raced back inside to fetch the keys, lungs burning from the effort.

Hopkins was on his knees, gasping for breath.

"The keys!" Pinkerton screamed. "Now!"

Hopkins turned, eyes streaming, face puce, finger pointing desperately to his throat.

Pinkerton stared blankly back at the awful sight, totally confused. "The keys!" he demanded again, heart racing.

Hopkins tried to mouth the words, but the nut held fast in his windpipe. He staggered to his feet, pointing to the bowl.

And it dawned on Pinkerton. He almost smiled. "Choke on it, you bastard!" he said, rifling through the dying man's pockets for Fines's car keys. "Your test, remember. Your rules."

Hopkins's bulging eyes made one last appeal for mercy, no sound coming from his blueing lips.

Pinkerton held the car keys in his hand. "I'd say this was a moral decision, Ben. Two lives to save, only one pair of hands." He turned and headed for the door, stopping one last time. "When you first came here, you said you wanted answers. Would I save the life of the man I despised most in the world?" He held the car keys aloft. "See these? I'm taking Fines to the hospital. Hopefully, it's not too late. And I hope that answers your question, Ben, I really do."

The last sound Hopkins heard was the cottage door closing.

THE ESCAPE

Anne Perry

Historical crime fiction made steady gains in popularity all through the 1990s and credit for increased readership in this subgenre must go primarily to writers like Anne Perry, who combines superb storytelling with scrupulous attention to historical detail. Now one of crime fiction's bestselling authors, Anne Perry broke into the field with a series of Victorian mysteries featuring a London detective inspector, Thomas Pitt, and his upper-class wife, Charlotte. It is the dramatic contrast between "upstairs and downstairs" that the author says caused her to choose the Victorian era as a setting for her tales, and she didn't venture much further back in time in creating her second successful series, the post-Crimean War William Monk mysteries. Though she has departed from her period of preference in the following story of Paris in the terror of the 1790s, readers will find in it the characteristic Perry flair.

THE RESCUE FROM the prison of La Force was very carefully planned. Sebastien had taken care of every detail himself, and no one had been told anything they did not have to know. By eight in the evening everyone was in his place.

Jacques was doing no more than driving the coach which had taken them all to La Force, where the man they had come for was lodged pending his trial before the Commander of Public Safety, and inevitably his execution by the guillotine.

He was a young aristocrat named Maximilien de Fleury who was there simply because his father's estates had been confiscated and it was necessary to indict him also in order that they could remain in the hands—and in the pockets—of the government. No other charges were known against him beyond those of idleness and wealth, in Paris in 1792, a crime unto death.

A bribe had been very carefully placed so that his family might visit him for one last time. A plea for clemency, plus several sous, had obtained the promise from a guard to find himself otherwise occupied, so that they might have time alone, during which some swift changes would take place. A very fine forgery executed by Philippe was to be substituted for their pass documents, and in the torchlight four of them would leave where three had come in.

Nicolette was very good indeed at distracting people's concentration by a variety of means, as seemed most suitable according to the nature and status of those whose attention was to be held. She was not a beautiful girl in the usual sense, but she could affect beauty in such a way that it beguiled the mind. One saw the grace and the confidence in her walk, the vitality in her, the imagination and intelligence, and a certain air of courage which intrigued.

She could discard it as quickly and be timid, gentle, demure. Or she could be weary and frightened and appeal for help. She had even aroused the respect of guards Sebastien had thought beyond the human decencies. It never ceased to surprise him, because over the last year he had come to know something of the woman beneath the facade. She had joined the small group in the beginning, two years ago when they had just banded together, tentatively at first, to rescue a friend from one of the many prisons in Paris, before he faced trial and death. There were five of them, Sebastien, Nicolette, Etienne, Philippe the forger, and now Jacques.

Another rescue had followed swiftly, and then a third. By the end of 1792 they had snatched several more people from the Committee's prisons, and failed with three. This year they had attempted more, and succeeded.

Now Sebastien was walking beside Nicolette, her head bent demurely, as they passed the guards and gave them their papers, identifying them as Citizen de Fleury's sister and brother-in-law, come, with the jailor's generous permission, to visit him a last time. A few paces behind them Etienne followed, named in the same document as a brother. All of them, as always, wore a slight disguise, so they would not easily be recognized again. Sometimes it was powdered hair, sometimes a false beard or moustache, a change of complexion with a little paint, a blemish, and of course different clothes.

They walked slowly; it was a natural thing to do in the cold, torchlit passages towards the entrance of the cells. Their feet echoed on the stone floor and the darkness beyond the flame's glare seemed filled with sighs and whispers, as if all the pain of the thousands of inmates was left here after their shivering bodies had been taken out for the last time. Nicolette moved closer to Sebastien, and without thought he put his arm round her.

They presented their identification and their notes of permission to the turnkey and slowly, every movement as if in a dream, he took them, perused them, and passed them back. Then he lifted his great iron keys and placed one in the lock. The bolts fell with a clang, and he pushed open the door.

With a barely perceptible shudder Sebastien went in, his finger to his lips where the guard could not see it, in silent warning. De Fleury looked round, his face white with fear, to see who had intruded on him at this hour. It was only too apparent he expected the worst: a hasty trial and summary execution at first light. It was not uncommon.

"Maximilien!" Nicolette ran to him and threw her arms round him, her lips close to his ear. Sebastien knew she would be telling him not to show surprise or ignorance, that they had come to rescue him and he must follow their lead in everything they said.

Sebastien went after her across the icy, straw-covered floor and wrung de Fleury by the hand, his eyes steady, warning.

The turnkey banged the door shut. Sebastien's heart was in his mouth, his ears straining. The lock did not turn. The man's footsteps died away as he went back up the corridor. Etienne stood guard, shifting nervously from one foot to the other.

"Quickly!" Sebastien took off his cloak, a large mantle of a garment, and held it out to de Fleury. "Put it on," he ordered.

"They'll never let me out!" de Fleury protested, his eyes wild as hope and reason fought in his mind. "Three of you came in, they'll know to let only three of you out. And if you think finding the wrong one will make them let you go, you are dreaming. They'll execute you in my place, simply for aiding my escape. Don't you know that?" Some innate sense of honour forbade him accepting on these terms, but he could not withdraw his hand from the cloak.

"We have passes for four to leave," Sebastien explained. "The turnkey has been bribed to be elsewhere, and it is the changing of the guard who let us in. Be quick."

De Fleury hesitated only a moment. Incredulity turned to wonder in his face, and then relief. He seized the cloak and swung it round his shoulders even as he was moving towards the door.

"Don't run!" Etienne hissed at him.

De Fleury stopped, twisting round to look back at Sebastien.

"You're supposed to be taking your last leave of your family," Sebastien reminded him. "You aren't going to gallop out!"

"Oh . . . oh yes." De Fleury controlled himself with an effort, straightened his shoulders, and walked with agonizingly measured pace out through the cell door and along the torchlit passage towards the entrance. Once he even looked back as if to someone he knew.

Etienne and Nicolette came close behind him, and Sebastien last, closing the cell door, the new pass papers in his hand, for four people.

Nicolette moved ahead to catch up with de Fleury, clasping his arm and clinging to it. Every attitude of her body expressed grief.

They were twenty feet short of the outer gates. The guards moved across the passage to block their way. Sebastien felt his heart beating so hard his body shook with the violence of it. It was difficult to get his breath.

De Fleury faltered. Was Nicolette leaning on him, or in fact supporting him?

One of the guards brandished a musket.

De Fleury stopped. Etienne and Sebastien drew level with him and stopped also.

"Here," Sebastien offered the pass to the guard. He took it and read it, looking carefully from one to the other of them. Their faces were full of shadows in the torchlight. Each one stood motionless, at once afraid to meet their eyes, and afraid not to.

This was the relief guard. They had not seen them come in. The paper was for the exact number of people, three men and one woman.

There was no sound but the guard's breath rasping in his throat and the hiss and flicker of the torches in their brackets.

"Right," the guard said at last. "Out." He gestured to the great archway and on shaking legs de Fleury went down, Nicolette still at his side. It had begun to rain.

Sebastien and Etienne increased their pace, passing into the wide street. Etienne took Nicolette by the arm almost exactly as the shot rang out in the air above them.

They froze.

One of the guards came running through the archway and across the cobbles, his musket held in both hands, ready to raise and fire.

Sebastien swivelled round. He was about to ask what was the matter, when he saw the turnkey behind them, and the ugly truth leaped to his mind only too clearly.

"Citizen de Fleury!" the guard accused breathlessly, looking from one to the other of them.

Before de Fleury could move, Etienne put his hand on his arm and stepped forward himself.

"What is it? Is something wrong?"

The guard stared at him, trying to discern his features in the erratic light.

Sebastien peered to see how far away the carriage was. Would Jacques have the cool-headedness to bring it forward even after he heard the musket shot? If not, they were lost.

The turnkey was coming out into the street as well, torch in his hand.

"Is it not bad enough we have to lose our brother, without bothering us at this time?" Etienne demanded, his voice shaking.

Sebastien heard the carriage wheels on the cobbles and saw the faint light on Jacques' pale hair. He turned back and caught Nicolette's eyes. He nodded imperceptibly.

Nicolette began to sink as if she would faint.

Sebastien started forward and picked her up, swinging past the guard and knocking the musket sideways and onto the stones. Etienne grasped de Fleury by the arm and as the carriage drew level, threw the door open, and pushed him in with all his might. De Fleury fell onto the floor, with Nicolette on top of him.

There were shouts of fury from the archway and swaying light as the turnkey came up, yelling for them to stop.

Sebastien knocked the barrel of the gun into the air, and then hauled himself onto the footplate at the side of the carriage just as it turned and picked up speed, and a moment later a musket shot rang out, and another, and another. One thudded into the wood-work, but it was nearly a yard away. Please God, Etienne was on the footplate.

They would call out the National Guard, of course they would, but by then de Fleury would be on the road to Calais, and they would be back in the familiar streets and alleys of the Cordeliers district, invisible again—if only they could elude them for the next hour.

The rain was heavier, driving in his face, making a mist of the dark streets, dampening torches, sliming the cobbles under the horses' feet. The wood under Sebastien's fingers was wet as he clung on while the coach swayed and lurched along the Rue Saint Antoine towards the Place de la Bastille. He could still hear the sound of gunfire behind.

Was Etienne on the footplate, clinging on as he was, or had he been flung off, and was lying somewhere on the road, perhaps injured, or even dead. Perhaps one of the shots had caught him?

Jacques could see better in the dark than he could! They were close to the river. He could smell the water and see the faint gleam of reflections on the surface. They must be on the Quai de l'Hôtel de Ville. There were still shouts behind them, and another volley of shots. They were far too exposed in the open.

They swerved left into the Pont d'Arcole. The huge mass of Notre Dame loomed ahead on the Île de la Cité. They must find the narrow streets soon, the winding alleys of their own district.

They swept through an open square, more shots splattering around them, some sharp on the stones, others thudding heavily into the woodwork of the carriage. The driving rain was making it desperately hard to cling on. Sebastien was slithering wildly, his fingers bruised, his body aching. All his muscles seemed locked.

He was all but thrown off as they careered over the Petit Pont, across the Quai Saint-Michel, and finally into the narrow streets behind the Church of Saint Severin.

When at last they stopped in the stable yard in the flaring torchlight, Sebastien was so numb he could barely let go. His fingers would not unbend. He saw Philippe's face white and streaked with rain as he ran out of the shelter of the doorway. The horses were shivering and streaked dark with sweat.

Sebastien dropped down onto the cobbles and almost fell, his body was so stiff, and hurt as if he had been battered.

"What happened?" Philippe demanded. "You look awful!" He looked at the coach, and his voice dropped. "It's riddled with splinters—a shot!" He lunged forward and yanked the door open, and Nicolette almost fell out. She was ashen.

Jacques scrambled off the box and came round the side. He too was soaked with rain, his hat was gone, and he looked exhausted and terrified. His eyes went straight to Sebastien.

"Etienne?" Sebastien asked the question which was in all their minds. "Where's Etienne? And de Fleury? Is he all right?"

Nicolette stared at him and shook her head minutely, barely a movement at all. "De Fleury's dead," she said in a small, tired voice. "One of the musket balls must have caught him. I don't even know when it happened. In the dark I didn't see, and he didn't cry out. In fact I never heard him speak at all. It could—it could have been the very first moment, when they were shooting at us before we even left the prison yard, or any time until we left them behind when we crossed the river."

There was a clatter of boots on the stones, and Etienne came round the back of the coach. He looked pale and very wet. There was blood on the sleeve of his coat, but he seemed otherwise unharmed.

Sebastien felt a surge of relief, and then instant guilt. He took the torch from Philippe and went to the coach, the door still swinging open as Nicolette had left it, and peered in.

De Fleury was half lying on the seat, the cape Sebastien had put round him in the prison crumpled, covering his body, his legs buckled as if he had been thrown violently when the coach had lurched from side to side as the horses careered through the darkness, shots screaming past them, thudding into the wood and ricocheting from the walls of the buildings on either side.

Sebastien held the torch higher so he could see de Fleury's face. With his other hand he moved the cloak aside. There was no mistaking death. The wide-open, sightless eyes were already glazed. He looked oddly surprised, as if in spite of all the terror of the prison, and then the sudden escape, the flight and the shooting of the guards behind him, he had not expected it.

Nicolette was close behind him. He handed her the torch and she held it, shaking a little, the light wavering, so he could use both hands to move de Fleury.

"What are we going to do with him?" she asked over his shoulder.

He had not yet thought as far as that. Other failures had stopped far earlier, before they had ever reached the prisoners, or else very soon after. Once before they had fled in rout, but the prisoner had remained behind, to face the guillotine. Decent disposal of the corpse had not been their responsibility. There were no churches open since the edict, and no priests in Paris openly. Religion was outlawed. You could go to the guillotine simply for harbouring a priest, let alone indulging in the rites of the faith.

Yet they could not simply leave him. They had offered him freedom, and now he was dead.

"I'll smuggle him outside Paris, as we were going to." It was Etienne's voice from the yard, behind Nicolette, his face wet in the torchlight, but he was beginning to regain his composure. "I'll bury him somewhere on the road to Calais." He grimaced. "At least that's better than a common grave with the other victims of the day's execution. Better a quiet coach ride towards Calais than a drive through the street mobs in a tumbrel."

"Yes, you'd better do that," Sebastien agreed. "Thank you." He leaned forward to straighten the cloak, to lift it and cover the face. In spite of the thousands who had died in the city since the storming of the Bastille nearly three years ago, the small gestures of decency still mattered—or perhaps because of them.

Etienne mistook his intention.

"Leave him there," he said quickly. "I'll take him out before dawn. Better in the dark. I'll make it look as if he's sleeping."

"Good," Sebastien acknowledged. "Thank you." He looked a moment longer at de Fleury's dead face. He felt guilty. Perhaps this death was better than the guillotine with all its deliberate horror, but that was little comfort now. They had still let him down. How had it happened? As always, no one else had known anything of their plans. They had been made only the night before. Why had the guard come back, and then followed them out to challenge them?

"I'm sorry," he whispered to de Fleury. He should leave him sitting up a little better. There was no point. It was a meaningless thing to do, but he still did it. It lent a kind of dignity.

Then he saw the hole in the back of the seat where the musket ball had come through. What an irony that the one ball that had penetrated through instead of merely splintering the wood and lodging in the upholstery, should have gone straight to his heart. There was blood on the seat, dark and shiny. Sebastien put his finger to the neat round hole, then froze. He had touched the ball, embedded in the wadding. That was impossible!

His mind whirled, bombarded with realisations that ended in one terrible, irreversible fact. De Fleury had been shot from the front, from inside the coach! That could only be either Nicolette or Etienne—or just conceivably Jacques, if he had somehow tied the reins for a few moments and swung down from the box, and in the confusion and the dark Nicolette had not seen him.

But why? why on earth would any of them, people he had trusted with his life over and over again, kill de Fleury?

Nicolette was standing at his elbow, still holding the torch. Etienne was still waiting.

"Yes," Sebastien said steadily, moving back and away from the carriage door. He slammed it shut, turning to face them. Nicolette lowered the torch. It must be getting heavy. "Yes, that's a good idea." He did not know what else to say. The question roared round in his head: which one of them—and why?

He did not want to know. The friendships were too deep and too precious. The betrayal was hideous. But he had to know. The suspicion would stain them all, and worse than that, they could no longer trust any life to whoever had done this. It explained the guard's return, the shots, everything else.

It was still raining. They were all standing there watching him. Nicolette, her hair wet across her brow, her clothes sticking to her, her dress sodden; Etienne with his arm still bleeding, holding it across his chest now, to ease the weight of it; Jacques frightened and puzzled; Philippe beginning, as usual, to get cross. He had been waiting for them since they left, not knowing what had happened.

Sebastien forced himself to smile. "Let's go inside and at least have something hot to drink. I don't know about the rest of you, but I'm frozen!"

There was a sigh of relief, a release of long-held tension. As one, they turned and followed him towards the light and the warmth.

Sebastien slept from sheer exhaustion, but when he woke in the morning, late and with his head pounding, the question returned almost instantly. One of them had killed de Fleury, coldly and deliberately. When the rescue had succeeded, in spite of the betrayal of the plan to the guards, they had shot him in the coach as they fled through the night.

How? None of them had taken a gun into the prison. It would have been suicidal. It must have been left in the coach, against the eventuality of the escape not being foiled by the guards. That still meant that any of the three of them could have done it, Jacques most easily, he had obtained the coach, that had been his task. But it would have been very hard for him to have left the box and come into the coach to perform the act. When they were in a straight road, Nicolette would have been likely to have seen him.

Nicolette would have found it the easiest. It was she who had ridden in the coach alone with de Fleury. When had she put the gun there? He sat at the table in his rooms eating a breakfast of hot chocolate and two slices of bread. It was stale, but bread was scarce these days, and expensive. He went over the events of the previous day, from the time Jacques had brought the coach until they had left from the prison of La Force.

There was no time when Nicolette had been alone. She had helped Philippe with the forged papers, getting them exactly right, then she had been with Sebastien himself.

The question that remained was why? Why would Etienne have wished de Fleury dead? How did he even know him? If he had some bitter enmity with him, why had he not simply said so, and refused to be part of the rescue?

There was no alternative but to confront him with the evidence and demand the truth, at the same time hoping against reason that there was some explanation that did not damn him.

It was early evening when Sebastien knocked on the door of Etienne's rooms in the Rue de Seine. He had put it off all day, but it could wait no longer.

The door swung open and Etienne stood in the entrance, smiling.

"Sebastien!" he said with surprise and apparent pleasure. "Not another rescue? It must be someone very important for you to try now, so soon after this fiasco."

"No, not another escape. An answer, if you have one."

Etienne's fair eyebrows shot up. "To what?"

"To why you betrayed us to the guard, and when that didn't work, why you shot de Fleury?"

Etienne stood motionless, his eyes unblinking. Seconds ticked by before he spoke. He measured Sebastien's nerve, weighed their friendship and all that they had shared, the dangers, the exultation of success and the bitterness of failures, and knew denial was no use.

"How did you know?" he said finally.

"The ball was still in the hole behind him. He was shot from in front."

"Careless of me," Etienne said with a very slight shrug. "I didn't see it. Thought it would be so far embedded in the wadding you'd never find it."

"I wouldn't have, if I hadn't put my finger in."

Etienne still had not moved. "Why not Nicolette? She was in there with him."

"You left the gun in the carriage . . . in case. She had no chance to do that."

"I see."

"Why?" Sebastien asked. "What was de Fleury to you?"

Etienne moved backward into the room, an elegant room with mementos of a more precious age, when it was still acceptable to be an aristocrat and have a coat of arms. One hung on the farther wall, two crossed swords beneath it.

"Nothing," Etienne replied. "Or to you either . . . compared with our friendship." He was not begging, there was something almost like amusement in his eyes, and regret, but no fear.

Then suddenly he darted backward with startling speed. His arm swung up and he grasped one of the swords from the wall and in an instant was facing Sebastien with it held low and pointing at him, ready to lunge. There was sadness in his eyes, but no wavering at all. He meant death, and he had both the will and the art to accomplish it.

They faced each other for a fraction of time so small it was barely measurable, then Sebastien threw himself to one side and scrambled to his feet as Etienne lunged forward. The blade ripped the chair open where a second before he had been standing.

There was no weapon for Sebastien. The other sword was still on the wall, ten feet away and behind Etienne. There was a silver candlestick on the table near the wall to his left. He dived towards it and his hand closed over it as Etienne darted forward again. The blade flickered like a shaft of light, drawing a thin thread of blood from Sebastien's arm and sending a sheet of pain through his flesh.

He parried Etienne's attack with the candlestick, but it was a poor defense, and he knew from Etienne's face that it would last only moments. The sword was twelve inches longer, lighter and faster.

His only chance was to throw the candlestick. Yet once it was out of his hands he had nothing left. He must work his way round until he could snatch the other sword. But if that was obvious to him, then it would be to Etienne also.

He picked up a light chair with his other hand, and threw it. It barely interrupted Etienne's balance, but it did bring Sebastien a yard nearer to the wall and the sword.

"You're wasting your time, Sebastien," Etienne said quietly, but for all the lightness of his voice, there was pain in it. He would not have had it come to this, but when he had to choose between himself and another, then it would always be himself. "I'm a better swordsman than you'll ever be. I'm an aristocrat, for whatever that's worth. I was born to the saddle and the sword. Don't fight me, and I'll make it quick . . . clean."

Sebastien picked up a Sevres vase and threw it at him.

"Damn! You shouldn't have broken that, you bloody barbarian!" Etienne said with disgust. He slashed and caught Sebastien a glancing blow across the other arm, ripping his shirt and drawing another thin line of beaded blood.

Sebastien jumped over the footstool and dived for the other sword. Etienne saw what he was aiming for and leaped after him, but his foot caught the stool and he crashed down, saving himself by putting out his other hand. Had he not fallen, he would have speared Sebastien through the chest.

Sebastien tore the weapon off its mounting and faced him just as he rose to his feet again. The blades clashed, crossed, withdrew, and clashed again. They swayed back and forth, dodging the furniture, first one slipping, then the other. Sebastien was stronger and he had the longer reach, but Etienne had by far the greater skill. It could only be a matter of time until he saw the fatal advantage, and Sebastien knew it.

There had been far too much death already. Paris was reeking with death and the fear of death. There was so much that was good in Etienne, far more than in many that were still alive. He had courage, gaiety, imagination, the gift for inspiring others to give of their best, to rise above what they had thought they were and find new heights.

Then Sebastien again saw in his mind's eye the surge of hope in de Fleury's face when he knew why they had come to La Force, the gratitude, and then the surprise of death as he knew he was betrayed.

He stepped back and with all his strength tore one of the tapestries off the wall and threw it at Etienne. Etienne swore, as much for the damage of the fabric as anything else. He ducked so that it did not entangle him, and at the same moment Sebastien lunged forward and sideways and his blade sank deep into flesh. Etienne fell, taking the sword with him, blood staining his shirt in a dark tide.

Sebastien stood still, looking down at him. There was surprise in his victory, and no pleasure at all, not even any satisfaction. Etienne was dead with the single thrust.

Sebastien pulled out the blade and let it fall towards the body. He felt empty except for an overwhelming sadness, a heaviness inside him as if he could hardly carry his own weight.

As he had with de Fleury the night before, he bent to the body, only this was different, this was a man who had been his friend, a man he himself had killed. He wanted to say something, but all that filled his mind was "Why?" Why would a man like Etienne have shot de Fleury? Why could he not have told Sebastien, if de Fleury were some bitter enemy from the past?

Then he saw the paper in Etienne's pocket, just a small edge poking out. He pulled it, then opened it up. It was a large sheet of high-quality vellum, written in a copperplate hand. It appeared to be a legal document, but quite short, taking up only two thirds of the page. After it were several signatures.

He began to read:

Versailles, 5th June, 1785

I, Maximilien Honoré de Fleury, Vicomte de Lauzun, do herewith offer myself and all I have in solemn covenant with Satan, Lord of Darkness and of Lies, Master of Destruction, King of the Nether World, and Heir Apparent of this Earth and all that is in it, that I may be of service to him, in the seduction of innocence, the indulgence of appetite, the sacrifice of human flesh to his will, and the bending of minds to his dominion. For my loyalty to his cause he will reward me with pleasure and riches here, endless sensation and variety, and hereafter a place among the Lords of his Kingdom.

I pledge my soul to this cause, and write my name in my own blood. Maximilien Honoré de Fleury.

In witness to this covenant we fellow servants of his Satanic Majesty do sign our names beneath:

Jean Sylvain Marie Dessalines
Jean Marie Victor Coritot
Stanislas Marie Delabarre
Donatien Royou
Joseph Augustin Barère
Etienne Jacques Marie du Bac
Ignace Georges Legendre

He stared at the page, unable to believe it. Etienne had been witness to this grotesque piece of . . . of what? Did these men really believe they had made a pact with the devil? Perhaps in 1785 it had seemed some kind of effete joke. Now no one joked about the devil, he was only too real. The stench of his breath was everywhere and the mark of his hand shriveled the heart.

People had turned on each other, killing and being killed. That Etienne, of all people, ironic, graceful, and brave, should have taken de Fleury's life to protect this grubby secret was tragic above all. If he had told Sebastien about it, Sebastien would have taken the paper from de Fleury, and made him promise on his life to keep silence. He could hardly tell his hosts in England of Etienne's complicity without exposing his own, and destroying his welcome also.

Sebastien shivered, cold through to his bones. Perhaps that was how pacts with the devil worked—you lost sight of the stupidity of evil, and the ultimate sanity of good. You destroyed yourself—unnecessarily.

He put the letter in his pocket. He would burn it when he got home. He turned round and went out of the door and closed it softly behind him.

JOYCE'S CHILDREN

Stuart M. Kaminsky

Of all the subgenres of the mystery, the celebrity whodunit may provide the most pure fun. Stuart Kaminsky writes one of the best and longest-running of the celebrity series, taking a nostalgic view of 1940s Hollywood with his detective Toby Peters in charge of cases that involve the likes of Judy Garland, Gary Cooper, and Howard Hughes. But Stuart Kaminsky is a versatile writer who also pens the Abe Lieberman police procedurals set in Chicago and the Rostnikov police procedurals set, originally, in the Soviet Union and, currently, in the new Russia—books with much darker themes than one would expect from the author of the Toby Peters romps. A few years ago, the Edgar Award–winning author began yet another series of stories about an unlicensed private eye, Lew Fonesca, the protagonist in the following tale. Kaminsky created much of this considerable body of work while also teaching in the film divisions at Northwestern University and Florida State University.

I DON'T LIKE theme parks, any of them—long lines, short rides, teens dressed like Mickey and Goofy or Bugs, in hot suits, trying to make the best of a minimum-wage job they thought was going to be fun and easy. And I don't like the high prices and robots that we're supposed to think look like Thomas Jefferson or Mighty Joe Young or Mighty Mouse.

"You're not a kid," said Dave when I gave him my opinion, which he had listened to with nodding attention.

Dave owns the Dairy Queen across the parking lot from where I live and work in a crumbling walk-up office building that had begun life as a 1950's motel and had gradually gone downhill till it was ready for me. I'm not supposed to live in the back room of my office, but the landlord doesn't care as long as I pay my rent on time and don't complain about the ancient air conditioner.

Dave looks like a dark, deeply weathered mariner, which he is when he's not handing out Dilly Bars. He owns a boat and is out in Sarasota Bay and the Gulf of Mexico whenever possible. The sun has leathered him. The boat has given him muscles and kept him trim.

Dave is about my age, early forties. I like to think that with his face and bleached-out hair he looks older than I do, but I'm dark, with a rapidly receding hairline that makes me look every minute of my age.

My name is Lew Fonesca. I live in Sarasota, Florida, where I drove a little over two years ago when I couldn't stand my job in the state attorney's office in Chicago and I wanted to get away from my ex-wife, who had drained me dry. My car had given out in Sarasota. I sold it for twenty-five dollars and made the first month's rent on the office overlooking the DQ and heavily traveled Route 301, which was named Washington Street. The office was the first place I had been shown.

Now I sat with Dave talking about theme parks at the white, chipped-enamel table with the umbrella. Dave was drinking water. I was working on a cheeseburger and a chocolate-cherry Blizzard.

I sat quietly digesting my burger and Dave's observation.

"I didn't like it when I was a kid," I said.

Dave shrugged, drank his water, and accidentally spilled a few drops on his white apron.

"When I get my kids for a few weeks in the summer," he said, "I have to take them to a theme park: Busch, Universal, Disney. I hate it. They love it. I agree with you. Most of all I hate the rides."

"Soul mates," I said, finishing the burger and giving my full attention to the Blizzard.

"Dus es shicksall giveren," he said. "It's fate."

Dave spoke five languages, all picked up when he'd traveled in Europe for two years when he got out of high school, over twenty years earlier. Dave was a quick study with not much ambition.

"Well," I said, finishing my drink with an unbecoming final slurp and getting up, "I'm on my way to Orlando."

"Wear a hat," he said as I headed for the rented car my client was paying for.

I had already packed my blue carry-on for a couple of nights and had my Cubs cap in the front seat of the Geo Prizm. I look like a big-eared dolt in the cap, but it protects my ever-growing forehead from burning under the Florida sun.

I headed down 301, turned at Fruitville, and drove to I-75, where I headed north.

Traffic wasn't bad for two reasons: It was summer, and the snowbirds had left, reducing the population of Sarasota and the entire state of Florida significantly. It was late on a Tuesday morning, when people who worked were at work and people who didn't were in their air-conditioned homes or at Siesta Key beach on the cool white sand, ignoring the ultraviolet index.

My business had picked up considerably. Most of my clients are lawyers or are referred by lawyers for whom I serve summonses or do legwork, including tracking down dads who haven't paid their child support and runaway teens, most of whom never ran very far. I'm not a private detective. I'm a man in a Cubs cap who asks questions.

This promised to be an easy job. Jason McConeky, one of the lawyers I work for, had sent me a client. The client and I had met at Raoul's, a bar and eatery just north of downtown. If there had been a Raoul, he was long forgotten. What he had left to several owners was a place with atmosphere, the look of an old Western saloon: grizzled old men and construction crews wearing yellow hard hats, drinking beer and eating burgers or chili at the round wooden tables.

His name was Kent Sizemore. He was a very burly two hundred and fifty pounds, with a pink, round face. He was in his late thirties and knew how to dress. When we met at Raoul's, he was in a neatly pressed light-weight tan suit, complete with a bold red designer tie. He was out of place in Raoul's, but he didn't seem to notice.

"She took the kids," he said to me to open the conversation. "Jason must have told you."

"Nice to meet you," I answered. "Mr. McConeky gave me a little information."

"She had no right," Sizemore said, leaning toward me and staring into my eyes without a blink.

I don't play "who blinks first." I'm an adult. Dave at DQ was always there to remind me of that fact. I sat back and placed my order: the chili, mild.

"The same," said Sizemore. "Hot, double order."

The waiter had nodded, brought us two beers, and disappeared.

"How old are the kids? Do you have recent pictures of them and your wife?"

"Yes," he said, reaching into his inside jacket pocket. "Jason said I should bring them."

He handed me a brown envelope with a clasp. I opened it and looked at the three pictures. There were individual color photos of a boy and a girl. The boy looked as if he was about eight. The girl was five at the most.

Both were smiling. Neither looked at all like their father. The third photograph told me who they looked like. The kids stood on each side of their mother, who wore jeans and a white shirt tied about her belly to reveal a very nice navel. Her hair was blond, just like both kids', and all three had the same smile.

"My daughter's name is Sydney, after my father. My son is Kent, Jr."

"Nice family," I said, returning the photographs to the envelope and placing it next to the chili which had just been brought to our table.

"Used to be," he said, looking down at the huge bowl in front of him. "Then. . . . Wherever Joyce has the kids, Bill Stark is probably with them."

"Friend of your wife?" I asked.

"More than a friend," Sizemore said, digging into the chili. He didn't turn red and his eyes didn't water. This was a man to be reckoned with.

"I see," I said.

"Stark worked for me," he said. "I have a real-estate agency on Siesta Key. Upscale property and boats."

"I know," I said, slowly working on my chili.

"I caught them on the phone," he said. "Joyce didn't deny it. Says it's my fault, that I've changed, that she needed attention not grunts."

"Have you?"

"What?"

"Changed," I said.

"Yeah," he said. "We've been married eleven years. I gained about ten pounds a year. It's in my genes. So Bill Stark is in my wife's jeans."

"What do you want?"

"My kids," he said. "I'd even take Joyce back if she'd come. But she had no right to run away with Stark and the kids."

"I can find them, maybe," I said. "It's hard to hide in the age of computers. But I can't force her to come back. I can tell the police."

"No," he said emphatically. "No police. Jason said they probably wouldn't do much even if I did involve them. I want this quiet."

"I can tell you where they are," I said. "And you can get a restraining order from a judge. McConeky can do that. And if she's in a hotel room with Stark and the kids, I can testify or tell a judge."

"I want my kids," he insisted.

"I told you what I can do," I said.

He thought about that for about a minute while he continued to eat. For a big man, he was a slow, dainty eater.

"Okay," he said.

We worked out the payment, and he gave me a cash advance. I told him

I'd check in with him every day, and if it started to take a lot of time he could reassess the situation, especially if I had to go out of town or out of the state. He agreed.

"Find them," he said, and dropped a ten-dollar bill on the table along with a business card. He left. His bowl was clean. His office number was on the front of the card along with his home number. I pocketed the card.

My regular computer hacker, who worked for one of my lawyer clients, was out of town. I went to my backup, Dixie Cruise, no relation to the actor.

Dixie was slim, trim, with very black hair in a short style. She was no more than twenty-five, pretty face and big round glasses. Dixie worked behind the counter at a coffee bar on Main Street. About six months back, I had sought her out to ask some questions about a straying husband and found that Dixie, who had as down-home an accent as any Billy Bob, was a computer whiz.

I called her at the coffee bar, had dinner with her at a new French restaurant, and went to her apartment in a slightly run-down twelve-flat apartment building. She had a two-room place. One room was devoted to her two computers and all kinds of grey metal pieces with lights.

It took Dixie ten minutes and cost me fifty bucks, which I would bill to Kent Sizemore. Stark belonged to AAA. Three days earlier he had purchased two adult and two children's tickets to Disney World, Sea World, and the Universal theme park. Dixie got a list of hotels in Orlando. It was a long list. She hacked into their computers and did a search for "Stark" and another one for "Sizemore."

"Embassy Suites on International Drive," Dixie said, pointing at the screen as if her right hand were a handgun. "Check out in three days."

In the old days, I would have gone to AAA, told a sad story, and hoped for the best. Then I would have tried airlines, travel agencies, and friends of Joyce and Bill Stark. Sarasota isn't huge, but it might have taken me days, which means that without Dixie they would have checked out before I found them.

That was why I was on my way to Orlando armed with three photographs and wearing a Cubs cap. There was construction on I-4 from the Tampa interchange to Orlando. I-4 is only two lanes in both directions, and it seems there are as many trucks as cars. Still, it only took me a couple of hours to get to International Drive, a street of glitz, restaurants, hotels, a water slide, plenty of places that sell T-shirts and souvenirs, and a Ripley's-Believe-It-or-Not house built at an odd angle as if it had just been dropped from outer space.

The hotel wasn't full, but all they had for me was a suite at almost two hundred a night. I took it, and the young man behind the desk did a great job of ignoring the fact that my luggage was a single blue carry-on.

When I got to my room, I threw my cap on the table, took the novel I was reading out of the carry-on, and went down to the atrium lobby. There were plenty of wrought-iron seats at tables and tastefully upholstered chairs scattered around the sun-filled area. I found a chair facing the front door and began reading *The Headsman* by James Harvey. I figured they were out at one of the amusement parks. I might have to wait a long time, but I was getting paid well and I had found them quickly.

Little kids ran screaming in their swimsuits, heading for the pool. Families went by speaking German, French, and something I couldn't place. I read, paused at seven to get a quick carry-out sandwich at the snack bar, and went back to my chair fairly certain that they hadn't come in during the minute or two I had been away. To be sure, I took my sandwich to the house phone and asked for their room. No answer. The machine asked if I wanted to leave a message. I hung up and went back to my chair with my tuna on white and a Diet Pepsi.

They came in a little after nine. Stark was carrying the little girl, Sydney, who was sleeping. Kent, Jr. was walking slowly, with a less than happy look on his face. His mother was definitely a beauty, but there was something less than ecstasy in her face. She was carrying a colorful shopping bag with a picture of the Lion King on the side.

There wasn't too much I could do to be inconspicuous. I don't have the kind of face people remember in any case. It is a blessing in my work and a minimal curse in my private life.

I managed to get on the elevator with the four of them, smiled, and pressed 8.

"Floor?" I asked pleasantly.

"Seven," Joyce Sizemore said, closing her eyes.

When we hit 3, she opened her eyes and looked at me.

"I know you," she said.

Stark turned to face me.

"I don't . . ." I began.

"Sarasota Y.M.C.A.," she said. "You workout there."

So much for my keenly developed internal storehouse of names and faces. How could I not remember someone who looked like Joyce Sizemore? How could she remember me?

"I do," I said with a grin. "Every morning before I go to work. I'm the menswear department manager at Burdine's in Southgate. Brought my wife and kids here for our annual week of torture."

"I know what you mean," she said.

The elevator stopped at 7, and they shuffled wearily out. When I reached the eighth floor, I got out quickly and headed for a spot where I could see them moving toward their room across the atrium.

After they went in, I waited for another hour, pretending my novel was a sketch book when anyone went by. I even drew a crude stick figure and a tree at one point. My watch hit ten, and I went to my room and set the alarm clock for five in the morning. I shaved, showered, shampooed, brushed my teeth, and slept. Everything was going just fine.

I had eaten the free Continental buffet breakfast and was at a two-person table slowly drinking cup after cup of coffee with *U.S.A. Today* in front of me. A little before nine, Bill Stark, Joyce Sizemore, and the kids came down. The kids were bouncing and arguing. The adults were just arguing. I couldn't hear them, but it looked as if the brief honeymoon was in trouble.

I followed them out after they breakfasted. The rest of the day was moppet heaven for the kids and nightmare alley for me. They went on and saw everything at the Disney-MGM Studios theme park while I watched from a discreet distance. I don't know what I was watching for. Possibly signs of intimacy in front of the children. A stolen passionate kiss and a little groping while the kids were in the Muppet Vision show.

We watched the Beauty and the Beast show, the Hunchback show, the Honey, I Shrunk the Kids show, the Indiana Jones Epic Stunt Spectacular, and had lunch at Disney's Toy Story Pizza Planet Arcade. By the time we hit the Voyage of the Little Mermaid, I was strongly considering calling Kent Sizemore, giving him what I had so far, and going back to Sarasota; but I wanted, I must confess, to squeeze at least another day's pay out of my client. The cable television bill was due.

They went on The Great Movie Ride and ended the day with The Making of Evita. I wished Stark would carry me or, better yet, that Joyce Sizemore would carry me.

They stopped for dinner at a seafood restaurant. I didn't eat. The chance of being spotted was too great and I didn't put much faith in, "Well, we meet again. Small world after all."

I wasn't hungry. I was tired.

When they went back to their suite, I followed and stood outside trying to listen through the window without giving the impression that I was an awkward Peeping Tom. I couldn't make out words, but the voices were hard and angry.

I went back to my room. My plan was to call Sizemore in the morning, give him his wife's room number, and let him do what he wished with the information.

Someone was knocking at my door. I sat up dizzy and looked at the clock with the red numbers. It was a little after three in the morning. The knock came again. I got off the bed, pulled on my pants, and went out of the bedroom to the front door.

"Yes," I said.

"Joyce Sizemore."

I opened the door. The children were both in pajamas and robes, crying. Joyce Sizemore needed a comb and a good dry cleaner. Her white robe was splotched with blood.

"Can we come in?" she asked.

I stepped back and the weeping trio came in. I closed the door and turned to watch them sit on the small sofa. Joyce Sizemore was trying to comfort them, kissing the tops of their heads, hugging her children.

"How did you know about me?" I asked.

"I called the desk after I recognized you," she said. "I said I didn't remember your name but that we knew each other from Sarasota. I described you. They found someone who remembered checking you in."

"I hope the description was kind," I said.

She didn't answer.

"Then I called some friends I can trust in Sarasota," she went on, looking at the dark television screen and hugging her sobbing children. "Found someone who knew you. My husband sent you, didn't he?"

"Yes," I said.

"Can I trust you?" she asked, continuing to soothe her children. "I have no one else to turn to."

"You can trust me. But I'm not sure why you should believe you can."

"No choice," she said with a shrug. "I want you to take Sydney and Kent, Jr. back to their father."

Both children said no, but Joyce wasn't listening.

"At three in the morning?" I asked.

"I just murdered William Stark," she said.

Kent, Jr. turned his head into his mother's shoulder. The little girl looked down and bit her lip.

"I've got to go back to the room and call the police," she said. "Take my children home. My husband, for all his faults, is a good father. I don't want them involved."

"How about you and I go out on the balcony?" I said. "The kids can watch television."

She looked at both children, seemed to understand, and told the children she would be gone for just a minute. They clung to her, but she managed to pull away gently.

"Be right back," she said, following me through the door after I handed the boy the remote control and checked my pocket to be sure I had my door card.

Even at three in the morning, the atrium wasn't empty. Five men were seated eight stories down, talking softly. A crew of cleaning people were sweeping and scrubbing. Joyce Sizemore was looking down across the open space at the closed door for her room.

"What happened?" I asked quietly.

She wiped her eyes with her sleeve, took a deep breath, and said, "He tried to take me in front of the children. He hit me, pulled my hair. He'd gotten up during the night. He was drunk. There was a knife on the table. We had forgotten to put the dishes outside the door after we had room service. It was a steak knife. I told him to stop. He didn't. He grabbed my wrist and laughed. We were standing there, just . . . I twisted my arm and pulled free and then I brought the knife down three, four times. He looked surprised. I hated him. I wanted to keep . . . You know the rest. I'll go back and call the police. You take care of my children, please."

"You're sure he's dead?" I asked.

"Yes."

"Then it won't hurt if I go take a look. You go back to your kids and give me your room card."

"Why?" she asked.

"Because I'm asking you," I said. "I won't take long. If the phone rings, it'll be me. Answer it."

She brushed her hair back with her long fingers and pulled the room card out. I took it and let her back into my room. The television was on. An old Dick Van Dyke rerun where Rob goes off to a cabin to write a novel was on in glorious black and white. The episode, as I recalled, was funny. Sydney and Kent, Jr. weren't laughing.

I went down the fire stairs, made sure I wasn't being watched, and made my way to the room on the seventh floor. I opened the door and wiped it clean with my shirt. Then I kicked the door closed. The lights were on and William Stark lay on the floor, bloody, eyes closed, in his T-shirt with the picture of a grinning cartoon turkey on the front. The turkey was covered in blood. Stark was naked from the shirt down.

I didn't touch anything. I looked around the room and into the bedroom and then I leaned over the body. I didn't try to count the stab wounds. There weren't a lot of them. The knife, not a particularly long one, lay bloody-bladed not far from the body.

There was a cot in the room with a pillow and blanket, and a Hide-A-Bed with a teddy bear and stuffed elephant lying back on a pink blanket. Some blood had splattered on the Hide-A-Bed.

I checked my watch and started for the door.

The moan wasn't loud, but it was clear, and it came from the supposedly dead William Stark. I went back to the body and knelt. Stark's eyes opened and moved in the general direction of my face. I didn't bother to tell him not to move as I lifted the bloody T-shirt to get a closer look at the wounds.

There were four of them. I should have just called 911, but a few minutes probably wouldn't make much difference. At least, that's what I told myself.

"You'll be all right," I assured him as I examined his wounds.

He looked around the room as if he had no idea of where he was.

Two of the stab wounds were to the chest. I gently touched them. Neither was deep. Both appeared to have been stopped by Stark's ribs.

The third wound was almost at his right shoulder. I couldn't tell how deep it was, but it was into muscle, not much chance of being fatal. The fourth wound was the problem. It was on the left side of his stomach. There was plenty of blood, but I couldn't tell how deep it was or what had been hit.

"You'll live," I said. "I'm going to try to stop some of this bleeding. Then I'll call an ambulance."

His right hand came up suddenly and gripped my wrist. For a dead man, he was damned strong. I tried to pull loose as he croaked, "No ambulance. No police."

"Noble," I said. "But you might be dying. You want to live?"

He took a second to think about it and then nodded yes and let go of my hand.

This was all wrong. I had known it from the moment Joyce Sizemore entered my room with her frightened children. Stark closed his eyes and I leaned over to be sure he was still breathing. He was.

I picked up the phone, not worrying about fingerprints any longer, and dialed my own room. Joyce answered before the second ring.

"Yes?" she said with a quivering voice.

"It's me, Fonesca. Get down to your room, fast. Leave the kids there."

"What . . . ?"

"He's still alive," I said.

She didn't answer and I had no time to talk to her now.

"Fast," I said.

I hung up, checked my watch, sat on the bed, and said, "Stark, you still with me?"

His groan suggested that he was. I checked my watch. Almost a minute passed. If she didn't show I'd have to call 911. My voice would be on tape. I'd have a bigger mess than I already had.

The knock was soft, but it was a knock. I let her in. She was a ghostly pale, beautiful vision of white and blood red. I closed the door and she walked over to Stark, who hadn't moved.

"Bill?" she asked.

He groaned in response.

She turned to me and said, "I've got to kill him."

"You've got to call nine-one-one," I said. "You've got to call now. Just tell them a man has been stabbed. Tell them where we are. Don't answer any more questions."

She shook her head. I picked up the phone and handed it to her. I hit the three buttons.

I could hear a voice on the other end because the phone wasn't close to her ear, but I couldn't make out the words.

She said exactly what I had told her to say and hung up.

"Good," I said. "I think we've got at least five minutes, maybe more. I'm going to be back in my room with the kids. You understand?"

She nodded again, looking at the half-naked, bloody man on the floor.

"You want to tell me what really happened here or you want me to guess?" I asked. "Faster if you tell me."

"No," she said, clasping her hands together to keep them from shaking.

"Okay," I said, determined to be out of there in three minutes. "You said he hit you. There's not a mark on you. You said he tried to attack you in front of the kids, but your robe is bloody and I don't see a tear in it or a button missing. You stabbed him while you were dressed. Which kid?"

"Which . . . ?"

"You woke up, heard sounds in here, and came in. Which of your children was he going to molest?"

Stark groaned again and something like words gurgled from his mouth.

"Kent," she said wearily. "The night-light was on. He was sitting on Kent's bed, his hand on Kent's chest. Kent was half asleep. I told you Bill had been drinking while I was asleep. I could smell it across the room. I took the knife and . . . the rest of what I told you was true."

"Does Kent know what Stark was trying to do?"

"No, I don't think so," she said. "He seemed to wake up, both of the children seemed to wake up, when I stabbed him."

I checked my watch and moved to Stark.

"Stark," I said. "Can you hear me?"

"Yes," he said with a groan. "Get an ambulance."

"One's coming. You were drunk. You tried to commit suicide. I'm going to give you the knife so your prints are on it."

He shook his head.

"Suit yourself," I said. "Then the whole thing comes out and you're labeled a pervert. Not a chance an Orlando prosecutor would take this case to court, especially if you don't die, which you won't. Mrs. Sizemore will walk away with her children and you'll be all over the newspapers and television. You want that?"

"No," he said, his face contorting in pain.

"We have a deal?" I said, checking my watch. Florida police had been under fire for months over not responding to 911 calls quickly enough. I had the feeling that my time was running out.

"Deal," said Stark, so softly that I could barely hear him. "Who are you?"

"Nobody," I said. "You've never seen me. Understand?"

He coughed and nodded.

I turned to Joyce Sizemore.

"You came out here. Saw him stabbing himself. You could tell he was drunk. He fell to the floor. Your kids were crying. You called nine-one-one and remembered that you had seen me, an old friend of your husband's, in the hotel. You called me, brought the children to my room, and came back here to wait for the ambulance and police. You understand?"

"I . . ." she said, looking at Stark, who was attempting to sit up.

"Mrs. Sizemore," I said. "If you want to keep your kids out of this, you better remember."

"I'll remember," she said.

I put the knife in Stark's hand and closed his fingers over it. I doubted that anyone would bother to check the story, but it didn't hurt to be sure. Some of the wounds might make a medical examiner think they weren't self-inflicted. Stark would have to insist that they were, but that he couldn't quite remember. Even if a smart cop thought something was screwy, he probably wouldn't pursue it. These people weren't rednecks in a cheap motel room. Class still has its privileges.

"I'm going," I said. "They'll be here any second. You'll be all right."

It wasn't a question, but she answered more strongly than I expected, "I'll be all right."

I moved toward the door.

"Wait," she said.

I turned toward her. She moved to the cot, picked up the teddy bear, and handed it to me. I understood. I went out and moved fast, without running, toward the stairwell. Below, out of sight, I could hear the sound of voices in the lobby. I ran up the one flight and came out close to the wall, where

I couldn't be seen by anyone eight flights below. I made my way to my room, opened the door, and found Sydney asleep on the sofa next to her brother, who was nodding off as he watched the end of the Dick Van Dyke episode. In her sleep, Sydney took the bear and clutched it to her chest.

"Mr. Stark is going to be okay," I said quietly.

Kent looked at me.

"He tried to kill himself," I said. "He had been drinking."

"I don't like him," the boy said. "Sydney doesn't like him. He smiles, buys us stuff, but he's a fake. We told Mom. She wouldn't listen."

"She's listening now," I said. "What did you see?"

Kent didn't hesitate.

"I was asleep, but I saw Mr. Stark stab himself and fall down. Then Mom took us to your room. Is that right?"

"It's right," I said.

"Sydney doesn't remember anything," the boy said, looking at his sister. "She remembers seeing Mr. Stark on the floor and Mom bringing us here."

"You want to get some sleep, Kent?"

"Yes," he said.

"There's a bed in the other room," I said.

"I don't want to leave Sydney. She might get up and be scared."

"I'll carry her in and put her next to you."

That seemed acceptable to him. I picked up the girl. She smelled clean. She smelled like a little girl. Kent walked slowly into the bedroom and watched me put his sister down. Then he climbed into the bed, put his head on the pillow, and fell asleep almost instantly.

It was just a question of how long it would take some cop to knock at the door to my room. My story would be simple, always best to keep it simple. Friend of Joyce's husband, taking a few days off to enjoy the Orlando glitz; ran into them in the elevator. Then she brought me the kids. I didn't know Stark. I didn't know what he was doing there. Joyce would have to swallow the truth on that one. It wouldn't be too painful. The cops would probably just go through the motions. No need to do anything else.

I was halfway through a Diet Dr. Pepper and an ancient rerun of a Bob Newhart show when the knock came.

"Chili here is great," said Kent Sizemore, Sr., digging into Raoul's special.

This time he had it with double onions and cheese.

Everything had gone pretty much the way I had laid it out. Joyce had told her story. Stark had told his tale of attempted suicide. I doubt if the cops believed it or cared. Stark's wounds looked worse than they were. He was in and out of the hospital in two days. I guess his insurance program wouldn't cover more unless he suffered life-threatening brain damage or decapitation. Stark hadn't come back to Sarasota. I'm fairly sure he didn't stay in Orlando or the state of Florida.

Meeting me at Raoul's had been Sizemore's idea. He had paid me in cash, including a generous bonus, before we ordered. I had gone for the regular burger with onion, tomato, and cheese.

"How are things?" I asked.

Joyce Sizemore and the children had been back for almost a week. I hadn't called him until the day before this meal.

"Not bad," he said. "Could be better. I think Joyce is going to leave me. I don't think she'll fight for the children after what happened."

"That what you want?"

"No," he said. "I want my wife. I want my kids to have their mother."

"No chance?"

He shrugged.

"You going to work on it?" I asked.

He paused, spoon almost to his mouth, and looked at me.

"Now you're a marriage counselor?"

"Let's say I've got an investment in your family now."

He cocked his head to one side, put the spoon in the bowl, and clenched his large fists.

"You're not going to shake me down for more money," he said.

"No. I like your wife. I like your kids. In an odd way, I think I might even like you."

Sizemore looked at the bowl in front of him, sighed, and pushed it away. "I'll do what I can," he said.

"A real marriage counselor might be a start," I said.

"Can't hurt," he said. "I'm going now."

He got up and held out his hand. I took it and he left. I was working on my burger and beer when Siegfried Donnelly, a small, skinny, grizzled old hanger-on in need of a shave and a comb joined me at the table and sat across from me. I ordered him a beer and burger.

"Struck it rich?" he said.

"Enough to pop for a brew and burger, Sig."

Sig had once been a pharmacist in Holland, Michigan. He liked to talk about tulips. He didn't like to talk about why he wasn't a pharmacist and why he wasn't in Holland, Michigan.

"Heard you went to Disney," he said with a serious look on his sun-dark face.

"Yeah," I said.

"Always wanted to go," Sig said, shaking his head. "Might make it some day."

"Good luck," I said, holding up my mug of beer in a toast.

He lifted his mug.

"Fun there, huh?" Sig said.

"I'll never forget it," I said.

Sig smiled with the few teeth he had left and his eyes went moist with a vision of magical rides and singing dwarfs.

OF COURSE YOU KNOW THAT CHOCOLATE IS A VEGETABLE

Barbara D'Amato

There are not many writers who cross the line between true crime and crime fiction. For Barbara D'Amato, however, the move was a natural outcome of her research on a true-crime book that ultimately pointed to the innocence of a man wrongly convicted of murder. The fictional creation that emerged as a result of her reflections on her true-crime research was an investigative reporter she called Cat Marsala. In virtually all of the Cat Marsala adventures, social issues come into the case. But if the author wants her readers to consider the serious issues she puts forward, she doesn't do it in a heavy-handed way. On the contrary, her books are marked, always, by a touch of humor. Barbara D'Amato is a multiple Anthony and Agatha award winner, and she won the Anthony, the Agatha, and the Macavity awards for the short story we've included in this book. Readers who are familiar with the Cat Marsala novels, which are consistently praised for the meticulous research that goes into them, will realize that the author is seeing a little of herself in the deadly protagonist of her story.

"OF COURSE YOU know that chocolate is a vegetable," I said.

"Lovely! That means I can eat all I want," Ivor Sutcliffe burbled, reaching his fork toward the flourless double-fudge cake.

Eat *more* than you want, you great tub of guts, I thought. The tub-of-guts part was rather unfair of me; I could stand to lose a pound or two myself. What I said aloud was, "Of course it's a vegetable. Has to be. It's not animal or mineral, surely. It grows on a tree—a large bush, actually, I suppose. It's as much a vegetable as pecans or tomatoes. And aren't we told to have several servings of vegetables every day?"

We were seated at a round table covered with a crisp white cloth at Just Desserts, a scrumptious eatery in central Manhattan that specializes in chocolate desserts, handmade chocolate candy, and excellent coffees. Just Desserts was willing to serve salads and a few select entrees to keep themselves honest, but if you could eat chocolate, why would you order anything else?

"I must say, Ms. Grenfield, it's very handsome of you to invite me after my review of your last book," Ivor said, dropping a capsule on his tongue, which then took the medication inside, his mouth closing like a file drawer. He washed the medication down with coffee.

I said, "No hard feelings. Reviewing books is your job."

"I may have been just a bit harsh."

Harsh? Like scrubbing your eyeball with a wire brush is harsh? I said, "Well, of course an author's feelings get hurt for a day or two. But we can't hold it against the critic. Not only is it his job, but, to be frank, it's in our best interests as writers to keep on pleasant terms. There are always future reviews to come, aren't there?"

"Very true."

Ivor's review had begun:

> In *Snuffed*, the victim, Rufus Crown, is dispatched with a gaseous fire extinguisher designed for use on fires in rooms with computer equipment and other such unpleasant hardware, though neither the reader nor the fictional detectives know this at the start when his dead but mysteriously unblemished body is found. The reader is treated to long efforts—quite incompatible with character development—on the part of the lab and medical examiner to establish what killed him.

"That's right; give away the ending," I had snarled to myself when I read this.

Snuffed had been universally praised by the critics and I thought I was a shoo-in for an award until the Ivor Sutcliffe review came out.

At the awards banquet, where I was not a nominee, fortune had seated me next to Sutcliffe. Just when the sorbet arrived, and I had happily pictured him facedown, drowning in strawberry goo, he began to wheeze. My mind had quickly changed to picturing him suffocating. But he had popped a capsule in his greedy pink mouth and after a few minutes he quit wheezing.

Since one has to be moderately cordial at these events, or at least appear to be, I asked courteously, "Do you have a cold?"

"Asthma," he said.

"Sorry to hear that. My son had asthma. Seems to have outgrown it."

"Lucky for him. What did he take for it?"

I said, "Theophylline."

"Ah, yes. That's what my doctor gave me. So proud of his big words, just like you. Standard treatment, I believe. I have been taking it for several weeks." He said this as if conferring a great benediction upon the drug.

I was about to relate an anecdote about the time my husband, son, and I were on a camping trip, without the theophylline. We'd left it at home, since it had been many months since Teddy's last attack, and we weren't expecting trouble. Then Teddy had developed a wheeze. As evening came on, it got worse. And worse. There's nothing scarier than hearing your child struggle for breath. We were two hours away from civilization, and my husband and I panicked. We packed Teddy into the car, ready to race for the nearest country hospital; then I had called Teddy's doctor on my cell phone.

"Do you have any coffee?" he said. Well, of course we had. Who went camping without coffee?

"Give him some. Caffeine is chemically similar to theophylline. Then drive to the hospital."

All this I was about to tell Sutcliffe when something stopped me. It was not more than the faint aroma of an idea, a distant stirring of excitement. So—theophylline and caffeine were similar. Hmm.

Teddy had been warned to take his theophylline as directed, but never to overdose.

Then and there I invited Sutcliffe out to a "good will" snack the following week. He accepted. Well, *my* will was going to feel the better for it.

Sutcliffe's review had gone on:

> I deplore the substitution of technical detail for real plotting. One could amplify the question "Who Cares Who Killed Roger Ackroyd?" by asking, "Who cares how Roger Ackroyd was killed?" No one cares what crime labs and pathologists really do.

"Agatha Christie cared," I had whispered as I read it, trying not to gnash my teeth. "And Dorothy Sayers and just about everybody then and just about everybody now on any bestseller list—Crichton, Clark, Cornwell, Grisham." In the first place, readers like to learn things. Second, technology is real and it's *now*. Third, it's exacting. Keeps a writer honest. You can't fake technical detail; it has to be right. You can't use the untraceable exotic poison these days. It has to be something people know about or even use every day. Or know they *should* know about. Then it's tantalizing.

But Ivor Sutcliffe wasn't scientific-minded. A know-it-all who knew nothing. A gross, hideous, undisciplined individual with bad table manners. I had once seen him, at a banquet, eat his own dinner and the dinners of three other guests who had failed to show.

So after the banquet I went home to my shelf of reference books, looking for something I almost knew about, or knew I should know about—just like a reader of fiction. I keep a large shelf of reference books. Having them to hand saves time, effort, and parking fees.

What would an overdose of theophylline do to a human being?

I turned first to the *Physician's Desk Reference*. This is a huge volume, 2,800 pages of medications, with their manufacturers, their brand names, their appearance shown in color pictures, their uses, their dosages, their effects, their adverse effects, and—overdosage.

An overdosage of theophylline was serious business. It said, "Contact a poison-control center." That was good. One didn't issue that kind of warning for minor side effects I read on. One had to monitor the dose carefully. Apparently the useful dose and dangerous dose were not far apart. I read on. Overdosage could produce restlessness, circulatory failure, convulsion, collapse, and coma. Or death.

Theophylline in normal use, it said, relaxed the smooth muscles of the bronchial airways and pulmonary blood vessels, acting as a bronchodilator and smooth-muscle relaxant. That was why it helped an asthma attack.

And then the punch line: "Theophylline should not be administered concurrently with other xanthines." And what were xanthines?

I turned to my unabridged dictionary. Why, xanthines included theophylline, caffeine (given Teddy's experience, this was no surprise) and the active ingredient of chocolate, theobromine Aha!

Hmm. Being similar, they would have an additive effect, wouldn't they? Synergistic, maybe? I turned to the *Merck Manual*, also huge, a 2,700-page volume, a bible of illnesses, their causes and treatments. In its section on poisons, caffeine poisoning was in the same sentence with theophylline poisoning. Among the symptoms of both were restlessness, circulatory-system collapse, and convulsions.

A medical text told me that fifty percent of theophylline convulsions result in death.

Isn't this fun? Research is so rewarding.

Well, I knew that theophylline was potentially deadly. Now what about the caffeine?

My book on coffees from around the world told me that a cup of coffee, depending on how it's brewed, contains 70 to 150 milligrams of caffeine. Drip coffee is strongest. Well, what about the extra-thick specialty coffees at Just Desserts? Could I assume they might have 200 milligrams?

What the book didn't tell me was how much caffeine would kill.

I pulled out the *Merck Index*, a different publication from the *Merck Manual*, the *Index* being an encyclopedia of chemicals. Here I found that if you had a hundred mice and gave them all 137 milligrams of caffeine per kilogram of body weight, half would die. This was cheerfully called LD 50, or lethal dose for fifty percent. My dictionary said a kilogram is 2.2 pounds. So if a man reacted like a mouse (although to me Ivor was more like a rat), that would work out to 13.7 grams of caffeine per 220 pounds. Of course, getting thirteen grams of caffeine into the 220-plus-pounds Ivor was not going to happen, but then caffeine was not the only xanthine that was going to be going into Ivor.

A volume for the crime writer on poisons told me that one gram of caffeine could cause toxic symptoms, but it didn't tell me how much would kill. Well, if one gram was toxic, two grams ought to cause real trouble.

Now what about theobromine, the xanthine in chocolate? The *Merck Index* informed me that theobromine, "the principal alkaloid of the cacao bean," was a smooth-muscle relaxant, diuretic, cardiac stimulant, and va-sodilator. My, my! Sounded a lot like theophylline and caffeine. It said chocolate also contained some caffeine. That couldn't hurt.

How could I find out how much chocolate was dangerous? Certainly people eat large amounts with no ill effects. But at some point, with the other two xanthines . . . ?

I turned on my computer, thinking to get on the Net and ask how much theobromine there was in an average piece of dark bittersweet chocolate. But I held my hand back. This could be dangerous. I could be traced. Somewhere I had heard of people receiving catalogues from companies that sold items they had queried the Net about. Like travel brochures when they'd asked about tourist destinations or smoked salmon when they'd asked about where to get good fish. Webmasters could learn everything about you. I certainly didn't want anybody to know I was the person making queries about theobromine in chocolate. Could I ask anonymously? No. How could I be sure the query couldn't be traced?

Then I remembered the library at the local law school. If you looked like you belonged there, you could query databases at no charge, although there was a time limit. And there was a per-page charge if you wanted to print out what you found, but why should I want it in black and white? Now, if they just didn't ask for names. I grabbed my coat and ran out the door.

Two hours later I left the library highly pleased. I'd asked two databases to find articles that used "chocolate" within ten words of "theobromine" and got all kinds of good stuff. Chocolate, it seemed, frequently killed dogs. Dogs and cats didn't excrete the theobromine as well as humans. The poisoned animals would suffer rapid heart rates, muscle tremors, rapid respiration, convulsions, and even death.

Dark chocolate, I learned, contains ten times as much theobromine as milk chocolate. Bitter cooking chocolate contains 400 milligrams in an ounce! And—oh, yes!—the amount in a moderate amount of chocolate is about the same as the amount of caffeine in a moderate amount of coffee.

In humans, theobromine is a heart stimulant, smooth-muscle relaxant, and dilates coronary arteries. So what if we eliminate it faster than Rover would? It still had to have an additive effect with the other two.

All three of my drugs caused low blood pressure, irregular heart rhythm, sweating, convulsions, and, potentially, cardiac arrest. What's not to like? Ha! Take that! I thought. Hoist with your own petard.

The *PDR* had said that oral theophylline acted almost as swiftly as intravenous theophylline. But I knew I would need time to get a lot of coffee and chocolate into Ivor. He'd better not feel sick right away and just stop eating. Well, the desserts themselves should slow the absorption.

At this point in my research I phoned Sutcliffe and suggested we hold our rendezvous at Just Desserts.

When the day came and we sat down like two friends at Just Desserts, I encouraged Ivor to try the dense "flourless chocolate cake" first.

"It's excellent," I said. "Like a huge slice of dark chocolate. I'll have a piece myself." The waiter brought the cake promptly and filled our coffee cups with mocha-java.

We tasted, nodded in appreciation, ate in companionable silence for a few minutes. Then I suggested he try the Turkish coffee, just for comparison, along with an almond-chocolate confection, for the blend of flavors. He agreed readily.

Now, since he was eating at my expense, he found the need to be borderline pleasant. "You know, I did say in the review that I've liked much of your past work."

Actually, no, you clot. His review of my first book, graven on my heart, said, "This novel is obviously the work of a beginner." And his review of my second book, also etched somewhere in my guts, said, "Ms. Grenfield has not yet got her sea legs for the mystery genre." The most recent review had, in fact, damned with faint praise: *This effort*, Snuffed, *is not up to her former standard.*

"Thank you," I said mildly.

"I suppose I should be frightened of eating with you, Ms. Grenfield. I've read so many novels where the central character, feeling wronged, invites his nemesis to dinner and poisons him."

"Well, Ivor, I was actually aware you might worry about that. I had thought of inviting you to my home. But it occurred to me that you might find it intimidating to be at the mercy of my cooking. Hence—Just Desserts."

Disarmed and possibly a little abashed, Sutcliffe said, "Well—you could hardly have found a more competent kitchen than this."

I nodded agreeably as Ivor finished his third cup of coffee—one regular, two Turkish so far—and pushed his cup within reach of the waiter. The calculator in my brain said that was 600 milligrams of caffeine now, give or take, and another two hundred on the way as the hot brew filled the cup.

Let's see. Add the capsule of theophylline just half an hour ago when he arrived. Didn't dare ask him the dosage, but it had to be either the standard 300 or the 400-milligram dose. Plus he had taken his morning dose, I supposed.

Ha! Well, me fine beauty, we'll just see how inartistic technology is. And we'll give you every chance to save yourself. Just a little paying of attention, Ivor. A morsel of humility.

Lord! That man could eat! *Schokoladenpudding*, which was a German chocolate-coffee-almond pudding served warm with whipped cream. *Rigo Jancsi* squares, dense Viennese cake that was more like frosting, which the waiter explained was named after a Gypsy violinist. And a slice of Sacher torte, a Viennese chocolate cake glazed with dark chocolate. *Shokoladno mindalnyi tort*, a Russian chocolate-almond torte made with rum, cinnamon, and, of all things, potato. Then just to be fair to the United States, he agreed to a simple fudge brownie with chocolate frosting, à la mode, as he put it, with coffee ice cream on the side. I had cherry strudel.

With each dessert he tried a different coffee. Ethiopian *sidamo*, Kenyan *brune*, a Ugandan dark roast. In my coffee reading I had noted that the *robusta* coffees have more than twice as much caffeine as the *arabica* species, and smiled indulgently as he drank some.

Two grams of caffeine by now, minimum. Clever of me to suggest he switch to the demitasses of various strong coffees. Just as strong and less filling. He could drink more of them.

Plus two to maybe four or five grams of theobromine from the chocolate.

"What are you working on these days, Ms. Grenfield?" Ivor said in his plummy voice. Could I detect a slight restless, hyper edge in his tone now?

"A mystery with historical elements," I answered, and almost giddy with delight, lobbed him a clue. "About Balzac, and the discovery of some unknown, unpublished, very valuable manuscript." Balzac, of course, an avid, indeed compulsive coffee drinker, died of caffeine poisoning. Let's see if this self-important arbiter, this poseur, was any better at literature than he was at science.

"Oh, interesting," he drawled in boredom. "You know, I *could* just manage another dessert."

"Of course!" I caroled in glee. "How about a chocolate mousse? And another Turkish coffee to go with it." The waiter appeared, beaming. "And I'll have a vanilla cream horn."

"This is very pleasant," he said, chuckling as he plunged a spoon into his new dessert and gobbled the glob. "Actually, I'm rather surprised."

"Why?"

He became distracted, watching as another waiter passed with a silver tray of various chocolate candies on a lace doily—the house specialty, glossy dark bittersweet chocolates with various fillings, handmade in their own kitchens. I raised a finger, said, "One of each for the gentleman," and pointed at Ivor. The waiter tenderly lifted the little beauties from the tray with silver tongs and placed them on a white china dish near Ivor's hand.

"Why surprised?" I reminded him.

He said, "I'd always thought of you as lacking in appreciation of the finer things."

"Oh, surely not."

"All those bloody and explicit murders, or poisons with their effects lovingly detailed. Hardly the work of a subtle mind."

"*Au contraire*, Ivor. I am very subtle."

"Well, I suppose it does require a certain amount of delicacy to keep the knowledge of whodunit from a reader until the end." He fidgeted as if nervous.

"Yes. Until the end."

Ivor began to cram the candies into his chunky, piggy cheeks. The pitch of his voice was rising, not louder but more shrill. Satiated, he pushed the dish away.

"Come on. Have another chocolate."

"I shouldn't."

"Oh, you only live once."

"Well, maybe just a taste or two." His fat hand, as he reached for the morsels, showed a faint tremor. He shifted his bulk. Restlessness.

Time for another clue, Ivor. Last chance, Ivor.

"Did you know that the botanical name for the cacao tree is Greek and that it translates to 'food of the gods'? *Theobroma*," I said, trying not to chortle. Last chance, Ivor, you who know so much.

"Nope. Didn't know that. Rather apt, actually," he said without interest. He didn't care about this detail, either, didn't care how close to theophylline it sounded. His flushed face was a bit sweaty, seen in the subdued restaurant light. In fact, he looked as if he had been lightly buttered. He cleared his throat, took another swallow of coffee, and said, "Odd. I'm feeling a little short of breath."

"Your asthma?"

"Could be."

"That's too bad. Well, you know how to deal with it, anyhow."

"Ah-whew." Puff. "Yes."

"Well, shouldn't you do something? Don't you think you should take one of your pills?"

"I already did when I got here. The doc says don't exceed two per day."

"But that's a preventative dose, isn't it? If you have an attack coming on—?"

"Probably right." He groaned as he leaned his heavy bulk sideways to claw in his pocket for the pill vial. Wheezing harder, he drew it out. He tipped a capsule into his hand.

"Here," I said helpfully, and I pushed his cup of *robusta* coffee toward him. The waiter topped it up again.

"Hmmmp," was all the thanks he managed as he popped the pill and swallowed the java.

For another minute or so, Ivor sat still, catching his breath or whatever. His face was flushed, and he moved his head back and forth as if confused.

"Are you feeling all right, Ivor?"

"I may have eaten just a tad too much."

"Well, let's just sit awhile, then."

"Yes. Yes, we'll do that."

Ivor sat, but his hands twitched, then his fingers started to pleat and smooth the tablecloth. He took in deep breaths and let them out. His face was pinker still, almost the color of rare roast beef.

"I'm not sure about that tie you're wearing, Ivor," I said. "It's not up to your former standard."

Ivor goggled at me, but his bulging eyes were unfocused. He blew his cheeks out, let them sag back, then blew them out again. His head began to bob up and down in a kind of tremor.

"And that suit," I said. "A fine, well-bred wool. Quite incompatible with your character."

No answer. I said, "But perhaps that's a bit harsh."

He leaned forward, holding onto the table. Very slowly he drifted sideways, then faster and faster, until he fell off his chair, pulling the snowy white tablecloth, silver forks and spoons, a china cup, the remains of brownie à la mode, and the dregs of *robusta* coffee with him.

"Oh, my goodness!" I shouted.

The waiter came running. I fanned Ivor with a menu. "Stand back. Give him air," I said. The waiter stepped back obediently.

The manager came running also. He tried the Heimlich maneuver. No luck. Several diners stood up and gawked. Ivor was making bubbling, gasping sounds.

"That's not a fainting fit," the manager said, obviously a more analytical chap than the waiter.

"I guess not," I said.

The manager wrung his hands. "What should we do? What should we do?"

"Maybe it's an asthma attack. He carries some pills for it. They're in his pocket, I think."

The manager felt in Ivor's pocket. He read the label. A genuine doctor's prescription in a real pharmacy container. "Yes. Here they are. At least they can't hurt."

"This coffee is cool enough," I said. "Wash it down with this." He did, even though Ivor choked a lot and showed no awareness of what was going on.

"Call the paramedics," the manager told the waiter, who bustled away. The manager slapped Ivor's cheek. I envied the man this role, but had to stand by. Ivor produced no reaction to being slapped, now well and truly in a coma.

The paramedics arrived with reasonable promptness. The one with the box of medical supplies knelt by Ivor to take vital signs. The second said, "What can you tell us about this? What happened?"

I shook my head. "I can't imagine. He was just eating a perfectly delicious chocolate dessert."

Ivor gasped, but did not rouse. His cheeks were taking on a purplish hue, the color of a fine old burgundy.

I thought of the last line of Ivor Sutcliffe's review:

In Snuffed, *the only thing deader than Rufus Crown is Ms. Grenfield's plot.*